HIGHLAND DESIRE

Glynis blushed under Robert's bold gaze, yet she wanted him as much as he wanted her, and she felt almost weak as she thought of him taking her once again.

"I can never get the sight of you washing in that stream out of my mind," he said, watching her. She had looked ravishing, and in spite of everything, she looked ravishing now. He wondered how he had resisted her for so long— and silently he thanked heaven that he did not have to resist her.

"Undress for me, Glynis."

Slowly, knowing how much he enjoyed watching, Glynis discarded her clothing. His gaze never left her and she felt as if her skin glowed under his gaze. Slowly, she stepped into the tub of water and felt its glorious warmth. She washed her hair first and sat up to wring it out. When she looked up, she was surprised to see that Robert had stripped.

Glynis took a brazen look at her lover. He was so handsome and strong. His broad shoulders rippled with muscles and his chest was wide and covered with light brown curls. She smiled, and without waiting for further invitation, he slipped into the water behind her, silently putting his arms around her. . . .

Books by Joyce Carlow

TIMESWEPT

A TIMELESS TREASURE

TIMELESS PASSION

SO SPEAKS THE HEART

DEFIANT CAPTIVE

HIGHLAND DESIRE

Published by Zebra Books

HIGHLAND DESIRE

Joyce Carlow

Zebra Books
Kensington Publishing Corp.

http://www.zebrabooks.com

ZEBRA BOOKS are published by

Kensington Publishing Corp.
850 Third Avenue
New York, NY 10022

First Printing: December, 1998
10 9 8 7 6 5 4 3 2 1

Printed in the United States of America

Chapter One

October 1743

The carriage bumped along the familiar rutted lane that led through Cluny Glen, winding its way toward the home of Duncan MacPherson, leader of this particular branch of Clan MacPherson. These lands, comprising hundreds of acres, had been ceded to Duncan MacPherson's ancestors by Clan Chattan, the Clan of Cats, which had spawned the MacPhersons, the MacIntoshes, the Davidsons, the MacBeans, and the Gillivrys.

Glynis MacPherson peeked out the carriage window. It was late afternoon, and the sun filtering through the trees cast light in between the shadows, giving the earth beneath them a mottled appearance.

The glen was as she remembered it, quiet and beautiful, with trees, thick brush, and hidden paths that occasionally led to small, surprising grass-covered clearings beside clear, rushing rocky-bottomed streams. In the midst of the glen there was a lake formed by a tributary of the River Spey. The Spey itself led to the Firth of Moray, an inlet of the turbulent North Sea. Cluny castle was built a short walk from the lake.

Glynis hugged herself in anticipation. How she wanted to get out of this carriage and run! And in her mind she did just that, dashing through the trees toward home, a thousand and one memories crowding her thoughts.

"Two years," she said aloud to no one. "Such a long time." Yet, she would have readily admitted, the time had gone by quickly. Far more quickly than she would have believed it would on the day she had left Cluny.

"I don't want to go!" she remembered wailing. But her father was a rock-hard man. Neither smiles nor tears would make him change his mind once it was made up.

"Some men don't hold with educating women, but I've always believed that a mother should be learned! So off you go, Glynis! The good Ursuline Sisters will tutor and teach you. You leave a girl, but you'll come back a woman. An educated woman and, I trust, a lady."

How she cried, Glynis remembered. She'd been fifteen and leaving home for two years seemed the cruelest of fates. She loved their country estate of Cluny fiercely. In a way, it was the mother she had never known.

Glynis was the youngest of four children and the only girl. Her mother had died in childbirth and she was reared by her father and by her three older brothers. Stewart, the eldest, was eight when their mother died, James was seven, and her youngest brother, Colin, the one to whom she was closest was only a year old.

There had been a nurse, or, more accurately, a procession of nurses. The last of the nurses, whose name was Bryden, called her "the wild one" and declared she was far harder to care for than were her brothers, and would clearly come to no good.

Exasperated, her father finally sent Bryden away. Glynis remembered that she was twelve at the time, so her father hadn't hired another nurse. Instead, Mrs. MacTavish, the housekeeper, had taken over. Mrs. MacTavish always said that she grew like a wildflower, untamed and unaware of how a lady should behave.

Glynis supposed Mrs. MacTavish was right. She had always climbed trees, gone swimming in the cold lake, ridden horseback, and hunted with her brothers. She was more skilled at hunting with the crossbow than any of them, and she was a dead shot with the pistol.

After the nurses, and before she went away, there had been a teacher, Michael McCormick. He tutored them all, showing favoritism toward none. In retrospect, she realized she had much for which to thank Mr. McCormick. His insistence on academic excellence had stood her in good stead. She achieved the highest marks in her class, and if the nuns were unimpressed by her unladylike ways, they were nothing less than enthralled by her intellectual accomplishments.

She sighed. It had been a difficult two years. The nuns were strict and she was constantly being disciplined for lapses in her manners. But after a time she learned how to act as they wanted her to act. But it was just that, an act, she thought, smiling. Nothing has changed, certainly not me.

Although she would no doubt wait until the following day, she wanted nothing so much as to ride her horse through the glen, go to the lake, and plunge into its cold, clear waters. Oh, and they would be cold now; clearly there had been several frosts. Summer was no more.

Glynis strained to see out the window as the carriage rounded the corner and the castle came into view. Home! she thought as her heart raced. Home! She could hardly wait to get out of these restrictive clothes!

The carriage came to a clattering halt and the driver climbed down and opened the door for her. He helped her out and was startled when she ran past him and bolted toward the great wooden doors that had been left ajar. "Father! Colin! I'm home! Stewart! James!"

It was Mrs. MacTavish who stood by the door. "Miss Glynis!" she said, looking her over.

Glynis hugged her and twirled her around.

"Stop now, you'll make me dizzy!" Mrs. MacTavish complained.

"I'm home! I'm really home!"

"So I see, and hear. I also see that while you look a lady, you're still a mischievous girl. You haven't changed your ways a bit. And from the size of the trunk on the coach, it looks like you must have bought out Paris before you left."

Glynis laughed. "And when will I have the opportunity again?"

"Glynis!" Colin bounded down the stairs and ran to his sister. He picked her up in his arms and hugged her. "By heaven," he whispered in her ear, "you're going to turn things upside down! My little sister with the braids has gone through a proper metamorphosis."

Glynis laughed again and Colin squeezed her. "Your laugh is like music to my ears. We've all missed you."

"And I've missed Cluny castle." Glynis peered over his shoulder. "Are you the only one here?"

Colin kissed her cheek. "I'm afraid Tavish and I are the sole welcoming committee." Tavish was what they all called Mrs. MacTavish. She was a rotund and motherly woman who had nine children of her own.

"Where are the others?" Glynis asked, her hands on her hips.

Colin could not help but smile. Hands on hips was a familiar stance for Glynis. As a child she had often stood so. It was sometimes to offer a challenge, more often to state an opinion, and still more often a sign of her supreme stubbornness.

"Father and Stewart have gone to Inverness, but they should be home soon. James is out hunting with Robert Forbes."

"Robert Forbes, is he visiting?" At the very mention of Robert's name, Glynis felt the color rush to her face.

"For another week," Colin revealed.

Glynis smiled again. "I suppose I had better get cleaned up. I've had a long journey." She turned to Tavish. "I'd like a bath," she said, discarding the thought of bathing in the lake just then.

Tavish nodded. "I'll have the tub filled. Dinner's at seven, and I suspect your father will be back by then."

"I want to hear all about Paris," Colin said, grinning.

Glynis squeezed his hand. "I shall tell you over and over. I shall speak of nothing save my wonderful two years in Paris. I shall tell you my stories so often, you'll beg me to be quiet."

Colin winked. "Begging never helped before." He turned and ran up the stairs and in mock anger Glynis chased him, shaking her fist and laughing.

"Nothing has changed," Mrs. MacTavish muttered.

Glynis stood in her robe and watched as the tub was filled. She added scented oil, and as soon as the maid closed the door, she discarded her robe and sank into the steaming water.

"So, Robert Forbes," she said to herself, "you're here for a week!" Immediately she closed her eyes and began reviewing her clothes. She had wonderful new gowns in her trunk, seductive, womanly gowns, gowns from the finest couturiers in Paris. Most of them were quite daring, but that was the style, and she felt herself to have a reputation of being daring above all.

The question, if there was one, was which of the gowns would Robert like best. Perhaps, she thought, the green one was the most appropriate. Its color matched her eyes and it had a breathtakingly low neckline and was trimmed in white lace. Yes, that was the right gown.

"Robert Forbes," she whispered his name and kissed the air, pretending she kissed his lips.

Robert was the same age as Stewart, twenty-five. He was Stewart's best friend and she had known him forever. He was tall and strong, broader of shoulder than any of her brothers, though roughly the same height as Colin, who was the tallest in the family, being six foot four inches. But as Colin still had the lanky build of a boy, Robert, even when she had left two years before, had the mature, filled-out build of a man. He was strong, and his blue eyes twinkled with merriment. He had sandy hair, which was unruly, and when he smiled, her heart pounded.

As a small child she worshiped Robert, who always helped her with everything. When she was twelve and he was twenty, he had taught her to use the crossbow. He had far more patience than any of her brothers. Glynis bit her lip. Yes, she had always worshiped him, but when she was fourteen, her feelings toward him had begun to change. She moved from childish hero worship to more womanly thoughts as she imagined them married with children, bound together always in eternal love.

Glynis sank deeper into the scented bathwater, her eyes closed as she conjured up the memory of the night before she left for France. She had just turned fifteen. Robert and she were walking by the lake. It was a wonderfully bright night, with a full moon.

"Let's stop here," Glynis suggested.

"So you can speak to the moon?" he asked, a broad grin on his face.

"Yes, of course. Look, it's perfect," Glynis said.

The full moon glimmered in the lake, its image reflected in the calm waters so it appeared as if it floated underwater. "It's the moon underwater," Glynis whispered. "You know the legend, if you ask the moon when it's underwater for a favor, your favor will be granted if you keep your wish a secret."

"And I suppose you believe this legend?"

Robert was twenty-three and clearly still thought of her as a child. "Of course I believe in it," she had answered, tossing her head back and putting her hands on her hips.

"I'll wait while you make your wish."

Glynis turned toward the lake, and with all her heart she wished for Robert to love her as she loved him.

"What did you wish for?"

"I can't tell you. If I do, it won't come true."

He only laughed. "Come along, we'd better go back. Your father will send out a search party."

Glynis turned suddenly, threw her arms around Robert, and kissed him. Not on the cheek, which is how she usually kissed him, and indeed how he kissed her, but on the lips—a womanly kiss, a kiss like the one she had seen Gillie MacAdam give her sweetheart, Kevin MacGee, in the barn one day.

At first Robert moved his lips on hers, and she remembered feeling the most incredible sensation, but then he had pulled away and stepped back.

"I love you," Glynis said.

Robert smiled and laughed a little nervously. "Of course—I love you too. But you're too young to be kissing like that, Glynis MacPherson. You're only a girl."

She remembered drawing herself up and looking at him boldly. "I'm not a girl. I'm a woman," she had protested.

But her protest was to no avail. He only smiled at her and in a split second he turned and began walking back to the house.

She had run after him and, catching him, taken his hand. "When I'm a woman, will you marry me?" she asked.

Robert had laughed. "Probably," he told her. "But you are still a girl now, and you might well regret that proposal."

Glynis opened her eyes. "Tonight I'll show you I've grown into a woman," she whispered as she plunged her thick raven-colored hair into the water. She knew she would have to towel-dry it for it to be dry before dinner, but that didn't matter. What did matter was how she would look tonight. What a wonderful homecoming! She had certainly not expected Robert to be there; she had thought she would have to finagle Stewart into inviting him.

Glynis finished her hair and, wringing it out, she climbed out of the tub and wrapped herself in a towel. She went into her bedroom and sat at her dresser. Vigorously she began to dry her hair, which was now a tangled profusion of dark curls falling over her bare white shoulders.

As soon as her hair was dry, Glynis unpacked her dress and shook it out. It was perfect! She hung it up and decided to lie down for a while before dinner.

She stared at the ceiling and pulled the soft sheepskin over her naked body. Vaguely, she wondered why her father had gone to Inverness when he had known she would come home today. But, of course, it was all politics. These days the Highlands were alive with politics and intrigue, intrigue that reached all the way to the French court. She knew about it all because she had heard the rumors in Paris.

It all had to do with the succession to the Austrian

throne. The Catholic monarchies of Europe, including France, lined up against Britain and Germany. The hostilities gave birth to the hope that an army could be raised to invade England and return the throne to its rightful heir, the Stuart pretender, James II. It was whispered that his son, Bonnie Prince Charlie, was prepared to lead the struggle.

"The Stuarts will rule again!" all the French courtiers predicted. Scotland's pains, desires, and the rebellions that had been fostered were part of a long-drawn-out history of religious warfare that had started in the sixteenth century.

It had begun with the Tudors and the rule of Elizabeth, and the beheading of her cousin, Mary Queen of Scots, the Stuart heir to the throne. Now it was said that James II, the pretender to the throne of England, was considering coming out of exile, raising an army, and trying to regain his throne. Yes, Paris was filled with rumors of a possible rebellion involving the Scots, the Irish, and English Catholics, and led by James's son, Prince Charles. Those who believed in the Stuart cause were called Jacobites, after James, *Jacobus* in Latin.

Yes, her father was most certainly involved in discussions with other clan leaders. The MacPhersons were one of the strongest Jacobite families in all of Scotland.

Glynis turned on her side and closed her eyes. If she kept thinking about politics, rebellions, and wars, she never would get any sleep. She forced her thoughts back to her childhood, back to the lake, back to the secrets she had confided to the moon underwater.

The loud knocking on her door, awakened Glynis, who did not immediately realize where she was. "Miss Glynis!"

"Yes, yes. I'm awake."

"Dinner is in one hour, and your father is home!"

Glynis jumped from her bed and shook her head to clear it of sleep. "I'm up," she declared.

"Do you want help dressing?" the maid asked.

"No, thank you," Glynis answered. "The last thing I want is advice," she said to herself. As she recalled, the upstairs maid was thirty years old with a mind slightly less progressive than that belonging to Mrs. MacTavish. She sighed. "It must be terrible being a prude at thirty!"

She sat down and looked into the mirror. "And now, Robert Forbes, I'll show you a woman and not a girl."

Duncan MacPherson lit his pipe and made himself comfortable in his favorite chair. He had taken refuge in his study on the second floor. A fire burned in the hearth, it was October, and the evenings were growing chilly. "A trying journey," he said to himself of his recent trip to Inverness to meet with the clan chieftains. "Trying and troubling," he said as he closed his eyes. It had been a meeting that brought back too many memories.

There was a light tap on his study door.

"Come in," he called out, and when Glynis came sailing through the door, Duncan MacPherson truly felt a sudden jolt of déjà vu.

"Glynis?"

His daughter's smile was absolutely radiant. "Don't try to tell me I'm unrecognizable," she replied playfully.

Duncan felt his throat go dry. No, she was hardly unrecognizable, but she was the very image of her mother. The girl he had sent to Paris two years earlier had returned, and while she had always borne a resemblance to Debra, now that she was mature the similarity was even more striking.

Glynis was tall and slender and she had her mother's thick, dark hair, ivory skin, heart-shaped face, and piercing green eyes. Her magnificent profusion of waist-length hair was swept up, yet it still fell to the middle of her back. She was wearing an emerald-colored off-the-shoulder gown, which from a father's point of view showed far too much cleavage. Her waist was tiny, and her skirts stood out, emphasizing her fine figure. For a moment he thought of saying something about the neckline on her dress, but he knew it was the style and he decided to keep the peace.

He stood up and Glynis came to him, hugging him tightly. "I'm so glad to be home," she said happily.

Duncan, though a reserved man emotionally, returned her hug. "Now it will seem normal around here," he said, holding her back and looking at her appraisingly. "You really do look like your mother," he said under his breath.

"That's a real compliment," Glynis whispered. "It's almost time for dinner. I came here so we could go to the dining room together."

"Have you seen your brothers?"

"Only Colin. The others were out hunting when I got home, so I had a bath and a short nap."

"Yes, Robert's here too. He was hunting with them."

"Just like old times," she said, turning to avoid her father's eyes. She didn't think that she hid her feelings for Robert at all well.

From afar, the dinner bell could be heard as Cook rang it to summon everyone to the table.

Her father bowed somewhat formally and grinned at her. "Your arm, my lady?"

Glynis smiled back at him and took his arm.

She and her father walked down the hall. Glynis suppressed a hundred questions about why he had gone to Inverness, just as he put off asking her about Paris.

They entered the dining room to find the others there.

"Glynis!" Both James and Stewart came and hugged her. When they released her, Robert Forbes stepped forward.

"Paris has done wonders for you," he said, bowing and taking her hand to kiss it.

Glynis blushed. Truth be known, she had really wanted a hug and a kiss from him too. But she supposed his kiss on the hand indicated that he now thought of her as a woman. Nonetheless, it seemed to her that his eyes lingered for a long while before he turned away.

"I think a real party is in order," Colin said as they all sat down.

Robert held out Glynis's chair and she smiled up at him.

"A welcome-home party," James suggested.

"You could use a party, brother," Colin poked his eldest brother, Stewart, in the ribs. "You're far too serious."

"How about it, Father?" James asked.

Duncan nodded his approval and added, "This old place could use some fiddling, dancing, and partying."

They all clapped, but Duncan only half smiled. His thoughts of foreboding would not take flight. And he couldn't help but think that it might be the last party ever held at Cluny castle.

The maid brought the soup, and for a few moments there was relative silence around the table while they ate.

"Join us on the hunt tomorrow, Glynis?" Stewart asked.

"Did you think you could keep me away?"

James laughed. "You haven't forgotten how to use the crossbow, have you?"

"I can still outshoot all of you."

Robert put down his soup spoon. "Are we making a wager?"

"Of course," she answered, an impish grin on her face. She thought of wagering a kiss in the glen, but it was far too bold a suggestion, especially with her father in the room. "How about a new shawl if I win?"

"And a new cravat if I win." Robert winked.

"The bet is set," Colin said cheerfully.

The soup dishes were taken away and soon platters of meat, potatoes, and greens were brought to the table.

"We'll have a fine haggis at the party," James said.

"What kind of party would it be without haggis?" Colin asked.

"An English party!" Robert said.

"Well, we don't want one of those!" Colin responded quickly.

They all laughed.

Duncan looked around the table at each of them. They were his family and they made him proud. Silently, he wished Debra had lived to know her children as he did. She would have been proud too.

It was just before dawn when Glynis heard the pounding on her bedroom door. She turned lethargically, then suddenly opened her eyes and sat up.

"Glynis! Sleepyhead! Did you get spoiled in Paris? It's the early bird that catches the worm and the early hunter who shoots the buck!" Robert's voice called to her tauntingly from the other side of the door.

Glynis threw her legs over the side of the bed and jumped to her feet. "I'm coming!" she shouted back, "Don't you dare go without me!"

She pulled on her undergarments and then her riding skirt, which although ankle-length and full, was divided. She put on an overblouse, and over that she pulled on a sweater. She quickly brushed her hair and tied it back. Lastly, she pulled on her socks and her riding boots. In a flash, without so much as a quick peek in the looking glass, she was off, flinging open the door to find her brothers and Robert gathered at the head of the stairs.

Her brothers were dressed in their hunting kilts, as was

Robert. The design of the plaid was the same as their tartans, but the hunting kilts had a darker background.

The five of them picked up a flask of hot soup and some bread and cheese that Cook had prepared, then they were off for a long morning in the woods.

Glynis inhaled the early morning air as they proceeded outside. She looked up at the sky. "Look, it's the morning star," she said to Robert, who nodded and smiled at her.

It was still dark out, not pitch black, but the purple dark that causes a unique glow in the sky just before dawn. Glynis felt the cold breeze, and to the east she could see a thin line of light.

"The ground's still wet," Glynis said as they walked toward the barn across the squishy ankle-high grass. She took Robert's arm and they walked slowly, lingering behind her brothers.

"You're so silent," Glynis commented. "I don't remember you as being as silent as Stewart."

"I was just thinking," he said casually. "Perhaps old age is creeping up on me."

"Old age? You're only twenty-five!"

He glanced at her out of the corner of his eye, and she caught the look.

"And you're only seventeen."

"I'll be eighteen in August."

"You look all grown-up."

Glynis wanted to stop walking. She wanted to look deep into his eyes; she wanted him to hold her and welcome her home properly. But that wouldn't happen as long as her brothers were around. Silently, she vowed to find a way to get him off alone. Surely, if no one were around, he would act as she was certain he felt.

"Have I changed?" she asked, "Did Paris change me?"

Robert laughed out loud. "I don't know about Paris,

but two years is bound to change a girl your age! Are you fishing for compliments?''

Glynis blushed and felt herself vaguely angered that he had called her a girl. But perhaps he hadn't meant it as it sounded, so she restrained herself.

Colin opened the barn doors and Glynis ran ahead of Robert and into the barn. ''Ah, Sampson,'' she said, running to the stall that held her horse. He was a splendid jet-black stallion.

Sampson nuzzled her and Glynis stroked his nose and gave him the carrot she had brought from the house. ''You do remember me,'' she said, stroking him again.

''Horses have good memories,'' Robert said. ''How about a lift up, my lady?''

He held out his hands, and Glynis put her foot in them and mounted the horse. ''I thought you might come back riding sidesaddle, as a proper lady should,'' Robert said.

Glynis looked into his eyes. ''I shall probably never be a 'proper' lady. This is the only way to ride.'' She had wanted to say that she was a woman if not a lady by this stilted definition. But again she thought she would wait until they were alone. When the moment was right, he would know she was a woman and not a girl.

She guided Sampson away and waited as the others mounted and gathered in front of the barn. Then, as if on some silent signal, they all rode off and into the thick brush. They would break up into one team of two and one team of three to hunt stealthily in the early morning light so preferred by deer.

Her three brothers went off together, at Colin's suggestion. ''Since it is you two who made the bet, it is you two who should hunt together.''

Glynis tried not to look as pleased as she was. She knew her brothers. They would go far afield, leaving her and Robert quite alone.

But from then on, there was no talking. They tethered their horses and began creeping through the heavy brush as silently as possible. It had been less than a half hour when Glynis caught sight of a magnificent buck; his antlers had eight points, showing him to be a mature beast.

Robert saw the buck too. Glynis put her finger to her lips, and she positioned her crossbow and took careful aim. Such a fine animal deserved a clean kill, a swift death. She waited a second, then she fired. The arrow went straight for its target as Robert, too, fired. If one arrow only wounded, the second would kill.

The buck was hit dead on and crumpled to the ground. Glynis let out her breath and both she and Robert ran toward the felled deer.

Robert looked at the buck. The arrow with Glynis's mark went right through the heart, while his own was in the buck's throat. "You win." He smiled. "A new shawl it is."

Glynis's eyes shone. "Make it a green one," she said offhandedly.

"I'll go for the horses, you stay with the buck."

Glynis nodded and watched as he walked off. Her heart was beating wildly. Soon, she told herself, soon she would feel his lips on hers.

Robert returned and tied the deer's feet together. He wrapped the animal in a huge heavy canvas bag and tied it tightly. Next he tied each end of the bag to a long, heavy rope and, using the horses, lifted the bag with the deer off the ground and suspended it between two large trees in order to protect it from marauding foxes and wolves. Robert marked the spot on his map. Later the servants would come and take the buck away, butchering it and preserving the meat for winter.

"I'm hungry," Glynis said. "Let's walk down by the lake and have some soup and cheese."

"A hunter's breakfast," Robert said. Again he took her

arm and they walked through the glen toward the shores of the lake. The sun was fully up now and it shimmered off the lake even as the trees that surrounded it were reflected in its calm waters.

"We were last here, on this very spot, the night before I went to Paris," Glynis said as she sat down on the flat rock.

"Ah, yes. I remember, you made a wish on the moon underwater. Did it come true?"

"I don't know yet," she said softly.

He tore off some bread and used his knife to slice a bit of cheese. He held out his offering to her, and in a moment opened a second flask.

Glynis took the bread and cheese. Her stomach was rumbling in anticipation of food just as her heart was beating in anticipation of a kiss, of hearing him speak the words she had waited so long to hear.

"Is that more soup?"

"Scotch, it's a chilly morning." With that he took a fine swig.

"May I have some?"

Robert raised his brow and looked at her quizzically.

"Well, I'm chilly too. Besides, I've had drink before— I mean besides wine."

"Are you sure?"

Glynis nodded and took the flask. She gulped down a large mouthful and felt it burning as she swallowed hard.

Robert watched her face flush and her eyes water. "You may have had drink, but not Scotch, I'll wager."

Glynis suddenly hiccuped loudly, and then she hiccuped again. Much to her embarrassment, she couldn't stop.

Robert laughed. "Good thing we got our buck. With hiccups like that, I imagine half the deer in the forest can hear you."

Glynis flushed even more. How could she kiss him now?

She wanted to stomp her foot and scream. Her morning was ruined, and so was this wonderful opportunity. Damn, she thought angrily, and damn him for laughing so hard at me!

Robert Forbes walked slowly down to the lake, leaving Glynis behind, and continued around the shore for half a mile. From the position of the sun over the distant rolling hills, he assumed it must be after three o'clock. The others had gone back to Cluny castle, but while he had no intention of hunting any longer, he felt a strong need to walk in the fall air, to be alone with his thoughts.

He perched on the same flat rock and stared back toward the castle. Its twin turrets were just visible above the trees. Cluny was indeed a castle, but it was also a house. He had no idea when the original part of the castle had been built, but he was sure that it was Duncan MacPherson who had built the house within the castle, covering the stone wall and floors, leaving only the stone staircases and the dungeons as they had once been. He smiled—the dungeon no longer housed prisoners, but was in fact a wine cellar with a collection of some note.

Cluny—it was a part of his life too. He thought of Glynis and unconsciously shook his head. She had left a lanky, awkward duckling and she returned a swan. Her dark hair and green eyes were a dazzling combination, her figure was wonderful, her voice musical, and, yes, her lips were inviting. Glynis was a stunning woman with brains as well. She was a temptress and he felt ill at ease with his own thoughts of her because he was a part of the family and until then had always thought of her as a sister. Now he found his thoughts about her to be disquieting.

His mind traveled back over the years. Suddenly he got off the rock and began walking down the path. He turned onto a narrower path, and stopped. To one side he saw it. It was coming apart now, but once it had been the playhouse he had built for Glynis. How he remembered her tears. She had wanted a playhouse, a place of her own. Her father was away on business and none of her brothers would build it for her. So he had built it though it took him more than a week. She was eight and he was sixteen.

Unconsciously he touched his lips. He thought of the kiss she had given him two years earlier. It had surprised him, taken him aback completely. He had not been prepared for little Glynis to kiss him that way, and he had responded at first—feeling guilty later.

"Why am I so consumed with thoughts of Glynis?" he asked himself. It wasn't right. She was his friend, and she was too young to think about the way he kept thinking about her.

You just need a woman, he told himself. And immediately he conjured up the image of Margaret Campbell. She was his age and they had been seeing each other. She was pretty and kind and mature. In all likelihood he would marry her. These feelings for Glynis were nothing—it was surely normal to notice anyone as beautiful as Glynis had become.

They returned from hunting at four in the afternoon and it did not surprise Colin to learn that Glynis had won the bet, and, indeed, that Glynis and Robert had bagged the only deer in three months.

Colin changed out of his hunting clothes and dressed casually in his kilt and a sweater, walked in the late afternoon sun through the garden behind the house, knowing that Robert was about somewhere.

Mrs. MacTavish was something of a wonder, Colin thought. He paused to look at what she called "my kitchen garden." It flourished under her loving care, and because of it they had fresh vegetables all summer and carrots, cabbage, turnips, and potatoes throughout most of the winter. But it wasn't just a garden. It was a disguised garden. Deeming the sight of growing vegetables to be less than aesthetic, Mrs. MacTavish set flowers among them and a hedge of wild roses around the garden. Some of the flowers she proclaimed to be quite edible, and naturally the rose hips were picked, and from them Mrs. MacTavish made rose hip syrup, rose hip tea, and rose hip jam. She insisted it was a wonderful tonic, and that it even cured and prevented scurvy.

Colin walked beyond the garden toward the lake and the small house where once they all played as children. Now the small house had a veranda that looked toward the shore. There were still chairs to sit on, but the house itself was boarded up and used to store scythes and other such equipment.

To his surprise, he saw Glynis sitting in one of the chairs, looking out toward the lake.

"Glynis!" he called out to her, and she waved back. He was closer to her than either of his brothers, perhaps, he reasoned, because they were almost the same age—and neither of them remembered their mother.

He draped himself over one of the chairs. Glynis had changed into a simple skirt, blouse, and shawl. Her hair was loose, and its red highlights shone in the afternoon sun. His sister, he thought, was a truly beautiful woman.

"And what are you doing out here all alone?" he asked.

"Being lazy—thinking, daydreaming—"

He smiled at her. "Who are you inviting to the party?" he asked.

"No one," Glynis answered. "Robert will be there."

Colin felt his voice catch in his throat. He hadn't thought of it before, perhaps because he had chosen to ignore it—

but quite suddenly he thought of how Glynis behaved when Robert was around, and he realized with brotherly naïveté that Glynis had a crush on Robert Forbes and wondered why he had not thought about it before.

Her expression when she made the bet with Robert flashed across his thoughts as did the way in which they had divided up to go hunting. He thought of how she had looked last night at dinner, and wondered if she would look as ravishing tonight.

He and Robert had known each other all their lives and he supposed that was the reason he had ignored what now seemed so obvious to him.

He felt suddenly uncomfortable and slightly depressed. She most certainly had strong feelings. Vaguely he wondered if he should tell her about Robert. Instantly, he decided he should not. It was Robert's place to tell her, and even so, he admitted he was a coward on this score. He didn't want to see the hurt in her eyes.

"Is something the matter?" Glynis asked.

"Not really." He had to protect her. Even if what she felt was just a crush on Robert, both her feelings and her pride would be hurt when she learned the truth. Silently, he vowed to invite several young bachelors to the party himself. At least they would be there; she would have someone. He pressed his lips together, wishing that Robert had already told her. But he knew it simply hadn't occurred to him. He certainly wasn't trying to hurt or deceive Glynis in any way. It was just that he thought of her as a sister and not as a potential lover. For her part, Glynis had always looked up to Robert, she had always adored him in a way that Colin now realized he hadn't understood. And if he hadn't understood it, surely Robert hadn't either.

"You're so quiet," Glynis pressed. "It's not like you."

"I was just thinking about Laurie," he said quickly. Yes, he had to talk about himself. It was the only way to get his thoughts off Robert and Glynis, the only way to prevent his blurting out something by mistake.

"Laurie?" Glynis questioned.

"Yes, you remember, Laurie Lewis."

"Oh, of course. What about her?"

"I've been seeing her," Colin confided.

Glynis reached over and poked him playfully. "You've been keeping secrets."

His face turned red and Glynis laughed. "It's all right. I expected you to find a girl sometime. But honestly, I can't remember much about her save her name. I know we met one summer in Inverness, but I'm sure it was at least four years ago."

"At least," Colin agreed. "You'll like her, she's very pretty."

"She had better be smart too," Glynis said. "I don't want you running around with just anyone."

"She's smart," he replied.

"Well, I don't suppose I have to ask who you're inviting, then. What does this 'pretty girl' look like, Colin?"

"She's not nearly as tall as you. She has red hair and brown eyes." He didn't mention her figure, but she was quite voluptuous, and while they'd only kissed and hugged passionately, he knew how her body would feel and he could easily imagine her naked in his arms. In fact, it was something he imagined quite often.

"Colin MacPherson, I do believe you're lustful."

His face went red again. He hated it when Glynis read his thoughts, but he was glad she had read his thoughts about Laurie and not about Robert.

"Are you going to laze here till dinner?" he asked.

"No. Want to walk down by the lake and look for unusual stones?"

"Okay." He stood up and stretched, then held out his hand and pulled his sister out of the chair. "As a matter of curiosity, how many rocks do you have now?'' He winked. Collecting unusual rocks was something they had done together for years, and seldom did Glynis return without at least two stones.

"Let's say I shall soon require a new cupboard.''

Chapter Two

In her room, Glynis stood in front of her mirror, admiring her gold taffeta dress. It was an off-the-shoulder gown with a tight bodice and a daringly low neckline. "He didn't notice me last night because I wear green too often," Glynis said. "But he will tonight." This dress with its suggestive black lace trim was much better, much more seductive.

And perhaps, she contemplated, her hair was too severe when drawn back. Tonight she would wear it loose; she would let it fall over her bare shoulders and all the way down her back.

She reached into her drawer and found a pair of small gold earrings. She put them on and tilted her head. No, they weren't quite right. She put on a gold chain choker and admired it. Much better. After a moment of consideration, she put on slightly larger earrings and decided they were perfect.

She picked up the perfume she had brought back from Paris. She dabbed it between her breasts and behind her ears. As a final touch, she pinched her cheeks till they were slightly pink. She did have hidden away rouge and eye makeup she had brought home with her, but she decided to save that for the party to come in a few weeks time. Frenchwomen wore makeup frequently, but as she had only a limited supply, she decided to keep it for special occasions.

She picked up her skirts and walked across her room. Without pausing, she opened the door and headed down the hall. Her brothers would all be in the study now. No doubt Robert would be there too. She contemplated joining them, but after a moment's thought decided not to. Instead, she went into the drawing room and sat down at the pianoforte to play before dinner. Her fingers danced across the keys, and she played some pieces she had learned in France, where pianofortes were far more common. Her father had spent a great deal importing this one for her to play. But she loved it just as she loved dancing, which so many frowned on. She sighed. All of France was dancing! Only in England were such things considered evil. Protestants, or what she knew of them, seemed to be utterly dull.

Glynis didn't turn around when she heard the study door open. She kept on playing, but she knew it was Robert. She could smell the sweet tobacco in his pipe.

"Don't stop," she heard him say.

She didn't stop, but played faster.

Robert came and stood by her side. He moved away again, looking around for a chair.

"Beautiful," he said.

She wondered if he meant her or the music. "Thank you," she answered as she finished the piece.

He had taken a seat in one of the chairs behind the pianoforte. "That piece is beautiful too," he said, clarifying his comment, much to her chagrin. He was being so—so aloof.

She turned and faced him. "Is there something wrong?"

For a very long while he stared at her. He shook his head. "Not at all. Do I get another song?"

He asked the question just as the dinner bell rang.

"Maybe after dinner," Glynis replied, looking up into his eyes. She felt certain he liked this dress better than the one she had worn the previous night. His look had been admiring, she was sure of it.

He stood up and held out his hand. "Dinner awaits."

Glynis took his hand and his arm as they walked down the center hall toward the dining room. "We're having lamb tonight. I know it's your favorite."

"It is indeed. Did you see your buck?"

Glynis shook her head.

"They took it to be hung several hours ago. It should provide a lot of meat over the winter."

"Half of it belongs to you."

"No, you won the bet, and it's your buck, not mine."

He opened the dining room doors. Everyone was there, and they looked up when the two of them entered.

Glynis glanced at Colin, who, she noted, had the strangest expression on his face.

"I could hear your playing," Duncan said. "You're very good now."

Glynis smiled flirtatiously at Robert. "I like to play," she said softly.

Ramsey Monroe spent most of his time at his town house in Inverness. It wasn't that he liked Inverness that much, it was simply that his work as an importer and proprietor of a store kept him there for most of the year. Not that he was as busy as he once had been. Goods from England and the Lowlands still came directly to Inverness by ship through the Firth of Moray, but goods brought surreptitiously from France more frequently were set ashore on the east coast of Scotland, where the British navy played hide-and-seek with French vessels in and around the many lochs, coves, and offshore islands. Of late, Loch Arkaig had found favor as a clandestine port.

"A curse on war," Ramsey muttered to himself as he looked at his sparsely stocked shelves. Fewer goods meant less income, and the continued fighting on the Continent meant fewer goods.

If I had money, he told himself, I would be able to charter French vessels to carry the contraband goods that were so popular. But he did not have the money needed to launch such an endeavor, therefore he struggled along, attempting to keep up appearances and gradually going into debt.

Not that he was totally against war. In fact, he was a Stuart supporter, a Jacobite. Not a sentimental Jacobite as so many of the clansmen were, but a Jacobite for practical reasons. He desired a return of the Stuart kings to the throne of Scotland and England simply because he deemed it good for business. A Stuart king would be allied with France instead of constantly at war. A Stuart king would favor stronger trading ties with France.

"I wouldn't always be so broke," he muttered as he turned away from his half-empty shelves to answer the tinkle of the bell on his door. "Twenty past nine," he muttered. Why couldn't people wait until he was officially open for business at nine-thirty?

Feeling annoyed, but not wanting to miss an order, he opened the door to find a messenger rather than a customer.

The disheveled messenger handed Ramsey a scroll, and Ramsey, in return, begrudgingly gave the man a few coins.

When the man had departed, Ramsey closed the door and undid the scroll, reading its message.

You are invited to attend a party at Cluny castle on
October 25th to celebrate the return of Miss Glynis
MacPherson from France.
Please let us know if you will attend.
Sincerely, Colin MacPherson

"Glynis MacPherson," Ramsey said aloud as he tried to
conjure up her image. After a moment he remembered
an attractive young girl who had come to Inverness in the
winters with her family—one of the wealthier clan families.

Duncan MacPherson, unlike many Highlanders, had the
business sense of a Lowlander. He had invested heavily on
the Continent and was known to keep sizable accounts out
of Scotland and in French banks.

"No doubt about it," Ramsey murmured. "Glynis Mac-
Pherson would be an excellent catch. She would have a
good dowry, and after a while Duncan MacPherson could
no doubt be persuaded to invest in his business. Thus
turning me into a proper gentleman of means." He envi-
sioned himself traveling back and forth to France once a
year and momentarily daydreamed about a château in the
wine country, about the luxury of the French court, and
about the exquisite women of France who so willingly gave
their favors. Yes, such a life appealed to him. Glynis could
remain in Scotland and bear him children, and he could
travel for months at a time, dallying with women of his
choice in France.

Hurriedly as well as enthusiastically, he penned his reply
to Colin MacPherson. When he had finished, he turned
to look in the mirror. He knew himself to be handsome,
handsome enough and charming enough to enchant
Glynis MacPherson.

* * *

It was the last weekend in October. The nights were already cold and the mornings frosty, but by midday the sun had burned through the mist and warmed the day.

"We're lucky," Colin said cheerfully. "It's usually colder by this time in October and ordinarily the fog is beginning to close in."

He was right, Glynis thought. In Scotland, one was never far from the sea. They lived on the shores of a lake from which a river flowed into the larger River Spey. In spring, as in fall, heavy fogs obscured the castle and covered the countryside like a soft white blanket. The seasonal mists came because in the spring the air temperature grew warm before the water; they came in the fall because the water was still warm when the temperature of the air grew cold.

"Don't talk about it," Glynis replied. "I don't like to think about winter coming."

"You'd just rather stay here than go to Inverness."

"You're right. I know it's only for a few months, but I miss it here. I don't know why we can't stay here."

"Because the clans are all far-flung, communication is difficult when the weather is inclement."

Glynis understood all too well. This year, of all years, communication between the clans was necessary. Most of the clan chieftains would winter in Inverness so that decisions could be easily made. And judging from the rumors, this was a year when decisions of great import were to be made.

"There, how does that look?" Colin asked from his perch atop the ladder.

Glynis looked up. He had draped a large swath of their bright red, blue, yellow, and white tartan across half the wall. "Very colorful," she replied. "And don't you think these flowers are a complement to your swag?"

"The room looks grand," Colin said, climbing down. "And with no help at all from Stewart and James."

Glynis made a face. "Don't you know? They're too old for such things. Oh, they'll come with their lady friends and drink and dance the night away. But they won't help at all in the preparations."

"Well, James will come and drink and dance the night away. I somehow doubt Stewart will. It's all much too close to enjoyment, and you know how Stewart avoids enjoyment."

Glynis laughed. "Aye," she replied. "Much too much like enjoyment." For years the two of them had made comments about their brother's dour nature. They loved him, but they knew him all too well.

"I guess that takes care of it," Colin said.

Just as he spoke, the clock struck the hour. "My heavens!" Glynis sang out. "It's so late! People will begin arriving by six!"

"Don't tell me it will take you two hours to turn yourself into a siren?"

"At least two hours!"

"And what expensive gown will you wear tonight?"

Glynis's eyes sparkled. "My surprise, you'll see."

Colin watched her as she disappeared up the stairs. He shook his head and walked toward the door. He needed a walk. Two hours of decorating the great hall with Glynis had been confining. He thought again of Robert, and again he wished that Robert had told Glynis about Margaret Campbell. Still, what did he himself know? He knew only that Robert had been keeping company with Margaret. It might not be serious, Robert might not even bring her to the party.

"I hope you don't," Colin said aloud as he walked down the path. He knew that he was right. Glynis felt strongly about Robert, and Robert, as always, seemed to regard her only as a little sister.

It occurred to him that the person who would know was

Stewart. Vaguely, he wondered why Stewart had not taken note of their sister's obvious infatuation with Robert. But the answer was clear, Stewart lived far too much inside himself. He was oblivious of relationships. He concentrated on politics; it was the center of his universe. And perhaps, Colin thought, it was a good thing. One day Stewart would be clan chieftain, and an understanding of politics would become invaluable.

"Colin!"

Colin turned around. James was coming down the path after him.

"Wait for me," he called out.

Colin stopped walking and waited for James to catch up to him. "Is something wrong?" he asked.

"Not at all. I just wanted to walk with you," James said. "I need some exercise."

Colin nodded. It was their habit to walk and hike not only through the woods but beyond to the pastures, where the land was like a rolling green carpet studded with jutting rocks. It was more difficult to walk in winter, so they all had a tendency to take advantage of the good weather as long as it lasted.

"You seem very thoughtful," James said. "Of course, I notice only because you're not usually thoughtful."

Colin glanced at James. It was an artful little barb, the sort that the four siblings exchanged often. They each knew the others meant nothing—it was a form of entertainment.

"I've been thinking about Glynis," Colin confided.

"And doesn't she look phenomenal! What a change, from tomboy into a—well, a very attractive woman."

"I wasn't talking about the change in her, though I admit it's quite noticeable."

"What were you talking about?"

"James, have you never noticed the way she looks at Robert?"

James frowned slightly and nodded. "What do you think?"

"I think she's smitten with him, that's what I think."

"What kind of detective work is that? She's always adored him," James said.

"She's older now, it's different. I can see it in her eyes, brother."

"She's in for a shock," James said, shaking his head. "Robert's bringing Margaret tonight. I'll wager he's going to announce their engagement."

"What?" Colin could hear the surprise in his own voice.

"Engagement, betrothal—you know, they're going to get married."

"She'll die," Colin said under his breath. "I think she loves him. She'll die."

James actually laughed. "I think it will be a short death. Glynis is far too spirited to be upset for long. I think the most one has to fear is a temper tantrum."

Colin did not look at his brother. Rather, he kept his eyes on the ground. James did not understand the depth of Glynis's feelings, he was a trifle insensitive and didn't realize how terribly hurt Glynis would be. But he did judge one thing correctly. Her reaction to the engagement would not reveal her true feelings—it could well result in a flare-up of her famous temper.

A good part of him wanted to disappear for the whole evening. But he had invited Laurie, and she wouldn't understand if he absented himself from the party. Yes, where such matters were concerned, he admitted to being a true coward.

* * *

Margaret Campbell was a year younger than Robert. She had ash-blond hair and cornflower-blue eyes with long, dark lashes. Her face was oval, and she wore her blond hair in a large roll around her face. She was a quiet, intelligent woman, an accomplished violinist and was known for miles around for her intricately woven shawls.

"You don't have to buy one of my shawls," she said, looking into Robert's eyes. "You know I'll give you one."

He liked that she did not ask for whom he was buying the shawl. She was not possessive, yet he knew she was loyal.

"It's for Glynis," he said offhandedly. "She won our bet. We went hunting, and her shot was more accurate than mine."

"Your Glynis sounds like a woman of many talents."

He bent down and kissed Margaret's cheek. "She is not my Glynis. She's Stewart's little sister. I've known her since she was a year old. She's a little sister to me too."

Margaret laughed lightly. "Did I ask?"

Robert smiled. "No, that's why I'm telling you."

"I'll meet your Glynis tonight," Margaret said. "I hope she likes me."

"How could she not like you?" He meant it with all his heart. He knew deep down inside he didn't feel that Margaret was the most exciting woman in the world, but she was close to the most likable. She was calm and cool, pretty and kind. She had a sensible way about her, and he judged her to be the kind of woman who would make a good wife and mother.

Margaret smiled. "Well, you never know. She's young."

Robert nodded. Glynis was that. She was young, beautiful, and spirited. He cursed silently. Now he was thinking about Glynis again, when he ought to be thinking of Margaret.

Margaret handed him the shawl, which she had wrapped carefully. "I'm ready to leave," she said.

"Our chariot awaits," Robert replied playfully. It wasn't really a chariot; in fact, it wasn't even a conveyance to be used on land. It was a small riverboat. Margaret lived far upstream from Cluny, but the trip was quick by boat, more so since it was downstream. They would spend the night at Cluny and he would take her to Inverness to join her family.

"I haven't been to a party in ever so long," Margaret said as he helped her into the boat.

"Well, not since last winter," Robert answered. Yes, winter was more of a social season because many of the clan chieftains wintered in Inverness.

"It seems like a long time."

"I'm glad we're going to this party. Anyway, I'm practically a member of the family, so you have to meet them."

"I daresay. Tell me about them. Tell me how you came to be an adopted member of Clan MacPherson."

"Duncan MacPherson's a wonderful man," Robert began. "He fought alongside my father in 1715, three years before I was born. My father and Duncan were very close. Duncan saved my father's life in battle and that bound them together and they became even closer. In 1718, when my mother was pregnant, my father was thrown from a wild mare. He was killed. Duncan and his wife, Debra, had my mother live with them until I was born. My mother died of diphtheria a few months later, and I was sent to live with my father's brother in Inverness. But the MacPhersons had me every summer and most of the winter until I went off to school. I was eight when Glynis was born and her mother died. It was as if my own mother had passed on. I was too young to have known my own mother, but I knew Debra MacPherson as a mother." Robert stopped for a moment; he could hear his own voice crack, and he knew he was filled with emotion.

"They must be a wonderful family," Margaret said in a near whisper.

Robert nodded. He thought silently that there weren't too many homes in the Highlands where Margaret would be welcome. He himself had thought long and hard before deciding to court her. The Campbells were a large and strong clan. They didn't always stand with the other clans, and many of those who had fought in 1715 disliked them. Moreover, there was bad blood between the Campbells and the strongest of Highland clans, Clan MacDonald. But he knew he could count on the MacPhersons to judge Margaret on her own merit and not by her clan. Margaret's family was not something of which they spoke often, and he decided to put it out of his head for then.

"Yes, I want you and Glynis to be good friends. I think she needs a female friend. A mentor, a guide. She's not had a mother, and she's a little wild."

"I shall do my best to please you," Margaret said. She changed the subject entirely. "Does it bother you that I wasn't educated abroad?"

"Of course not! Whatever made you ask?"

"I don't know. I just wondered."

"Well, wonder no more. You're soft and beautiful, Margaret Campbell."

She was looking into the water shyly, and he knew he had embarrassed her. She was a modest woman, not a great intellect, but smart enough.

"I think I shall want many children. What do you think, Robert?"

"I like children, perhaps four."

"Oh, I'd like more than that. Six at least."

"You should have as many as pleases you," he replied without really thinking about it. Vaguely he did wonder if she had ever seen another woman give birth. He had been present at birthings, and he wondered why anyone would want to do it more than once. But surely she had seen a birthing. He couldn't imagine a woman who hadn't.

Margaret didn't say anything more for a while, and she craned her neck. "I see lots of lights. It must be Cluny castle."

They had come around the bend in the river. "Yes," he answered. "That's Cluny."

He entered the calm lake and rowed to the dock. He secured the boat and stepped out, then lifted Margaret up and onto the wooden dock.

He set her down and watched as she smoothed out her skirt. "You look wonderful," he said. "Let me steal a kiss before we join the others." He bent down and kissed her. It was a long, slow kiss, but not a kiss that set him afire. He looked into her clear blue eyes and wondered what was the matter with him. He didn't feel as he should have, he felt, and it occurred to him that not once in their whole courtship had he told her he loved her.

"Most of the guests have arrived," Colin told Glynis as he watched her poke at her hair and once again pinch her cheeks. "You hardly need to do that when you're wearing a bright red dress. You glow just from the reflection."

"Is it too much? I could wear the lavender dress."

"I can't imagine anything more exciting than that dress." He was her brother, but even he had to admit she looked stunning. Her raven-colored hair fell over her incredibly white shoulders and caressed the low back of her red taffeta gown, a gown trimmed in black lace. Her green eyes were luminous.

"Are you ready to have me escort you down?"

She nodded and smiled. "I'm ready."

Colin paused, wondering again if he should tell her about Robert and Margaret, and once again he decided against it. There seemed nothing left to do but let nature take its course.

She looped her arm through his, and he led her down the long upstairs hallway to the winding staircase. She walked with a regal stance, her head high. Colin glanced sideways at her; he knew that even among beauties, she was going to be the most attractive woman in the room.

They reached the grand hall, the largest room in the castle. It was a colorful sight—over fifty young clansmen all wearing their dress tartans and nearly the same number of women, all wearing beautiful gowns.

Glynis looked about the room, scanning it from corner to corner. She saw Robert. He had a lovely blonde on his arm. She stared hard at them and felt, as she did so, as if she were turning to butter.

"Who is that with Robert?" she whispered, pressing Colin's arm hard enough that he almost winced.

"Margaret Campbell," Colin answered. He turned toward his sister and looked her straight in the eye. "They've been keeping company, Glynis. They're about to be engaged."

Glynis felt her throat and mouth go dry. "What? Why didn't someone tell me?"

Colin took a deep breath. "I should have."

Glynis bit her lower lip. Strangely, as shocked as she was, she didn't feel like crying. It just couldn't be. Colin was mistaken. Naturally Robert would go out with other women while she was away, but now that she was back, he most certainly would not marry another woman! It was preposterous.

"Are you all right?" Colin asked. It was like waiting for an explosion. But it didn't come.

"I'm fine," Glynis said, amazed at the calm in her own voice.

"Come on, I want you to meet a couple of friends of mine," Colin suggested nervously. "And when Laurie gets here, please take some time to talk with her."

"Of course I will," Glynis promised. But she was mouthing the words, feeling as if she were in a trance.

Colin took Glynis's arm again and guided her across the room toward Ramsey Monroe and Bruce Macleod. "Ramsey, Bruce, I'd like to present my sister, Glynis, who's just returned from France."

"How glad we are you returned, Glynis MacPherson." Ramsey Monroe bowed from the waist and took her hand, kissing it and holding it too long.

"Indeed," Bruce Macleod added. He, too, kissed her hand, but he seemed a little shy to Glynis. Yet this Ramsey had possibilities, Glynis thought. He was tall with red hair and brown eyes. He was broad-shouldered and had a square jaw. He was quite handsome. Handsome enough to make Robert jealous, in any case.

"May I have this dance?" Ramsey asked.

"Of course." Glynis smiled devastatingly, and Colin yielded her to Ramsey, feeling a bit confused.

"She's quite beautiful," Bruce said as he watched them dance away.

It was a wild Highland fling, and the fiddlers played with passion.

Glynis saw Robert with Margaret. She turned her head to one side as she flew by with Ramsey, and smiled at him.

The dance ended, but Ramsey did not let her go. He continued to hold her around the waist.

Stewart MacPherson climbed up on a stool and shouted out for silence. A hush fell over the crowd of young people. "Silence!" Stewart called out. "My good friend Robert Forbes has an announcement to make!"

Robert came forward. His face was a trifle flushed from a combination of the reel they'd been dancing and the wine. He took the stool as Stewart climbed down. "I want to announce my engagement to the loveliest of all her clan, Margaret Campbell."

Everyone clapped and Robert jumped from the stool and drew a blushing Margaret into his arms. He bent and kissed her on the mouth, and everyone shouted, clapped, and stomped their feet.

Glynis stared at them. She was as stiff as a board. Knowing was one thing, but seeing Robert kiss another woman the way she dreamed of him kissing her was too much. She turned toward Ramsey and squeezed his arm. "Excuse me for just a few moments," she whispered. She turned and fled through the side door and out into the courtyard that surrounded the castle. All she could think of was the fact that she had to get away before anyone saw her, before she began to cry, or scream. . . .

She ran down the steps and across the dewy grass toward the lake. "Damn!" she cried as soon as she was far enough away. "Damn! Damn! Damn, you, Robert Forbes!"

Colin was across the room when he saw Glynis leave. Laurie had just come, and he couldn't excuse himself immediately.

"Colin, have you met my Margaret?" Robert called out. He brought Margaret over and introduced her. Colin kissed her hand and in turn introduced her to Laurie Lewis.

"Where's Glynis?" Robert asked. "I saw her dancing."

Colin frowned. "Robert, can I speak with you for a moment in the study?" He turned toward Laurie. "Could you keep Margaret company till we come back?"

Laurie smiled warmly. "Of course."

"Just man talk," Margaret said cheerfully.

Colin led Robert out of the main hall, down the corridor, and into the study. He silently poured him a brandy.

"Will I need this?" Robert asked, half in jest and lifting his brow.

"No, I need it," Colin said, taking a long gulp. "I don't exactly know how to start—I should have spoken to you much earlier."

"I take it this is about Glynis."

"Yes. She didn't know about Margaret."

Robert frowned. "And she's upset that I didn't tell her?"

Colin couldn't believe that Robert was so dense, so unobservant. "Yes," he said, nodding. "Good heavens, man. Don't you know she's in love with you?"

Robert stared at Colin. Was Glynis in love with him? "I know she has a girlish crush on me, but it's not love," he stammered.

"I don't know what it is," Colin answered. "I know only how upset she is about you and Margaret."

"Good heavens, I'm too old for Glynis! Of course I adore her—but not that way!" Yet no sooner had the words escaped his mouth than he wondered if he meant them.

Colin shrugged. It seemed odd to him that Robert had not noticed the woman Glynis had become. Even he was aware of the changes—and they weren't all physical. But again, maybe Robert was right. Maybe what she felt was a girlish crush.

"Maybe if you talked with her," he suggested. "Maybe if you explained—"

"Of course. Where is she?"

"Down by the lake, I imagine. It's where she goes."

Robert nodded. "Thanks, Colin. Would you look after Margaret for a few minutes. Just tell her I went to find Glynis and speak with her."

"Glad to," Colin replied. Robert left through the door

in the study. For a moment Colin watched as Robert's silhouette disappeared across the expanse of grass and onto the path that led to the lake. He hoped he had done the right thing.

Robert followed the winding path down to the lake. He reached the shore and looked around. There, on the flat rock, he saw Glynis sitting in the moonlight. She was beautiful, and for a long while he stared at her, aware of the disquieting thoughts that crossed his mind. Thoughts about Glynis, about his inability to tell Margaret he loved her.

"Glynis!" he called out.

She slipped off her perch and turned to face him.

"You're going to ruin that beautiful gown climbing on rocks," he said, shaking his head.

It was only as he got closer that he saw the tears in her eyes. "I'm sorry," he said. "I should have told you."

She looked into his eyes with disbelief. "You don't love her," Glynis said firmly. "You love me, Robert Forbes. We were meant for each other. You can't marry her—you can't marry anyone but me."

He stepped closer and put his hands on her shoulders. "Glynis, little Glynis—"

She stood on tiptoe and threw her arms around his neck. She pressed her lips to his and moved them till she felt him kissing her back. He held her tightly and quite suddenly let her go. "Glynis!"

"You wanted to kiss me," she said defiantly. "You do love me!"

"Glynis, you're beautiful. And I warn you that any man would find it difficult not to respond to you. But I'm engaged to Margaret and I am marrying her. You just think you love me. I'm too old for you, too much of a brother

to you. Soon you'll find someone closer to your own age
and forget me."

"No! I will not! I will never forget you!"

"You have a girlish crush, that's all!"

"It's not all! It's not! And you're only eight years older
than I am! It doesn't matter, I'd love you if you were a
hundred!"

He smiled. "I'll remember that when I'm old and gray."

"Stop making fun of me! We were destined, you and I.
And the moon promised . . . remember, before I left for
France we stood here and saw the moon underwater. I
made a wish."

"It's a legend," he said, looking into her eyes, trying to
forget the kiss, forcing himself to remember her age and
trying in his mind to conjure up Margaret's image.

"I wished for you and me to be—" Glynis couldn't
finish. "You just can't marry her," she finally said.

"Glynis, you will forget me. Please, I want to be your
friend. I want Margaret to be your friend."

Glynis stared at him. "You love me and you don't know
it! I'll show you!" she shouted. She picked up her skirts
and ran back through the woods and up the path toward
the castle. She didn't look back because she knew he wasn't
following her. She ran into the kitchen and up the back
stairs to her room on the second floor. She bolted the
door and threw herself on the bed.

Robert turned and walked slowly back to the castle. Yes,
he remembered that night before she left. He'd been
twenty-three and she'd been fifteen. He hadn't dreamed
she had feelings for him other than the kind of emotions
one has for a brother. But there was the kiss she had given
him that night. It wasn't at all sisterly.

He felt terrible, and he was aware of feeling guilty. But he also felt something else, something like regret.

When he returned to the party, Margaret and Laurie had gone to the ladies' powder room. "Where's Glynis?" Colin asked.

"She came back. She must have gone to her room."

Colin did not need to ask how their talk had gone. It was evident from Robert's mood. "I'll go and see to her," he said after a moment. "I'll be down in a moment."

Colin banged on Glynis's door. "Come down, Glynis."

"No!" she shouted back. "I'm not coming back."

"You're missing a good party."

"I don't care, leave me alone."

"Ramsey wants to call on you when we return to Inverness. What shall I tell him?"

There was a long pause and Glynis answered, "Tell him to call."

He breathed a sigh of relief. She would be all right. She just had to get used to the idea that Robert would be getting married, that things would change.

For a long while Glynis lay on her bed. She got up and undressed, then hung up her gown. She put on her nightdress, washed her face, braided her long hair, and thought about morning. Margaret Campbell would still be there. "I'll just stay here till she leaves," Glynis promised herself. "I'll stay here forever if I have to." After all, her window looked out on the front of the castle. She would see them when they left.

Finally, she went to bed. It would be hard to sleep, but sleep was a form of escape.

* * *

Each time Glynis heard a carriage she peeked out the window. Finally, she saw Robert and Margaret leave at ten-thirty. She quickly dressed and went down to breakfast. Stewart and James were both gone, but Laurie Lewis and Colin were still in the kitchen, talking over tea and biscuits.

"Feeling better?" Colin asked diplomatically.

Glynis nodded. "A bit of a cold," she said, sitting down and pouring herself some tea. She turned and smiled at Laurie. "Forgive me. We haven't been properly introduced, but I know you're Laurie."

"It's I who should apologize," Colin said quickly. "I forgot you two didn't meet last night."

"Yes, you do look as if you've a cold. Your eyes are all red," Laurie said.

Glynis nodded. "My eyes have been watery." She wondered if Colin had confided the truth to Laurie, or whether Laurie was being genuine. In any case, she would continue the lie; she would tell anyone who asked that she had left the party because she felt unwell.

"I truly missed you," Laurie said, blinking her dark lashes. "Colin invited two men for you, and when you disappeared, I had to take turns dancing with them."

"Thank you," Glynis said, thinking she didn't know exactly what to say. Laurie was quite pretty, and she seemed nice enough, but there was something about her—Glynis couldn't think just what it was that made her feel as if she should be a bit reserved with Laurie. She chastised herself; they had, after all, just met.

"Father said we'll be going to Inverness next week," Colin confided. "Laurie's staying till we leave so she can go back with us."

"Good," Glynis said, smiling at Laurie and vowing to try to get to know her. "I'll have to decide what to take with me."

"It must be difficult moving back and forth," Laurie said, sipping her tea.

"Especially as I just got home," Glynis said wistfully. She didn't want to leave. And, she realized, she also had misgivings about going to Inverness.

Chapter Three

November 1743

It was nearly ten P.M., an unusual hour for Glynis to be in the barn. But then, she had been keeping strange hours as she tried to avoid conversations with her brothers and with Laurie.

Glynis stood in Sampson's stall. The barn was one of her favorite places. She loved the smell of hay and the sounds the animals made. Even as a child this is where she had come when she wanted to be alone.

"We've hardly been riding at all," Glynis said as she brushed Sampson's luxurious mane. The horse nuzzled her and she patted him. "I'm afraid you'll have to stay here," she told the horse. Not that she ever took her horse to Inverness. There was no room to keep a horse except in the communal stable, and that idea did not appeal to her.

Inverness was a town of some three thousand and consisted mainly of three roads that converged in the center of town. The square surrounding the crossroads was where the market was held, and it was also where the town fathers came to do business.

Inverness had over five hundred houses, most of which were town houses belonging to the clan chieftains. The houses were row on row and made of sandstone. They had gabled roofs and almost none had windows on the first floor. The reason there were no first-floor windows was simple: The clans—more so in days past than then— fought a great deal among themselves and glass was an expensive commodity.

On each door the name of the clan was carved into the wood, and on many the clan crest appeared in the form of an iron knocker.

In Inverness there was no boating on the lake, no hunting in the woods, no days spent with the flocks. And yet, she thought, Inverness did have its advantages. Friends were close at hand and the weekly market offered many items one could never find in the countryside.

Glynis put down her brush for a moment and listened. She tilted her head slightly. Voices, she heard voices. "Shh," she whispered to Sampson. She extinguished the lantern and crept toward the door. It was strange enough that she was out at this hour, and she wondered who else was about.

One of the voices was that of a woman, the other was a male voice, a voice Glynis was sure she had never heard before.

Glynis crept silently toward the door of the barn. She crouched down and peered outside. The moon was still full, so the night was bright. Glynis frowned. The woman was Laurie and she faced a tall man. Glynis could not see his face, as he had his back to her.

Who was he? Laurie and the stranger were standing very

close and talking in low voices. She could not hear what they were saying. And yet from the way they were standing, from the closeness, and from the way they were taking turns speaking, she could tell this was no casual conversation.

Should she ask Laurie who the stranger was? She discarded the idea. If she admitted she had seen them together, if she asked questions, Laurie would surely accuse her of spying. Then, too, if Laurie had something to hide, it would make Laurie take more care next time—if there was a next time. No, it would be better to say nothing, better to wait and see if Laurie confided anything to her.

Am I being too suspicious? she asked herself. She wasn't at all sure how she felt, or why. But something inside, some instinct, cautioned her against totally accepting Laurie. Perhaps, she thought, it was only because Laurie had spent so much time with Margaret Campbell, or perhaps she didn't really believe anyone was good enough for Colin.

She looked outside again. The two were parting company. The stranger disappeared into the woods and Laurie headed back toward the castle.

The MacPherson town house in Inverness was larger than many, but from the outside it looked much the same. The front door opened into a central hall, off which was a large drawing room, a study, a kitchen, and a parlor. At the end of the hall a door opened into a small secluded walled garden. On the second floor there were five bedrooms, and there were three more rooms in the attic, where many items were stored.

Glynis stood in the middle of the attic and looked at the collection of old trunks. One contained her mother's dresses, which her father had never been able to throw out. Another contained clothing that had belonged to various servants. Yet another held her own childhood toys and dresses, and still another the clothing of her brothers. Vaguely she wondered why her father kept everything— but she knew the answer. He could not bear to throw out things that had once meant something. At heart, her father was a sentimental man who cherished the past.

"Glynis?"

Stewart popped his head through the attic opening.

"Yes, it's just me."

Stewart pulled himself through the opening, but once in the attic he could not stand because he was too tall. So, instead, he sat down on the floor cross-legged. "What are you doing up here?"

Glynis shrugged. "It's time someone went through some of this—"

"It seems to me that you did this every year before you left for France, and now you're starting again."

"I used to come up and look around every year. But this time I'm going to clean some things out. There's children's clothing here that should go to the poor."

"Don't touch Mother's things."

"I know better," Glynis replied. "How about some of these old things of yours?"

"Leave them. At least for now. I'd like to go through them myself."

Glynis could not suppress her smile. "I got Colin and James to get rid of some of their old things, but you— you're just like Father."

He lifted his brow. "You seem to be feeling a bit more chipper."

Glynis looked at her older brother. He wasn't one to notice whether a person was better or worse. "Did Colin tell you I wasn't well?"

"He told me you were upset about Robert's engagement."

Glynis felt her skin flush. "I wish he hadn't told you."

"Well, more to point, he told me you would be upset."

Glynis tossed her head. "If I was, I'm over it now."

"I imagine he'll be here for dinner tonight," Stewart said without emotion.

Glynis didn't dare look at him. She wasn't as close to Stewart as she was to Colin. As a matter of fact, no one was close to Stewart. He was a loner, a man who seemed much older than he was, a young man who clearly felt his future responsibility as clan chieftain already. She didn't want to reveal the depth of her feeling or the extent of her hurt to Stewart. Stewart, of all those in the family, would understand least of all how she felt.

"Is he bringing Margaret?" she asked.

"No, he's coming alone."

Glynis felt a surge of relief. Perhaps Margaret had returned to Argyll. She wondered if she should again try to talk to Robert or if she should continue to ignore him. She decided to ignore him. In fact, she decided to invite Ramsey to dinner too.

She turned and opened a trunk. It was full of little-girl dresses that had once been hers. She fingered her white communion dress and touched the veil she had worn. Then she picked up Lucy, a wooden doll that Robert had carved for her when she was eight. She bit her lip as she touched the doll. No, this was not for throwing away. This was for keeping. She laid it gently back down in the trunk.

"Anything you want me to take downstairs?" Stewart asked, intruding on her thoughts.

"Those dresses," Glynis answered. "Give them to Cook. She'll know whom to give them to."

"Are you sure?"

"Yes, I'm quite sure."

Stewart crawled over and took the bundle of clothes in his arms, then he carefully backed down the ladder. "Don't be too long up here," he called out. "Colin said Laurie is coming."

Glynis didn't answer. She waited till she heard Stewart leave the second floor before she climbed down. She hurried right to the study and there she penned a quick note to Ramsey. She sealed the note and called Rolf, the manservant who worked for her father. "Take this to the Monroe house," she instructed. "See that Ramsey Monroe himself takes it."

"Yes, Miss Glynis."

Glynis watched as Rolf made off. Ramsey Monroe was good-looking and suave. He, too, was older than she, though only by two years. And clearly he was quite interested in her, as he had asked Colin if he might call on her. Well, she thought, what better thing to do than to invite him to dinner? Robert would be surprised. Maybe, she reasoned, he might even be jealous.

"You'll see, Robert Forbes! You'll see that I am definitely not a child!" she thought for the hundredth time.

Duncan MacPherson sat at one end of the table and Glynis sat at the other. Colin, Stewart, and Robert sat on one side while Laurie, Ramsey, and James sat across from them.

The table was laden with food. The mutton stew was served in a huge bowl, and ladled into smaller individual bowls by the serving girl.

"Ah, my favorite dish," Duncan MacPherson said in a loud voice.

"Mine as well," Ramsey agreed.

Robert studied Ramsey Monroe, who sat opposite him. Ramsey didn't take his eyes off Glynis, and Robert thought to himself that he didn't like the way Ramsey looked at her at all. It was a look that conveyed nothing so much as pure lechery. But it was more than lechery that caused Robert not to like Ramsey. Ramsey seemed to be playing up to Duncan MacPherson, trying to ingratiate himself. Yes, on the one hand Ramsey leered at Glynis, and on the other he lapped at Duncan MacPherson's boots, clearly trying to impress him. It was all very annoying.

Robert forced his eyes away from Ramsey. Instead, he stared into his stew, asking himself silent questions. What right did he have to be annoyed with Ramsey? It wasn't as if he were in love with Glynis. Still, Glynis was like a sister to him, and surely their long relationship gave him the right to want to protect her, to see to it that someone like Ramsey didn't take advantage of her. A certain guilt filled him. It was he who had told her to find someone her own age, and now that she had, he found himself not approving of the person she had apparently chosen. Was it just disapproval? He forced his thoughts away from more probing questions and tried to concentrate on what others were saying.

"The clan heads are meeting next week," Duncan Mac-Pherson said matter-of-factly. "You'll accompany me, Stewart. And, Robert, Donald Cameron asked specifically that you attend."

"Then I will certainly be there," Robert replied.

Laurie looked up from her stew. "Is it true that this time the French will really help to restore our king?"

"I've heard that the troops are already assembling in Brest," Duncan replied confidently. "Yes, I think that Louis has finally seen the light."

"In Brest and not in Dunkirk?" Laurie asked.

Duncan MacPherson looked at her steadily. If he was surprised by her interest and geographical knowledge of the coast, he didn't show it. "Perhaps both," he answered vaguely.

Laurie smiled at him. "I was just curious. I traveled once along the French coast."

"I see," Duncan said, returning her smile.

Colin, too, beamed at Laurie, and Glynis watched, thinking that she still felt ill at ease with Laurie. Yet, Laurie was obviously intelligent and she was certainly attractive. But Glynis still felt that there was something ingenuous about Laurie, something she simply could not define but that gave rise to her ill ease.

"Will you attend mass with me on Christmas Eve, Glynis?" Ramsey suddenly asked.

Glynis looked up. She wanted to look at Robert. She wanted to see the expression on his face, but she could not turn without seeming obvious. "I should be delighted," she replied. She continued to look at Ramsey, careful to appear smitten with him and wondering how her actions made Robert feel. She was all too aware of the importance of the invitation she had just accepted. Midnight mass was followed by a gay celebration at the Inverness town hall and, finally, by breakfast on Christmas morning.

"Perhaps," Glynis said, "you will help me deliver baskets to the servants before mass."

"It would be my pleasure."

Robert lifted his glass of wine and drained it. Ramsey was a womanizer, and he decided that he would have to warn Glynis at the first opportunity. In his own mind there was no doubt that Ramsey was completely unsuitable for Glynis, and he decided to tell her so.

Without hesitation, Duncan MacPherson opened a second bottle of wine. He filled everyone's glass and then lifted his own. "To Bonnie Prince Charlie!" he toasted loudly.

"To Bonnie Prince Charlie," they all repeated in unison. For years now that had been the toast made by loyal Highlanders, Glynis thought. Now it seemed their dream of restoring the Stuarts to the throne of England, Scotland, Ireland, and Wales was closer to coming true.

December brought much colder weather. Glynis wandered through the market, stopping at each stall to examine what was being sold. Cook was shopping for Christmas dinner, so Glynis was concerned only with the purchase of a few gifts, since most of the presents were brought back from France. She had a fine Italian pipe for Stewart, a leather pouch for James, a wide, splendid leather belt for Colin, a pair of knit gloves for her father, and a miniature painting of herself for Robert. At the time she had been sitting for the painting, she had not imagined it might end up sitting on a table in the home of Margaret Campbell. Even now she refused to recognize the possibility that they would actually marry. No, they would not. Robert would see her with Ramsey and grow more and more jealous. Then, realizing his own feelings for her, he would end his relationship with Margaret and return to her. Eventually, they would be married and he would carry the miniature painting of her with him wherever he went.

We have a love that cannot be denied, she told herself. *Margaret is only a temporary obstacle.*

But of course she now had to find a suitable gift for Ramsey, as he would be taking her to mass and would be with her on Christmas morning when the festivities ended. At last she stopped at a book stall, and after considerable searching, selected a volume of French poetry by Voltaire, *Discours en vers sur l'homme.* It seemed a suitable gift.

"Ah, Glynis, are you shopping again?"

Glynis whirled around to face Robert Forbes.

"I rarely shop," she said in as cool a tone as she could

muster. Then, deciding the moment was perfect, she smiled. "I was just buying a little gift for Ramsey."

"I should like to speak with you, Glynis. Could we walk for a bit?"

"If you're not afraid someone will tell Margaret. I shouldn't want anyone to misunderstand or have her misunderstand our friendship. You are, after all, engaged."

"Margaret knows how much you mean to me, Glynis."

Glynis said nothing, but let him take her arm and guide her away from the book stall and then from the market. A cold wind swept down the street, and she let go of his arm and pulled her long cloak closer. "I'm sure it will snow for Christmas."

"It's getting colder every day," he agreed. "But I didn't want to discuss the weather."

He took her arm again, and guided her inside the city hall. The foyer was deserted and he took her to one of the benches. "This seems like a good place."

"You're being very mysterious."

"This isn't Paris, there are no cafés to which I could take you. And frankly, talking on the street does not excite me, the wind is far too cold."

Glynis undid the top button of her cloak. The building was not heated, so it offered respite only from the wind, not from the damp cold.

"I want to talk with you about Ramsey, Glynis."

Glynis looked up into his eyes. "What about Ramsey?" She felt suddenly defiant. Her plan was most certainly working.

"Glynis, he's not the man for you. He's very much of a ladies' man, and I don't like the way he tries to ingratiate himself to your father either. To tell you the truth, I think he is very much of a fortune hunter."

Glynis lifted her brow. "A ladies' man and a fortune hunter, is he?"

Her sarcastic tone shot through him. "Glynis, I'm very fond of you. I just want to protect you."

"First you tell me to find someone my own age; then, when I do, you tell me he's a fortune hunter and a ladies' man. You're saying these things only because you can't admit how you feel about me, Robert Forbes."

"I feel like a brother to you. I feel a responsibility for you."

Glynis stood up and stomped her foot. "You don't want me, but the truth is you don't want anyone else to have me either! Well, Robert Forbes, it doesn't work that way! You're going to marry Margaret, and I don't care! I thought I did, but I don't. Who knows, maybe I'll even marry Ramsey!"

"Glynis, don't be foolish!"

"I'm a grown woman! Leave me alone. I don't need your advice!" Glynis felt as if her blood were boiling. She turned away and walked toward the door without saying another word.

Robert turned restlessly in his bed. Then, tossing on his back, opened his eyes and stared at the slanted ceiling. Reluctantly, he admitted that he felt uncomfortable in the Campbell household even though the woman he was to marry slept in the bedroom below, and her parents, brothers, and sisters would soon be his own family.

But the Campbell household was not like the MacPherson household, where he was so much a member of the family that he thought nothing of coming and going without bothering to tell anyone. He thought it would be good if, indeed, he stayed there tomorrow. If only Glynis did not feel as she did. When he was at the MacPherson house, he felt her anger and he was well aware that it was the first time he had felt any kind of friction in that household at all. And then, too, he sadly admitted, he had to deal with his own mixed and now deeply confused emotions.

The Campbells were a household of argumentative types. It seemed as if one were always feuding with the other. Margaret was calm and uninvolved in her family's ever-changing loyalties, but she was too quiet sometimes. She lacked Glynis's spark. It would not occur to her to enter into a discussion among the males of the house, or to argue with any of them.

Not so with Glynis MacPherson, he thought as her image came into his head. Glynis was a fighter, she teased her brothers and tried to out-do them at every turn. She argued politics and philosophy, and she was well equipped intellectually to do both.

He conjured up the picture of her as she had looked in her Paris gown, the one trimmed in black lace that made her look not only older, but more seductive than she should have. Her figure was wonderful, her hair thick and rich, her eyes penetrating. For the first time in his life, he let his thoughts wander and began to imagine Glynis in a way about which he had never before thought of her. He began to wonder what she would be like in bed, and exactly how she might look and feel if they were making love. She had such passion! He drew in his breath, this was insane! He was engaged to Margaret Campbell and Glynis was seeing Ramsey. In fact, she had not even spoken to him since Christmas.

But he still could not shake the vision of her and he realized that the thought of her tossing beneath him had caused him to harden and that he was truly excited by the vision of her he had created in his mind. "Insane," he muttered as he forced himself to think of something else, anything else. But his ill ease lingered even as Glynis's assertions to him came back. She believed he loved her, not as a sister, but as a woman. Now, not for the first time, he wondered, if, indeed, she might be right.

Robert Forbes walked down the narrow street, crossed it, and knocked on the door of Donald Cameron. Donald Cameron of Lochiel was the leader of a group of influential Highlanders who had formed an "association" to further the Stuart cause. The others in the association included the Duke of Perth; his uncle, John Drummons; Simon Fraser, and Lord Lovat, who was the chief of Clan Fraser. The secretary of the association, William MacGregor of Balhaldie, had spent many months traveling a circuit from Scotland to Rome, then to Madrid, to Versailles, to London and back to Scotland. He had met with the old pretender James II and with the most prominent Jacobites in Paris, London, Madrid, Rome, and Scotland.

In less than an hour's time, the clan chieftains would arrive for a meeting, but Cameron had asked Robert to come alone and to arrive early.

Donald Cameron was a cautious man. He was not given to undue optimism or flights of fancy. It was the fact that he was levelheaded that drew Robert to accept his invitation and to listen to his views.

Robert was directed into a small study. It was filled with books, largely on the subject of medicine. Archibald, Donald Cameron's brother, was a medical doctor, and he spent considerable time at this town house in Inverness.

"Ah, Robert Forbes!" Donald Cameron smiled broadly as he entered the study. He held out his hand and shook Robert's energetically.

"There's talk of a decision regarding our position," Robert said.

"If talk were worth gold, we'd be a rich people," Donald Cameron joked. "Sit down, lad. Share a whisky with me."

Robert sat down, albeit on the edge of his chair. He watched as his host poured two fingers of single malt whisky into a glass.

Cameron handed Robert the glass and then sat down. "Tell me what talk you've heard."

"I've heard talk that the French may invade England and that they support the return of the rightful heir to the throne."

Cameron stared into the golden liquid in his glass and swished it around a bit. "One cannot always count on the French to follow through. It's no secret that Louis XV is deeply angered by the British victory at Dettingen and just as angry that the British gave Maria Theresa more than five hundred thousand pounds to finance her defense against Louis's armies."

Robert nodded. Though France and England were not yet at war, most of Europe was engaged in fighting. Three years before, in 1740, Charles VI had died, leaving his daughter, Maria Theresa, sovereignty over his huge domain. His body was not cold in the grave before Prussia, Bavaria, Poland, and France moved against Austria. Britain, where there was considerable sympathy for Maria Theresa, prepared to go to Austria's aid. First they did so with money and then in June, an Anglo-Hanoverian army under George II's command marched to engage the French. The battle took place at Dettingen, and the French had been soundly trounced.

"The French are furious over their defeat," Cameron said, shaking his head.

"Are they angry enough to invade Britain?"

"Confusion reigns supreme," Cameron answered honestly. "Our cause benefits from England's turmoil. Yes, I'm given to understand that Louis is angry enough to provide an invasion force and finance a rising. Even as we speak, troops are gathering at Channel ports in France."

"Then the rumors are a reality."

"Now, yes. But young Prince Charles, who would lead such a force on his father's behalf, first must be taken safely out of Italy. This is where you come in. You're young, you're educated, and you're known to be a most dedicated supporter."

"My father died in the last attempt to restore the Stuarts to the throne," Robert said solemnly.

"I know that, and King James himself suggested you."

Robert drained his glass. "Suggested me—I don't understand."

"He wants you to travel to Italy and to—shall I say—assist the prince on his journey to Paris."

Robert swallowed hard. It was a dangerous assignment but he would not turn it down. "I would be honored to so serve my king."

"Good. When the others arrive, during our meeting, I'll let it be known that you're willing."

Cameron settled back in his chair. "Have you been with MacPherson?"

"Yes, I just left Cluny."

"I saw Glynis when I was in Paris. She's turned into a very beautiful woman."

Robert pressed his lips together and nodded. Her image crossed his mind all too often, and the memory of her lips lingered. But each time he thought of her, he forced himself to think of Margaret. He reminded himself that he was engaged, though even as he sat in Cameron's study, he knew their engagement was over.

"She is indeed a beauty," he acknowledged.

"But you're still seeing Margaret Campbell," Cameron hedged.

"Yes, we're engaged—though I will have to break it off now."

Cameron nodded. "I must ask you to keep our discussion this morning strictly confidential."

"Of course," Robert said.

"And by that I mean that you should not discuss it even with Margaret."

"I won't," he answered. It came as no surprise to him that Donald Cameron was suspicious of John Campbell even though both Cameron's mother and wife were from Clan Campbell.

"Old feuds make the Campbells less than trustworthy," Cameron imparted.

Robert knew what Cameron meant, so he did not comment. But he knew he would have to speak to Margaret that day, directly after the meeting.

The clan leaders sat around the table. It was time for decisions.

"Is it agreed, then?" Cameron asked. He had reluctantly agreed to chair the meeting.

"What of Clan Campbell?" Bruce Chattan asked.

"They won't join any rebellion. Indeed, I have cause to believe they will stand with the British."

That the Campbells would not participate in an effort to put the Stuarts back on the throne of England was not surprising, but everyone in this room had hoped for their neutrality. As blunt as Cameron had been earlier, he had not mentioned the possibility of the Campbells fighting for the British. Robert shook his head; this definitely meant he would have to break his engagement. And even if he had been willing to marry Margaret, her father would never allow it.

Then, after a long silence, it was MacDonald who posed the question. "And you, Robert Forbes, where do you stand?"

"With you. I pledge my loyalty to the Stuart cause."

Cameron drew in his breath noisily. "We're to send Robert on a mission. King James himself has asked that he come."

"I can think of no one better," MacDonald said, offering his confidence.

"Then I believe we have agreed," Cameron summed up.

There was much mumbling around the table. But there was no objection. The plan was set.

As the meeting broke up and the clansmen streamed onto the streets of Inverness, Robert headed directly for the Campbell house. He knew he had to see Margaret immediately. He had to say good-bye to her.

The Campbell house was one of the largest in Inverness, though it was rarely occupied. The Campbells preferred their estate in Argyll, which was well to the south of Inverness.

As Robert approached the house, he was not surprised to see wagons in front. Clearly, the decisions taken by the others had made life too uncomfortable in Inverness and they were headed home.

Robert knocked and was admitted by Margaret. She was dressed to travel and silently ushered him into the reception room, which was filled with boxes.

"We're going home to Argyll," she said needlessly. "But I'm being sent to London."

Robert nodded. "Is this your decision?"

"Yes, Robert, I cannot defy my family." She fumbled with the ring on her finger and then handed it to him. "I'm sorry."

He took the ring and turned it slowly in his fingers. "I'm to leave for Paris immediately."

"You to Paris and I to London." She shook her head. "Don't be sad, Robert. It is for the best."

He said nothing, but looked at her questioningly.

"Ah, Robert, don't lie to yourself. I've seen the way you look at Glynis MacPherson. Don't deny yourself. You love her, and she loves you. I'm not hurt, truly."

He felt his face flush. "She's young . . . she's my best friend's sister."

"And? She'll quickly mature and you will still love her."

"I'm off on a dangerous mission. When I come home, if she still feels the same way, then we'll see—"

Margaret smiled at him and then, standing on tiptoe, kissed his cheek. "Don't lose her, Robert. Glynis is a strong woman, and in my heart I fear for all of us. Only the strong will survive."

Robert embraced her and then let her go. "Safe journey, Margaret Campbell."

"Safe journey to you as well."

The hall that had been so cold and stark the day she and Robert had gone there to talk was now warm from the fire burning in the two huge fireplaces on either side of the room, and it was festooned with greenery and boughs of holly with bright red berries. On a platform, a group of fiddlers played familiar Highland tunes while dancers whirled about, doing reels. These were not the formalized, slow, and deliberate dances of the French court, but were rather fast and wild with the dancers breaking free now and again—sometimes groups of men, sometimes groups of women—to perform a special step dance in the center of the floor. These were dances that left the participants breathless and panting. These were dances that required energy and athletic ability, dances that gave rise to passion.

Glynis was not dressed in one of her Paris gowns, but,

rather, in a full woolen skirt and a crisp white top. Across her shoulder, from left to right, she wore her tartan, the bright red plaid of Clan MacPherson. Her tartan was held in place by a wide leather belt with a gold buckle. Just below her left shoulder, she wore a pin on her tartan. It was gold, and bore the family crest, a cat sejant. The clan motto, printed around the edge of the pin in Latin, read "Touch not the cat without a glove."

"You're a woman of great energy, Glynis MacPherson!" Ramsey called out as he clasped her tiny waist and grinned down at her. They whirled down the aisle between two sets of dancers.

"And you're a very good dancer," she responded. Robert was a fine dancer too, she thought. But she pushed all thoughts of him from her mind. He was gone, and rumor had it that Margaret Campbell had gone with him.

"You're a beautiful woman," Ramsey said, drawing her as close as he dared.

Glynis said nothing, though she was aware of a warm, glowing feeling. It was pleasant to see the admiration in his eyes and to know it was for her. She had longed forever to see that look in Robert's eyes.

Ramsey guided her to the edge of the dancers and then to the far corner of the room.

"Are we not going to dance anymore?"

Ramsey looked down into her green eyes. Her skin was like cream, smooth and soft. Her waist, cinched by her wide belt, was tiny, and her breasts, as he well knew from having seen her in more seductive dresses, were full and rounded, their hidden treasure a temptation. He smiled at the very thought of undressing her and of bending her to his will. She was proud and spoiled, the child of a rich and indulgent father. Still, she would be a desirable wife. She would bring a large dowry, stature in the community, and her father was a man of influence. Other women who might also bring power and fortune were far less attractive than Glynis MacPherson. Whatever her drawbacks, she could be tamed. And the taming, he decided, would unquestionably be worth the effort.

"I just thought we'd rest for a moment. In any case, I want to ask you if I might continue to call."

"You're welcome anytime," Glynis said, looking up into his handsome face. What on earth was it that Robert didn't like about Ramsey? Surely he was jealous, surely his warnings had no basis past his own desire to have her for himself, to keep her in reserve, so to speak. He might well have gone away with Margaret, but that did not mean that they would marry.

"I didn't mean just to visit, Glynis. I want to court you. I want you to seriously consider becoming my wife."

She could hardly say she was surprised. Still, she had not expected Ramsey to declare himself quite so soon. She looked into his eyes and then smiled, trying to appear shy, which in fact she was not. "I would be flattered," she whispered even as she thought about just how to get the news to Robert that Ramsey was courting her.

She felt Ramsey's hand drop slightly from her waist to give her buttocks a furtive caress. The feeling was not unpleasant, and so she decided to say nothing.

"I'll come on New Year's," he said, squeezing her hand.

"I shall be expecting you."

It was all very formal.

"We'd better go back," Glynis suggested. "People will talk."

Ramsey said nothing, but he led her back into the crowded hall.

Glynis looked about the room and then she saw Robbie MacInnis. He was to journey to Paris, there to attend the Scots College. It was impossible that he would not see Robert and bring him news from home.

"I want to dance," she said, pulling Ramsey forward.

Again they entered the fray. But in seconds Glynis broke loose and went to the center. She clicked her heels on the wooden floor, the rhythm of her clicks augmented by the music of the fiddlers. She whirled about wildly, tossing her head and her long, dark hair. Her skirt whirled out, revealing petticoats and trim ankles. This was a Highland step dance, intricate and intoxicating, rhythmic and wild. She turned and turned, faster and faster, clicking her heels to the clapping and shouts of onlookers. When she came to her breathless finale, she looked about quickly and danced into Ramsey's waiting arms.

Chapter Four

January 1744

Robert glanced out the window into the courtyard where the men who made up the royal hunting party had begun to assemble with their horses. Most were older men, and Robert realized that apart from Prince Charles himself, he was the youngest. Ironically, he was one of the few who knew exactly what was to transpire. He had arrived from Scotland only the previous day, but he had spent a few hours talking with the prince, and already the two of them had become friends and confidants.

Robert recalled part of a conversation he had with the young prince only a short time before. "I'm twenty-three years old and I've lived my entire life in exile in Italy," the prince had said, shaking his head.

The prince was a tall, slender young man with an oval face, soft brown eyes, and a rosy complexion. He was well trained and able to fight, yet confided that he felt he had been overprotected and stifled in his desire to be independent.

"Today," he told Robert with growing enthusiasm, "all that will end. Today, with your help, I'll break out of this sheltered royal cocoon and emerge a man."

By the time the sun rose, they would both be launching out on a new adventure.

"It seems today that my long-awaited destiny might soon be fulfilled," the prince told him dreamily.

One thought almost always leads to another, and the prince's use of the word "destiny" caused Robert to think of Glynis. What a fool I am, he silently thought. She was right, they were destined to be together. His heart ached for her and he wished he had gone to see her before he left. At least then he could have told her that he wasn't marrying Margaret and that he loved her.

Robert let his mind wander for a minute, then he looked outside, toward the courtyard.

The window was fringed with frost, a sure sign that it was cold. Both men and horses expelled their breath in white puffs. Robert put on his scarf and went outside to join them.

"Where's my brother?" the prince asked, looking around.

Robert could see that the prince was eager to get started. It was as if he feared something or someone would stop him needlessly. All the plans were in motion, he wanted to be in motion too.

"Prince Henry is not ready yet," one of his hunting companions replied. "Perhaps he is still at his prayers."

His brother's reverence was well known. Henry had a tendency to linger in chapel. "I shall go on ahead," Charles announced. "Henry and the rest of you can catch up with us at Albano." Charles waved his hand for the postilions to lead the way, and he signaled two servants, Robert, and his tutor, Murray. Everything was going according to plan.

Charles mounted his horse and fell in behind the others. It was not unusual for him to head out before the rest of the hunting party was fully assembled.

Robert smiled to himself in the predawn darkness, they would be surprised. Everyone would be surprised.

They rode for several miles and Charles, Robert, and the two servants pulled ahead of the rest.

The plan was simple. Murray would pretend to injure himself and most of the others would stop to tend him.

"Oh!" Murray called out. He drew his horse in and slipped from the saddle.

Charles, Robert, and the two servants widened their lead. After a time, when they came to the crossroads, they turned. Instead of heading toward Albano, they headed northeast toward the border with Tuscany.

The sun rose, but it did not brighten the cloudy day. The roads were winding and covered with snow. Traveling on the snow and ice was treacherous, but not as dangerous as lingering, Robert told himself.

It was well known that Tuscany was filled with British intelligence agents, and informers were as plentiful in Florence as the fine leather goods for which the city was famous.

Several months before, a British agent named Dixon had intercepted one of James II's guards. The guard, a man, named Chamberlayne, fought hard. He left Dixon for dead. But Dixon survived the attack, even though he was wounded so badly that he was no longer of use to the British. In this instance the guard had triumphed, but such was not always the case.

Tit for tat, the clandestine little battles between the

agents of Britain and the Jacobite agents and their supporters continued. But at this moment more was at stake. This was no mere member of the king's guard crossing Tuscany. It was the young prince himself. If British agents recognized and captured the prince, it would be a disaster. It would, in fact, end everything. Charles, and those with him, would be either killed or imprisoned.

Ahead, Charles saw the hut he had been seeking, and he reined in his horse, signaling Robert and his loyal servants to stop too. He dismounted, tied the horse, and quickly opened the unlocked door. It was no more than a one-room shack, but there, piled on a table, were the necessary clothes. Charles quickly discarded his own clothes and bade Robert and his servants to do the same. All four of them shivered, and Antonio, Charles's manservant, could do nothing to stop his chattering teeth.

Charles put on the uniform of a Neapolitan courier and found in the pocket a passport identifying him as one Don Biago, an Italian officer in the service of Spain. His two servants had been provided plain clothes that bore no resemblance to what they normally wore in the royal employ. Robert also had the uniform of a Neapolitan courier.

"We change horses in another two miles," he advised. Quickly, the clothes they had all four worn were discarded and put into the fireplace. Antonio started a fire, and for a moment they all stood and watched as their garments were consumed in the flames.

"Pity there is no time to stay and warm up," Antonio muttered.

Robert shook his head. "No time," he said, turning quickly. "We must ride until we can ride no more."

* * *

Colin slipped his arm around Laurie's shoulder. The fire burned steadily, keeping the small parlor warm and cozy in spite of the wind that howled outside, whipping around the corners of the houses and depositing fine ice pellets on the ground.

They were alone in the Lewis house except for the servants, who moved silently about, not entering the parlor, and for all purposes seeming invisible.

When she felt his warm fingers caressing her bare shoulders Laurie looked up into Colin's eyes. A half smile covered her lips, and Colin bent slightly and kissed her. She made no attempt to break the kiss, as she sometimes did, and he felt emboldened by her keen response. He withdrew reluctantly from her lips and kissed her neck. She squirmed against him, and he felt aroused by her movements and by the low, kittenish noise she made when he kissed her ear.

Colin felt his own skin flush with desire. He had dreamed often of being alone with Laurie, of exploring her curves, of touching her swelling breasts. His intentions were honorable, he wanted to marry her. But still, she kept putting that off, while at the same time allowing him certain liberties.

She nuzzled him back and his hand moved to her breast, which for a long while he held before dipping his head still lower and kissing her cleavage intimately. She did not object, but again moved seductively and even kissed his neck in return. Waves of desire flooded over him. How he wanted to dip his hand into her bodice, but he dared not even think of such a thing for long.

"Please, darling," she breathed into his ear even as she pulled away slightly, breaking the absolute passion of their embrace.

"Oh, Laurie. You taunt me so. For heaven's sake, why can't we be married? I want you so!"

She looked up at him with sadness in her eyes. "I know," she said softly. "But, Colin, how can we know what will happen?"

"We can never know what will happen," he answered.

"You know what I mean. If there is another rebellion—we can't know how it will turn out. Try to understand. I don't want to be married and with child and have you march off to fight the Saxons."

It was her perennial answer, and it was one with which he could not argue. He nodded and released her.

"How close is it?" she whispered as her fingers touched his cheek.

Colin looked into her eyes. "It is in motion," he answered vaguely.

"In motion? What do you mean, in motion?" A wave of absolute excitement filled Laurie, but she fought to maintain control, to appear interested but not anxious.

"The plan has been initiated."

"What plan?" Laurie asked, and as she let the words escape her lips, she realized she had revealed far too much interest.

"You know I can't tell anyone."

She continued to look into his eyes, then moved closer to him and took his hand. "Colin, I love you. I want to be your wife, truly I do. Darling, it's just that I'm afraid."

Colin looked at her in sheer amazement as she put his hand back on her breast and held it there.

"I like the way it feels when you touch me here," she whispered. "Oh, Colin, you don't know how much I want you to loosen me, to hold me naked in your arms—Colin, I want you so much, it's hard for me too. I fear for your life, for our lives."

He felt dizzy with desire at the renewed thought of holding her naked in his arms, more so now that he had the knowledge that she imagined them in such an embrace.

"It makes me sad that you cannot share everything with me," she whispered.

She was holding his hand hard against her now and looking at him imploringly. "I hate secrets too," he said softly. "If I tell you, you must promise not to breathe a word to anyone."

"Of course."

Her other hand was on his thigh, and she moved it between his legs, causing him to rise and feel incredible frustration. He wondered if—given her innocence—she knew the effect she was having on him. It was sweet torture, and had they been somewhere else, somewhere he did not have to worry about being interrupted, he would surely have tried to seduce her completely and utterly, hoping that once involved, she would lose her fear of "the situation" as she called it.

"Tell me, Colin," she pressed.

"The prince has left Italy. He will proceed to France and onward to where the invasion army is being prepared."

"And where might that be?" she asked.

"Gravelines, I believe. But perhaps Brest as well."

Laurie nodded and leaned her head against his chest. "It excites me and frightens me," she said softly. "Colin, I do love you, but you must be patient with me. Perhaps in a few weeks, when we know a little more of what is to come, then we could at least set a date."

It was the most she had offered, and he felt encouraged by it. "I love you," he whispered.

Laurie looked up and down the street. It was early in the morning and no one was around. Still, she was unprepared to throw caution to the wind simply because it was unlikely that someone would appear.

Certain, though, that no one was coming in either direction, she ducked into the narrow passageway that connected the two sets of row houses. Laurie let herself into the house on her left by the side door. As there was no window, the inner hall was pitch black. She cursed silently and ran her hand along the wall, walking slowly until from beneath a door at the far end she saw a light. She turned the knob and let herself into the well-lit kitchen.

Angus Ross, who preferred to be called only by his last name, sat at a long wooden table. When she came in, he looked up from his tea. "Ah, I thought I heard footsteps."

"The least you could do is to put a lamp in the hall."

"Why, are you afraid of the dark?"

"I am afraid of very little, as you well know. It is simply awkward."

"Have you brought me news?"

"Yes. But it is not news that will make you at all happy."

"All news makes me happy. I don't deal with the outcome or meanings of information, only with the value it has to others. You would do well to learn this principle. Once you become emotionally involved with either side in any given situation, you become infinitely less effective."

She did not argue with him. Ross was a hard man; he withheld his emotions and yet—she blushed ever so slightly at the memory that flitted across her mind—he always brought her great pleasure. "The prince has left Italy," she said.

"The players on the chessboard are all in motion. Is there more?"

"He will go to Paris and an invasion army is being assembled in Gravelines."

Ross smiled and stood up. Without a single word he pulled her into his arms and held her tightly. "What may

I ask did you have to give in order to obtain this information?"

"Kisses," she answered, deciding to leave out the rest.

"Only kisses?" He undid her cloak and pushed it away. She was dressed simply in a low-cut woolen dress with a tightly laced bodice. It displayed her charms admirably.

"Colin wants to marry me."

Ross covered her breast with his large hand and squeezed it hard. "Did he touch you here?"

"If he did?" She raised her brow slightly.

He squeezed her still harder, and she winced.

"Don't taunt me! I am not one of your lapdogs!" Ross hissed.

She opened her mouth to protest, but he was too strong and too quick for her. He pushed the top of her dress down with incredible strength; in fact, he nearly tore the material. He bared her to the waist, and hungrily nibbled at her breasts as she squirmed in his arms. Her arms were around his neck even as he lifted her to the table and explored beneath her skirts. She breathed heavily and groaned as she felt him pull down her undergarment. He paused for a moment as he lifted and folded his kilt.

She groaned loudly as he forced himself into her, all the time kneading her breasts roughly with his hands and sucking hard with his mouth on her right nipple.

Laurie heaved her hips upward, pressing hard and panting with exertion as he moved his hands from her breasts and held her buttocks tightly.

"Tell me what you like, my dear."

"You," she whispered.

"Say what I want you to say." He pinched her nipple and squirmed.

"That I like it when you—"

"When I what?"

"Take me—take me like this."

Even the words excited her and she let out a moan as she felt herself tumble into fulfillment. He shook above her, and as soon as he himself had finished, he turned her over and spanked her bottom playfully. "You're a very bad young woman," he said harshly. But he smiled. "You do need so much discipline."

Laurie shivered. He excited her so much, she could not contain herself. She would do anything for him, and regrettably he knew it.

The fire burned steadily and Glynis sat with her eyes glued to it, watching as it slowly consumed the wood, causing it to glow bright red, as if burning from the inside out. Although there were no windows in the downstairs room, she knew that a light snow had fallen during the night and that the windows on the second and third floors were white with frost.

Unable to sleep in spite of the darkness, she had gotten up before the sun rose and decided to take a long walk in the predawn silence of the town.

Now that she thought about it, it seemed almost providential that she had woken and gone out. It was not the only time she had walked in the early morning in Inverness, but it was not a part of her usual routine either.

Inverness was laid out like the spokes on a wheel. She had walked down her own street and around the outer rim of the town and down one of the several long streets that led to the square. That was when she had seen Laurie Lewis. For some reason, she herself had stepped behind a hedge and watched with fascination as Laurie, looking around with what seemed apparent caution, slipped into the side entrance of the house belonging to Angus Ross.

She had been so taken aback that rather than risk encountering Laurie, or being seen herself, she had retraced her steps and returned to her house the way she had gone. Now she sat in front of the fire and thought about what she had seen. This was the second time she had seen Laurie meeting with Ross—though, of course, this time she had not actually seen them meet. The question in her mind was simple, why were they meeting? And if their encounters were harmless, why bother with such subterfuge?

Glynis closed her eyes for a moment. The image of the fire remained, and she felt on the edge of falling back to sleep curled in her father's chair, when she heard footsteps on the stairs. It was Colin. She knew because among her brothers he was the one who was usually up first.

"Colin?" she called out softly.

"Glynis, what are you doing up so early?" He poked his head into the study.

"I went for a walk. Come in, I have tea in here."

He came into the room and saw the tray on the desk. He poured himself a cup of steaming tea and sat down.

"Could you not sleep?"

"No, I went for a walk."

"It's cold outside."

"Invigorating," she said. "Colin, I saw Laurie."

"Yes, like you, she enjoys early morning walks."

"She went into the house of Angus Ross."

Colin's face clouded over, and Glynis sensed his anger even before he spoke. "What's wrong with you?" he asked. "I love Laurie and I trust her. I'd like it if you'd stop spying on her."

"I'm not spying! I was just walking down the street."

"Glynis, I know how upset you are about Robert, but I can't allow you to be jealous of Laurie."

Glynis felt her temper rising. How could he think such a thing? "I felt I had to tell you," she protested.

"Angus is her cousin. Perhaps she was having breakfast

with her aunt. I don't know, and I don't care. As I said, I trust her.''

Glynis looked at her tea. She was afraid to pick up the cup for fear her hand would shake. Colin was her favorite, they were terribly close—how could he think she wanted anything for him except happiness? She swallowed her temper and simply nodded. Perhaps he was right. Perhaps her own confusion was causing her to misinterpret situations. Robert was engaged to Margaret, and now he had abruptly left for France. Strangely, Margaret had disappeared too, and it was widely assumed that she had defied her father and gone with Robert so they could be married in France. Ramsey had told her that the rest of the Campbells had retreated to Argyll but that Margaret was not with them and that fact had been confirmed by everyone she knew who has passed through Argyll.

No doubt Robert would be gone for many months, and when he came home he would be wed to another, Glynis thought miserably. She felt older, defeated, and suddenly very tired.

On arriving in Paris, Prince Charles and Robert went directly to the home of Lord Sempill. He was rotund, a man as round of girth as he was tall. His smile was infectious, and his attitude one of perennial optimism. They had been there only a short time when they were joined by Murray, who, after pretending to be hurt so as to delay and confuse the rest of the hunting party, traveled by a different route to Paris.

Lord Sempill was the Paris agent of Prince Charles's father, James II. His lodgings in Paris were modest, yet far better than those of many other Jacobites who lived in exile.

His house had three floors, and he could entertain as

many as fifty comfortably for a reception or seat twenty for dinner. The top floor was a separate apartment, always prepared for the unexpected guest of rank and influence.

Robert and Murray were lodged in rooms on the second floor while Prince Charles stayed in the apartment on the third floor.

Lord Sempill welcomed the young Prince Charles with enthusiasm and with his usual optimism. "You look so well," he gushed. "I cannot tell you how long I have waited for this moment. I know you must hardly remember me. After all, you were quite a bit younger when I visited in you in Italy."

"I do remember you," Prince Charles said gracefully.

"That is so flattering. I cannot tell you how excited I am to have you here, staying in my house."

"It is I who am indebted for your hospitality and loyalty. But, please, let me introduce my companions."

"Of course, of course," Sempill burbled nervously.

"This is Robert Forbes. He traveled from Inverness to Italy to help me with my escape."

"I'm honored," Lord Sempill said politely.

Prince Charles smiled and motioned them all to be seated. "As we'll be living under one roof, we must put aside all these formalities."

Lord Sempill smiled and his round, shiny face turned red. He pointed Charles to a chair and immediately poured snifters of fine French cognac for his guests. "I am completely confident that when the invasion force lands in England, Londoners will rise up as one and overthrow King George—King George? I don't even know why I call him that. He is nothing but a Saxon usurper. I know you will overcome all the obstacles and take the throne. I know the time is right. After all these years I feel it in my bones."

Robert lifted the cognac to his lips and thought to himself that Lord Sempill talked a great deal.

"I, too, feel optimistic," Prince Charles agreed. "I have received messages of great encouragement from the king of France, and he seems prepared to support our cause to the limit. Tell me, when do you think I will meet with him face-to-face?"

Lord Sempill frowned ever so slightly, and the frown made Robert feel uncomfortable.

"I'm truly not certain. There are messages from him, but you know that our friend, Cardinal Tencin, is only one of Louis's advisers. It may be that in order to mislead the British, he will decline to meet with you at all," Lord Sempill suggested.

"I would understand that," Charles said.

It seemed to Robert that the prince refused to allow anything to interfere with his good mood. He wished he were the same. He wanted to be there, to do all he could. But truth be known, he could bear no long delays. He thought of Glynis constantly and he wanted to get home to her.

"If the king does not wish to see you," Robert suggested, "perhaps we should proceed in a few weeks time to Gravelines so we can be at the heart of the invasion army as it is being formed."

"That could be dangerous," Lord Sempill warned.

Prince Charles laughed. "I live with danger. Besides, with so many strangers in the town, one more will not be noticed. It is easy for me to disguise myself simply as another soldier. I want to be there, so if it is pointless for me to stay in Paris, then I will go. Forbes is right, it is where we should be."

"But you will stay a few days in Paris, won't you? There are so many of your followers who want to meet you—and besides, your journey has been arduous. You surely need to rest."

Charles finished his cognac and took Sempill's hand. "Yes, and it took far longer than I expected."

"Another cognac? Let us drink to the success of this venture."

Charles nodded and they all watched as Sempill poured more cognac. They toasted with a click of their glasses.

Robert drank his slowly and continued to observe Prince Charles. He seemed gracious, earnest, and dedicated. Clearly, Lord Sempill was impressed.

Robert, who had traveled with him on his difficult and most dangerous journey, knew that Prince Charles did not complain about his circumstances or the absence of those amenities with which he had grown up. He seemed an adjustable sort, and well he would have to be if he was to deal successfully with the French king and, after him, the Highlanders.

Robert wondered if Louis would see the prince. Who could understand the French? To him it seemed as if Louis ran hot and cold. He promised the world, but he did not want to meet with the person to whom he had promised it.

"Is something the matter?" Charles asked, turning to Robert.

"Nothing, no, nothing at all. I know things will go well."

"To the future," Charles toasted.

"To the future," they all repeated.

Outside, the March winds howled and pellets of hard rain fell relentlessly. Inside, the house seemed gloomy, and certainly their host's constant lectures and pessimistic outlook added to the atmosphere of melancholy, Robert thought.

Robert sat on a high-backed chair in the study of George Keith, Earl of Marischal. Vaguely, he wondered if his feel-

ings were evident in his facial expression, or if he looked
as bored and miserable as he felt. Nothing had gone right,
nothing. He knew without a doubt that Prince Charles
shared his mood, though doubtless for different reasons.
Prince Charles wanted to get on with his proposed "invasion," and while he was eager for that, he wanted to get
back to Scotland and to Glynis. He couldn't shake thoughts
of her from his mind. He dreamed of her nightly and even
during the long days he thought of her.

For over two months they had been besieged with bad
luck and subjected to subterfuge and intrigue. He felt tired
of it all, yet no less dedicated to his monarch.

"These are little intrigues for Mr. Fisher's amusement,"
Charles had told him. Prince Charles was "Mr. Fisher"—
that was the name he was currently using.

But of course it was not just the fighting, bickering, and
little plots among the prince's followers that proved so
frustrating. There was much more. The French themselves
had done an about-face, and Prince Charles was obviously
unsure of exactly how he should respond.

First, there was a last-minute decision to change the
invasion site from Malden to Blackwall in the Thames
estuary. Next, the invasion was temporarily delayed, but at
the time they had all firmly believed that the final steps
would be taken in a matter of days when the men were
due to assemble at Dunkirk. From there, the plan was to
launch transport vessels. The French would sail up the
Channel to engage the British.

But they delayed too long. The British had time to prepare and to secure London. They forced Catholics to sign
loyalty oaths, and those who refused were exiled to the
countryside.

Next, the French admiral, Roquefeuille, led his ships up
the Channel from Brest. When he did not sight any British
warships, he made the fatal error of deciding that this

meant the British had not left Portsmouth. Unexpectedly, the French encountered the British fleet at Dungeness. It was late afternoon, and the tide was low, so there could be no engagement. Moreover, Roquefeuille was dismayed at the size of the British fleet. To add to the miserable situation, a storm was coming up. Roquefeuille made for the French coast. The storm continued. It battered his vessels and did much damage; worse yet, the bad weather did not cease. As if the British controlled the weather, fierce winds blew across the Channel and many of the transports anchored at Dunkirk were severely damaged.

Robert sipped his brandy and continued to think about what happened next. The prince asked him to accompany him, and the two of them were aboard the vessel captained by Marshal Saxe. Saxe had already embarked when the storm arose, and even he knew they had been fortunate to make it back to port.

The bad weather continued on and on, and it continued even now as Robert grimly listened to the wind and rain from inside the shelter of Keith's house. The upshot of the entire misadventure was that France could no longer delay declaring war on England. Moreover, it was clear to all that the battles of this newly declared war would be fought in Flanders. The French would not invade England, and Prince Charles and his proud Scots entourage would not be able to lead a triumphant army into London. They had watched as their opportunity evaporated and King Louis turned away to pursue other matters. Louis would fight the British without thought for the Stuart cause. This was apparent to Robert, to Murray, and most certainly to Prince Charles.

But Charles still considered sailing for England alone, even though the French advised him not to do so. And as if to ensure none of them did anything reckless, they had been sent to Keith and advised to stay out of sight.

Keith was in his seventies. He had sheltered James II in 1715. He was loyal to a fault, but he was also a terrible pessimist.

"To go alone would destroy the Stuart cause," Keith declared again and again.

Prince Charles didn't respond. Indeed, he had confided to Robert that he suspected Keith had gone behind his back to discourage the French.

"Well, we're in limbo," Charles said, filling the silence.

"It's better to be in limbo than to make a mistake that would cost you everything," Keith said, looking up.

"It's nearly April," Charles observed as he finished his brandy. "I see no point in remaining here. The army has even left and gone to Flanders. I think we should all return to Paris."

Keith shrugged. "I suppose you need some diversion."

Diversion? Robert could see Charles bristle, but to his credit, the young prince held his temper. They would not have needed diversions if things had gone as planned. And the truth was, they did not need them now. Nonetheless, the three of them—the prince, Murray, and he had already decided that they were returning to Paris with or without Keith's approval. What they all needed was to get away from the unending pessimism of this man who was completely unable to take risks.

"I hope you won't listen to the clan leaders and try to overtake England with their help."

"At least they still offer their help," Charles said, unable to disguise his sarcastic tone as he looked at Murray and then at Robert.

Keith shook his head and muttered.

Charles pulled himself up and out of the chair. "I'm going to my rooms to pack."

"I shall arrange for transportation."

"I would appreciate it."

Yes, they would go back to Paris. Obviously, Charles was going to consider depending solely on the Scots. Robert was unsure himself about this course of action. Murray was convinced it was right. He argued that with the English fighting on the Continent, an invasion from the north could be most successful. "And we'll gather followers as we go," he predicted. As it seemed the prince would choose to accent the offer of the clansmen, Robert could only hope Murray was right.

Years earlier Glynis had asked her father to build her a window seat, and finally he had acquiesced. She sat in it now, her arms around her knees, her eyes on the street below.

It was April, and as usual in April the Highlands were cold and rainy with an occasional day of icy sleet.

"Robert, oh, Robert." His name escaped her lips as she thought of him in Paris. It would be beautiful along the Seine, warmer by far than the Highlands. Flowers would be blooming and the grass would have turned green. Then she imagined Margaret at his side and she commanded her vision to disappear. If she thought about them together, she had to fight back tears. It wasn't right. It was she who belonged at Robert's side. Once she had questioned herself, but now she did not. She knew deep in her heart that he loved her. She cherished the dream that he would come back to her, unencumbered and ready to declare himself.

As her daydream evaporated, a reality came into view. From her vantage point, she could see the corner of the street and on the corner she saw Laurie and—yes, it was Angus Ross. Laurie was wearing her blue cloak and Angus his familiar tartan. But Laurie's hood had blown off and her red hair blew in the wind.

Glynis watched them and her mouth opened in surprise when she saw Angus bend and kiss Laurie. It was not, even from this distance, a family sort of kiss. "Kissing cousins," Glynis said to herself. She bit her lip and tried to think what she ought to do. The last time she had spoken to Colin concerning her suspicions about Laurie, he had been furious and more or less told her to mind her own business. But how could she overlook this? How could she not tell him?

"Oh, Colin." Why didn't he realize she had his best interests at heart? He was so smitten by Laurie, he couldn't see that she was hoodwinking him.

As she saw Laurie approaching the house, she thought that perhaps it was time to confront Laurie herself. Perhaps she would tell Colin, perhaps she would not.

Glynis stood up and smoothed out her skirt. She hurried down the back stairs and was behind the place where the back hall jutted into the main hall, just as Tavish was opening the front door.

"I'm to meet Colin here," Laurie said to Tavish.

Laurie was a frequent visitor and Tavish opened the door wide and directed her into the parlor. Glynis, whom neither of them could have seen, waited a moment before she entered the parlor. Colin wasn't home yet and, in fact, she thought he would be at least another half hour.

"Oh," Laurie said. "I thought you were Colin."

"He's not home just yet," Glynis said, trying to think exactly what it was she felt she had to say.

"I don't mind waiting," Laurie replied, smiling.

"Good. I think it's time we talked. In fact, the time is overdue."

Laurie frowned. "You sound angry."

"I think I am, Laurie. You know, Colin and I are very close. If anything or anyone threatens him, I take it badly. He is the same with me."

"Is someone threatening Colin?" she asked, making her big brown eyes even wider.

"I think so. Laurie, three times, including today, I've seen you with Angus Ross."

Laurie's face flushed ever so slightly. But her eyes were still wide, still filled with innocence. "He's my cousin."

"And you seem very close for cousins, Laurie. Close enough that he would visit you at Cluny late at night outside the barn and not so much as say boo to the rest of us. Close enough that you would be sneaking into his house at the crack of dawn, and, it seems, close enough to be kissing in broad daylight on the corner of this very street."

Her skin alone reflected her discomfort, Glynis thought. It was tinged with pink. But her eyes were very wide, unblinking. "You've been spying on me!" she said with a tone of shock.

"Not spying. On all three occasions it was simply an accident that I saw you. But considering your relationship with my brother, I think I'm justified in asking what is going on between you and Ross."

"I think you were spying. I don't think you like me, or think I'm good enough for Colin. You hate me and you're trying to ruin my relationship with him."

"I'm trying to protect him. What is your relationship with Angus Ross?"

"He's my cousin, I told you! There is nothing between us save that we are family."

How well she lied, Glynis thought. Should she tell Colin? "I was sitting in the upstairs window, Laurie. That did not look like a family kind of kiss to me."

"You're mean and suspicious and you're jealous because Colin loves me and Robert Forbes left you for another woman!"

Glynis scowled at her. That she brought up Robert infuriated her. She trembled with anger at Laurie's obvious attempt to distract her, to avoid the question. "That's not so," Glynis said, struggling for control.

At that moment the door opened and Colin came into the room. To Glynis's surprise, tears filled Laurie's eyes and she ran into Colin's arms, sobbing.

"What is it?" he asked, embracing her.

"Glynis! She hates me! She keeps asking me about Ross. She thinks I'm up to something."

Glynis was stunned. She had anticipated many reactions, but not this one. It was completely devious.

Colin glared at her. "Glynis, how could you?"

"Colin, I saw her kissing Angus Ross. And it was no family kiss! In the name of heaven, wake up!"

"Wake up! I should wake up? I'm not the one harboring a deep, dark love for a man who's left Scotland with another woman. Leave Laurie alone! If you can't be kind to her and accept her, then just be kind to her. I love her and I intend to marry her."

"Oh, Colin, I'm sorry," Glynis said. His anger was palpable and his eyes flashed. She didn't want it to be this way between them even though she was angered by his comments. She picked up her skirts and fled the room. Laurie's expression was triumphant and Glynis thought that if she lived to be a hundred, she would never forget Laurie's look.

Chapter Five

July 1745

The lake shimmered in the moonlight, its rippling waters reflecting the trees and even Glynis's own elongated shadow. The night was clear and the moon full, a full moon that appeared to dance beneath the water, beckoning her, calling her to move forward, to act.

So much had happened! She had been back in Scotland for nearly two years, and in a month's time she would be nineteen. Her days in France were a distant memory, though she knew the streets of Paris were a part of Robert's present. He'd been gone since December 1743, seventeen long months traveling with and serving the prince. Since England and France were now officially at war, there were no letters, only stories from travelers about what was happening, and what was not.

As the war dragged on, it sapped the French of the will, as well as the means, to help restore the Stuarts to the throne of England. And yet the rumor was still that Bonnie Prince Charlie would return and lead his followers to overthrow the Hanoverian king who now ruled England, Scotland, Ireland, and Wales—the disUnited Kingdom, as the joke went.

Glynis sat down on the flat, smooth rock that was her favorite perch. She stared at the moon's reflection and her mind wandered as fragmented thoughts filled her head.

Most of the time she was able to force the thought of Robert and Margaret together out of her mind, but sometimes at night she dreamed of Robert, and at such times she awoke in a cold sweat, reminding herself again and again that in all likelihood he was in the arms of another woman.

It isn't fair, she thought. He's made a horrible mistake. And then she thought of Ramsey. She wasn't being fair to him either. She let Ramsey go on courting her even though she did not love him. Yet, she admitted, she found his adoration was some small comfort.

"Glynis!"

Glynis turned slowly at the sound of her name on the silent evening air.

"Glynis! Are you out there?"

It was Ramsey's voice calling to her from the rutted path that led from the castle down to the lake.

"Yes, on my rock by the lake," she called back. He knew where her rock was, he knew the shore of the lake and the glen as well. Throughout the summer months he'd been a frequent visitor to Cluny. He knew everything except about the moon underwater.

In a few seconds he was standing next to her, the reflection of his tall shadow dwarfing hers. "When did you arrive?" she asked.

"Just a few minutes ago. Your brother said you were down here."

He slipped his arms around her shoulders and Glynis said nothing. He bent down and kissed her neck, and after a second, her cheek. She didn't move. He wanted to kiss her lips, but she didn't turn her head.

"I have stunning news," he whispered. "Important news."

The name Robert formed on her lips, but she squelched her own question. "What news?"

Ramsey leaned over. "The prince and his entourage have left France. He's on his way!"

Glynis felt her whole body go numb. Robert was with him! He would be coming home now! Perhaps he had enough of Margaret . . . perhaps he now knew they were not for each other. Perhaps Margaret wasn't even with him.

"I have other news too," Ramsey revealed. He was glad it was dark. He was an accomplished liar, but it was always easier in the dark when one could not see his eyes.

"Tell me," Glynis pressed.

"The messenger told me that Robert Forbes married Margaret Campbell in Paris."

Glynis felt her heart sink. It was no surprise, it was just confirmation of her worst nightmare. It was worse than when she had heard they were engaged. This news had a finality. It was truly the end of her dreams. How she had feared this very revelation.

Ramsey put his hand on her shoulder and slowly moved it upward and around her neck. He moved his fingers on the back of her neck, and the sheer physical sensation caused a chill to pass over her. "I'll be going to fight with the prince soon," Ramsey said slowly. "Glynis, I've been courting you for over a year. I want to ask your father for your hand in marriage."

Her father would most certainly give his permission if she told him it was what she wanted. A feeling of resignation flooded over her. And why not? Robert was gone, he belonged to another. She would marry a man she did not love simply to avoid being a spinster. Perhaps, she fantasized, she would have children she would love, children who would love her. Silently she felt herself nodding, and she whispered, "Yes, ask him."

Ramsey bent down and sought her lips. His mouth was prodding and urgent, and though she did not respond passionately, she did not withdraw either. He was to be her husband. She had to get used to him kissing her, holding her, making love to her. She closed her eyes. Maybe if she thought of Robert—

Duncan MacPherson lit his pipe and billows of smoke filled the study.

Ramsey sat opposite and marveled at his own feeling of ease. "I've been courting your daughter for some eighteen months," he said slowly. "I love her very much. She is everything a man might want in a wife."

"I'm well aware of your arduous pursuit."

"Sir, I will be leaving soon to fight with the prince. Glynis and I should like to be married right away."

"If it is Glynis's will, I can think of no impediment to a swift marriage. We live in troubled times."

"We do indeed," Ramsey agreed.

"As I'm sure you know, Glynis comes with a good dowry. Combined with your own means, it should offer you both a fine start in life. And an especially great future will be yours when the Stuarts are restored to the throne."

Ramsey did not want to press, nor did he wish to explain the true state of his own finances. "I should want to marry her even if she had no dowry," he lied confidently. The truth was, he wanted her in his bed with or without her dowry, but without it he would have attempted simply seducing her and not bothered with the encumbrances of marriage.

"Nonetheless, she has a dowry, and we will have to sit down before the marriage and go over the terms."

"Could we do that as soon as possible?"

"But of course. Tomorrow afternoon would be fine. You two can be married on Saturday in the chapel."

Ramsey felt his face flush slightly. It was even easier than he had imagined. Of course Glynis still had feelings for Robert Forbes, but he would make certain she never thought of him again.

The chapel at Cluny was tiny and was used primarily by the family. Father Carlyle came to the vicinity once every two weeks to hear confession and perform mass. Then, as now, the pews were all filled with clan members, servants, and nearby neighbors. There were some twenty-seven in all.

Ramsey stood in front of the altar, wearing a kilt of his family's dress tartan. Its deep hues were in stark contrast to the bright red, yellow, blue, and white tartan of Clan MacPherson that Glynis wore in the form of a sash over her left shoulder.

Ramsey, Glynis acknowledged as she stood at the back of the chapel, was handsome, though not to her eyes as handsome as Robert. Ramsey stood slightly over six feet tall and had an angular face and rather sharp features. Ramsey's dress kilt was made in the short style known as a *filleadh beg* in the Gaelic tongue; in addition, he wore a balmoral, which was a kind of beret, and a fur and leather sporran in the front. His long stockings were trimmed with his tartan and a sash that was also made of the tartan was worn right to left and held fast by a brooch on his left shoulder.

Glynis wore her mother's wedding gown, a plain ivory dress draped with a sash of MacPherson tartan. An ivory veil covered her face and dark hair.

Duncan MacPherson also dressed in full formal Highland wear. He held his daughter's arm proudly, and as the pipes began to play, they walked slowly down the aisle of the chapel.

Colin, Stewart, and James all sat in the front pew. Colin watched his sister carefully. She was stunningly beautiful, but although she looked intent, he could not feel her enthusiasm or excitement. He himself felt uncomfortable, unable to shake the desire to interrupt the ceremony and try to make her see reason. How could she marry Ramsey Monroe when she still truly loved Robert Forbes?

Not that he hadn't heard that Robert was married. Over a year ago he had given up all thoughts of Glynis having her way and ending up with Robert. But that did not mean she should marry someone she did not love. It was a mistake, and he knew it.

His mind wandered back over the past few days. He had argued with Glynis for hours, but she would not listen to reason. In the end she only sniffed that she had to build a life of her own now that Robert had taken a wife.

"I was a silly girl," she admitted. "Life can't be what we want it to be."

The sound of the pipes drowned out Colin's thoughts as Duncan MacPherson, with Glynis on his arm, reached the altar.

Glynis was breathtaking, and she was settling for second best, he thought. Ramsey Monroe was no Robert Forbes. In fact, Colin admitted to himself that he had to fight to like Ramsey. But then, he reminded himself, Glynis did not like Laurie either.

In a muffled tone the priest began to recite the vows, asking each the vital question, then cautioning about the difficulties of life. They promised to each other and kissed, and even before the kiss was broken, the pipes again began to play.

As they left the chapel, it was understood that all those present would adjourn to the house for drink and refreshments before the bride and groom left. Ramsey had made it clear he intended taking Glynis that very day to his own house in Inverness.

Colin watched Glynis and Ramsey as they walked toward the house. They were married, but somehow Glynis did not seem herself. It's a mistake, he thought again. A terrible mistake. But both he and Glynis knew that marriage was not something to be taken lightly. It was a pledge, and pledges were to be honored.

It was unusually clear and stars filled the night sky. When Glynis and Ramsey reached Inverness, it was well after midnight, and the houses, even those that were occupied this time of year, were in darkness.

Glynis felt nothing so much as sheer weariness. It was a long and arduous trip that started late after a wedding feast and considerable drink.

The house was dark inside and deserted. It was also dank, Glynis thought. No doubt because it had been closed up. Her father's house was not closed during the summer months. Instead, a small contingent of servants remained there in case some member of the family needed it.

"This way," Ramsey said, leading her up the winding staircase to the second floor. He carried a candle and the flickering light cast weird shadows in the darkness of the night.

Ramsey opened the door to a large room. Against one wall was a large bed and at its foot a wooden chest. On the opposite wall was a fireplace.

"I'll fetch our bags," he said. "Then while you ready yourself, I'll fix us something to eat."

Glynis said nothing. It was as if his words hung in the air like a vague threat. She immediately wanted to postpone what she knew awaited, but words failed her. What was she to say? In all truth, she was truly tired. But weariness was no excuse. She was a married woman and Ramsey was her husband and wanted to claim her. She nodded, and when he had left the room, she sat down on the edge of the bed. She felt a strong feeling of trepidation, or was she afraid? Certainly nothing in his attitude put her at ease. He seemed so—expectant. Not excited, not adventurous, but expectant.

In a few moments he returned with her bags. He looked at her but did not smile. "When I come back, be ready."

Glynis did not answer. He did not ask her if she felt like it. He only issued his order. Something in her stiffened, rebelled. He had not even kissed her or welcomed her to his home. He had shown her no tenderness. And yet he ordered her. He had not been like this before the ceremony. He seemed different.

Glynis waited till he had gone again before she went to her trunk and opened it. On top was her nightgown, the one she had chosen for this night. It was long and white, made of thin material with a low bodice trimmed in ribbons. Quickly she put it on, and she sat back down, wishing she could cover herself up.

It was not long enough before Ramsey came back. He had a bottle of whisky and some oatcakes on a tray. He was dressed as he had been, in his kilt.

He set the food and drink down on the chest and stared at her.

"Loosen your hair, Glynis."

Glynis held her silence. She undid her hair, and it fell on her white shoulders in a profusion of curls.

Ramsey stared at her. She was beautiful! Ravishing dark hair on white shoulders, green eyes—eyes that if he was not mistaken held a look of fright. And her diaphanous gown left nothing to the imagination. Beneath its thin, gauzy material her full breasts seemed to strain against the cloth. Her nipples were hard, perhaps from the night air, perhaps from fear or excitement.

He poured himself a glass of whisky and drank it down. He walked to her and pulled her to her feet and into his arms roughly.

Glynis shivered slightly. The buttons of his jacket were uncomfortable, and he held her too tightly as he bent and pressed his lips against hers, pushing his tongue into her mouth while his hands held her buttocks tightly.

Glynis wiggled in his arms and pushed him away with all her strength. "You're hurting me," she said. It was true, but she knew in her heart she had pushed him away for other reasons as well.

"Bitch!" he said in a low, menacing voice. "Would you pull away from Robert Forbes?"

Glynis was stunned. Her voice had deserted her. Why did he mention Robert? What had she done to betray herself? His eyes were hard; he was angry and his anger frightened her.

"I'll not have you making love to me and thinking of him, you spoiled little bitch!" Ramsey said in the same tone. "I'll teach you a lesson, Glynis MacPherson. I'll teach you to be a good wife, my wife!"

He took a long step toward her and seized her wrist. He pulled her hard against him and again kissed her roughly. She refused to open her mouth and he let her go, delivering a hard slap to her face.

Glynis felt her skin sting from his blow. She touched her face in sheer amazement. He had struck her!

"I'll beat you till you learn your lesson, woman!" He lunged at her and pushed her across the bed.

Glynis struggled with all her might. She screamed, but he forced her legs apart even as he tore away her nightdress and took one of her nipples in his mouth.

"No!" Glynis cried out. "No!" All she could smell was the whisky and all she could feel was sheer pain.

He was hurting her. He bit at her flesh, and he held her so tightly, she knew she would be covered with bruises from her struggle. And yet he was her husband! She should yield to him, but she could not. This was all a terrible mistake! Ramsey was a man she did not know!

"Let me go, Ramsey. Let me go!" She was pleading now.

He let go of her nipple and sat up. He struck her again across the face. He struck her hard enough that she felt a slight dizziness. His anger was turning to fury, and strangely, her own guilt fled and she felt only the instinct to defend herself from this man who had hidden his real self from her for so long. She pushed him hard and struggled from beneath him.

He staggered to his feet and began taking off his own clothes. First his heavy leather belt, then his kilt and jacket. In a moment he was naked, his organ hard and menacing. He gripped his belt in one hand, and she could plainly see he did indeed mean to beat her with it.

He rolled her over so swiftly, her cry stuck in her throat just as his first blow fell across her bare buttocks. It stung terribly and she rolled away, aware that he could not hit her and hold her at the same time. She rolled off the other side of the bed and without a second thought ran around the bed, seizing the discarded pistol he had been carrying in his belt. She held it firmly and stared hard at him.

"Don't move!" she ordered. "I'll kill you if you come a step closer to me. I'm a good shot, you know that."

"If you kill me, you'll hang by your pretty neck!"

Glynis let the pistol drop slightly. "Then I'll aim a little lower than your heart," she said, her own green eyes flashing. He had intended raping her, though she knew full well that as they were married, no one would see it that way. But he had also hit her. Her father would not allow her to divorce, but he would protect her.

"Lie down on the floor!" she ordered. She seized the blanket in one hand and threw it over him. He rolled around, and as he struggled to throw it off, she hit him with the pistol butt as hard as she could. He slumped unconscious, his chin hitting the floor.

She grabbed her cloak and the candle. She also took his clothes and backed out of the room.

She ran down the stairs and, without stopping, out the front door onto the dark street. She paused only to discard his clothes and pull her cloak around her. She tore barefoot through the streets she knew so well and straight for her father's house. When she reached the door she banged on it loudly till one of the servants answered.

"Miss Glynis!" the servant girl exclaimed in surprise.

Glynis brushed past her and into the sanctuary of the house. She bolted the door behind her and leaned against it, panting, even as hot tears began to run down her face. "Send someone to fetch my father," she whispered breathlessly. "Now, right now."

Glynis sat in the study, wrapped in a heavy blanket in spite of the fact that it was late July. Her dark hair was a tangled mass of unruly curls and her face was ashen. She looked up when the study door opened and her father came in.

"What's happened to you, lass?" His face knit in an expression of concern.

Tears filled her eyes and Glynis made no attempt to stop

them from flowing down her face. "I've made a horrible mistake," she sobbed. "A horrible mistake."

"You're a married woman," her father answered. "You've sworn an oath."

Glynis shook her head. "Oath or no oath, I'll not live with him. He tried to beat me—he slapped me and he hit me with his belt."

Her father's expression was cold and serious. "No man should ever hit a woman."

Glynis could not lie. "He was drunk and very rough with me. I—I rebuffed him."

"Is there more?"

"He accused me of loving Robert. He hit me and said he would teach me a lesson."

"Aye," her father replied. He scratched his chin. "And do you love Robert Forbes?"

Glynis nodded. She could not deny it. "I never should have married Ramsey."

"But you did, and wedding vows are sacred, Glynis."

"I'll not live with him. I can't."

Her father shook his head. "Under different circumstances I would kill him for hitting you, but you are his wife and you would not perform your duty."

His attitude did not surprise her. Her father was a man of honor and tradition. He knew the rules and he obeyed them. She knew them too.

"Of course you can remain here, in this house. But you cannot divorce or live with another man, Glynis."

Glynis said nothing. Robert was married to another. There was no man with whom she wanted to live. "I understand," she said. "I want to stay here."

"I shall write Ramsey and tell him."

"I don't want to see him. I won't see him."

Duncan MacPherson nodded. "I'm sorry, Glynis."

Glynis bit her lip and looked away. His gray eyes were

not accusative, but, rather, sad. No doubt he had looked forward to grandchildren. But even more than that, she knew she had disappointed her father. He had expected more of her than to make a bad marriage because she was angry with another man.

Her father left the room and Glynis continued to stare into space, her thoughts full of self-recrimination and the nightmare of her reality.

The servant girl appeared in the doorway. "Shall I draw you a bath?" she asked.

Glynis nodded. If she stayed in the bathtub forever, she could not wash away the last few days, she thought. In a haunting, horrible way, she could still feel Ramsey's hands on her body and his mouth on her breast. She thanked heaven that she had narrowly escaped having her bad marriage consummated.

Robert Forbes, the prince, and the rest of his entourage had left the French vessel, the *Du Teillay*, that morning. Now they were ensconced in a comfortable farmhouse on the shores of Loch nan Uamh in the village of Borrodale. Charles himself oversaw the unloading of the ship and Robert took care of the distribution of the guns and broadswords. There weren't enough arms, of course, but it was obvious that they would have to make do with what there was, and to the arms those loyal to the young prince would bring with them. Robert had long ago realized that Charles was far more energetic than he appeared. Furthermore, he was committed to his task, and given the difficulty of that task, his optimism was nothing short of inspirational.

They worked for hours, and at last Robert sat down in the warm sun to rest for a while. The last month had been a nightmare of uncertainty, and once again their plans were laid asunder by both weather and circumstance. Once again his personal desire to see Glynis was postponed together with everyone's desire to get on with the task of forming a credible fighting force.

A month ago they had all traveled from Paris to Nantes. They had each gone their own way, traveling separately to avoid suspicion. Charles himself had been staying in Normandy at the château of the Duc de Bouillon. He took his leave, ostensibly to tour the Normandy countryside. Once gone, he assumed the name of Mr. Douglas, and traveled incognito, telling one and all he was a student from the Scots college in Paris. They waited impatiently for weeks in Nantes till favorable winds allowed the *Du Teillay* to sail. They sailed from Nantes to Belle-Isle, where they waited a week and took on provisions. They were also awaiting the arrival of the *Elisabeth* from Brest. The bulk of the recruits and arms were on board the *Elisabeth,* though even these were a fraction of what the French had originally promised.

On July 16 they sailed. Robert stayed with the prince on the *Du Teillay* while others boarded the *Elisabeth*. None of the French crew understood the mission. All they knew was that England and France were at war and so they were all on alert for British ships.

The first few days of the voyage were peaceful, peaceful enough to forget the war, Robert remembered. None of the crew questioned them. They simply appeared to be an ordinary group of travelers whom fate had brought together. Several of the men were elderly, and the prince posed as the son of one of them. There were three Irish soldiers and a poor-looking English gentleman together with one Scots gentleman.

Their plan was simple. There were enough men and weapons to establish a sort of beachhead. They would take various strongholds occupied by the British one at a time. As they did so, their numbers would swell with loyal High-

landers who would join the rebellion. As they drew closer
to England, British Catholics would rise up and join them.
Eventually, the royal House of Hanover would fall, and
the Stuarts, the rightful kings of England and Scotland,
would be restored to the throne.

The trouble started a week out of Belle-Isle, just as the
raging sun had dropped beneath the horizon, bathing the
sky in a sweet purple and pink and turning the sea to inky
darkness with only the shimmering light on the far horizon
to serve as a reminder that the sun had just been there.

They were a hundred miles off the Lizard, headed
around Cornwall and planning to sail up the west coast of
Ireland, when a phantom ship was spotted. It drew closer,
then it disappeared.

The next morning it appeared again. This time it came
close enough to be identified as H.M.S. *Lyon*—a vessel
recently refitted. She was sailing from Spithead to the Bay
of Biscay. The *Elisabeth* was larger, the *Lyon* more maneu-
verable. But they were two ships and the *Lyon* was one.

The two captains of the French ships conferred. If they
attacked now, another British ship might appear.

The plan was simple. The *Du Teillay* would attract the
Lyon and the *Elisabeth* would close in and both ships would
fire on her.

Warning shots were fired, but the *Lyon* wanted to do
battle. As the *Lyon* came alongside, the *Elisabeth* fired her
sixty-four guns and made direct hits on the hull of the
Lyon. The *Du Teillay* withdrew out of the range of gunfire.

Thick black smoke veiled both ships. They were, unfortunately, equally matched. Both did vital damage to the
other. The terrible battle continued for hours. Walsh, who
commanded the *Du Teillay*, would not allow her to fire.
Rather, Walsh kept a safe distance. At ten P.M. the *Lyon*,
a wounded vessel that was just barely seaworthy, sailed off
and the *Elisabeth*, her sails in ribbons and her rigging look-

ing like a child's broken toy, had no choice but to head
back to Brest.

Charles had stood by the rail long into the night. The
ship that carried most of his men and arms was gone, and
he struggled to maintain hope for his cause.

But the next morning he made the best of things. All
was not lost, he said over and over. They sailed northward
up the coast. The chests of gold louis d'or were almost all
there was to show French backing. The *Du Teillay* carried
only fifteen hundred guns and eighteen hundred broadswords, hardly sufficient arms to conquer England.

For ten days they limped northward till at last they
approached the remote island of Barra in the Outer Hebrides. It seemed like sheer providence to Robert. No sooner
had they laid anchor than a horrible storm whipped the
waves with high winds, and torrential rains fell from dark,
swirling clouds.

When the storm subsided, they sailed on and finally
Captain Walsh sailed up Loch nan Uamh, which divided
Arisaig from Moidart. So here they were, in one of the
most isolated parts of the Highlands, isolated, but safe,
Robert thought. At least they were safe for now. "Dreams,"
Robert whispered to himself, "are almost never executed
as dreamed." He thought that statement, spoken to himself in the heat of the day when he was on the edge of
sleep, was a truism. Prince Charles's plans were not going
as hoped, his own life seemed pointless, his personal plans
dashed. Not for the first time on this long trip he pushed
his thoughts away and forced himself to return to what
had brought him to this farmhouse.

"Be that Robert Forbes?" a deep voice asked in a thick
brogue. Robert turned around.

It was true enough, as least according to outsiders, that
they all had a brogue, but Robert knew that those from
this place spoke with a thicker and even heavier brogue

than others. Robert prided himself on being able to know where a man came from by his speech. He had a good ear, and thus it was without surprise that he looked up into the face of the one man he knew who came from this area, Aeneas MacDonald of Keppoch. Robert grinned and stood up. He reached out and found himself in a bearlike grip. Aeneas was tall and stout. He had a rough red beard that seemed to cover his whole face save his forehead, bright blue eyes, and freckled nose.

"It's been six years since we were in Paris at the Scots college together!" he thundered.

"I've not forgotten you," Robert responded, punching Aeneas roughly, or at least as roughly as he himself had just been hugged.

"I've come to join the prince," Aeneas said.

Robert smiled. "Have you heard anything from Inverness?"

"Indeed. I've heard that Glynis MacPherson has wed Ramsey Monroe and left him to return to her father's house on their wedding night! Stories like that travel fast on the tongues of women."

Robert felt his mouth go dry. He looked at Aeneas and wondered if he looked as anguished as he felt. Objectively, he could understand the fascination with the story, but as he was so close to the MacPhersons, and to Glynis in particular, he was jolted by MacDonald's words. But it was much more than that. He had been coming home to Glynis! His sleep was filled with dreams of Glynis, and not a few of his waking hours were spent thinking of her.

Deep in a corner of his mind he feared she might marry Ramsey. He cursed himself for letting her go, for not realizing that she was right about them, about the fact that in spite of the age difference, they were fated. But now she had married Ramsey. Why? Didn't she know that Margaret had left him because of his loyalty to the prince? It was true that he liked and respected Margaret Campbell, but he did not love her and clearly she did not love him. Even before she left him, he had been planning to break off the engagement. Too many doubts filled him, too many dreams of Glynis filled his head.

For a long while he had thought it was a brotherly kind of love he felt for her, but now he knew better. During his long eighteen months away from home, he had come to understand himself better. He and Glynis were matched to each other, each was attuned to the other's moods, and physically he realized he had been fighting his feelings toward her for years. Now he felt stunned.

"Did you hear why she left Ramsey?" He asked because he wanted to be prepared. But of course there was no hope for him—her father would not allow it. She may have left Ramsey Monroe, but she was still his wife. Glynis, another man's wife! He hated the very thought.

"I heard he tried to beat her."

Robert felt himself go rigid. He drew in his breath. "I'll kill him if he hurt her," he said.

Aeneas raised a bushy brow. "Do I detect something hidden here?"

Mindful of the fact that the Highlands seethed with rumors and stories of all sorts, Robert grinned, and, attempting to cover up his feelings, laughed. "Well, only if her brothers don't beat me to it."

"Aye, I remember. You're a good friend of the MacPhersons, and particularly of Stewart."

"A blood brother," Robert said. "To Glynis too, I've known her since she was a child."

"They say she's the most beautiful woman in Inverness, a rare one with raven black hair and green eyes."

Robert said nothing even though the description certainly fit Glynis. Another wave of longing shot through him.

"Well, enough of women. Let's get to the drink. I've some really good whisky. Care to share it?"

"Of course," Robert answered. He hoped they would discuss the coming military campaign. Right now he had no desire to think about his own lost opportunities.

"Stewart!" Glynis ran down the path toward her eldest brother. His clothes were a little disheveled from his long ride, but he looked up and acknowledged her as he finished tethering his horse.

The July sun was hot, the ground dry. "What have you learned?" she asked anxiously.

"The prince has landed. They're encamped at Borrodale. An army is forming. I'll be riding back in the morning with the men from hereabouts. We're to rendezvous at Glenfinnan."

"Did you see Robert?" Glynis asked, barely able to keep the anxiety out of her voice.

Stewart was like their father, a man of quiet principles. A man who was sometimes too strict. "You're still a married woman, Glynis. And while I don't like your husband, I'll tolerate no foolishness."

Glynis felt her face flush red. "Robert's a dear and old friend of yours and of mine too. He's been gone eighteen months in the service of the prince. What foolishness is it to ask after him?"

Stewart saw the flash of anger in his sister's eyes. "No harm. No, I didn't see him. But I hear he's well. Glynis, he is not married—Margaret was apparently sent to London. But you understand that you're not free."

Glynis stood stock-still and stared at Stewart. How could he just stand there and tell her this—didn't he know how she felt? She was filled with absolute and utter confusion, with warring emotions, with the desire to stamp her foot and cry, with the desire to dance. Robert was free! She was tethered like Stewart's horse. Tethered by a vow she knew she never should have taken. She fought back hot tears, turned away from Stewart, and ran back to the house, back to the sanctuary of her room. Damn honor! Ramsey had lied to her. If he had not, she would not have married him. Honor indeed!

"I don't care if the whole Highlands call me a slut, a whore, and a harlot—I love you, Robert Forbes, and if you'll have me, I'll be yours," she whispered when her bedroom door was safely closed and she was leaning against it, letting her tears of anger flow freely.

Glynis sank to the floor and covered her face with her hands. Her angry tears turned to sobs as she thought of her terrible mistake. From outside her open window she could hear horses and riders. They were being dispatched and some were arriving. By tomorrow Colin, James, Stewart, and her father would have left for the rendezvous at Glenfinnan. Doubtless Ramsey would go too, though he would probably not ride with her kinsmen. Glynis bit her lip. She would be alone at Cluny—alone with her fears and her regrets.

Chapter Six

August 1745

It was August 19 when Prince Charles and his entourage arrived at Glenfinnan, the rendezvous for the formation of the Jacobite forces. They found a mere hundred and fifty men from Clanranald camped in the valley.

"More will come," the prince declared confidently.

They waited for hours, talking and swapping stories of battles past. Robert was sitting with Ian MacArthur, one of the Irishmen come to fight with the prince when the distant wailing of the pipes was first heard.

"They're coming," MacArthur said, looking off across the valley.

The sound of the pipes was low and mournful, a sound known to Irish and Scots alike. The pipes grew louder, and in the distance, Cameron of Lochiel appeared on the top of the hill. He led all the men of Clan Cameron and those who worked and lived on Cameron land two abreast. There were hundreds of them. They were big men, frightening-looking in their full war regalia. And behind Clan Cameron were others, including the hundreds and hundreds of MacDonalds. They were the largest of all the Highland clans and had over one hundred septs.

Robert watched as the numbers of men grew, and tears filled his eyes when they all halted on the banks of the loch. The eldest of their number, supported by two younger men, stepped forward, and they unfurled the red, white, and blue banner of the House of Stuart. James was proclaimed king, and Charles was named his regent. As one, every man present threw his war bonnet into the air and everyone shouted.

When the cheering stopped, a proclamation was read. It stated the terms under which King James would take his throne. First and foremost, it was declared that all those who had rebelled against the Stuart monarchy since 1688 would be pardoned if they declared their allegiance to the new king and renounced the Hanoverian usurper. This included soldiers. It was further stated that the government would continue as presently constituted, that a free Parliament would be summoned without any degree of duress from King James. All were to remain in office as long as they gave allegiance to James, and all religious persecution was to be opposed.

Stewart MacPherson made his way to Robert's side, and the two gave each other a customary bear hug. In a moment, James and Colin joined them.

The proclamation was finished, and the prince ordered the kegs of brandy opened so that all could toast his father, King James.

"May our numbers grow," Stewart said, looking around.

"British defenses are low here in Scotland. It can be taken easily," Robert said with confidence.

"The prize is all England," Stewart replied. He was look-

ing straight ahead and his expression was one Robert
Forbes knew well. It was a look of resignation, of fatalism.
"We'll take Perth first," Stewart predicted. "After that,
victory depends on our resolve."

Robert looked at his friend's profile. Though Stewart
had always been a contemplative, dour sort, he had now
given himself so completely over to fatalism that it was
distressing. Perth was the first city James had ridden into
during the last rebellion—the first and the last, as the
rebellion was quickly put down. But the situation was different now.

Robert looked around him and tried to concentrate on
the differences between this effort to restore the Stuarts
to the throne and previous efforts. These men were better
armed and far more rested than those who had fought
with James. This prince was young, energetic, and inspired,
whereas James had not been. But much depended on how
hard the British fought, on how many British Catholics
joined them, and for the moment, on how prepared was
Lieutenant General Cope, the British commander in chief
for Scotland. Rumor had it he was not at all prepared.

Glynis reached up and touched Robert's face, running
her hand over his forehead, nose, and smooth cheeks. She
looked into his intense blue eyes and lifted herself to allow
him to kiss her deeply. She sighed in his strong arms, arms
bulging with muscle, arms that held her tightly, pressing
her to his naked body even as his hands ranged over her,
loosening her bodice, freeing her breasts so that he could
devour them with passionate kisses.

His hands were swift and sure, soft and prying as he
touched her intimately, stroking her till she breathed heavily and writhed in his embrace. "Robert, Robert . . ."

Glynis opened her eyes suddenly. She was bathed in

perspiration and still felt the pleasurable gentle pulsating that accompanied such night dreams, dreams in which Robert was her lover.

It was early morning, and light streamed in through the window. She turned over on her back and stared at the ceiling of her room. A long, jagged crack ran the length of the ceiling with small cracks radiating outward like a tree branch. She thought of having it repaired, a mundane thought, all things considered. And who would repair it? She and the women were the only ones there. Virtually all of the men, save those too old to ride, were gone. Her brothers, her father, many of the servants, and all the heads of families that lived on MacPherson land had gone to fight with Bonnie Prince Charlie.

Glynis sat up in bed and pulled the pillow up behind her. She felt incredibly isolated and alone. The castle was as quiet as a tomb, and even Inverness, more than a half day's journey away, was greatly depopulated of males.

Ramsey had also gone to fight. She tried to conjure up his image, but it would not come. She had purged him from her thoughts, from her imagination, and even from her memory. I'll always be alone, she thought unhappily, and even though she loved her father, she wished he were not so intransigent. Her marriage had not been consummated—why could it not be annulled? She had heard of such things, though in fact she knew it would take a long while. But her father insisted that almost no marriages were annulled.

She felt wretched, destined to live out her life alone, unable to have the man she loved. And if this was not bad enough, she had been left alone. Even Tavish had gone. She went home to the Hebrides to take care of her dead sister's children.

Glynis thought of riding to join the Highland army where it was encamped. Not a few of the men had taken their wives. But, of course, she could not join her husband, and her presence would only cause problems between the Monroes and the MacPhersons. Her brothers upheld her father's view that she could have no other, but at the same time they were deeply angered by Ramsey. Moreover, she reminded herself, the journey to the Lowland encampment was too dangerous. The Highlanders were not well liked by Lowland Protestants, and it would be quite unsafe for her to travel alone. There was nothing to do but to stay and contemplate her situation.

After a few minutes she pulled herself from her bed and began to dress. "I really do feel sorry for myself," she said aloud. This attitude was accomplishing nothing. She decided to go hunting; at least she could provide some food for the women and children left behind. It was mid-September. Not quite rutting season, but still a time when the deer would be around, fattening themselves before the long winter.

Glynis was midway down the stairs, when she heard the pounding at the door. The servant girl had already answered it, and when Glynis reached the bottom of the stairs, she saw that it was Tilly McSwain, a messenger.

Glynis eagerly took the letter that he held out. "Have you ridden far?" she asked.

He nodded. Tilly was mute, although he was not deaf.

"Go to the kitchen and have some refreshment," she offered. "Take some time, rest if you like."

Tilly grinned a toothless grin and disappeared with the servant girl.

Glynis tore open the letter and eagerly hurried back upstairs to the study in order to read it in privacy. It was from Colin, who although no doubt still angered with her over Laurie, had at least taken time to write.

Glynis sunk into her father's chair and unfolded the parchment.

Dear Glynis,

A man should not do battle angry, so let me say I'm sorry we fought. You have to realize that I love Laurie and a good part of our love is the trust we have in each other.

Ramsey is here, too, and though we try to ignore him, he talks too much of private matters. He must know how we feel because he stays away from all of us.

The prince is a finer man than any of us hoped for. He is brave and ready to fight. With such a person leading us, we will surely know victory. We'll soon be heading for Edinburgh, since our spies report the Hanoverians are unprepared and have left the Lowlands defenseless. I know how unhappy you are, Glynis, but remember that life takes strange twists and turns. I know things will work out for you. Pray for all of us, my beautiful sister. The time for us to face our enemy is at hand.

Love,
Colin

Glynis felt tears in her eyes. "Oh, Colin," she said softly. He had written no news of Robert, but his own feelings toward her situation were implied and she felt an immense sense of relief that he had forgiven her. She got up and decided to go to the small chapel to pray. Perhaps they were doing battle even now.

"Let them all be safe," she said to herself.

It was just after dawn, and the day that had just been born was obviously to be cloudy and cold. Summer was gone, and the unpredictable fall weather would now begin.

It could be sunny and warm, or it could turn cold and nasty without warning.

"It was too easy," Stewart MacPherson said as he led his horse through the nearly deserted streets of Edinburgh.

Robert silently agreed with Stewart's assessment. The city of Edinburgh had capitulated, and its would-be defenders had either fled or discarded their weapons and taken a peaceful stance.

For several days the Highland army had been camped near Slateford some two miles away. General Cope and his alleged army were not to be seen, nor as yet had they attempted to even engage the Highland army.

Charles had issued a declaration commanding the provost and magistrates to summon the town council of Edinburgh in order to discuss how best to turn the city over to the forces of King James. In response, a delegation had come to the camp in order to request terms, as well as for time to think them over. Clearly they hoped General Cope's forces would arrive—rumor had it that having come by sea from Aberdeen, they were near the Firth of Forth, and would arrive in time to defend the city.

But Charles, too, knew of the rumors and thus refused the city officials more time than that to which he originally agreed. At dawn, unwilling to allow them to stall, the Highlanders had entered the city and within minutes there were Highland guards at every city gate. There was no resistance, and as Stewart had remarked, it seemed too easy.

"Perhaps you're being overly gloomy," Robert offered.

Stewart shook his head. "Our prince landed only a month ago. He came without soldiers and more or less without arms. Now we have crossed Scotland and taken the capital without any significant battle. It's been too simple, my friend. The Hanoverians will fight and fight hard. That they have not done so already is lulling us all into a false sense of strength."

Robert again nodded. He certainly could not disagree with Stewart. He had always expected more in the way of resistance. As it was, the main difficulty so far had been the squabbling among the clans. The MacDonalds argued with Clanranald, and both displayed nattering jealousy of the Camerons. The Irish argued with the Scots and the Lowland Catholics among them argued with the Highlanders. Around their campfires at night there was a constant round of fighting, and if cooler heads prevailed, it was by strength rather than logic.

"Once we've been battle-tested, you'll have more faith in our victories," Robert said.

Stewart shrugged. "I'm here because I believe in the cause. I don't for one moment believe we'll win in the long run. Our days are numbered, my friend. Only a blind optimist would think otherwise."

"No one will accuse you of being one of those," he said with irony. He wanted to cajole Stewart out of his black mood. But Stewart did not even respond with a smile as he might once have done, Robert thought.

"Let's try to find some breakfast in this place," Stewart suggested.

"Yes, before the pomp begins. A prince cannot enter a capital without pomp," Robert said.

At that comment Stewart did smile. "The genteel prince and his army of savages—that's what they think, you know. Behind the walls of their houses the people of Edinburgh are cringing because the savages are now in control."

Robert knew that Stewart was right on that score. The Highlanders were for the most part rough and ready. Their culture was completely different from that of the Lowlanders—at least most of them. Of course there were exceptions among the clan chieftains and their relatives—there was wealth, education, and even refinement. But on the whole, the climate and the way of life molded the people. They were tough, they had to be. They were educated for survival, not for the drawing rooms of the south.

Undoubtedly Stewart understood the Highlanders, but was he right about other matters as well? Robert knew he was born more of an optimist than Stewart MacPherson. Still, he knew there was a certain truth in Stewart's gloomy fatalism. They would head south soon, and they needed more money, more men, and more arms. If they were to maintain their momentum, keep up their victories, and truly put James on the throne, the long-promised help from the French and the Spanish would have to come— more promises would not be enough.

Robert let his thoughts drift away from the morning's easy conquest. He thought of Glynis and realized that he now often sought escape from reality by conjuring up her alluring image. He reminded himself to look for Colin. Colin wrote to Glynis often and he decided to at least send her a message—perhaps through Colin.

Glynis watched as the fire flickered in the hearth. Outside, the January winds howled. It seemed to her as if tonight were the culmination of weeks and months of inclement and unusually cold weather.

She had closed up the entire castle save for a few rooms on the bottom two floors. She slept in her father's study on the second floor, her crossbow and pistol at her side. Her horse, Sampson, was tethered not in the barn but in the small storage shed off the kitchen. If necessity dictated, she wanted to be able to ride at a moment's notice.

The study was her private domain; the other downstairs rooms housed the women who lived on the estate. The women had all been left alone. Their husbands were fighting by the side of her brothers and father. Glynis believed that the situation demanded they be there and remain as long as necessary. She was quite convinced it was what her father would have wanted. Simply put, the Jacobite army had conquered and moved on, but they had left no force to hold and govern what was taken. There was a British commander in Inverness, though he could not have controlled the population even had he been unwise enough to try. So, even though the number of government troops who remained in the Highlands was small, there were other threats. Marauding bands of dangerous men, gangs of wretched youth, hungry soldiers, and criminals roamed the countryside and made it unsafe for anyone to remain alone. Hence the women banded together with their children, hoping at least that there would be safety in numbers.

Glynis scanned the room. She was surrounded by messages, some as old as five months, one as recent as yesterday. Today was January 25. The New Year was less than a month old, yet in her heart Glynis knew it would be a year that would change everything.

For months and months the Highland army, now with over forty-five hundred men, had advanced across Scotland and south into England and onward toward London. They reached Derby, not far from London, without facing any opposition. Indeed, their only real fight had been in Scotland when General Cope finally met them in battle at Prestonpans. Cope's travel-weary, unprepared army had been defeated easily.

Glynis smiled faintly in spite of the situation. Colin, the most optimistic of her brothers, had written often. He felt certain of victory and had even predicted that by the New Year, James would assume the throne.

But such was not the case. Indeed, it might never be the case.

The Duke of Cumberland, King George's youngest son, had been placed in charge of the army. By all accounts he was a worthy enemy. Moreover, his army was swelled by battle-seasoned mercenaries from the Continent as well as by thousands of new recruits. According to Colin, rather than face defeat on British soil, the Jacobite leaders had, against Prince Charles's wishes, decided to retreat.

"None of us can understand this," Colin wrote. "We've lost our momentum, and now we retreat to Scotland, down-hearted, confused, and angry with one another. Even the prince wanted to continue, but we are headed home, and Cumberland's army, which grows larger by the day, is in full pursuit."

To Glynis it was obvious what would happen. As soon as the Highlanders reached home, they would dissolve into the glens, return to their families, and to a man deny they ever served in the Jacobite army. They would fight only if the Highlands were invaded. The conquest of British soil did not hold the urgency that defense of Scotland held.

Glynis closed her eyes. Perhaps she should feel relieved. Everyone she loved was still alive. Perhaps, she reasoned, they would be spared bloodshed. Perhaps Prince Charles would remain as king of Scotland and the British and Hanoverians would stay in England and would choose not to invade Scotland.

Glynis looked up in response to the knocking at the door. "Come in," she called out.

It was Sheila, one of the women whose family lived on the very edge of MacPherson land. "I've a message," she said, a smile on her face. "The Highland army is on its way to Inverness."

Glynis felt her heart rate increase. Politically, heaven knew what it might mean, but no matter. What it meant to her was that Robert was coming home at long last, and so were her brothers and her father! She put Ramsey out of her thoughts. It was Robert she had to see, Robert she had to talk with, Robert who held the key to her future.

"Finally," she said under her breath. Maybe things

would return to normal. Maybe war and hardship would fade away and life would resume . . . but, of course, there *was* Ramsey.

"I'm going to Inverness," Glynis said suddenly. "You and the others stay here."

"It's a dangerous trip alone," Sheila warned.

Glynis nodded. She would dress as a man and take both pistol and crossbow. Sampson could run like the wind, even in bad weather. "I'll take precautions," she replied.

Sheila continued to look serious. "You're very brave," she said a minute later.

Glynis could hear the admiration in her voice. "Not really, I'm just driven," she admitted.

And driven she was. At that moment seeing Robert was all she cared about. He was no longer engaged to Margaret. She sensed he knew he had made a mistake just as she knew she had made one. She was unsure just what could be done about it, but in the corner of her heart she was sure they would find a way to be together.

It was bitterly cold and the wind whistled through the leafless trees as Glynis carefully guided Sampson down the far side of the road that led to Inverness. The snow-covered hills were still shrouded in partial darkness as the dawn had just begun to light the eastern sky. It was a strange morning, cold and crisp with a lightly frozen mist hanging over the valleys.

Glynis started and reined in Sampson. She had reached for her pistol when she realized that the source of her panic was a heavily antlered buck. It had sprung from one side of the road and sprinted in front of her, crossing the road at breakneck speed in its desire to escape detection.

"Not this morning," she whispered under her breath. No, there was no time to hunt, and even if there had been, there was no way to butcher the animal and preserve the meat.

But the sight of the stag had caused her to bring Sampson to a halt. In the silence of her momentary stillness, she heard noise in the distance. She listened carefully and quickly ascertained that the sounds were coming toward her. She prudently guided Sampson off the road and into the trees. Unhappily, the area was not thickly wooded, and even more unhappily, her tracks in the snow were quite evident.

She hurriedly took her horse down a slight incline. Yes, from there she could not be seen from the road. She dismounted and gently patted Sampson. He moved off, still farther away, and out of sight. Glynis crouched behind a large rock and put her crossbow beside her even as she readied her pistol. Perhaps because this was an ill-traveled road in the winter they would not see her tracks . . . but if that were the case, it would be only because they were not looking. Perhaps whoever they were would pass on by. It crossed her mind that she should have stayed at Cluny, but in reality it was no safer there. And she was glad she had not brought one of the other women with her. It would just mean someone else to protect. At least she had only herself to worry about.

The sounds grew louder. And because the riders were not trying to be silent, she could hear them talking as they rode. They were government troops leaving Inverness— yes, they were no doubt circling the city in order to avoid the incoming Highland army.

Glynis sucked in her breath. There was no way to tell how many there were.

She froze as she heard one of them shout, "What's this?" and she knew they had seen her tracks that now led directly into the sparse brush. She waited, her whole body alert, her fingers on the trigger of the pistol.

They were close, and she peered out from behind her rock cautiously.

Three men on horseback appeared. They had left the road and now halted to study the tracks. She knew full well that there were more of them on the road—they would all come if they heard shots.

"Just a lone rider," one of the men said. Glynis thought he sounded relieved.

"Here, there are deer tracks too—maybe the tracks are from a hunter."

There was general agreement that the tracks had been made by a hunter. They all turned around. "No use wasting time," the man who was apparently their leader muttered. "We'd best be on our way before the whole Highland army is on top of us."

Glynis watched as they left the brush. Letting out her breath, she leaned against the rock and tried to regain her composure. She had run from them, but they were running from the Highland army. She waited for what seemed like an eternity, she waited till she heard them no more, and then some. When she was absolutely certain they were gone, she made a soft clicking sound and in moments Sampson appeared. She mounted him and resumed her journey. She didn't know what she would find in Inverness, but at least she knew where to find protection were it necessary.

It was late afternoon when she entered Inverness, the unofficial capital of the Highlands. But she did not stay there; instead, she joined the throngs of women and children who headed out across the heath to welcome the homecoming army. Virtually every thought of her situation was erased from her mind as she rode forth, Robert's image filling her imagination.

"Father! Colin! Stewart! James!" Glynis called out their names as soon as she saw the MacPherson standard, which

Colin carried proudly. Robert was not with them, and she knew immediately that he must be with Prince Charles.

Glynis circled them and they each touched hands, then they formed a line and rode toward Inverness.

"I've missed you," she said, speaking to all of them.

"And we've missed you and our warm beds," Colin said. He was looking around. "Where's Laurie?" he finally asked.

"I only just arrived in Inverness myself. I haven't seen her," Glynis answered honestly. She did not ask where Robert Forbes was because she was sure she knew, and just as sure that such a question would anger her father. Ramsey, her husband, she knew full well, would be riding with the Monroes and in all likelihood returning to their land rather than staying in Inverness.

"Where is Prince Charles?" Glynis asked.

"In one of the wagons," her father replied. "But you'll see him soon enough. He'll be brought to our house. He's quite ill."

"Should I ride ahead and prepare for him?" Glynis asked.

Duncan MacPherson nodded. "And summon Dr. Cameron as well."

Glynis turned Sampson and galloped off. If the prince was coming to their house, Robert might well come too. Her heart leapt at the thought of being under the same roof with him, of being able, at last, to talk with him.

Outside, it rained tiny pellets of ice. They hit the wooden shutters, making a sound like small pebbles hurled from the street below. Upstairs, on the third floor, a loose shutter banged in the wind.

The prince, pale and ill-appearing, was put into a large bedchamber on the second floor. He lay in the center of the canopied bed, covered with a warm sheepskin while steam spewed from a kettle over the fireplace. The bed had been imported from France—it seemed a relic of better days.

Archibald Cameron, brother of Donald Cameron of Lochiel, looked down at the prince.

"I'll be leaving him in your care, Glynis. But I'll be coming every day."

Glynis had expected as much. Clearly he could not be moved, especially with the weather as it was.

The prince seemed groggy from some medicine he'd been given. He was a man with a gentle face and delicate features. Yet he was well respected by the Highlanders he led and it was said that his appearance belied his inner strength and sheer athletic ability.

"It seems more than an ordinary cold," she ventured.

"Aye. It's pneumonia. He needs to be kept very warm indeed, and he needs lots of liquid."

"I've many dried rose hips in the larder."

"Good, make rose hip tea. It always helps. And, Glynis, you're as ferocious a woman as I know, so see to it that you keep people away from him. He needs to rest, not to be chattered at till dawn by his loving followers."

"I'll do my best."

Cameron laughed. "Do better than that, his life might depend on it. By the way, that order includes your brothers and father."

She watched as Archibald Cameron repacked his doctor's bag, then she smoothed out the prince's pillow and followed Dr. Cameron out of the room.

She stopped short as she saw Robert at the head of the stairs, first because it was a shock—she had not seen him since his return, and second because she was unprepared at that moment to say all that filled her thoughts.

Archibald Cameron nodded at Robert and brushed past him. "I'll see myself out, Glynis."

"Thank you," Glynis called after him without taking her eyes off Robert. Most certainly the good doctor realized she wanted to see and talk to Robert. Archibald Cameron, like everyone else, knew about her and Ramsey. Gossip, gossip, gossip. Everyone seemed to know about everyone else.

"Did you get my letter?" Robert looked into her beautiful face. Was it his imagination, or was she even more lovely than he remembered?

Glynis shook her head and frowned. "No . . . I would like to have heard from you."

"I did write, Glynis."

She nodded. She felt her chest tighten and it was like being wrung out from the inside. All her words were caught in her throat, all of her long-felt emotions suppressed.

"I've made a mess of things," she said softly.

"Did he hurt you?"

Glynis shook her head. "He lied to me. He told me you were married. On our wedding night—" She stopped. The memory of Ramsey as she knew him, as she had seen him, was so repulsive, she couldn't even explain her feelings. "I'd have never married him if I'd known you hadn't married Margaret."

"Glynis, I'm sorry."

She wanted to fling herself into his arms and once again declare her love for him. But she could not. If he felt about her the way she felt about him, surely he would say something now. Instead, he said nothing. He was only sorry that she had made the mistake of marrying Ramsey. Perhaps it was true that he did not love her. Perhaps she was no more than a childish dreamer.

Robert looked at her and was filled with pain. What were they to do? "Glynis, we must—"

He didn't have the opportunity to finish his sentence. She turned and ran down the hall. He had wanted to say: we must speak honestly. But she was gone and he wondered if it was possible for them to speak honestly. They could not have each other; she was married to another man. He cursed Ramsey under his breath.

March was a month of continued howling winds and icy rain. Inside the MacPherson house Glynis stood by the window in the room occupied by the prince. Dr. Cameron was completing his examination, and she stared out at the small back garden, wondering if the grass would ever again be green.

"You are quite well," she heard the doctor say to his patient.

"I feel totally restored, thanks to you and to my fine nurse."

Glynis turned and smiled. She curtsied lightly, though she felt neither like smiling nor curtsying. She had seen Robert only once, and at no time in the last two months had they time, or, more important, opportunity to talk with each other.

"I'll be leaving now," Dr. Cameron said. "But you can resume all of your normal activities."

In fact, the prince was already dressed. He had been up and around for the better part of a week. He walked with Dr. Cameron to the door, and when the good doctor was gone, he turned to Glynis. "I think I should like to entertain. In fact, a royal ball at the town center would help break the spell of winter. I'll wager you'll be the belle of the ball, Glynis MacPherson."

Glynis shook her head and bit her lower lip. "I thought someone had already told you," she said softly.

"Told me? Told me what? You are far too pretty to be harboring a dark secret."

"I'm married," Glynis confessed. "Very unhappily—it was a terrible mistake. It was never consummated, I don't love him. Still, the fault is all my own."

Charles frowned and tilted his head slightly to one side. "I'm so sorry, my dear."

"I should like to have a proper annulment, but it's so difficult and takes so long."

"Yes, by proper channels you would be an old lady," he said. "I could intercede on your behalf, but not until after my father is restored to the throne."

It had not occurred to Glynis to even ask him. "Would you?"

"I will, if you assure me it was not consummated."

"It was not," Glynis said. "I swear."

He smiled kindly. "I believe you. Yes, I should like to see you smile—really smile."

Glynis continued to look down. "I'm sorry my gloom was so obvious."

"I'm glad to know the source of your unhappiness, my dear. Now, do you think you could help me plan this ball?"

Glynis nodded, and it occurred to her how odd it was to have him call her "my dear," as he was not at all old himself. But, of course, he was a prince, he was well educated, and she presumed had considerable experience.

"I should be most happy to help you," she replied. It would at least serve to distract her.

The hall was decorated not with the holly boughs of the Christmas season nor with the flowers of spring, since one had passed and the other not yet arrived. Instead, long swaths of tartans hung from every wall with the Stuart tartan larger than all the others and in the center of the far wall.

Tables were laden with the best food available, though during the winter months many dishes were unavailable. Still, the pride of the Highlands, haggis, was served on huge silver platters and blood puddings filled bowls, as did pies made from stored vegetables and fruits. And from his own stores the prince provided wine and scotch whisky of a finer variety than was normally to be had.

Glynis, dressed in one of her Paris gowns, did not dance, but, rather, served as hostess for the prince, assuming, as her father insisted, a somewhat matronly role that suited neither her dress nor her age.

At first her father had objected to her even attending. But the prince interceded and a bargain was struck. She would not dance—such would not be proper for a woman separated from her husband.

It would have been horrible, Glynis thought ruefully, had Ramsey been in attendance. But he was not. He had gone home to his estates, there to fume and fuss on his own. As long as her father gave her refuge, he could do nothing but complain.

"You look lovely, Glynis."

Glynis turned around, surprised that Robert had stepped up behind her and half whispered in her ear. It was instinctive that she glanced about before turning. None of her brothers or her father were in sight, nor, she noted, was the prince, who had suddenly disappeared from the festivities.

She looked into Robert's eyes and thought that he looked sad. "Thank you," she whispered.

"I've wanted to see you, Glynis."

She nodded and at the same time felt as if some invisible hand were pulling her toward him. No one was looking at her, and she motioned him to follow as she headed toward the cloakroom. She reached the silence and privacy of the cloakroom and whirled around. Robert was a few steps behind her.

Without a word, he drew her into his arms, and she did not resist when he bent and kissed her lips. Glynis shuddered. It was a forbidden kiss, but a kiss she had longed for, a kiss she now knew he had longed for too. His lips moved sensuously on hers and his hands caressed her lightly, as she had so often dreamed he would caress her.

He kissed her neck. "God, I do love you, Glynis. But it's not right."

She pulled back slightly and felt the tears in her eyes. But she didn't care now if he saw them. "I spoke to the prince. He will intercede for me when his father is king—perhaps I can get an annulment."

There was hope in her voice, and he wanted to feel it too. But instead he was possessed of Stewart's pessimism. "Glynis, something has happened."

"What?"

"The Duke of Cumberland now leads the army. He is camped at the Nairn. At this very moment the prince and his advisers are choosing the place of battle. Scotland's been invaded, Glynis. It's going to be a fight to the death, one I am afraid we won't win."

She felt stunned by his words. At the very worst she had thought the Highland army would simply fade away. "Won't win? But you were almost in London. Our Highlanders defeated the Hanoverians at every turn."

"It's different now. They've had time to build their army, time to bring in fresh seasoned troops from the Continent. Glynis, we're fighting to the death, we're fighting now for our whole way of life."

There was a terrible urgency in his voice. "Oh, Robert . . ." She leaned against him, and he held her for one brief moment.

"Glynis, we have to go back inside. We'll have to wait, for now."

She stepped away from him and nodded. Inside, she felt as if everything were churning around. He did love her! She knew it, and yet they could not be together, she knew that too. She turned away and hurried back into the main room. Nothing was as it should be and, perhaps, if Robert were right, it never would be again. All her misgivings had been correct—everything would indeed change.

Chapter Seven

April 1746

The April rain fell in sheets, flooding the streets of Inverness, carrying the accumulated refuse away, washing the city as it did every spring. Not that it felt like spring. It was a cold, unrelenting rain, and in the mornings the puddles were covered with a thin layer of clear ice, so that when a man walked, he could hear the crunching beneath his boots, like thin glass breaking.

Angus Ross paced the length of his library, then turned and retraced his steps. He talked out loud, his words escaping his lips in short, rapid sentences.

"It could hardly be better. It will be over soon. Half of the prince's followers have returned to their drinking—"

Laurie's hair fell over her shoulders. She was perched on the edge of a straight-backed chair and her eyes followed him as he moved. She hated it when he was excited like this. He paid no attention to her at all. It was as if she were simply a fixture in the room. He wasn't even talking to her, he was talking aloud to himself.

"But Colin told me the prince is well. He's strong enough to fight, strong enough to lead."

"Lead what?!" Ross turned and shouted at her angrily.

She blinked up at him, taken aback by his attack. "I'm only giving you information," she said softly. "Is that not what I am supposed to do?"

"I hardly need your comments as well. They're finished. Prince or no prince. They'll be forced to fight on Culloden Moor and it is exactly the kind of place the Jacobites should not fight. It is a place for artillery and formal battle, not for the kind of attack-and-run tactic used so well by the Highlanders. They've mucked it up, my dear, they've snatched defeat from the jaws of victory! If they had stayed on the road to London, we might all be living under the rule of James."

This time Laurie kept her silence.

"I'll write to the Duke of Cumberland and you will ride to the Nairn and deliver it."

It was over twelve miles to the banks of the Nairn, where the duke's army was encamped. Twelve miles through the mud and in the cold rain. But she supposed that the message was one of import.

"After it is delivered, you will stay away until the battle is over. You will not return to Inverness until victory is ours."

Laurie nodded silently and closed her eyes. She opened them when she felt his hands on her, drawing her close. He kissed her bare shoulders. "But, of course, I must warm you before you go," he said, slipping his large hand into her dress to feel her breasts. "Do bend over the footstool, my dear, and raise your skirts."

Laurie felt a surge of heat pass through her whole body. His words excited her; his rough lovemaking always left her wanting more. She bent down and looked back up at him. "And when I do return?"

He smiled. "I'll be waiting."

Glynis stared into her mirror, and her image stared back at her. The house was empty save for a few servants. Her brothers and her father were gone to the encampment on the edge of Culloden Moor.

"I'm growing to be like Stewart," she said aloud. And it was true that she was filled with foreboding, with a feeling that soon the world as they all knew it would not just change or become more difficult, but that it would come to an end. She bit her lip. It really wasn't fair that the men had gone off without her. It wasn't fair that they had gone to fight at the side of the prince and in defense of their country and left her to wait.

"I can ride as well as any of them," she said aloud. And she knew she was as skilled as any with the pistol and the crossbow. She could not, of course, wield the broadsword. She contemplated Lady Anne Mackintosh, whom she did not know personally, but whose name was growing in fame. Lady Anne's husband had gone off to fight for the Hanoverian king, George II. Clearly, there was no love lost between Anne and her husband. As soon as he was gone, Colonel Anne, as she was now known, had set out to raise an army of Mackintoshes to fight for the prince. Now she led her own men though she was only twenty years of age. "The same age as I shall soon be," Glynis said.

"I don't want to stay here," Glynis said aloud, again speaking to her own mirror image. Abstractedly, she comtemplated her gold brooch with its cat in the center.

I'll go to fight with my brothers and with Robert, she vowed. And what did it matter? She had left her husband and was now condemned to a life of solitude, a life without the only man she had ever loved. Her only hope lay in the prince interceding, and if this battle was lost, there would surely be no intercession. Moreover, she would be trapped in Inverness with the enemy in power. This was no life, it was better to fight by Robert's side, better to be doing something rather than nothing.

But of course her father would object. Her brothers would make her go home. "I shall disguise myself," she said, leaning close to the mirror. It would not be all that difficult. Thousands of young men were joining the prince. She would simply be one more recruit. Dressed as a boy, she would blend in, and besides, even if she was discovered, she would not be the only woman fighting. She would just have to be careful to avoid her brothers and father.

She thought for a moment and remembered that Stewart had clothes that would probably fit her, clothes long out-grown but not thrown away. When she had been cleaning out the attic he had told her to leave them.

The army was camped at the moor, and rumor had it that men who had gone home for the winter were arriving from near and far to swell its ranks. "Now there will be one more," she said aloud as she headed for the attic to retrieve the clothes.

It was a gray dawn. There was light but no sunlight. The moving sky was filled with dark clouds, and a heavy, cold dampness hung over Culloden Moor.

The heather blew in the wind, dancing to and fro like a deep purple canvas in motion. Glynis thought that it was a strange, silent world out there on the moor, a world of dying fires and still-sleeping men. But there was some activity.

The sodden ground was covered with puddles of various sizes, and to one side of the moor a river ran over rocks and twisted like a snake. In the distance, a large black crow cried out and its lone complaint filled the silence of the morning.

Glynis looked around her in disbelief. This was not what she had expected, not at all what she thought she would find when she had ridden out to the moor. She had expected a proud army, assembled to fight, weapons at the ready. Instead, there were some four thousand Highlanders, most of whom appeared weary and hungry, tired beyond all belief. They had been encamped, waiting for the duke and his army for nearly two days now, and the weather was hideous and obviously food was in short supply. She closed her eyes and thought of all the food there had been at the ball only a few days ago . . . but of course among so many even that excess would not have gone far. As she rode along in search of the area where the mixed clans were assembled, more men awoke and took their places in the formation of this ragtag army.

Almost spontaneously singing began, though in fact she would not really have called it singing. It was more of a drone, a kind of humming. It was the Twentieth Psalm; "Let the Lord hear thee in the day of trouble; the name of the God of Jacob defend thee; . . . They are brought down and fallen: but we are risen and, stand upright . . ."

It was a potent verse and Glynis could only hope that it was prophetic. But the sight of the defenders frightened her. The mood frightened her.

At the far north of the field were Clan MacDonald, the most powerful clan supporting the Jacobites. They were led by Ranald MacDonald, their chieftain. They were all experienced cattle thieves and renown fighters, a bellicose lot from the far Highlands. Next to Clan MacDonald were the Roy Stewarts, a regiment of mixed clans. Next to them were the Farquharsons, Clan Chattan, which stood together with her own clan, the MacPhersons, to whom they were closely related, Clan Fraser, Clan Appin, and the Camerons. The second line of fighters were positioned in front of the prince. They included the Picard Irish, the Scots Royal, the Duke of Perth, Clan Gordon, and the Ogilvys.

Robert would surely be either with her brothers or with other members of Clan Forbes. Her father had gone on a mission for the prince and had not yet returned. As she looked at the faces around her, she was glad he was gone, glad he would not be a part of this battle. The mood in the air was not one of victory, but one of presumed defeat.

She rode on. If she went to where her own clan stood, someone was certain to recognize her horse, and she deemed it was equally important that Robert not see her either.

Glynis shivered slightly. She was full of nervous energy. She felt a terrible kind of apprehension, and that combined with fear as well as with her desire that they should emerge victorious. But the men were tired, the odds unfavorable, the weapons murderous. She had never fought in a battle, never even seen one, but she knew that many, perhaps even she, would die. Now, at this moment, she realized she had come here for romantic reasons, but that there was no romance in war. "God help us all," she whispered under her breath. She thought if anyone ever asked her, if she survived, she would say that this was the moment she had truly grown up. This was the moment when she saw herself as the silly girl she had been and knew the woman she had become. A part of her wanted to run, but she knew she would not.

Far back, on knolls overlooking the battlefield, women and children watched and waited. In the distance, through the fog, a sound could be heard. It was the low rumbling roll of drums. The enemy was approaching.

Glynis peered off into the fog and mist. Out of it emerged

a solid line, a frightening line of men with cannon, men led by drummers.

From nearby, the drumrolls were quickly drowned out by the whining glory of the bagpipes. The story went that they had been invented to frighten the enemy. But Glynis realized sadly, this enemy, which she now saw, included Clan Campbell, and they had their own pipers. Yet this was not to be a battle of pipers.

The artillery began firing, and in moments it seemed as if the two armies merged and dissolved into combat. The Highlanders had broken rank, and moved between their own artillery and the enemy.

Sampson reared and Glynis turned to see a British foot soldier. He slashed at her legs, but she raised them and drew her pistol, firing and hitting him. He crumpled and fell to the ground, and she turned her horse, her hand shaking and her heart beating wildly at the very thought that she had most probably killed someone. Tears began to form and run down her cheeks. Surely he had been no older than she.

Time seemed to pass quickly. It grew lighter, the two armies came together, and the smell of blood seemed to rise from the ground. There was complete disorganization, total chaos.

Glynis fought her way out of two desperate situations. But there was no rest, no looking around. She moved now toward her brothers, never mind if they saw her. It was too late, she wanted to be with her family.

"Close up!" Robert yelled out. "Close ranks!" But his voice was lost in the noise of battle. It was more horrible than he had imagined it would be. The Highland army was completely unready for this kind of fight. They completely lacked the discipline necessary. It was as if the MacDonalds were alone on the field of combat with the Campbells, their old enemy. They ignored everything else and fought alone, each seeking a hundred years of vengeance on the nearest Campbell, who did the same.

Robert turned in time to see Stewart fall from his horse. There was no time to get to him. He was beheaded with a single slice of his opponent's sword.

James MacPherson had ridden to the prince's side, and Colin was nowhere to be seen.

Robert had no time to think and less to mourn. He was besieged himself. He fought his way out of a circle of men who had surrounded him, only to see something that so stunned him, he almost lost control of his horse.

It was Sampson, and the person riding Sampson was clearly Glynis. Her war bonnet had fallen off in battle, her hair was loose, and she gripped her pistol, clearly trying to reload before she was run over. He spurred his stallion on, and leaning forward used his sword as a staff, toppling one of those who threatened her. "Glynis! Get out of here!"

She looked up and saw that her foe was dead. She opened her mouth to scream, but it was too late. Robert was hit from behind, his leg gashed. She seized her bow, took aim, and fired. The deadly arrow found its intended victim and hit him with such force that he toppled off his horse.

Robert was wounded not just in the leg but also in the arm. Glynis saw that he was slumped in the saddle, the horse's reins hanging loose. She reached his side and grabbed the reins. The hell with all of it! She saw an opening and took it. She guided Sampson away from the fray, pulling Robert's horse with her. She rode as fast as she could for as far as she could, and only when they had reached the safety of the knoll did she turn around and look behind her.

The field of battle was a sea of bodies. Men screamed in pain, women shrieked and tried to drag victims to safety. The prince and those with him had left, and Glynis knew that in a very short time the victorious English would come looking for survivors. She leaned over, and using a length of leather she had in her bag, she secured Robert to his horse. He was bleeding badly, but she had time only to tie a scarf around his leg. She again took the reins of his horse and galloped off.

"Home, Sampson," she whispered as she leaned forward in the saddle.

Glynis was not certain how far she had ridden, when she knew she had to stop. Sampson needed to rest for a few minutes, and he needed water as well. More important, she had to dress Robert's wounds or he would bleed to death, if indeed he was still alive.

She stopped by the river and let Sampson drink. She hurriedly bandaged Robert's arm, which was cut less deeply than his leg. She tore strips from her cloak and bound Robert's gashed leg. He moaned now and again, but he did not regain consciousness. Her only comfort was his heavy breathing. He was strong. She felt certain he would survive.

"I must get to Cluny," she thought. There were supplies there, and clothing, and most important, a wagon. It was the only way they would escape, since Robert could not continue to ride this way. By tomorrow, the day after at the latest, the Highlands would be crawling with patrols. There would be no mercy for any of them. Her mind was a muddle, but she knew Cluny had to be her first stop.

Glynis's eyes snapped open when she heard Robert groan. Not that she had been deeply asleep, she was far too uncomfortable to have rested well. She had stopped around ten to take refuge in a crofter's small, deserted hut. All of Scotland was dotted with such huts. Some were used by hunters, others by poor squatters, and still others—usually better than this one—were homes to those who worked the land and tended the sheep.

This particular hut was of the most primitive kind. The floor was dirt and the hut itself was made of twigs, straw, and branches. Still, it offered some shelter from the wind if not the dampness.

To make matters worse, she had nothing but her saddle blanket. This she had wrapped Robert in, while she herself made do with her ragged cloak, the same cloak from which she had torn strips to bandage his now-blood-soaked wounds.

He seemed to have stopped bleeding. The bandages were soaked but stiff with dried blood. His face was pale, but his heartbeat was strong. It was imperative that she wash his wounds and properly dress them. But this was not the place for such an undertaking. It was dark and she had no candles. It was dirty and there was no hot water.

She had tethered both horses outside and now she wondered how she would get Robert back on his horse. She knew she was not more than a two-hour ride from Cluny, and it occurred to her that if she left him, she could come back with the wagon. She sat up and listened. The night could not have been more quiet. Most certainly trouble would not start until tomorrow. The British would be celebrating tonight in Inverness. They would drink long into the night, and tomorrow, when they had rested, they would begin to search for stragglers. There was no doubt in her mind that vengeance would be taken; it always was.

Robert moaned again, and she leaned close to his ear. "Robert, can you hear me? Are you awake?"

"Glynis—"

His voice escaped in a gasp.

"Yes, it's Glynis. Robert, listen to me, don't try to talk. You're hurt. We're in a crofter's hut. I have to ride on alone and bring back a wagon. You must stay here, you must not try to move while I'm gone."

"Can't move," he said slowly, painfully. "Glynis, I can't feel my leg."

"It's going to be all right. Please, stay here. I have to go and get the wagon."

He nodded in the darkness and she felt his head move. It would all be much easier alone. She pulled herself up and staggered back out into the night. She had probably slept two hours at least. She was rested enough not to fall asleep while riding. She went to Sampson and untied and mounted him. She marked her location and began making her way to Cluny.

Glynis rode for nearly two hours before she reached truly familiar territory. When Sampson realized they were on the road home, he broke into full gallop in spite of his own weariness.

Glynis took him around the side of the castle to the shed where she had been keeping him. His feed was there, and he ate while she gathered up the necessary things.

Glynis slipped into the kitchen and lit a candle. The others were probably still sleeping. She wasted no time. First she gathered a store of food, which she assembled in the kitchen. Then she hurried to her room and got sheepskins and clean clothes. From Stewart's room she got clothes for Robert, and she took candles, a lantern, her flint, more bullets for her pistol, and extra shoes. She went to the safe and emptied it of her own jewelry and a hundred pounds of British currency. She also got medical supplies . . . bandages and some powders for pain as well as a medicinal alcohol. Just for good measure, she emptied her father's liquor cabinet as well.

She could hardly think about it, but deep inside she felt

her brothers were alive. Nonetheless, they would not return here. They would head directly for the Outer Hebrides, where they would seek refuge on the untamed land belonging to Clan Chattan.

Glynis went back downstairs, passing the rooms of the sleeping women and wondering if she should wake them. She decided against it. No one should know where she was—that way they could tell no one. The British were sure to want the clan leaders, not the wives of crofters.

She went to the barn and hitched two horses to the wagon. Sampson could follow behind. She hurriedly put in the food, clothes, sheepskins, arms, medical supplies, and liquor. She covered everything she had gathered with loose straw and attached Sampson to the back of the wagon. She clicked and jiggled the reins and the wagon clattered off and down the road. She realized with concern that just gathering the supplies had taken her two hours and that it was a two-hour ride back to the hut. That would leave them only four hours of travel time before dawn.

Carefully, marking her way as she went, she retraced her earlier ride on Sampson. At last, after what seemed an eternity, she reached the crofter's hut.

"Robert," she whispered, jostling him slightly.

He opened his eyes and looked up at her. What a pitiful sight he was! His face was encrusted with dirt and there were streaks of white where the rain had run down it. She forced a smile. Surely she looked no better. Her hair was a tangled mass of dark curls, and it seemed doubtful she would ever get a brush through it again.

"Glynis—I was worried."

"Come along. There is no time to waste. We must go."

He nodded and pulled himself into a sitting position on his good arm. She pulled with all her strength and he struggled up onto one foot, wincing in pain. She let him lean on her, and they staggered forth with Robert hopping.

At last they reached the wagon, and he threw himself over the back end. She pushed him the rest of the way in and he rolled under the straw. "Cover yourself," she whispered.

"Where are we going?"

Glynis bit her lip. "I don't know where we should go. Just away. I know they'll be looking, I know there will be no mercy."

"You're right. Glynis, there will be no mercy for any of us. Let's go south around Inverness. Head for Nairn. Most of those who escape will go north and so will those searching for them. We'll be safest going south. I know a place we can hide."

Glynis did not question his logic or his suggestion. She climbed onto the wagon and they were off. South it would be.

Colin lay on the damp dirt floor of the overcrowded cell in the Inverness jail. Meant to hold a few prisoners only, it now held fifteen, and all the other cells were as full.

Those who were not mortally wounded had been rounded up like cattle and marched into town. There were soldiers billeted in every house, and some of the prisoners had been moved into the cellars of homes and were being held there. It had been five days since the battle, and the number of prisoners was now so large that he heard many were being held on British ships anchored in the river.

Outside, the ominous hammering kept him awake. It was only days after the battle, but already the scaffolding that would be used to hang the traitors was being erected.

Unconsciously, Colin felt his neck. Being hung was hardly a pleasant thought. But, he assumed, it would not be right away. And who could predict which prisoners would be hung and which would not? If he knew his jailers well, it would be haphazard, but that alone would serve to terrorize those who were held.

Colin pulled himself to an upright position. Beyond the walls of the prison he could hear the sound of drunken singing. The victorious were still celebrating.

When first captured, he had been in another cell, until he had been thrown into this one tonight. "Who shares this cell with me?" he said in a loud voice. "I'm Colin MacPherson."

"Thomas Chattan," one of his cellmates returned.

"William Chattan," another put in.

"Donald MacDonald . . ." One by one, each of them gave their name. But it was too dark to see the faces of those who responded.

"Are you the brother of Stewart MacPherson?" one of the men asked in the darkness.

"I am," Colin answered.

"I saw him killed," the man said.

Colin could not immediately answer. He made a sound of acknowledgment and crossed himself.

"Better off than those wounded," a voice in the darkness muttered. "They've been left to die slowly, their bodies picked at by animals and those ghouls who waited to rob the dead and wounded."

"And better off than we. We'll be starved or hung."

Colin didn't answer. He was sure the man spoke the truth. He was just as sure that James must have escaped. "Did the prince get away?" he whispered.

"Aye," someone replied. "But let's not discuss it. We don't know who's listening, or even who might be among us in this darkness."

There was mumbling agreement. Colin pulled himself over to the wall and sat leaning against it. The air was already foul, and he knew it would get worse. He wondered what Laurie's fate had been—indeed, he wondered about most of those who had been in Inverness.

At some point, Colin fell asleep. He was startled into wakefulness by the sound of gruff voices in the prison corridor, and then suddenly the dungeon door was opened and two men stared into the cell, while behind them heavily armed guards pointed guns at those inside.

"What a stench these savages have!" a very British voice proclaimed.

"They don't wash often," a Scot's voice replied.

Colin blinked in disbelief. The British voice belonged to an officer, but the Scot's voice was none other than Angus Ross's, Laurie's cousin. His mouth felt a trifle dry as he stared at Ross in the dim light. This was the man Glynis kept reporting she saw Laurie with—yet he was with British soldiers and was clearly a traitor to the Jacobite cause.

"Ross! Are you one of the spies who was among us?" a man from Clan Chattan called out.

Ross did not look at the man directly, and Colin knew he did not see him. "I prefer to think of it as patriotism."

"And so it is," the British officer added. "It is most of you who will hang."

"What happened to justice?" someone asked.

"You'll all be properly tried for treason," the officer said crisply.

Colin could see it all in his mind now. It would be as it had been before. They would be lined up and brought before a magistrate. Their so-called trial would last no more than a few minutes, and they would be sentenced either to be hung or, if the judge were feeling merciful, to rot in prison.

"A disgusting lot," Ross said. His eyes searched their faces and came to rest on Colin. "Is that you, Colin Mac-Pherson?"

Colin did not know whether he should answer or not, but after a moment he did. "Yes."

"I should thank you for all your help. Without the information you so kindly gave Laurie, we might not have won so handily."

"Laurie!" Her name escaped Colin's lips in a cry that was half howl and half scream of disbelief. Ross's words cut through him, and doubly so because he recalled how angry he had been with Glynis.

"The trials will begin tomorrow," the British officer said.

The door slammed and the prisoners were once more alone.

"Was your lover a spy?" one of them asked. Colin supposed he might be in danger from them, but it did not seem the case. He nodded dumbly, the reality and depth of Laurie's deception still too difficult for him to understand.

"You're a young lad, women can be deceptive," one of them said sympathetically.

Colin could not speak. Learning of Laurie's activities was worse than the sting of defeat, this feeling of having been betrayed by a person you loved a kind of hell. For the first time in his life he felt tears in his eyes. "I loved her," he said in a hoarse voice.

There was a mutter of sympathy. "We'd have been beaten anyway," someone said in a halfhearted attempt to make him feel better.

Colin again slumped against the wall. Inside, he knew he would not feel the same tomorrow, but at that moment his fate did not matter.

Glynis guided the wagon into the woods and toward the small lake. She knew they were some nine miles south of Inverness. Robert appeared to be right; thus far they had encountered no patrols on this previously conquered ground.

"We'll reach the Nairn before dark," she said.

"I think it's safe enough here for a while," Robert replied from the back of the wagon. "Glynis, you need to get some sleep."

"Your wound needs dressing more than I need sleep," she said firmly.

"That's why I directed you here. Follow this road and take the first left. There's a small hut there, one suitable for our purposes."

"Is the lake nearby?"

"Just a few steps beyond the door."

She followed his directions and in a few minutes the hut came into view. "It looks better than most."

"It's on my family land," Robert answered.

Glynis brought the wagon to a clattering halt, then she climbed down and, clutching her pistol, made sure there was no one around. She took what she needed from the wagon and helped Robert inside.

"First I'll see to your wounds," she said. "I'll have to get water though, and we'll need a fire."

He did not protest when she built a fire. This hut was one clearly used by hunters. It had a dirt floor, but it also had a small hearth and a place where the smoke could exit.

When her fire was burning, she went out with her bucket to get water. She returned and began heating it.

"I'll have to soak that bloody cloth from your wound," she said matter-of-factly.

Robert did not answer. His leg throbbed and so did his arm. But at least he could feel both of them. He knew the removal of the cloth would be painful and that he might begin bleeding again.

Glynis worked silently, and when the water was warm,

she began soaking the cloth. Layer by layer she removed the strips of her cloak from both wounds. She worked slowly so as not to cause the wounds to begin bleeding again. The arm was, as she suspected, far less serious, and the cloth came off easily. She applied alcohol and though Robert winced, he sat still while she bound the arm in clean bandages.

His leg took much longer. She had to cut away his clothing completely rather than just remove it. The gash was deep, and it seemed obvious to her that it needed stitching up. Since that was impossible in their present circumstances, she cleaned it and pulled the skin together, binding it in a way she hoped would allow it to heal. He would have a deep scar, a terrible scar, but she felt certain he would be all right.

"You're a good nurse," he said when she finished. "I'd like to wash," he said, smiling for the first time. "Then get dressed in clean clothes."

Glynis nodded. It was only April, so the water in the lake would be cold, but she was used to cold water. "I'm going in the lake," she said. "When I come in I'll wash you with hot water. It will take a few minutes to heat anyway."

Robert said nothing. He knew she had an enormous tolerance for cold water. He bit his lip. He had not yet told her about Stewart, and he decided to wait.

Glynis went outside and quickly stripped. She walked into the cold water and shivered at the temperature. Still, in a moment she was aware of how good it felt, and she quickly washed her hair.

She hurried back inside wrapped in a sheepskin. "Brrr . . ." She glanced at Robert. He was sitting up and looking at her. It was a peculiar look, a look of admiration, of longing.

Slowly, she let the sheepskin drop to the floor.

Robert's eyes widened. He should turn away, but he could not. He was transfixed by the sight of her, frozen by her singular beauty and the very nearness of her. "Glynis—" Her name escaped his lips. He had started to tell her how very beautiful she was, but he could not find the words to describe her. Her skin was like alabaster, white and smooth. Her breasts were full and high, and in the cool evening air, and no doubt as a result of the cold water, her nipples were hard and erect, rosy and inviting. Her waist was tiny and her hips angular. Her legs were long and shapely, and as she bent to dry herself, her breasts hung invitingly.

She was like a wild creature, this beautiful young woman with the tangled dark hair and the flashing green eyes. His mouth felt dry and even without seeing her backside, he knew her buttocks were rounded and firm. She was everything any man could want and more.

"You tempt me," he said.

"I have to wash you," she said in a low voice.

He sucked in his own breath. She undressed him carefully and began to slowly wash the top half of his body.

And she was close, so close. She knelt by his side. He reached up and took her breast in his hand. Her face flushed pink and her lips parted as he felt her firm nipple. Her skin was soft, so soft.

She removed the sheepskin that had covered him when she had dressed his wound. He was strong and ready and she touched him in wonder, moving her hands slowly over him, holding his manhood in her hand.

"Glynis—" There was no stopping now. She bent and took him into her mouth and kissed him gently.

He felt he would burst. Her touch was sure, but he knew it was guided by instinct and not experience. Ramsey had called her a cold bitch, but she was anything but cold. He thought of the old saying, "One man's virgin is another man's whore," and he knew that Glynis would reject other men, but still be his with all the wild passion that was hers to give.

"Woman, you will make this far too fast," he said, trying to think of other things.

She looked up at him, her green eyes steady. "Please, take me, Robert Forbes. Hold me and kiss me. Make me yours, for I belong to you."

Her declaration came in a soft voice. Her eyes were wonderful, her mouth irresistible.

"Robert, our whole world changed yesterday—our world is different now, nothing is the same."

She was right and he could not deny that she was right. Nor could he any longer deny his love for her. "Glynis," he whispered as he drew her down to him and kissed those lips that were so freely offered.

He sought her breasts with both hands now. He was drawn to her as if she were a magnet, unable to resist her beauty, her soft vulnerability, her eagerness to please him. She possessed, he now recognized, all these characteristics and more. So much more. She was intelligent and talented, and above all brave. Marrying Ramsey was a terrible mistake, a mistake he caused her to make by not recognizing what was in his own heart.

"Oh, Robert." Her hands were on the floor of the hut and she shivered as she straddled him. She did not shiver from cold, but from excitement.

Her full breasts were above his face, and he drew one of her erect nipples into his mouth. It was tight and hard and a wonderful rosy pink, a pink that grew deeper as he nursed on it, causing her to surge above him and moan.

He moved his hands over her bare skin. It was silky and warm, glowing with the intoxication of their lovemaking. It was all wrong because of Ramsey, and yet it was right and he could not withdraw now or stop his urgent caresses.

With his lips still on her breast, he ran his hands over her buttocks and then circled around to the front and touched that area he knew to be her most sensitive. Her response was instant as she automatically lowered herself to receive him.

" 'Tis you who will have to come to me," he whispered.

She said nothing, but she was careful to avoid all contact with his wounded leg. "This is good," he said, touching her nipples and again nursing on one.

Glynis closed her eyes and moaned again as he touched her again, caressing the inside of her long, slender thigh with his warm hand, allowing his fingers to slip into her. She was soft and moist and ready as he continued to toy with her breasts.

"Please," she whispered. "I want you."

"It is all the more pleasurable to wait," he returned, even though he himself was having difficulty. He moved his hands again to her buttocks. Round and soft, they undulated as he caressed her, again returning to her thighs, then to her place of hidden pleasure.

"I can stand it no longer," she breathed even as she lowered herself to him.

"Glynis, you're a virgin. It will hurt." He pushed gently up into her, she let out a little gasp, and he withdrew.

"Lie down for a moment at my side," he said.

"I'm not afraid," she whispered. "Robert, I love you."

"I will not hurt you," he said gently. "You must be totally ready, Glynis. Lie still, let me ready you."

She said nothing, but lay on her back next to him and closed her eyes, giving in to all her emotions and all the sensual feelings his touch created in her.

Softly, tauntingly, he moved his hands over her whole body, sometimes hardly touching her, while at other times pressing gently. Again she felt his fingers between her legs, gently parting her and entering her. First one finger, two. He moved his fingers and she wriggled and groaned.

He slowly moved down, still caressing her nipples with his fingers. To her delight and astonishment, she felt his lips on that place—when he touched her there, chills went through her whole body, a feeling of incredible tension.

"Oh," she murmured as his tongue flicked against her. His fingers were still on her breasts, pressing and rubbing, rhythmically caressing her even as his tongue moved in that other place. Her hips were undulating now as she reached for his touch. Her whole body was glowing hot and she felt only a terrible longing, a tension, as if she were on the rack—and yet it was a pleasurable tension, a desire for the throbbing of her dreams. But he continued to toy with her till she thought she would shriek, and suddenly she felt it. It was as if the demon of pure sensual joy had suddenly inhabited her whole body. It was the wonderful pulsating of her dreams, yet a hundred times stronger. He held her fast now, and she shook violently in his arms, clinging to the sensation of this wild, free throbbing that seemed to consume her whole body.

When it finally stopped, she looked into his face. In the candlelight she could see he was smiling. "Now you're ready," he said softly. He waited for only a few minutes before he began again. He stroked her slowly, purposefully. He caressed her breasts in many ways—with his fingers, with his mouth, even by rubbing against her with his growth of beard. Each movement held a promise, each helped to once again bring her to a fevered pitch. But this time there was a new element, the element of expectation.

When again he touched her she moaned, "Now, please, now," and he laughed lightly and breathed into her ear, "You're beautiful and fiery and I love you."

Again she positioned herself over him, and again he touched her, but this time so lightly that she knew she wanted more. Again she lowered herself onto him. He pushed upward and there was only the smallest feeling of discomfort as she felt him fill her. It was a wonderful feeling! An indescribable feeling! It was as if they were one person. He moved within her and his movement caused the same wonderful feeling she had experienced before. The mounting tension caused her to moan again, and when he grasped her undulating buttocks and shivered, she felt it again and reared back, her mouth open in the ecstasy of fulfillment.

Glynis collapsed onto him, then carefully moved to his side, curling herself in his arms. He leaned over and blew out the candle even as she pulled the sheepskin over them.

In the darkness, long after he knew Glynis was asleep, Robert lay on his back and stared at the ceiling of the hut. He knew he had just experienced the most pleasurable moment of his life. But it was a troubling experience as well. What if Ramsey were still alive? He knew he could never give her up, and yet, she was not truly his. Now there was no question about what had to be done. If Ramsey had survived the battle, he would have to duel him.

Chapter Eight

Late April 1746

Outside the Inverness town hall, gray clouds moved across the sky but now and again, a spot of blue shone through. It was one of those days so familiar in Scotland, a day of clouds that would almost inevitably end in a brilliant sunset.

Inside the town hall, a stone-faced magistrate sat high on a pedestal overlooking two rows of unkempt prisoners. Behind the prisoners, crowds of jeering soldiers and civilians had squeezed into the hall, there to see justice meted out to the Jacobite rebels.

Colin drew in his breath. The air in this makeshift courtroom was superior to that in his cell, but it was nonetheless far from fresh. No doubt the odor was a result of the number of filthy bodies crammed inside, all eagerly waiting to learn who would live and who would die.

Colin looked around him. Could this be the same place

where only a few weeks ago a gay, carefree ball had been held? He thought of dancing with Laurie, of holding her in his arms, of looking into her deep brown eyes. He shook his head, feeling defeated spiritually as well as bodily. She had betrayed him. She had betrayed all of them.

And what had become of all the others? Of his family? He wondered if James and the prince had gotten away and if Robert Forbes was alive or dead. He wondered where his father was, and where Glynis had gone. He could only pray that they were safe. He knew Stewart was dead and he thought as he looked at the magistrate that he would soon join his brother.

The gavel came down with a thundering finality. "Stephen MacDougal! Guilty. You shall be hung by the neck until dead. May God have mercy on your soul."

How many before him? He wasn't sure just how they were being called, alphabetically, by clan, or by some random method. All he knew was that when they were called a few questions were asked, the judge conferred briefly with two British officers, and the sentence was handed down. The prisoner was then led away, out into the courtyard, where the scaffold waited. The sentence was apparently carried out immediately. In fact, the judge's proclamations were often punctuated by the sound of the trapdoor outside as the hangman's noose claimed yet another victim. It wasn't the outcome, Colin thought. It was the waiting. And in spite of his feeling of defeat, in spite of Laurie's betrayal, in spite of knowing he might never see a member of his family again, he knew he still wanted to live.

Laurie sat nervously across from the Duke of Cumberland. If Ross knew she were there, he would surely beat her, but guilt filled her. She had never loved Colin, but he loved her and she had used him. Now, because he loved her, he was going to be hanged.

"How may I help you, Miss Lewis?"

The duke was a rotund man, short of leg but with strong features and a strangely long nose. When he talked, he used his hands expressively. But his hands were pudgy and his fingers short, so the result of his gyrations was more comical than impressive.

Unhappily, the duke's odd movements did not ease her own anxiety. She felt extremely nervous, not just because of Ross, but because the duke himself was formidable and definitely not known for his kindness.

"I've come to beg a favor," she said in a voice he had to lean forward to hear.

The duke pursed his lips and frowned. "A favor? Well, I suppose you are owed a favor for all the information you provided. What will it be? A dress from London?"

Laurie shook her head. "No, your highness."

He did not correct her as he would have corrected one of his officers. He was not her highness or anyone else's. "I'm a duke," he offered.

"Yes, sir. I've come to ask mercy for one of the prisoners."

Again the duke frowned. "Why?"

"He gave me much information."

"And did he know how this information would be used?"

"No, sir."

"Then why should I offer him mercy?"

Laurie bit her lip. She had no answer. "Only because I ask it," she said softly.

"And why do you ask?"

"Because he loved me and I betrayed him."

"A matter of conscience." The duke rubbed his chin with his stubby fingers which, she noted, were bitten to the quick. It had not occurred to her till then that he was a very nervous man. Perhaps even more nervous than she.

"Yes, that is it, it is a matter of conscience. It haunts me and I can't sleep."

"I'm not sure you should feel any remorse at all, my dear. But as you ask, I will grant it. Where is this person?"

"Being tried at this moment. His name is Colin Mac-Pherson."

The duke made a noise deep in his throat, then he took a paper and wrote a note on it. He rang a bell and one of his men came in, snapped to attention, and stood waiting.

"Take this note over to the town hall and give it to the judge. Make swift, or you might be too late."

The man turned on his heel and left.

"Thank you," Laurie said. "What will happen to him now?"

The duke smiled. "He will be mercifully deported."

"Thank you," Laurie murmured. Deportation was surely better than hanging. She had heard that life in the colonies was difficult, but that with hard work and perseverance one could not only survive but get ahead.

"You are quite welcome, Miss Lewis. I trust Mr. Ross will be in touch with you about future work."

Laurie, who had stood up, looked at the duke and nodded dumbly. What future work? Was it not over yet? But she could not bring herself to ask those questions aloud. Instead, she forced a smile and left.

Colin saw the young officer come into the courtroom and hand the judge a note. He watched as the judge read the note and nodded. He heard his name called and knew the noose awaited. It was as if small chunks of ice were suddenly running through his veins.

Colin forced himself to stand and walk to the front of

the room. He listened as the charges of treason were read
out. They were the same charges read for all the prisoners.
Midway through the droning accusations he heard the
trapdoor fall and he knew the man who had preceded him
was dead. Could any of the others see him shaking? Did
they know how dry his mouth was? Could they tell he was
afraid? He forced a passive expression, standing tall and
straight. But a voice within him was screaming. No! No!
No!

The court clerk finished. "How do you plead?" the judge
asked.

"Not guilty," Colin said clearly. How could he be guilty
for supporting the true king? But he did not add to his
statement. Others had tried to make statements and been
silenced.

"I sentence you to deportation in the colonies, there
to serve as an indentured servant for a period of fifteen
years!"

Colin blinked. He had been so certain of his fate, he
could hardly believe his ears. There was some jeering in
the courtroom, but two guards stood on either side of him,
pushing him forward.

"Have him put with the prisoners being sent to London,
there to await transport to the colonies."

Colin was marched away, his head still reeling. He was
not to be hung! Most assuredly he did not want to be
sent away from Scotland, and the prospect of indentured
servitude was none too pleasant, but it was certainly better
than hanging. He felt suddenly alive, and though he was
sure the conditions of his travel would be horrendous, he
silently vowed to live. He who was not dead could live to
fight another day. Perhaps he could escape. Perhaps he
could find Glynis and James . . . perhaps he would have a
life after all.

* * *

Both the moon and stars were obscured by low clouds. James MacPherson, who was more tired than he could ever remember being, was glad the night was dark.

"Here is as good a place as any," he heard Cameron call out. James reined in his horse and for a moment sat in the saddle, too weary even to climb down.

His mind was still filled with horrible images, images he could not chase away or forget easily. The loss and suffering on Culloden Moor was unbelievable. He had seen his own brother slain and he was not sure if his other brother, Colin, was dead or alive. And what of Glynis? She was alone at Cluny. Would she have the sense to hide? At least, he thought, she had a chance. Had she been in Inverness, she would have had no chance to avoid arrest. Most of the clan women in Inverness had been rounded up, and rumors abounded. In hushed tones people spoke of beatings and rapes. The two most common rumors involved their own fate; they were to be deported to the colonies in the Caribbean and there they were to be made servants. Yes, had Glynis been in Inverness, she would surely have been arrested too. Their father was one of the leaders of the rebellion, and he was a wanted man. James shook his head. All he knew for certain was that his father was leading a regiment, and was on his way to meet Ogilvy, who was leading another regiment, when the battle had occurred.

A third of the Highland army had not been at Culloden. Perhaps they could rally—but James's optimistic thought was fleeting. A rally was impossible. The British had taken all the stores of both food and arms at Inverness. There was no way to clothe, feed, and arm a force of some fifteen hundred men. In any case, they would be outnumbered.

He shook his head sadly. The losses had been terrible. He and a few others had just saved the prince, leading

him away from the battleground. For two days it was as if
the prince were in a hypnotic trance. He hardly seemed
to have realized what had happened. That such a tragedy
had occurred seemed to him to indicate that the British
had been in possession of detailed information concerning
their numbers and strength.

"Come along," Cameron called out.

James dismounted and felt the full effects of the day's
long ride and the weeks of deprivation. They had slept on
the ground, in dank huts, and in a miserable damp root
cellar. They had eaten only biscuits, some hard cheese,
and stale bread. They had drunk only weak tea.

When they left the field of battle, they had ridden like
the wind southward toward Forthleck on Loch Mhor,
where now they had mercifully arrived. It had not been a
direct ride. They had circled around glens, separated, and
met up again, and led their horses over narrow rocky paths.
It was all an effort to confuse their pursuers.

Cameron led them to a small, dark cottage. He knocked
loudly on the door and was greeted by a woman bearing
a rifle.

"Cameron of Lochiel," he said, looking at her steadily.

She peered into his face, dropped her rifle, and
motioned them inside. The four of them went in, and she
lit a lantern. She held it up and examined each of their
faces. When she came to Charles, she suddenly dropped
to her knees. "Your highness! I would know your image
anywhere."

Charles smiled. "Thank you, dear lady, but what we need
is shelter for the night."

The woman was still on her knees. "My humble home
is yours, I am so honored."

Charles took her hand. It was worn from hard work, and
rough. He smiled warmly. "I thank you, my lady."

Never had the crofter's wife been called a lady, James

thought. But that was part of Bonnie Prince Charlie's charm. He treated his subjects with an equality they found endearing.

In moments they had lit a fire and were cooking over it. Tonight they would have rabbit soup and then some strong hot tea.

The woman asked a few questions, and they told her about Culloden. She wiped tears from her face and told them that her husband had been there.

"Perhaps the survivors can reorganize," Alexander Macleod suggested.

James shook his head. He was the youngest there, but he intended to speak his mind. "We haven't the means," he said firmly.

"We have near fifteen hundred men," Macleod declared.

"And no food, clothes, or arms for them," James said. "It might well be better if our prince returns to France and tries to raise funds and troops there."

Charles himself listened to the conversation. He turned. "It is too late, far too late. I think we must order the others to disband. Each man must seek his own safety."

James muttered his agreement. Getting the prince out of Scotland would not, in any case, be an easy matter, but somehow they had to find a way.

"The sun is out," Robert said as he hobbled toward the hearth.

Glynis stirred the soup. It wasn't really her choice of breakfast, but it served to fill the stomach and give strength for whatever lay ahead.

Robert smiled at her. She had finally succeeded in brushing the tangles from her hair and now she had braided it. She wore clean clothes, plain clothes, but they were not plain enough to cover her magnificent figure, a figure he now knew well. As he looked at her he was aware of a sudden growing excitement, a desire to possess her yet again.

"I know what you're thinking," she said, looking into his eyes.

"Do you?"

She moved closer to him and sat down. "It will be a while before the soup is ready."

"By heaven, Glynis, our lives may depend on our riding swiftly. On our putting as much distance as possible between us and the soldiers who will be combing the Highlands."

She lifted his hand to her lips and kissed it. She held it on her bodice and closed her eyes. "I cannot forget the last few weeks—I've never known such a feeling."

Her honesty was overwhelming, her desire obvious. "Glynis, we ought to think about this. We really don't know about Ramsey."

She pressed his hand harder to her swelling breast. "Touch me," she said, looking into his eyes. "Make me feel as I did last night, please. I don't care about Ramsey, I don't care about anything or anyone except you."

Glynis took her other hand and touched him, she smiled. "You want me too."

There was no denying his own passionate desire. He quickly unlaced her bodice and pushed away the material so that he could once again taste the sweetness of her magnificent breasts. Her skin was ever fresh, and she glowed, looking more lovely than she had ever looked before. Raven hair on alabaster skin, deep green eyes, lips that yielded everything . . . he kissed her mouth, then her breasts. He lay down and pulled her with him, feeling under her skirts, exploring even as he himself felt he would burst.

"I love your hands on me," she whispered. "When you touch me there I—I can't control myself."

Her words further inflamed him as he pulled down her undergarments and grasped her exactly where she wanted. She groaned in his arms and began to writhe in a newfound drunkenness. Now, he thought, he knew the meaning of drunk with desire. He could see the intoxication in her eyes and feel it in her movements.

He moved slowly, sucking her breast while she squirmed, exciting him even more. He lifted his kilt and their skin touched.

"You're quite wonderful," he whispered as he again sucked on her nipple till it was as hard as a pebble. She was a gift given at a time when most of life's pleasures had been withdrawn. She was young, and yet she was a woman—all woman, he thought as he grasped her mound and let his fingers dance on her flesh. She was more than moist, she was damp all over, an anxious, writhing mass of pleasure.

"Now," she whispered urgently. "Now."

He laughed gently and continued to caress her, though he moved away slightly, not wanting her to know pleasure so soon.

He managed to climb atop her and easily enter her. She breathed in his ear and moved beneath him while he grasped her buttocks. In moments she let out a little scream of delight and pure wanton pleasure. He allowed himself to take his own pleasure, and then he held her tightly. There was no leaving this woman, there could be no giving her up.

After a short time Glynis pulled herself up and relaced her bodice. She pulled up her undergarments, leaned over, and saw once again to stirring the soup.

After a short time she dished up the soup, and both drank it quickly.

"We've got to keep heading south," Robert said.

"I've money," Glynis revealed. "And my jewels."

Robert nodded. His mind was on neither money nor jewels. "Glynis, I can't give you up even if Ramsey is alive."

She looked deeply into his eyes and nodded. "My family—my father would make me go back to him or live without you."

"I love and respect your father, but I still could not give you up."

"Nor would I let you," she said, still looking deep into his eyes.

"Maybe we should try to leave," Robert suggested.

"Leave Scotland?"

"Yes. We'll go to London. I hear there are people there who would help us. We could book passage and go to the colonies."

"The English colonies—we'd be persecuted."

"We could make our way to the French colonies. I know it would be a hard life, Glynis. But we'd be together."

"I don't know . . . I love Scotland. I love Cluny."

"So do I, but I love you more than life itself."

Glynis put her head on his shoulder and he wrapped her protectively in his arms. "We'll do what you think best," she said, softly. "Oh, Robert, I do love you so."

Colin cursed the sun. It beat down on the rotting timbers of the ancient vessel and heated the hold to unbearable temperatures. But with or without the sun, the innards of the old ship were hell, and each and every day he questioned his vow to survive the circumstances of his imprisonment.

The vessel on which he was held was anchored in Loch

Ness. At some time, he presumed, it would sail into Moray
Firth and from there into the North Sea. He assumed they
would sail south to London and then Portsmouth. There
they would be put on another vessel to be shipped out to
the colonies.

If they lived that long. Every day a few of his fellow
prisoners died. They had little room, hardly any fresh air,
little water, and only one meal of watery gruel a day. Even
among the hapless prisoners rumors flourished.

"A hundred or more have been hung," he was told. But
that was hardly the whole tale. Many were hunted down
in the glens and shot. And as he could personally testify,
many were dying in prison.

"We're to be sold as indentured servants. We'll probably
be treated like slaves." Rumor after rumor, story after story,
as men clung to hope in spite of everything.

Colin soon gave up listening to the rumors. He didn't
care where he was sent. He would escape and somehow
he would return to Scotland to find the rest of his family.
It was all that kept him alive.

He sat in the far corner of the filthy hold, his eyes closed
against the sight of the place. He tried to concentrate on
something more pleasant than the stench that filled the
overcrowded room.

"Colin MacPherson!"

Colin started at the sound of his name. Had there been
a mistake? Had they decided to hang him after all? He
had struggled to remain anonymous even from his fellow
prisoners. Now he felt betrayed once again, given away.

"Colin MacPherson!" There was no use hiding. He
stood up, walked forward, and looked upward to where
the hatch to the hold had been opened.

"You've a visitor," he was told by a sailor who sounded

angry. The man peered at him from above, a round face surrounded by light.

"A visitor?" Colin was dumbfounded.

"You're unfit to see anyone," the sailor said gruffly. "Follow me. Get up here and follow me!"

Colin climbed the ladder though he felt he might fall. He staggered out of the hold and followed. He was led into a small closetlike room with a drain in the middle of the floor. There he was ordered to take off his clothes. He did so gratefully and was rewarded by having several buckets of hot water thrown on him. He washed quickly and two buckets of cold water followed. At that point he was given clean clothes, ill fitting though they were.

Again he was led down an inside passage and he was prodded up another ladder. Colin blinked in the sunlight and looked around in disbelief. There, by the rail, talking to the captain of the vessel was Laurie Lewis. She was dressed in a long blue dress and her red hair was tied in ribbons.

"Ah," the captain said. "Here he is. Be brief."

Laurie nodded at him. "Colin, I had to see you."

He looked into her eyes and wondered how he could ever have allowed her to fool him so. "Why? Did you wonder if they had killed me? Or perhaps you wanted to see if I was being treated well."

"Yes, I wanted to see if you were being treated well."

"And did you ask the bodies on Culloden Moor if they were being well treated? How about the wounded who died slowly that night?" He could hear the bitterness in his own voice. He knew it grew even more bitter as he contemplated the enormity of her deception.

"I suppose I deserve that," she said coolly. "I know you must consider me a traitor."

"Is there another word?" he asked.

"I was loyal to my king. Many would say *you* are the traitor."

Colin did not answer her. He had no intention of giving her the satisfaction of an argument.

"Are they treating you well?" she repeated.

"Below this deck there is a stinking hellhole of the dead and dying. They cleaned me up before bringing me up here."

She looked at him and pursed her lips. "I got your sentence changed from hanging. I'm trying to help you."

Of course, that was it. He owed his life to the woman who had betrayed the whole Highlands. But he couldn't hate her. He just shook his head. "Please, I'm sure you will understand if I don't thank you."

"I shall speak with the captain. Perhaps you won't have to go back below."

Colin just stared at her. His eyes narrowed. "I should rather go below than remain here with you. Go back to Ross, Laurie. You're not just a traitor—you're a slut too."

Her mouth opened in shock and she whirled around and left him standing by the rail, inhaling the blessed air. In a few moments he was again prodded down the ladder and back into the wretched filth of the hold.

"Look at you," one of the others commented.

"A mistake," Colin said as he again sat down. Vaguely he wondered how much longer it would be. Perhaps they wouldn't sail till everyone was dead.

He closed his eyes again and sucked in his breath. Above him there was the sound of tramping on the deck. They were bringing still more prisoners for the overcrowded hold. Fresh bodies to replace the dead. And news—all the newcomers brought news.

* * *

James MacPherson shivered in spite of the fact that it was the first week in June. Since April 27 he and a small group had remained with the prince, circling the glens, hiding in the rock-strewn mountains, and making do with nothing more than dried fish, birds they could shoot, and a little brandy. Hunted, all with a price on their heads, they had finally reached the rugged coast and boarded a vessel.

The drenching rain poured down on a slant, owing to the wind that so often attacked this coast. They were to sail to the Hebrides, judged by all to be a safer locale—if, of course, they lived to get there.

The boat on which they traveled to the outer isles was eight-oared with a sail that could carry it across the water at great speed. The mast was just forward of midships, and the sail was a loose-footed square on a yard.

There were several other passengers besides their group of four. Two of them, James thought uneasily, looked as apprehensive as he felt. He came from farther south, where the sea was kinder and the weather slightly more benevolent. He had never ventured as far as the Outer Hebrides, but the Minch, which had to be crossed, had a vile reputation.

"Take shelter," the captain had warned less than a half hour earlier. "Beyond the entrance to the loch, the wind will be very strong." It was an understatement.

The bay that guarded Loch nan Uamh was calm, sheltered by islands. It had looked like a lake, placid and still under the moon and the stars. But the calm beginning of the voyage was a deception, and by the time their boat had reached the Sound of Arisaig, the wind had increased in velocity and was blowing at near gale force. Moreover, the moon and stars had disappeared as if wiped out of the sky by a giant eraser.

"We should turn back," James said weakly. "We'll all drown."

"To turn back would be to risk being dashed against the rocks. We've no choice but to go forward," the captain shouted.

The crew struggled to hoist the sail. It caught the high wind and they began to cut rapidly through the black water. James crossed himself, as did the others.

The prince gripped the seat beneath him as if he expected that at any moment the boat would be swamped by the high waves. The water was foamy and the whitecaps seemed to have teeth, as if the sea were a wild animal that wanted to eat them alive. James could not close out the sickening rolls and heaves, but he closed out the sight of the water by shutting his eyes tightly.

His stomach churned and vomit rose in his throat. He became sick and opened his eyes to see that one of the others had shoved a pail between his legs.

"I'm going to die," he moaned, wishing at that moment he would, and momentarily completely forgetting the cold wind, their flight from the British, and the terrible danger that pursued them.

"Nonsense," the captain said. "You'll do no such thing! Lift up your head and focus your eyes on the far horizon."

"It's too dark," he groaned.

"Do as I say, no matter that you can't tell where the sky ends and the sea begins. Look up and out!"

Ashamed in front of the others and mollified only by the fact that his monarch looked as ill as he, he tried to follow the captain's orders, and true enough, in a few minutes he did begin to feel a little better.

"Good man," the captain praised him.

James forced a smile, which soon faded. A great crack caused him to grip the side of the boat as it lurched dangerously.

"The arm has split in two!" one of the seaman called out. The sail sagged, leaving them at the mercy of the sea.

James sat rigidly while the little ship tossed helplessly. The prince, who was next to him, was stoic, and somehow his stoicism made James feel somewhat better. Hours passed and James closed his eyes. A light sleep overcame him.

How long he slept he wasn't sure, but when he opened his eyes he could see the thin line of the rising sun. Dawn widened gradually till he could easily distinguish the dark clouds from the angry sea. The storm was still all around them, yet somehow it now seemed less ferocious. He glanced at his compatriot, MacDonald, who was asleep, his arms wrapped around himself, his unruly red hair damp with the sea mist. The prince, too, had nodded off and snored ever so slightly.

Captain MacRae stared into the distance, his beard and bushy eyebrows seemingly alive with glistening droplets of ocean spray, his large, pawlike hands firm on the wheel. The man had clearly spent his life on the sea, and that, James thought, was the only reason they were all alive.

In the early morning light James studied the captain. The man's features were like the craggy rocks, his skin weathered from wind, salt, and sun. This captain, James decided, was more than just an experienced seaman though. He had worked a miracle! The vessel, disabled though it was, was still afloat. They had survived the long night.

The prince opened his eyes and stretched. He leaned forward and squinted into the distance. "I see land," he said suddenly.

Neither the captain nor the other passengers knew he was the prince. He was traveling under the name of O'Sulli-van, and he looked as unprincely as it was possible to look.

"It's Benbecula, the island that lies between North and

South Uist," the captain shouted loudly. "And we'll be headed for it. We can go no farther in these seas unless repairs are made."

"I'll be glad to be on land," James admitted. Let other Scotsmen sail the seas, he was no seaman and he didn't mind admitting it. "Sorry I got sick."

"You've nothing to be ashamed of. You did well," the captain roared.

The waves that pounded the shore splashed over the sides of the vessel. James surveyed the desolate beach. The wild surf danced on the rocks, and in spite of the wind, the fog obscured the high ground above the beach. He could see that great care would have to be taken as the beach was covered with slimy, slippery seaweed.

After a few moments the three members of the crew, all of whom were dressed in oilskins and wore high boots, were out of the boat and pushing the vessel ashore. As soon as the water became shallower, the other adult passengers went over the side to help. Together they pushed and pulled with each shorebound swell, till the boat rested high on the deserted beach. Once there, it was secured with heavy lines so it would not be carried away with the high tide.

They dragged their packs from the boat and the captain carried a huge iron pot. "There's cattle nearby," he announced. "We're not too far from Rossinish. We'll slaughter ourselves a fine fat cow and have plenty of meat." His words were greeted by grunts of enthusiasm from the unkempt clansmen and a half smile from the pale prince.

They all headed farther inland, trudging along on the soggy ground. It scrunched beneath their feet as if complaining of their weight. The captain led, taking them to a deserted stone house. "It's not the first time I've been forced to land here," he told them. "The currents often force landings of small craft." He laughed loudly. "Even large ships have trouble in the Minch!"

James looked around. This place had a proper wooden floor and it was sturdy and strong. There was wood piled neatly by the fireplace and there was a table and even six chairs. A large pile of sheepskins in the corner was evidence that people often slept here. "This place seems to be waiting for us," he said.

"It belongs to my brother," Captain MacRae revealed. "He's away but he won't mind our taking refuge here."

"Fit for a king," Mr. O'Sullivan, who was in reality the prince, intoned with a smirk.

They made a fire to dry their clothes and the captain and the crew went to find a cow from among the herds that roamed the island.

James sat before the fire, soaking up its warmth, grateful again to be on dry land even though it was barren, lonely, and cold. The captain of the boat had promised the damage would be repaired in three days time and added, "It's a short trip from here to South Uist."

And then what? James wondered silently. Were they to wander forever, living off the land, trying to save their necks from the hangman's noose? But there were no answers to his questions. He knew by comparison to others that he was fortunate indeed. So far, luck had been his companion.

Colin inhaled deeply, savoring the fresh air, knowing it would be a long while before he again stood on deck and felt the salt spray against his cheek. Above, the sun was shining, and as far as he could see, the ocean stretched like a carpet shimmering in the sunlight. Most of the prisoners huddled on the deck area near the entrance to the hold. Only a few stood by the rail in order to feel the ocean spray on their filthy skin. It was only every few days that they were allowed out, and then only so that the buckets provided for waste could be emptied. But on this occasion the captain was merciful. He allowed them to remain on deck longer and had promised them more time each day if there were no outbreaks of fighting. Once, Colin thought, when they had first been captured, they had fought. But now the fight was gone out of all of them. Too many had died; they had been ill fed for too long; the air was too foul. Now they were like animals clinging to life, hungry and blinking in the sunlight because they had been in the darkness too long.

"Colin?" a hoarse voice whispered.

Colin turned to face a fellow prisoner, an emaciated yet grizzled fellow. He squinted at him, sensing a familiarity, yet still unsure of the man's identity.

"It's me, Rory MacGregor. I wouldn't blame you for not knowing me."

"Rory!" Colin embraced the man whose name was so familiar and whose appearance was so strange. Rory was an old classmate, but in those days Rory weighed in at over two hundred pounds and had a red face, plump and round as the full moon.

"How is it we've been in the hold together for weeks and not known it?" Colin asked.

"I came in the last group. I was put on board just before we set sail."

Rumors spread like fire in a dry field; still, they were the only news, the only information available and every man clung to the stories that best suited him. "Did you see my brother, James?" Colin asked.

Rory shook his head. "No, but I saw your friend Robert Forbes. He was dragged off the field of battle by a woman with long, dark hair—a beautiful woman from the look I got. She rode well, and shot a man who threatened Forbes. I'll not forget her green eyes! Forbes was wounded."

"Glynis?" Colin was stunned. The description could be only Glynis, but what was she doing on the moor? His heart leapt into his throat even as the answer came to him. She had come to fight! Yes, Glynis would. She would not have been satisfied to remain at Cluny. Angered though he was that she had been on the moor to fight, he was in some sense relieved. She was alive and she was not alone at Cluny, which in the end might have proved extremely dangerous from what he had heard. And she was with Robert. If he knew his sister, she would will Robert Forbes back to good health.

"I never met your sister, but it could be that the woman I saw was indeed Glynis."

"What else did you hear?"

"I think the dead are to be envied," he replied gloomily. "The Duke of Cumberland has decided to deport, starve, or kill practically everyone in the Highlands. There's a rumor they'll forbid the wearing of the kilt and the playing of the pipes. They've laid waste to villages, killing men, women, and children and burning everything."

Colin shook his head. He couldn't bear to think about Scotland's reality.

"Have you a guess as to where we're headed?" Colin asked in spite of the fact that he had his own thoughts on the subject.

"London town, I imagine. There to be displayed like vicious animals. We'll be put in jail to await passage to the colonies. In the end, we'll be sent to some godforsaken place and sold into indentured servitude."

Colin nodded his agreement. But he kept his silence because it was not good for his jailers to overhear a conversation that revealed a man to have too much fight left in him. It was better to play the weakling and await the right moment. Maybe it would come in London, maybe he would have to wait till he got to some colony. But he knew that no power on earth would keep him from returning to Scotland and claiming his ancestral lands. It was his duty to his brothers James and Stewart. It was his duty to his aging father. It was a duty he was pledged to fulfill.

Chapter Nine

June 1746

The blue sky was filled with puffy white clouds and the sun shone brightly as Glynis drove the wagon ever southward toward the Lowlands. Robert lay in the back, his wounded leg outstretched.

When others approached, he buried himself in the straw. Glynis, to her credit, he thought, kept a steady pace and managed to appear nothing more than a casual traveler. Sometimes she even waved at passersby, and her warm friendliness dispelled any suspicion they might have had. Happily, they encountered no soldiers. When no one was around, which was usually the case, as they were traveling down a rutted country road in the mountains, they talked.

"I'm so glad it's stopped raining," Glynis said. "In spite of everything, the sun makes me feel better."

Robert studied her profile. She was a strong woman, and although he knew she was shattered by Stewart's death, she was bearing up well. Of course, they had each other, and he did not underestimate what that meant to both of them. As well, Glynis took heart because she seemed certain that both Colin and James had survived and in all likelihood, her father was also alive.

"It would be much faster and safer if we could travel to England by sea," Glynis suggested.

"That's why we must head for Aberdeen," Robert told her. "I have friends there. If they haven't been arrested, they will help us." For more than four weeks they had been progressing slowly, keeping to less-traveled roads, staying one or two nights in the same place.

Glynis did not ask what they would do if his friends had been arrested. They had both heard rumors of Catholics being arrested everywhere. Yet she also knew there were networks of Catholics in both the Sottish Lowlands and in England proper who helped Highlanders. They had existed even before this rebellion, and she was sure many of them survived. Some British Catholics were extremely wealthy and influential. To save themselves, they had pledged their allegiance to King George, but that did not mean they would not help those in need. But, of course, there were spies everywhere and they had to be extremely careful whom they approached.

"I have enough cash for passage to London," Glynis said. "But once in London, I'll have to sell some jewels."

"I don't like to have you do that," Robert replied.

"You may be sure I'll sell Ramsey's wedding ring first," she said. It wasn't like her family jewelry. It meant nothing to her.

Robert smiled. Glynis did not wish Ramsey dead, nor did he. But he knew he might well end up fighting a duel with Ramsey were he still alive. Yes, he had no trouble understanding how she felt about the ring. Ramsey had lied to her and mistreated her. Still, they were married, and he knew that somehow, in spite of the ecstasy the two of them experienced together, Ramsey was still between them and would be between them until the marriage was annulled or Ramsey was dead.

"We'll have to be careful in London. For that matter, we'll have to be careful in the Lowlands," Glynis said. "We must stop speaking Gaelic and we must do our best to sound as if we come from the Lowlands."

"At least we both know how we should sound," Robert said with a smile. Glynis and he were educated, which many Highlanders were not. As a result, their accents were more refined. It would be easier for them to disguise their brogues.

"I've never really understood it all," Glynis said thoughtfully. "The English once had a Stuart monarch. Prince Charles is the rightful heir to the throne."

"Ah, Glynis, but the Stuarts are Scots. Think of England, think like the English in order to understand them, and truly, you must think like them if we are to survive in London. To them, Scotland is remote, sparsely populated, a bleak land with few trees."

"We have trees, forests, and mountains and—"

"I did not say their image was real. Some people think it is most disagreeable when the heather is in bloom."

"Some people are blind," Glynis replied curtly.

"They see it as a wilderness. Even the Scots Lowlanders refer to us as Irish."

"It's where we began," Glynis said matter-of-factly. She knew full well that many of the Highland customs originated with the Irish who had migrated across the sea to settle the Highlands. She knew too that Highland life had far more to it than most visitors realized. "What matters most is our land, our land and our name," she said dreamily.

"Ah, Glynis, you and I are of one mind."

"I think we're coming to a village," Glynis said suddenly, peering into the distance.

Robert pulled himself up and looked down the road. "It must be Pitloch, we're near Loch Tummel."

"That means we're near the land owned by the Athollmen."

"To our left, I imagine," Robert answered. The hills were getting higher, the glens more heavily wooded. Certainly they were not the only ones who would have headed south. Deep in the mountain glens he supposed the land was crawling with Highlanders, men who had survived, men who had quickly returned to take their families out of harm's way.

"I'm going to let the horses drink from that stream," Glynis said, pointing off to where a row of trees stood. She could not see the water, but it was surely a stream, and as they got closer, she could see that the trees by the water's edge dipped down as if they were drinking from the rushing little stone-bottomed stream.

Glynis climbed off the wagon and led the horses to the water and fine grass that grew nearby. "They need to rest," she said, patting Sampson. "The road is getting steeper."

Robert slipped from the back of the wagon and hopped toward her on his good leg. He had carved a walking stick the previous day, and now he leaned on it and watched as Glynis tended the horses.

"What will you do with Sampson?" Robert asked. He knew how much the animal meant to her. She had raised it from a foal.

"I don't know. I'll try to find him a good home. I don't want to think about it now."

Robert nodded. He could see the pain in her eyes. Parting with Sampson would be one more change in a world of changes. Sampson was one more thing to be left behind. Glynis took one of their blankets and spread it out on the grass. In a moment, she took out some bread and hard cheese. "We might as well rest too."

Robert hopped over to her and tumbled down beside her.

"Are you all right?"

Robert looked into her green eyes and saw concern. He laughed and touched her cheek with his hand. "Just the most practical way of sitting when one is in my condition. Though it is healing."

She smiled back at him and he touched her neck with his hand. "I can't keep my hands off you," he said in a low voice as he moved closer and kissed her waiting lips even as he pressed her breast with his hand.

Glynis returned his kiss with equal passion. "I don't want you to keep your hands off me."

Robert smiled as he felt her hand on him. She knew he had only to think of her to be ready to make love to her. And she was right. The memory of her body, the scent of her skin, the feel of her beneath him was more than sufficient to arouse him.

"Here? Now? Before lunch?" He smiled mischievously and slipped his hand into her dress.

Glynis felt her face flush with anticipation. He made her feel in a new way, a way she had never before known, a wonderful way. When he touched her breasts she wanted him to rub them, to suck on them, to make her writhe in his arms. And when he caressed her in that magical place, she wanted to scream with pleasure. He knew exactly how to touch her and where; he knew how to make her yearn for him. And he felt her pleasurable release. It was divine, and even though he had just begun to touch her, she already wanted that feeling again, she already wanted him declaring his love while he devoured her with kisses.

"Such sweet pleasure," she breathed. "Oh, I do love you, Robert Forbes."

"And I you, Glynis MacPherson. I will always be yours."

The cottage of Annie Roy was better than many, but modest considering she was the sister of the Duke of Atholl. It was located some three miles beyond the village of Pitloch.

Robert knocked on the door, and in a moment a woman answered, pistol in hand. Her face was pale and her graying hair disheveled. She looked quite prepared to use her gun.

"Annie Roy, it is I, Robert Forbes."

"Robert Forbes—" The woman let the pistol drop to her side and she opened the door wider, admitting both Robert and Glynis.

Annie Roy brushed her hair off her face. "You're a sight for sore eyes."

"Glynis, Annie was my teacher for many years. She's a learned woman who runs a school for children six to twelve."

"Days long gone," Annie said, motioning them to chairs.

"Have the English been here?" Robert asked.

"Weeks ago."

"Did they harm you?"

Annie shook her head. "They questioned me for hours, but they let me go. I was lucky, they raped a lot of Atholl women and even killed some of the herd boys."

Annie Roy was in her mid-forties. She was a tall, straight woman with bright blue eyes and graying hair which she wore in a bun atop her head. But now much of it hung down in strands, as if she had not arranged it for some time. Her angular face looked weary, and it was obvious from the way she had greeted them that she was also wary.

"I assume you're running from the soldiers," Annie said. "I'll fix you some tea."

"Thank you, Annie. This, by the way, is Glynis Mac-Pherson."

Annie looked at Glynis and smiled. In a moment she shook her head. "Keep her away from the soldiers," she cautioned.

Glynis wanted to say that she could take care of herself, but she did not. In truth, she knew that Annie was right. No matter how good a shot or how strong a woman might be, the soldiers could be dangerous. Rape was a favorite activity if only because it humiliated the women as well as made their men feel powerless. It was a timeworn form of punishment for the vanquished even when the clans fought among themselves.

Annie took the boiling kettle off the fire and poured it into a small pot. After a few minutes she poured hot tea into the cups she had set out.

"We haven't had anything hot for days," Glynis said as she sipped her tea.

"The Highlands are filled with those trying to escape and those just trying to stay alive. Stories say the prince and those with him are living in the rocks and eating nothing but raw fish."

"My brother is with him," Glynis revealed in a near whisper.

"Oh," Annie breathed. "You're one of *those* MacPhersons."

"I'm Duncan's daughter."

"There's a heavy price on your father's head. I saw it posted. May God give him the strength to escape."

Glynis murmured, "I think of him daily and pray for him."

"We're headed south, into the Lowlands," Robert told Annie.

"It's smart to head south. Were I young like you, I'd head right for London and from there to one of the colonies."

"Just what we had planned, but it's a long and dangerous journey to travel overland to London."

"And you want my advice?"

"Annie, you've taught many. You have lots of friends and considerable knowledge."

Annie smiled. "Flattery will always get you what you want, Robert Forbes."

"I meant it, you're a knowledgeable woman."

"Take your wagon east and travel to Aberfeldy. Go to the home of Carrick Roy. His house is a mile east of the village on a knoll. You'll know it by the stones that mark the road leading up to it. There are three boulders of considerable size on each side."

"And just who is this Carrick Roy?" Robert asked.

"My late husband's cousin. He has a boat and often goes down Loch Tay. From there you must follow the river to Loch Lomond. Carrick will give you the name of someone who will see to it you get a vessel to Bristol. Each person will give you the name of another until you find refuge in London."

"I knew you would know the way," Robert said.

"I'm assuming you have money."

"Yes," Glynis replied.

Robert drained his teacup. He had known for a long while that there were several networks set up to assist those leaving Scotland. But when he had gone to France, as when he returned, he had been picked up by a French vessel.

Nonetheless, people often traveled to France via Ireland, but just as often they went south and crossed the Channel. Wealthy Catholics and Stuart sympathizers provided lodging and transportation all along the route. This particular route pleased him. It would not be well traveled by those escaping Culloden. For the most part, they would head for the Hebrides, as it seemed the prince and his entourage had already done. From there they would try to arrange to have French ships pick them up and take them to France.

"You've been a tremendous help, Annie."

"You can stay as long as you wish, but I'm sure you want to be on your way."

"The sooner we get out of Scotland, the sooner we'll be safe," Glynis said. "Thank you, again." She reached over and gently hugged Annie Roy.

When she stepped back, Robert embraced Annie and planted a kiss on her cheek. "Take care," he said sincerely.

"You take care," Annie said. Then, taking a long look at Glynis, she smiled. "She's much too pretty for you, and I have a feeling she's smart as well."

Glynis blushed and Robert grinned. "That she is," he replied as he hopped off toward the wagon, leaning on his crudely carved walking stick.

William Pitt looked around the room with considerable satisfaction. It was filled with his compatriots, who were known in the Parliament, and indeed to the people, as the "boy patriots." Not that at the age of thirty-eight he considered himself a boy.

His climb to power had been difficult, and in the process he had alienated the king, who had appointed him to his present position only because he had been forced to do so. When the appointment was made, the king cried with rage.

Pitt was well aware of what had caused his estrangement from the king. It was because of his reaction to the actions of John Carteret, the Earl of Granville, who had followed Walpole as chief minister. The earl had pursued the War of the Austrian Succession on the Continent. His sole purpose was to protect King George's Hanoverian interests. To

Pitt's way of thinking, the earl was sacrificing the interest of Great Britain to those of the king's Hanoverian possessions, and he was outspoken on the matter—so outspoken that the king had grown furious with frustration. But no matter, Pitt thought. The king was now forced to recognize his talents, forced, indeed, to seek his council as well as the council of the other "boy patriots."

Although his present position was as paymaster general to the forces, it was a far more powerful position than it sounded. Powerful enough so that he was included in this meeting with the king's ministers and the king himself.

"Why hasn't he been captured yet?" the king asked, the irritation obvious in his nervous quivering voice and the way his mouth twitched.

George II was sitting at the head of a long, highly polished table. His seat was a trifle higher than the others, and he was fully dressed in his royal robes and white powdered wig. His face was a near-perfect oval, and while he was not as handsome as the hunted Bonnie Prince Charlie, there was something similar about them even though, as far as he knew, they were in no way related.

"Because the Scots population is tight-lipped and because he keeps moving," one of the king's ministers ventured.

"It's ferocious countryside, your highness. Very hard on our troops," another muttered.

"I know what a barbaric place Scotland is!" King George scowled at all of them.

"Perhaps fate has smiled on us," Pitt offered. He held his chin and waited for their collective attention to focus on him. His eyes fastened on the long golden drapes that framed the window behind the king. If the king could avoid looking at him, he decided he could avoid looking at the king by simply gazing at the window behind him.

"What do you mean, smiled on us?" the king demanded.

Pitt shrugged. "Your highness, consider for a moment exactly what we would do if we captured the bonnie prince."

"Do not call him that! That usurper, that creature!" The king's voice thundered through the room and the others looked studiously down at their papers.

"We are not happy!" George added with a scowl.

A silence followed, and at last Lyttelton said without looking up, "Your highness, it is a good question. What would we do?"

"We could hang him," Pitt offered. "Of course, if we did, half the kingdom would be up in arms. A pretender to the throne is one matter, a full-fledged young martyr is another," Pitt said purposefully.

King George narrowed his eyes. "He could be put in the Tower."

Pitt sighed heavily. "Your highness, he would be a martyr in the Tower. Worse yet, he would be a living martyr. He would be a rallying point for all Catholics, and even a few Protestants."

"He could be deported!" George thundered.

"Your highness, he's trying to escape. Must we spend months trying to catch someone who is trying to escape to France, just to have him deported to the very place he wishes to go?"

"What are you suggesting?" the king asked in an angry, exasperated tone.

"I am suggesting that we allow him to escape. He will present a very difficult problem for the French as well. We might have some luck if they decide to rid themselves of this, shall we say, loaded diplomatic gun. Louis has been known to speak from both sides of his mouth . . . . I suggest letting him deal with Prince Charles."

The king turned away from Pitt and looked to the others. "What do you think?"

There was a muttering around the table. Finally Lyttelton looked up. "I think we are in agreement with Mr. Pitt."

The king stood up. His lips were pursed and he spit his words out like little bullets. "I'm delighted to know that my ministers know exactly what to do. Just do it!" He turned and spun toward the door, and Pitt watched him, thinking to himself that there would be many more enjoyable confrontations with this king, whom he privately considered to be something of a Hanoverian tyrant. At length, he himself stood up. It was time to send some trustworthy informants to Paris. Rumors and counterrumors needed to be started. The king of France or those who opposed war with England must be made to take certain suggestions, to follow a logical path.

The June sun shone brightly all day, but it could not make any of them smile, James thought. And now that it was evening, they were facing yet another move. For weeks they had all been posing as Orkneymen and the prince had traveled under the names Mr. Sinclair and Mr. O'Sullivan.

They were on Long Island, and it seemed to him that they had covered every rocky inch of it. The inhabitants were willing enough to let them know if the army was around, but they were too frightened to give them refuge. As a result, they had slept among the rocks and eaten little. But now the island was literally crawling with militiamen, all spurred on by the thirty-thousand-pound reward being offered for the prince.

Flora MacDonald, like all the MacDonalds, was braver than most people. She came to Glynis and Robert and fed them, and tonight she sat with them and spoke seriously.

"You must leave this island. You'll be safer on Skye, there's no question about it," Flora said intently. She was a serious woman with a triangular face and a long nose. She was far from pretty, but she was highly intelligent.

"If I try to board a vessel, I'll surely be discovered," Charles said earnestly. "They watch for me on every vessel, it would be most difficult."

"Where there is a will, there can be found a way," Flora said, and James could hear that MacDonald determination in her voice.

"Do you have a suggestion?" Charles asked.

"I do. I propose to have you dress as my maid. It is a trifle undignified, but more dignified than losing one's head to the ax."

Charles smiled. "I quite see your point."

No one said it, of course, but Charles could easily pass for a woman. He looked incredibly like his mother even though he was completely masculine. Still, his oval-shaped face, light growth of facial hair, and delicate features would make the farce far easier.

"Come to my house, your highness. Let me outfit you and coach you. If all goes well, we could be sailing for Skye by midday."

"We'll wait here," Cameron grouched.

"I'll go with the prince," James volunteered. His mouth watered slightly. It was possible that Flora MacDonald had hidden stores. He decided he could use a good meal and, in any case, the prince did indeed require someone to help him.

Flora MacDonald looked at James appraisingly. "I think you will rouse little suspicion. The prince shall pose as my maid and you shall pose as my maid's husband."

"So we'll remain close," the prince said, smiling.

James could not but admire him; after all he had been through he still retained his sense of humor. And though he dared not say it, he did think the prince would make a handsome woman.

* * *

After a fine meal, Flora took them to her bedroom, where she produced clothing from one of several trunks.

Charles stripped to his breeches and waistcoat and Flora handed him some undergarments. "You'll wear this quilted petticoat and one of my favorite gowns."

James found he felt like laughing. Flora held up a calico gown that was covered with embroidered lilacs. Then she held up an Irish-style mantle, a cap, and a headdress. "I think you will look quite fine," she commented with a completely straight face.

The prince gamely adorned the entire outfit. "I think it prudent to carry a pistol under my petticoats."

Flora shook her head vigorously. "Heavens, no! If you're searched and they find a pistol, we'll be in jail faster than you can say my name. A pistol would betray you."

The prince's face reddened. "Madam, if I am searched that carefully, I suspect we would be discovered in any case. There are things about my anatomy that would give me away."

Flora blushed too, but she was not prudish. She enjoyed the joke. "Quite right," she murmured. "Now your name will be Betty Burke. And you, James MacPherson, will be Mistress Burke's husband, James. If you use your own first name, at least you'll respond when spoken to."

"I'll do my best."

"Perhaps if you are going to continue to smirk so, you had better not drink any brandy."

James cleared his throat and forcibly erased the expression of bemusement from his face. "I shall be the consummate actor rather than give up my brandy, madam."

"I really will have difficulty with these petticoats," the prince complained.

"You are here to practice," Flora reminded him as she

obligingly poured some more brandy. After this drink, we should get our rest. It will be a rough crossing.''

James thought of the night they had crossed the Minch, and he wondered if there was any other kind of crossing. He had begun to think of the Irish Sea as a caldron stirred by the devil.

''When we get to Skye, what shall we do?''

Flora smiled. ''It's a dangerous trip. But you will go to Coir d'Chair and join the Glenmoriston men. They're outlaws, but they'll take care of you as few of us can. You'll be safe there, at least till the right arrangements can be made.''

Flora MacDonald did not have to explain what she meant by the ''right'' arrangements. She meant until it could be arranged for a French ship to pick them up. But when and how this would happen was anyone's guess.

The room was bathed in a half light, and Laurie, sitting before a mirror, brushed out her long, red hair. She wore only her white petticoat and a thin camisole.

Behind her, Angus Ross paced nervously. This manic mood, which she had seen often, usually preceded some revelation, and she waited now for him to confide in her.

''All the king's horses and all the king's men—can't find the usurper, Charles.''

''I would suppose there are plenty who are ready to help him,'' she offered.

''Rumor has it he escaped Long Island just ahead of the militia! Dressed as a woman!''

Laurie thought of the young prince's looks. He had a very clean-shaven, ''pretty'' face to her way of thinking. Everyone said he was very masculine, but the only time she had ever seen him she had found his appearance somewhat effeminate. That was the night of the ball he held in Inverness, the night before the Highland army was summoned to fight. Ross had sent her away the next morning, so she had seen the prince only that one time.

Ross sneered at her comment. Doubtless he agreed with her.

His image grew larger in the mirror as he stepped closer to her. He stood for a moment, then ran his hand over her shoulders. "We're going to Paris," he said evenly.

Laurie felt her heartbeat increase. "Why?" she asked in a low voice. In fact, she was afraid to hear the answer. She could tell by his voice that it involved more clandestine activity. It was activity that frightened her. Deceiving Colin had made her miserable even though she did not love him. But he was a decent man, and she had suffered guilty feelings since his arrest. She had arranged for clemency— for him to be deported rather than hung. Ross did not know; he would kill her if he had known.

"Why? You are never supposed to ask me why. You are simply to do as you are told."

Ross's eyes had narrowed, and she felt a surge of apprehension. "I'm sorry," she whispered. She would never know why, but he both frightened and excited her.

"We have a new assignment," he said, answering the question he had chastised her for asking. "The prince is to be allowed to escape. He will be assassinated in Paris. That's much more convenient for the British government. After all, if he were captured, he would either have to spend the rest of his life in the Tower, be hung, or be beheaded. These alternatives are all very awkward considering the number of papists there are in England."

Was she now to betray a prince? She shuddered at the thought. If they were caught, they would be hung. But she was too afraid of Ross to say anything.

He grasped her shoulders firmly. "You may be required to sleep with other men, my dear."

A chill swept through her. "Would you allow such a thing?" She felt totally shocked.

"Allow it? I should want to watch!" His hand dipped into her camisole, and she felt ill with excitement as he pinched her nipple. She closed her eyes, not sure she was capable of pretending to the extent he wanted her to pretend with others. "Look at that, you're excited already."

She opened her eyes and saw that although he had removed his hand, her nipples were hard and erect and pressing against the thin material of her camisole.

"Actually, I find the very thought of you with other men exciting," he said, bending to kiss her neck. "Take off all your clothes and walk around a bit. Then go and lie on the bed."

She stood up as if she were in a trance, and slowly, while he watched her, she removed the rest of her garments. She walked around self-consciously, doing what he asked. After a few moments she went to the bed. In seconds he was there, ravishing her in ways that gave her the pleasure that bound her to him.

"How long had it been?" Colin MacPherson was unsure. They had sailed away from Inverness, and while they were at sea they had been allowed some time on deck. At last, after a long and wretched voyage, they had sailed up the Thames. There the captain left the ship, a new captain came, and they laid anchor.

More than half the original prisoners taken with him were now dead. More were sick, and he himself had long bouts of diarrhea and fever.

He was certain they had been at anchor in the Thames for at least thirty days, perhaps longer. In the darkness of the hold there was no night and no day. Only ongoing misery. Some days he felt they would just keep them all there till they died. It was a slow death, one that made the hangman's noose seem merciful. Still, Colin felt some small hope, and he knew that as long as he was still breathing, he would go on feeling it.

For hours at a time he concentrated on what it might be like in one of the colonies. He didn't want to go to the Caribbean, though he knew that is where he would go. There were many stories about it. He wanted to go to the New England colonies. From there, he reasoned, he could find a way to join other Scotsmen who had gone to Quebec. But all this was a distracting dream. What he truly wanted was to go home to Cluny, to restore it, and to claim his family land. He felt certain Glynis would want that too, though no doubt the time was not yet right for either of them to go home.

Colin was lost in thoughts about the colonies, which he alternated with memories of Cluny, when suddenly the hatch to the hold was opened and a waft of blessed air swept into the putrid atmosphere. A tunnel of light also caused the denizens of the hold to blink and rub their eyes.

"Topside!" a voice shouted.

Colin could hardly believe his ears. They were taking them out on deck! His heart beat wildly as he headed for the ladder. In a short time such necessities as fresh air and clean water had translated themselves into simple pleasures given at the behest of a generous captor.

Colin clambered up the ladder behind others and in front of some of the slower captives. When he reached the top, he helped two or three others up and out into the air. Overhead, gray clouds shrouded the towers of London in a heavy mist. It felt wonderful on his skin, moist and clean. He ran his tongue around dry lips and savored the taste of the moisture.

"What a filthy lot!" someone uttered.

Colin sought the speaker. He was a paunchy man in a fine suit with a ruffled shirt. He stood next to the ship's officers and wrinkled his nose in disdain. Small wonder. Even Colin recognized that through no fault of their own, they were indeed a disgusting-looking lot.

"Take these men ashore!" the man commanded. "See to it that they are bathed and fed. They can't stay on these vessels any longer, the conditions are appalling!"

The captain saluted. Whoever this man was, he was one of influence, Colin thought.

"Then," the man of influence continued, "take them to Newgate Prison. As transport becomes available, they will be deported."

"Yes, Mr. Pitt."

Colin repeated the name to himself. He did not want to forget it.

"Form a line!" one of the officers commanded.

Hurriedly, they did as requested. Those who were able to walk on their own assisted those who were too weak. Pale, dirty, and starving, they descended the gangplank to the dock and were marched onto the cobblestone road. They were loaded into wagons and were soon on their way through the streets of London, headed for Newgate Prison. Colin felt hopeful again. Perhaps this ordeal would, after all, come to an end.

Glynis poked her head out of the cottage and inhaled the sea air. It smelled more heavily of salt than usual because today the wind was blowing directly off the water. In the distance, she could hear the waves crashing on the rocks as the tide came in.

For a long time she and Robert had remained in a cottage on the banks of Loch Lomond, some distance from where they now were. Loch Lomond, one of the most beautiful lochs in all Scotland, was a peaceful lake. It lay in the center of a grass-covered valley surrounded by rocky, rolling hills in the distance. But as tranquil as the setting, it soon became turbulent. The soldiers came, so Robert, Carrick Roy, and she had moved on.

Judging the area around the port of Glasgow far too dangerous, they traveled, at Carrick Roy's suggestion, down Loch Long through the Argyll forest, and onward to the village of Intellan on the shores of the Firth of Clyde. From there they had traveled by boat to the larger port of Ayr on the shores of the North Channel. Now, in Fisherton, a small village south of Ayr, they had taken refuge in yet another cottage and here they had been for several months. Carrick did not live with them, but, rather, in the village.

In one respect, Glynis thought, the Lowlands were no different from the Highlands. Everyone knew everyone, and unless one were in a very large town, it was necessary to keep up a believable facade.

In order to account for Robert's limp, he was disguised as an older man. He dressed shabbily and walked with a cane. He had grown a beard and mustache, which he allowed to become very long. He faked a cough and so no one got too close. Glynis, on the other hand, braided her hair and wore pinafores. As a result, she looked considerably younger than her twenty years. The idea was to age Robert by ten or eleven years and to make Glynis appear sixteen or so in order that they might masquerade as father and daughter. Thus far, no one had seemed at all suspicious.

They told the locals that Robert had been injured in an accident and had lung trouble. They carefully explained that their doctor had suggested the fresh, clean sea air, thus making it necessary for them to move from Glasgow to Fisherton.

The cottage they rented had only one room, but unlike many in Fisherton, this one at least had a wooden floor and a proper hearth. There was nothing inside except a bedroll made of the sheepskins, a table, and two straight-backed chairs.

Feeling that others would find them suspicious if they bought all their food, Glynis purchased a goat from which to get milk and three laying hens to provide eggs. She had also planted a small garden so that their neighbors would think them permanent.

The truth of the matter was, Robert's leg was nearly healed and he no longer required a walking stick. But his limp had become a part of their facade, so he maintained it whenever he went outside.

Sometimes, bundled from head to toe in cloaks and scarfs, Robert went to the pier to fish. It gave him the opportunity to speak with others and hear whatever rumors were making the rounds. This sometimes resulted in a fresh fish for dinner, a welcome relief from their usual fare of turnip soup and rabbit stew.

Glynis was outside when she saw Robert, afraid to let down his guard even though he was close to home and no one seemed to be around, limping down the road.

Glynis stood still, waiting for him to reach her. When he did so, he looked around warily and motioned her inside.

"What is it?" she asked, sensing immediately that he had something to tell her.

He half smiled at her and took off his fisherman's hat. "I'm surprised I have to tell you anything, my woman. You're damnably good at reading my mind. I shall have to be careful should I take another lover."

"Very careful," she said, raising her brow. He was right.

She could tell when something was on his mind, just as he could tell when something was on her mind. It was a part of the bond they had together. It had been that way ever since she could remember. And now that she thought about it, she had been ill at ease when she'd come home from France—before she knew about Margaret. And in her heart she had always known that he did not love Margaret. She looked up at him. "Yes. I can tell you have something to tell me."

"It's not good news," he said, hesitating.

"Tell me," she pressed.

"I've learned there is a large price on the head of one Duncan MacPherson of Cluny. That means he is still alive. It also means he is in considerable danger."

Glynis nodded. "I knew he would have a price on his head. Better he is alive. My father is a survivor. His tenants love him and will hide him if he stays on our land."

"There's more. The soldiers are near. They may not come here, but they aren't far off."

"Should we move on?"

Robert shook his head. "Not yet, my love. Let's wait and see what develops."

"I think that's best too." The fact was, she didn't want to move on just yet. They had been there over two months, and it was restful not always running. Carrick, who had been forced to move too, was still attempting to arrange passage to England. He now intended going with them. Until the time was right, they had to wait. Of all their temporary dwellings, she liked this best and preferred to wait here.

Robert touched her shoulders and she spun around and into his arms. His rough beard tickled her skin and she shivered as he held her.

"I must be careful not to make your delicate skin red," he said, looking into her eyes.

Glynis put her arms around his neck. "I rather appreciate the roughness of your beard in certain places," she said in a low voice.

Robert felt his own face flush. "You are a little tart, aren't you? You like having me brush your breasts with it, don't you?"

Glynis laughed lightly. "And even other tender places."

He slipped her bodice down, bent, and nuzzled against her. She giggled in delight, and he slung her over his shoulder. "You're much too tempting," he said, depositing her on the bedroll.

Glynis laughed, this time more throatily. "I've not yet even begun to tempt you."

Chapter Ten

September 1746

A cool September breeze swept across the land. For six months they had been hiding, living under assumed names, trying to arrange passage out of Scotland. But Carrick felt passage could be had soon. He wanted them to travel in a good-sized vessel, and so they had waited.

Glynis put down the sheepskins she had just brought from outside, where she had been airing them. Robert was once again fishing, and she hoped he would bring home a good catch.

Glynis stopped suddenly and listened, all her senses alert. She heard hoofbeats and she quickly stood up to peer outside. Across the back field, headed for the cottage, were three soldiers. She thanked heaven that Sampson was tethered some distance from the cottage. He was not the sort of horse people such as those they were pretending to be would own.

Should she try to get away? But reality ruled. There was place to run or to hide.

For a moment indecision seized her—should she arm herself? No, there were three of them and they would surely overcome her, pistol or not. They would most certainly arrest her if she resisted. "I'll just have to brazen it out," she said to herself.

The soldiers pounded on the door and Glynis paused for only a second. She decided to pretend she was a bit simple-minded. She opened the door a crack and was surprised when it was simultaneously kicked in. She fell backward and looked up into the eyes of the three soldiers. One was a big man with a growth of beard, hard, small dark eyes, and a narrow-set mouth. He wore the uniform of a sergeant. The second one was a thin blond with pale blue eyes. The third had pockmarked skin and a long, thin nose. It was he who stepped forward and helped pull her to her feet.

"Pretty little piece," the sergeant said as he grabbed Glynis's arm and yanked her toward him.

His odor was foul, but Glynis forced herself not to react.

"What's your name, girl?" he asked, still not releasing her arm.

"Glinnie MacDougal, sir."

"Are you a rebel?"

Glynis shook her head vigorously. "No, sir. I'm a loyal subject of his royal highness the king of England."

"You alone here?" the sergeant asked gruffly.

His eyes were fastened on her breasts, and he was all but drooling. His intentions were clear, but Glynis forced herself to be calm. "My father's away. Would you kind gentlemen and representatives of the king like a cup of tea?"

"I'd like more than that," he said, gripping her arm harder.

"Sir, if she is a loyal supporter, we could get in considerable trouble. Perhaps we should take her to headquarters and question her there," the pockmarked soldier suggested.

The sergeant glared at him, but begrudgingly loosened the grip on her arm slightly. All Glynis could do was silently pray that Robert would not come back. No matter what happened to her, she could endure it. But if he returned, he would defend her to the death and she would lose him.

"I swear I'm a good girl," she said, wide-eyed. "I'll go, but I don't know the answers to many questions. They all say I'm not bright."

"All right, we'll take her to Ayr," the sergeant muttered.

"Could you leave a note for my father? Then he'll come and fetch me home. I can't write."

"As this was your idea, you write the note," the sergeant said angrily to the younger man. He supposed if he did anything to her, one of the other two might tell. Possibly, he thought, the opportunity would arise once she was in jail.

Quickly, the younger man wrote the note and put it on the table.

The sergeant pulled Glynis outside and lifted her into his saddle. He climbed up behind her. Her ankle-length woolen skirt rode up her legs, exposing her long, white thighs. The sergeant could not resist slapping one.

As they rode off, Glynis closed her eyes and gritted her teeth. He was in a perfect position to fondle her, and he wasted no time in doing so. He roughly touched her breasts and tried to touch her in other places at every opportunity. He whispered in her ear, telling her what he would do when they were alone. She tried to ignore his words and his ever-prodding hands. She tried to think of something else, anything else.

* * *

It was nearly five o'clock when they entered Ayr. They rode up to the town hall and dismounted. Glynis all but fell from the saddle. She feigned stiffness, staggering till she was supported by the young man with the pockmarked face. It was important not to betray herself in small ways. A woman used to riding long distances, as she was, would be most suspicious.

As they approached the doorway, a young lieutenant was coming out. "What have we here?"

"A prisoner, sir. A girl to be questioned."

The lieutenant turned about and motioned them inside. The sergeant, whom he did not like in any case, looked thoroughly lustful, and the young woman was far too attractive to be safe in his company.

"Why have you brought her?" he asked.

"She seemed suspicious. The neighbors said she and her father were new in the neighborhood, there for the sea air or some fool thing."

"Father's sick," Glynis said. "The doctor said he needed the fresh air."

The lieutenant pulled his watch from his pocket and looked at it. "I haven't time for all this now. You—" he said, pointing to the pockmarked soldier. "Lock her up in a cell alone. And all three of you keep your hands off her. I'll question her in the morning."

The young soldier led Glynis quickly off down a long corridor. He locked her in a tiny cell. As he did so, he whispered, "Watch out for the sergeant."

Glynis nodded. It was not a warning she needed. Wearily, she sank into a dark corner of the cell. In a moment he returned and gave her a blanket.

"Thank you," she said as she settled down. She heard the door lock. It was a temporary reprieve. She had heard the army was trying to stop the atrocities, but that it was difficult for the officers to control their men. She felt certain that the young lieutenant would let her go. But Robert would find the note—he would know where she was and he would almost certainly come looking for her. She prayed he would be careful and not do anything rash.

Laurie Lewis sat rigidly on the end of the tapestry-covered chaise longue and tried to adjust to her strange surroundings. For the moment, she had been left alone in a luxuriously furnished bedchamber in the magnificent palace at Versailles. Her arrival in Paris, the trip through the city, and the grandeur of its buildings had left her awestruck. Soon they left Paris and went there, to Versailles, a palace so splendorous that she could not even have conjured it up in her imagination. She was not simply a world away from Scotland, she was a universe away from the home she had always known. It was true that she had studied and knew French, as many Highlanders did. But she had never dreamed she would come to France, and if she had, she could not have imagined it as it was.

On her way into the palace she had been taken on a tour of the gardens. Even though it was mid-September, the patterned paths were ablaze with the color of extraordinary blossoms and lined with exquisitely trimmed shrubbery. And throughout, she had been able to view the commanding sculptures brought from Italy by Catherine de' Medici when she had married Henry II of France.

But this room was not the taste of one of the earlier French kings. The furnishings in this room were new, distinctly the taste of the present king, Louis XV, who had set about refurnishing Versailles in order to make it even more sumptuous.

Abstractedly, Laurie felt the material in which the chaise

longue was covered. It was truly a beautiful piece of furniture, and the seat was well padded for comfort. But it was not the only chaise in the room. She had been told that each room was decorated with the whole palace in mind and thus contained an ensemble of pieces intended to create a given impression. Her guide was a strange young man whom she and Ross had met at the palace gates and who had taken charge. He seemed to feel it his duty to explain her surroundings as they went. He told her that the furnishings were influenced by Oriental designs, by nature, and by carvings that represented creatures of the imagination.

She touched the end of the chaise longue and ran her finger over the intricate carving. It was some sort of animal surrounded by what looked like tulips.

She inhaled and tried to overcome her feeling of utter insignificance. It was such a large room with such high ceilings. In the center of the ceiling a crystal chandelier with twenty-four candles hung from what appeared to be a gold sunburst. The walls were partially covered with a light turquoise paper that had an intricate design that looked like white lace. The mirrors were all gilded and their frames were tiny masterpieces of metal craft—all curlicues and tiny flowers.

On one side of the room there was a draped alcove, and inside it on a dias stood a huge double bed with a canopy the same color as the drapes surrounding the alcove. Several ornately carved chests, a dressing table, a large freestanding mirror, three tables, and a number of chairs completed the furnishings.

Laurie returned her hand to her tartan skirt. She savored the rough material but thought it looked worn and a trifle faded. The swath of tartan over her shoulder was also worn, and her brooch was made of metal rather than gold. She had felt out of place since her arrival, and now the feeling was even more acute.

Laurie looked up as the huge double doors of the chamber opened. A statuesque woman came toward her. She was extremely attractive and her long, thick hair was worn up, in great rolls that framed her angular face. Laurie stood up, smoothing her long tartan skirt as she did so.

"Are you Laurie Lewis?" the woman inquired in French.

"Oui," Laurie replied.

"I am Madame de Pompadour, royal mistress of his highness Louis XV."

Did one bow to a royal mistress? Laurie was not sure how to respond. She lowered her head respectfully.

Madame reached out and touched her hair. "Very pretty. French men like women of your coloring. Of course you will need instruction, and you will have to wear more suitable gowns."

Laurie nodded. Ross had told her very little. He had simply brought her there, told her she was expected, and instructed her to do whatever was asked.

Madame walked around her slowly. "Open your blouse and take off that tartan. Pull it down like a gown so I can see your shoulders."

Laurie did as she was asked.

"Good, good. You have good skin and full breasts. Yes, you are most attractive, as I was told you would be. You will most certainly do."

Laurie was afraid to ask "do for what?" Was she to be one of those women of the court who was available to entertain wealthy, influential men? Ross had told her she would have to sleep with other men. He had even told her it would excite him to watch. The idea did not truly appeal to her, but she knew she would do anything Ross asked.

"Many important men come to court," Madame said. "It is essential that the king know certain things—it is necessary to know about the various intrigues—beautiful women are able to—shall I say—hear useful information? Do you understand?''

Laurie nodded. Long ago Ross had told her that pillow talk was involved in the art of spying. But she felt confused. It seemed to her that there was more than one thing happening. Ross wanted her to find out all about the prince when he arrived. He wanted her in place now so that she could be in a position to learn where the prince would be, and when he would be there. It seemed that Madame wanted something else from her. But for the moment she decided not to ask. When Ross came back to talk with her, she would ask him.

"I shall send in one of the other women. She will see to your bath and help you select a suitable gown.''

"Thank you, Madame.''

Madame de Pompadour smiled and turned away. She seemed to be a busy woman.

No sooner had she left than servants began coming in with hot, steaming water. They passed through the bedchamber and into a smaller room off the main room.

In another moment, a stunning woman with long, curly dark hair and golden skin came in. She was striking-looking and her eyes, while soft, were slightly slanted and almost golden in color. Her figure was perfect and her low-cut gown emphasized it by lifting her breasts and drawing in her tiny waist.

"Laurie Lewis, I am Aimée Doucet,'' the woman said, smiling. "Madame sent me to see to you. Come along, the bath must be filled now.''

Aimée led her into the smaller room. In its center was a large porcelain tub with hand-painted flowers decorating its edges. It was filled now with steaming water and Aimée poured some essence from a tiny bottle into it. In seconds the steam carried the heady perfume all over the room.

"I will wash your hair and style it," Aimée said.

Sensing her protégé was shy, Aimée smiled again. "Call me when you're ready to have your hair washed."

Laurie nodded and watched as Aimée disappeared. Quickly she undressed and sank into the wonderfully warm, scented water. She scrubbed away, and when she was finished, she called Aimée back into the room.

"I'm ready now," she said. Then, curious, she asked, "Is Madame the only royal mistress?"

Aimée laughed lightly and shook her head. "Madame is a very important and influential woman. She is far more than a mistress. She makes appointments for the king, she issues his orders, and she completely runs the court. Louis would do nothing without her advice. She is far more than his mistress. She is a woman of great intellect. She is even assisting in the writing of an encyclopedia. No, Madame is not the only royal mistress, and, of course, there are many women in court.

"And what am I to do?" Laurie asked.

"You are to entertain those men whom you are asked to entertain. Above all, you are to listen and report what you hear and what you are told to Madame. But she will give you further instruction at a later date."

"Thank you," Laurie said. She leaned back as Aimée began pouring warm water over her hair. Perhaps when she was dressed differently and her hair was done, she would look more as if she belonged there. She could not say that she didn't like it. In fact, she felt like a fairy-tale princess.

James MacPherson looked out on Loch nan Uamh. It was, he thought, a special night in more than one way. For days and days a coastal storm had forced ships into harbor; for days and days they had waited for the storm to abate.

Now it had, and the dark clouds in the west were illuminated by the dying sun, giving the impression that each one was edged in gold. It was an unusual phenomenon and gave the early evening a special beauty. Loch nan Uamh was incredible bathed in this light. Sparse yet tall trees served as a backdrop to its rocky, stone-studded beach while its rippling waters reflected the gold of the clouds giving the whole scene a gilded Midas touch.

James MacPherson stood by the rail of *L'Heureux,* taking in the scene, trying to commit it to memory. Nearby, a second French ship, the *Prince de Conti,* was anchored peacefully. The prince had just returned from the *Prince de Conti,* where he had been meeting with a few clan chieftains. At dawn, when the tide rose, the two heavily armed ships would be off to France, bearing some one hundred clansmen and Prince Charles.

"What are the likes of us to do in France?" a voice said.

James turned to see David MacDonald, a tall, heavyset member of Clan MacDonald. David was a bear of a man, a champion of the caber toss. If he closed his eyes, he could picture him now at the last Highland games. He had gripped his tree hard, and in a display of great strength tossed it forward like a spear.

"I don't know," James said. Although, in his own case, he did know. But MacDonald had never been out of Scotland. He was not among those educated on the Continent and fluent in French. James knew full well that in Paris MacDonald would wither like a flower in January. No matter what the risks, MacDonald would be back in Scotland in no time, unable to adjust to the life of a gentleman, unable to stand the stuffy indoor parlor games so popular in France. He was a man of the Highlands, a man who walked barelegged in the snow and who tossed full-grown trees for sport.

"A grown man shouldn't cry," MacDonald muttered as

he wiped a tear off his cheek. "But I hate leaving. It's our land, not theirs."

"We'll come back to it," James said with determination. He knew full well he intended coming back. Cluny had been in his family for generations. It would be reclaimed and rebuilt. He would not give it up, his exile was temporary.

MacDonald turned away from the scenery. "I'm going below to drown my sorrows in good whisky, join me?"

Again James nodded. Leaving was painful. He didn't want to ask the others how they felt; he was certain they all felt the same way.

As he walked toward the cottage, Robert felt ill at ease. Glynis was used to his comings and goings. So used to them that she was usually on the path to greet him when he returned, since he nearly always came home at the same time. But she was not there this evening, and he quickened his step, dropping his limp because there was no one around.

"Glynis!" he called out, and when she did not open the front door he ran to it and flung it open. "Glynis!" The cottage was empty and he ran outside and around the tiny dwelling. She was nowhere to be seen. He hurried back inside, and that was when he saw the note on the table. It was scrawled in a childlike hand, and he knew even before he read it that Glynis had not written it.

It read simply, *We have taken your daughter to the town hall in Ayr for questioning.*

He frowned. Somehow Glynis had tricked them into leaving a note for him. They no doubt agreed to do so in order to capture him when he came for her. Still, he knew where she was and he had every intention of getting her. He drew in his breath. God help any soldier who touched her, he thought. A shiver ran through him. She was far too beautiful to be left in custody.

He forced thoughts of anyone molesting her out of his mind and concentrated on how to rescue her. He needed a bold plan, a clever plan, and for that he needed to observe the comings and goings in the town hall, he needed information.

He decided to take Sampson, who was far faster than either of the horses that drew the wagon. He took their packs from their hiding place. They contained some clothes, their money, and Glynis's jewelry. He also took the pistol, and hurried off to get Sampson. Time was of the essence. Every minute she was incarcerated she was in danger.

It was near midnight when Robert arrived in Ayr. It was once the most important Scottish port on the west coast, but now it was surpassed by Glasgow and other ports along the River Clyde. The main part of the town was centered around High Street, Sandgate, and a few streets that ran off of it like the spokes of a wheel. The town hall and Loudoun Hall were the two largest buildings in town.

Robert headed for the town hall. He circled it several times and ascertained that the cells were in the rear, and he felt there was no doubt Glynis was in one of them.

He checked his pocket watch. It was ten minutes to twelve. If there was an officer in charge, he would likely be going off duty at midnight. He shivered, it was just as likely that another would not appear until morning. Usually there were only two. One from early morning till around five and another from around seven until midnight. That meant that Glynis would be in the most danger between then and the morning. But he had to have time to execute the vague plan that had formed in his mind.

Danger or no danger, it was no good if both of them ended up dead. He crouched down in the bushes and waited.

At a few minutes past midnight an officer did indeed come out of the town hall. Better yet, Robert thought as he watched him, they were roughly the same size. He glanced heavenward and half smiled as if in thanks, then began silently to follow the young officer.

He followed him to a small cottage down one of the side streets off Sandgate. He watched as the officer fumbled with the door and finally went inside. Robert watched and waited, crouching down in the back garden. He saw candles lit in the house, but after a short time they were extinguished.

Finally, he crept around to the front and entered the cottage through the unlocked front door. He passed through two rooms and in the third room he found his prey, snoring loudly and sprawled across a wide bed. Another stroke of luck, Robert thought. The officer lived alone—he had no family that also had to be subdued.

Robert drew his pistol and crept up to the bed. At the feel of the cold steel of the pistol barrel on his forehead, the young officer opened his eyes and blinked in terror.

"Shh," Robert cautioned. "Just relax and you won't be shot."

The fellow nodded, his eyes wide like saucers. Robert moved his hand away. "What's your name?" he asked.

"Watson—Brickston Watson."

"Tell me how many prisoners there are in your cells."

"Not many. A Carrick Roy who's being sent to trial in Glasgow and three Highlanders—"

Carrick! They had Carrick too. Robert did not react, but he did notice that the frightened young lieutenant did not add the usual epithet, "Highland trash," because he no doubt suspected he was a Highlander and knew full well it was not a good idea to call a man who had a gun to your temple trash.

"Is that all?" Robert prodded.

"No, there's some daft girl. She'll be questioned by the day officer tomorrow."

Robert digested the information. Glynis must be putting on some act if they thought she was daft. Daft like a fox, he thought with pride.

"You're not going to kill me, are you?"

The young officer was trembling. Robert shook his head. "No, but I am going to tie you up and gag you. Lie down on your stomach and put your hands behind you. When does the day officer come on duty?"

"Around eight in the morning."

In order for his plan to work, he would have to get to Glynis before eight, but he also knew he could not go too early without appearing suspicious.

The lieutenant was obedient. He rolled over immediately and put his hands behind his back. Robert took the rope he had brought off his belt and proceeded to tie the young officer. When he was finished, he gagged him.

Before dressing, Robert looked around some more, and finally found the shaving gear. He shaved off his mustache and gave his beard a military trim. That finished, Robert gathered up the lieutenant's clothes and took them into the center room. There, he quickly changed. He wished there were a mirror, wanting to know how he looked as a British officer.

He covered the uncomfortable-looking lieutenant with a blanket and hurriedly left. It was almost dawn. He had to wait near the jail, but he could not reasonably appear until morning since no officer would come in the middle of the night to claim prisoners.

It was all going to be more complicated than it had been originally. Retrieving Glynis was difficult enough, but he had to get Carrick out as well. Moreover, there would be no waiting around for a larger vessel. They would have to leave the vicinity by boat immediately. They would have to head for Solway Firth and hope to get a larger vessel there. Now, he thought, their choices were limited, and to succeed, luck had to be their constant companion.

Robert shifted restlessly and checked his watch far too often. Time had never passed so slowly.

Inside the enlisted men's quarters, the sergeant pulled himself from his cot. He'd had a restless night, and he had awakened in a sweat, thinking about the girl and how much he wanted her. Never had he touched a girl that beautiful.

Throughout the long ride to Ayr he had fondled her full, ripe breasts and occasionally he had stroked her long, white thigh. She was a prize and he hungered for her and had throughout the night.

He dressed quickly, pulling up his dirty breeches and putting on his shirt and jacket. He ran his fingers through his hair and beard, then quietly left the others sleeping and crept down the hall toward the cells.

He stopped to peer out the window. It was near seven, but the lieutenant who was to examine the girl would not come till nearly eight. By that time he would be finished with her, he thought, smiling. But when the lieutenant examined her, she was bound to tell him what had happened. It occurred to him that if he was to have her, he had two choices. He could kill her afterward so she couldn't talk, or he could spirit her away, rape her, and leave her. She would probably run home, glad to be free and too frightened to say anything to anyone. He settled on his second choice. He would drag her out of the cell and take her into the woods. There he could take his time with her.

* * *

Glynis opened her eyes when she heard the door of the cell open. There, in the half light, she saw the sergeant, and she shuddered. There was no doubt in her mind why he had come. But she closed her eyes and pretended to be asleep.

"Get up, little beauty." The sergeant ran his hand over her. She didn't move, and he shook her more roughly.

Glynis opened her eyes. He slipped his hand down to her breast and squeezed it. "Remember yesterday?" he whispered. "Well, today I'll give you the full treatment. Come on, you'll like it."

She shook her head, but he yanked her roughly to her feet and into his arms. His hands were on her buttocks now, and he was squeezing her hard and pressing her to him.

"Feel that, it's all for you. Come on, come with me."

Again he tried to pull her along. It occurred to Glynis that he didn't want to rape her there. Instead, he wanted to take her away. All the possibilities ran through her mind.

"No," she said, standing her ground. At that moment she decided it was time to stop play-acting. She would not go without a fight. If he was afraid of being punished, he would probably kill her. "No!" she said loudly.

"Bitch!" He swore at her and pushed her with force against the wall. He was breathing hard and he grabbed both her breasts and kneaded them. "I can hurt you," he said evenly. "I know how to hurt you."

"Touch not the cat without a glove." Her family motto once again darted across her mind, and she lifted both her hands and raked his face with her long, hard nails. She screamed as loudly as she could, not once, but twice, before he hit her so her so hard, she slumped to the floor, partially losing consciousness as her head hit the hard surface.

Robert heard the scream. He knew it was too early, but now he had no choice. He walked toward the town hall. He walked up the steps and past the sleepy guard who just managed to salute. He wanted to break into a run, but he did not want to arouse suspicion.

He reached the desk; the man on duty was fast asleep. Robert leaned down very close to his ear. "Private!" he shouted. The man's head jerked up, and fright filled his eyes.

"I am Lieutenant Franklin Marshall from Glasgow. I've come for your prisoners."

The private frowned. "Sir, our lieutenant won't be in till eight."

"That was not a question I asked you," Robert said angrily. "I have no time to waste. Who are you currently holding?"

The private consulted his list. "A Carrick Roy, four members of Clan MacDonald, and some girl."

"Show me your cells!"

The private saluted and led Robert down a long corridor. "Take me to the girl first," he said, trying to sound calm when in fact he was far from it.

The private led him farther down the corridor, but he stopped short. "Damn," he muttered as he stared into the cell.

Inside the cell, Glynis was unconscious on the floor. She was naked to the waist and her skirts were pulled up. Her hands were tied together and a large barechested man whose face was bleeding badly loomed over her—he had either just withdrawn from her or was about to enter her. He looked at the two of them and his mouth fell open. "Just Highland trash," he slurred.

Robert did not hesitate for a second. He withdrew his

pistol and shot the sergeant in the forehead, dead center. Then he quickly reloaded. The sergeant had a surprised look and he toppled backward. The private stood stunned. Paying no mind, Robert hurried to Glynis. He quickly undid her hands and cradled her for a moment. "Glynis, Glynis—"

She opened her green eyes and looked up into his face. She was dazed. "Robert—" she whispered.

"Did he—?" he asked, looking into her pale face.

Glynis shook her head. "He was about to—" she whispered.

"Can you walk?"

"I think so—help me up. I'm just a little dizzy."

"What's going on here?" the private asked.

Robert turned around, his gun still drawn. "Sorry, Private. I'll have to relieve you of your keys."

The openmouthed private handed over the ring of keys. "I don't understand, sir."

"It may be just as well."

Glynis leaned against the wall for a second, covering herself with her hands. Then she quickly retrieved her clothes and put them on. "I'm going to have a bump on my head," she said. She was still aware of her dizziness, but there was no time. She had to force herself to keep going. She would be able to rest later, or at least she hoped she would.

"Take the pistol, Glynis. Don't hesitate to shoot if there's trouble."

She took the pistol and watched as he tied the private and gagged him. "I am sorry about this, old man," Robert said in his best British accent. "But we do need a bit of a head start, you know. Now, when you get freed, I suggest you go to your night lieutenant's house and free him. You'll find him in the bedroom—alone, I'm afraid."

Robert turned and took the pistol back. Then they both

went from cell to cell. They freed the MacDonalds and they found Carrick.

Robert again checked his watch. "We've got an hour's head start at the most," he said. "Let's go."

Carrick smiled. "There's no waiting for a larger vessel; we'll meet by the dock a mile east of Fisherton."

Robert nodded, and he and Glynis mounted Sampson. "I'm afraid this will be your last ride on Sampson," he whispered in her ear.

"I know," she said sadly. But she couldn't think about it now, so she concentrated on how wonderful it was to have Robert's arms around her.

On their way, Robert and Glynis retrieved their packs and he took one of the other two horses. It wasn't a long ride, but there was no time to waste.

James could feel the autumn air as he alighted from the prince's carriage and prepared to storm the palace at Versailles. It had been a tiring trip from the port to Paris, but now he felt well rested.

As he climbed the steps with Prince Charles, he thought of the coach ride. The prince had commented sadly that "my greatest adventure is now over." And it was over, James thought. Whatever happened next, it seemed evident to him that the Stuarts would never again rule the United Kingdom. Still, the prince had to be protected.

The prince had not yet seen Louis, but money had been forthcoming for both the prince and the Highland exiles. He himself had not taken any. Instead, he had accessed his family's bank accounts in Paris. He judged himself one of the few exiles of independent means, although it was his desire to build on the MacPherson investments, not spend them frivolously.

Many of the other exiles, the prince included, were staying with the prince's uncle, the Duc de Bouillon, who had a spacious house. But James preferred his own apartment. It was small, but he was alone and he did not need to talk all day and all night about past glories and recent defeats. In fact, he preferred not to speak too much of the past.

"My, this is impressive," the prince said. He sighed deeply. "I have loved Versailles since the moment I first set foot in it. It is the most magnificent palace in all Europe."

There were few who would disagree, James thought. The Hall of Mirrors, which they were walking down, was stunning. Every room was furnished in exquisite taste, and the gardens, even in winter, were a sight to behold.

They stepped into the grand reception room and were greeted by yet another assault on the senses. There was a rage of color everywhere, from the ornate paintings on the walls to the women's gowns. Added to that was the aroma of rich food and the soft tinkle of fine crystal.

It was a large room with a high ceiling and a winding staircase. Waiters circulated with trays of filled wineglasses and plates of hors d'oeuvres. A great crowd of influential nobles, writers, painters, and newly arrived clansmen who were special guests mingled with the full court of Louis.

"Here is the place to look," the prince said.

"Look for what?" James asked cheerfully.

"A woman. I keep telling you, you need a woman."

James laughed good-naturedly. Perhaps the prince was right, but he was not at all sure this was, in fact, a good place to look.

The prince excused himself and quickly disappeared with Madame de Pompadour.

"James? Is that James MacPherson?"

James turned to face Conwin Roy, the brother of Annie Roy who had been one of his teachers.

They embraced and Conwin grinned at him. "It's good to see you, James MacPherson. I may have news for you."

James guided Conwin to a quiet corner. "Let's be mindful of the number of spies that wander about," he cautioned.

"Right you are, and the longer you're in Paris, the more careful you become, my friend."

"Tell me, what news do you have?"

"Actually, I've been on the lookout for you. My sister wrote that you were with the prince."

"And how might Annie know that?"

"Your sister and Robert Forbes were with her. She sent them to Carrick. They're headed for London and ultimately for the colonies."

"That's good news indeed. Tell me, have you heard anything of Colin?"

"Yes, he's in London. In Newgate Prison."

"He's alive," James breathed. He had been sure Glynis and Robert were alive—he had not been at all sure about Colin. Still, it was good to know about all three of them. "Thank you so much." He pressed Conwin's hand.

"He might be headed for the colonies as well. He was sentenced to be deported."

James took in the information. All three of them might leave for a time, but he had faith that they would all want to return to Cluny, just as he did.

Conwin pressed James's hand back. "I must get back to my woman," he said, grinning. "These French girls have no patience at all."

James waved him away, then rejoined the party.

Chapter Eleven

October 1746

Glynis lifted her skirts to avoid dragging them through the puddles that seemed to be everywhere. "Strange, I always thought of London as being—well, richer than the Highlands."

Robert glanced around. He had been to London before, but this was Glynis's first time, and he thought, given the circumstances, it would be her last. He had no trouble understanding her comment. Because it was distant, because it was the seat of power and the home of the king, one supposed it was a grand place and that the poorest Londoner lived far better than most Highlanders. But it was not the case. Poverty raged in London, and in a way it seemed worse than in the Highlands. Worse because one could not live off the land, worse because there was overcrowding and disease, worse because there were people who were fabulously wealthy and whose wealth reminded the poor on a daily basis of their position in life.

"It is pretty grim," he allowed, "made worse by the existence of staggering wealth."

"Well, there's no evidence of staggering wealth around here," Glynis said in a near whisper.

Overhead, the sky was as gray and the air was chilly and damp. They were standing in a cobblestone lane with two-story brick buildings in great disrepair on either side. On the corner, a collection of ragged children jumped rope and loudly recited a ditty—"Catholic, Catholic, ring the bell. When you die, you'll go to hell."

"That's disgusting," Glynis murmured. "They're just little children and already they're learning to hate."

"Shh," Robert advised as he guided her away. "Let's not advertise who and what we are."

Glynis nodded and they plodded on. "There are so many mews. You can't get a carriage down any of them."

"Along with the shoes one is made to wear, London seems to have been created to torture visitors. But let me assure you, there are sights worth seeing—there is a commendable side to London."

"There must be," Glynis said. She smiled at Robert and felt admiration for him. The British were his enemies, but he could still appreciate their accomplishments. His mind was not closed and he judged every man not by where he came from, but by how he acted.

They turned a corner, and Glynis let out a little gasp. As suddenly as they had found themselves in the slums, the slums disappeared and they found themselves on the street that ran parallel with the Thames. A short distance away, London Bridge stretched out across the river that divided the city.

As she looked at it, Glynis thought that it was as much

a small village as a bridge. Shops lined both sides of it, and over the shops were houses.

In spite of the constant traffic of wagons, carts, and fine carriages, the view was awe-inspiring. The Thames was filled with craft. Long rafts piled high with merchandise floated lazily, while sailboats tilted with the wind. Rowboats moved along with the current, and many of the vessels sported colored flags. In the distance, the dome of St. Paul's Cathedral was etched on the horizon, and the buildings of Parliament stretched out, their spires reaching toward the angry sky.

They walked along until they came to a riverside pub called the Duke of Kent. There they waited.

In less than five minutes Carrick appeared. He grinned from ear to ear. "Found her," he said. "Tonight we'll be tucked into clean beds."

"That sounds good," Glynis said. How she wanted a bath! Their escape from Ayr had been a long, dismal nightmare, one she knew she would long remember.

Once they had retrieved their packs from where Robert had hidden them, they had ridden down the coast to a fisherman whom Carrick knew. Finding him a good man, she had tearfully left Sampson in his care. There was nothing else to do, he could not be taken.

They sailed the fisherman's small vessel down the coast to another wretched little village. From there onward it was one small village after another, until finally they were able to take a larger vessel to Portsmouth. From Portsmouth they made their way by common coach to London.

The three of them had been together during the entire trip, and only that morning had Carrick left them to go in search of the woman who would give them shelter in London.

"It's a fair ways to her house," Carrick said. "I suggest we hire a carriage, it's much too far to walk."

Glynis smiled at the very suggestion. They had been most frugal with money; now she felt like splurging a little. "Good, I've had enough of these cobblestones."

As they traveled through the streets of London they left poverty behind and were soon in an area of elegant town houses with large trees and thick green lawns. Beyond that were huge estates owned by the nobility. All around those streets were elegant houses with wild land, which she learned was a part of the Royal Hunting Reserve.

"Mrs. Pinkney is a splendid woman," Carrick bubbled. He seemed more relaxed than he had throughout the entire trip.

"She's very attractive and she's most loyal to the Jacobite cause. I don't know if she survives because she's beautiful, rich, or influential. Perhaps all three. They say she sleeps with a dozen or so wealthy men and one member of the royal family."

"You sound quite enchanted, Carrick," Glynis teased. In truth, she did not think she had seen him happy since their adventure began. He was normally quite glum and certainly not given to optimism.

"She must be very rich indeed," Robert said, looking out the window of the carriage. "We're in Mayfair."

Their carriage traveled along a lane adjacent to the hunting reserve. Finally it came to a halt in front of a well-kept, expansive, and gracious home. "My," Glynis said. "It is grand."

Robert paid the carriage driver and Carrick directed them around to the back. "Let me assure you, we're honored guests," he whispered. "But we must go in the back or we'll attract undue attention."

A small woman with dark hair wearing the uniform of a house servant silently admitted them. Without further ado, they were taken upstairs and shown to their rooms. "Dinner will be at seven," the maid told them. "Madame will meet you then."

"May I bathe?" Glynis asked. It was bad enough to have nothing to wear, but she most certainly had to bathe.

"Yes, madam. I'll have water brought."

Off the bedroom was a bath, and shortly a procession of servants came and filled the ample tub.

"I've been looking forward to this," Glynis said enthusiastically.

Robert looked at her and smiled a slightly crooked smile. "Lo these many weeks of travel with Carrick, I've missed having you, lass."

Glynis blushed under his bold gaze, yet she wanted him as much, and she felt almost weak as she thought of him taking her once again.

"I can never get the sight of you washing in that ice cold stream out of my mind," he said, watching her. She had looked ravishing, and in spite of everything, she looked ravishing now. He wondered how he had resisted her for so long—and silently he thanked heaven that he did not have to resist her now.

"Undress for me, Glynis—"

Slowly, knowing how much he enjoyed watching, Glynis discarded her clothing. His eyes never left her, and she felt as if her skin glowed under his gaze. Slowly, she stepped into the water and felt its glorious warmth. She washed her hair first and sat up to wring it out. When she looked up, she was surprised to see that Robert, too, had stripped.

Glynis took a long, brazen look at her lover. He was so handsome and so strong. His broad shoulders rippled with muscles and his chest was wide and covered with light brown curls. His hips were slender, and that which gave her so much pleasure was large and strong, waiting to fill her. She smiled, and without waiting for further invitation, he slipped into the water behind her.

Silently, he put his arms around her and slowly began to wash her breasts, rubbing the nipples gently with the rough washcloth.

Glynis leaned against him, giving in to her sensations, her eyes closed, her lips slightly parted. He was taunting her, and she adored it. "I couldn't stand it when I saw that man touching you," he whispered in her ear. "You're my woman, Glynis. I'm so stupid, I almost let you go—I almost lost you."

"I love you so," she whispered as he continued to toy with her nipples. He moved his hand over her. Though one hand remained on her breast, the other rubbed the insides of her long thighs, then ventured between her legs, exploring slowly, torturously, as she squirmed with him in the water, reaching for her pleasure while he teased her with light touches and silent, sweet promises of fulfillment.

Her breath was beginning to come in short gasps, and she was pink not just from the heat of the water but from excitement when he lifted her and carried her from the tub. He wrapped her in a towel and gently began to dry her, even as he taunted her, this time with the towel.

"Please," she whispered as she gently bit his ear.

"You're not playing fair," he said, feeling himself as if he might burst. "It's been too long, Glynis. Much too long."

He carried her to the bed and lay her down.

He kissed her most intimately, causing her to move seductively in his arms. "Not there—yes, there . . . oh . . ."

He moved on top of her and felt her close around him. Her hips undulated to a wonderful rhythm, and he moved within her till she clung to him and cried out, till he felt her shivering beneath him. Then he allowed himself his pleasure.

It was all right. Everything would be all right. They were together and that was all that mattered.

King Louis moved the court to Fontainebleau, which was one of his favorite châteaus. It was some forty miles from Paris and two miles from the left bank of the Seine, situated in the quite wonderful forest of Fontainebleau. Originally, the ornate palace had been the royal hunting lodge.

The ballroom was filled with the visiting elite of Paris, an entire entourage of Highlanders accompanying Prince Charles, and the most influential members of the court and their ladies.

Like Versailles, Fontainebleau was a symbol of the royal extravagance of Francis the First, and its redecoration was an extravagance of Louis. Primaticcio and Cellini, the famous Italian artists, had embellished its interior, and its famed gardens were designed by Le Nôtre, a well-known landscaper. It was impossible not to admire its perfection or the beauty of its art and furnishings.

James, who had never been to Fontainebleau before, was taken aback by its opulence. He had been admiring the wall paintings by Primaticcio, when Prince Charles approached him. "I have a special bond with you," the prince confided as he took a glass of wine from a passing waiter and offered James one.

James smiled at the prince. He was a down-to-earth fellow in spite of his appearance, and James liked him, not because he was a prince, but for himself. "I'm certainly not of royal blood," James said.

"Not that kind of bond, my friend. No, we share a bond because we have been together in two different worlds. We've been in the wilderness together and shared uncooked cold fish for food. And we've drunk champagne here, in the world's most elegant dwelling. I've walked with kings and with paupers, and you and a few others have remained at my side. That is the bond of which I speak."

"It is indeed a bond," James agreed.

"Please, enjoy yourself tonight. It's been a long road for all of us. Look, my friend, Louis, king of France, has provided many beautiful women. Find one and truly enjoy yourself."

James drank his wine slowly. "And you?"

The prince laughed. "I shall find one too. And if you have difficulty, ask Madame de Pompadour. She is that most wonderful-looking creature over there."

"Thank you," James said, amused that the prince wanted him to find a woman. He glanced up at Madame de Pompadour. She was indeed a wonderful-looking woman and she was already famous all over France.

The prince moved away, and for a moment James stood alone before he began to walk around the room. Suddenly, as if hit by a bolt of lightning, he stopped and stared into a secluded alcove. There, in a most lavish and revealing gown, was Laurie Lewis, the woman to whom Colin had been betrothed—the woman of whom Glynis had been so suspicious.

He stepped quickly behind a column, not wanting her to see him immediately. What was she doing there? He braced himself; there was only one way to find out. He reminded himself to be careful. He had been warned about spies, and Glynis had been so suspicious of Laurie. Now he wondered if her suspicions were justified.

James circled the room. Surprise was always good, and he decided to come up behind her, to catch her off guard.

"Laurie," he said in a reasonably loud voice.

Laurie fairly jumped as she turned around.

It wasn't difficult to see why Colin had been so smitten by her. She was wearing a blue gown the color of the sea.

Its neckline was so daring that it bared both breasts save for the nipples. The Frenchman she was with was in uniform, but James was unsure of exactly who he was.

"James MacPherson," Laurie said, taking a moment to recover from what was obviously shock.

"In the flesh, my dear. Might we talk privately?"

Laurie turned to the young officer and in perfect French explained he was an old friend from Scotland and that if he would excuse her for a few minutes, she would return to him. Where, James wondered, had Laurie learned French? As he recalled, she had never mentioned that she spoke French. But apart from family dinners and what Colin had told him, he didn't know Laurie all that well. Still, if she were well educated enough to speak French, it seemed like the kind of thing Colin would have mentioned. Although, he did recall her mentioning she had been in France—on the coast.

He took Laurie's arm and walked with her toward the balcony. It was too chilly to go outside, but there was a small antechamber near the door. He guided her there.

She turned to him and asked the first question. "When did you get here? I'm so glad you're alive."

"I came with the prince," he answered. There was no secret about his arrival. "How is it you came to Paris?"

"With my cousin, Angus Ross."

"Ah, yes, I remember. Laurie, I need to know about my family. What's happened to Colin? Did you see or hear anything of my father or Glynis?"

"Colin's dead," she said, turning her head and biting her lip. "He was hanged before I left Inverness. Do you think I would be here—with other men—if he were alive?"

James looked into her huge eyes. They looked at him steadily, begging him to believe her. She was an accomplished liar, and he knew now with absolute certainty that Glynis had been right about her.

He forced himself to looked pained. "Dear heaven," he said, hanging his head.

"I'm sorry to have been the one to give you the news. I can honestly say I know nothing about Glynis. I do know your father is free but that there is a price on his head."

James nodded. "Are you staying at court?"

"Madame de Pompadour has taken me under her wing. As I've never been in France before, I'm most grateful for the help."

James did not say what came to mind. He had heard all the rumors. Madame de Pompadour kept an eye on all things that went on in court. She was the eyes and ears of the king and her women were her eyes and ears. A woman as beautiful as Laurie would have no trouble at court. She would in fact be kept quite busy by rich, influential men. Soon she would also be well off. But he wasn't at all sure that was what it was all about. He sensed something more, something far more Byzantine and something far more complicated. Moreover, Laurie had now told a second lie. He now remembered the full conversation—she had asked where the troops were being readied and then said she had been on the coast of France.

"I'm sorry I interrupted you," he said. He stepped into the shadows. "I should like to grieve alone now."

"Of course," Laurie said. She turned and fled the antechamber with apparent relief.

This, he thought to himself, was a kingdom where important matters were decided in bedchambers. He smiled slightly. The prince was right. He needed to find a woman.

Glynis opened her eyes in response to a light tapping on the door of their bedroom. She carefully moved herself away from Robert, who had fallen asleep with his head on her breast, and wrapping herself in a sheet, opened the door a crack.

"Madame sends these clothes for you to wear, miss. I am asked to inquire as to whether you require help dressing?"

"No, no. It's quite all right. I can manage alone."

The girl handed her a large bundle of clothes. Glynis closed the door and set the bundle down in order to examine each item.

First was a lovely red gown, and Glynis smiled. It had been so long since she had been dressed up! She didn't care if it was frivolous! If only for a night, she yearned to look herself again, to look like the woman Robert made her feel like. Beneath the dresses were the necessary undergarments, including three slips and a corset. Beneath that was a gauzy nightdress and below that a pile of men's clothing.

"What was that?" Robert asked, propping himself up on one arm.

"Well-chosen clothes from our hostess."

"The servant girl must be very good at judging sizes. They look as if they might fit."

"I believe this means we are to dress for dinner. Come on, get up, my lazy one!" Glynis laughed and threw a pillow at his head.

Robert sprang from the bed and grabbed her, pulling her roughly into his arms and savaging her with kisses. "If you're not good, my girl, I shall be forced to spank you."

Glynis squirmed in his arms, "Careful, I might like that."

He grinned at the very thought of her round, firm buttocks, which he now lovingly squeezed. "Dress up, my beauty. I need to see you looking as you deserve."

Glynis dried her hair and pulled it back, allowing curls to fall around her face. She put on the red gown and stood before the mirror with satisfaction. It was the first time in many months that she had really looked at herself.

Robert watched her with admiration. The red dress suited her as it made her skin seem whiter and her raven hair even more lovely. Her green eyes were steady and clear—she was a stunning woman, a woman who enjoyed lovemaking and who could laugh and tease. She was also accomplished and bright. And brave. He thought of her on the battlefield and in the jail with her tormentor. She had kept struggling, kept fighting, kept her common sense. His heart was filled with love and admiration for her. She was no longer a child, but a true woman. His woman, the only woman he would ever love.

"Are you ready?" Glynis asked.

He took her arm. "I love you, Glynis MacPherson."

She heard the emotion in his voice. It was like a pledge, and she knew he had spoken from the heart. "And I you," she replied.

At the foot of the winding staircase they were met by a tall blond woman in a black dress trimmed with red lace. She had a long neck and an angular face. She was surely in her forties, but her skin was unlined and her brown eyes danced with merriment.

"Did you rest well, my dears?"

"Most assuredly," Glynis replied. "I cannot thank you enough for lending me these clothes."

"Posh, you must keep them. Especially as you are headed for the colonies. I doubt you can buy much of anything there."

Mrs. Pinkney had leaned over to speak, and she had whispered.

"I take it we must be discreet," Glynis said.

"Yes. Very. We will talk later, about your trip and the arrangements."

"Yes, of course."

"Come, come. We'll have some wine and a fine dinner. Please, I want you to meet my other guests."

Carrick was already there and he had a brandy in his hand. He looked completely different, and he nudged Robert in the ribs and whispered, "I'm beginning to feel British already, lad. How about you?"

Robert laughed. "A bit."

"In there, you useless piece of shit!" The great iron door slammed closed and the burly guard half kicked and half shoved Ramsey Monroe into the filthy cell. There were already others inside. They were clinging to the walls like spirits. It was a terrible place with only one small window, a hole in the ground for human waste, and low, uneven wooden benches around the room.

"Another ruddy Scotsman, I'll wager. Soon there won't be any room for good old London pickpockets," one of the spirits against the wall complained.

"Quiet!" a stronger voice with an unmistakable brogue shouted. "Our only crime was trying to get you a rightful king!"

"Rightful? That Italian-raised papist foppet? The hell you say!"

Ramsey sank onto the bench as the argument continued. The two of them didn't begin a physical fight. They just swore and shouted at each other till one of the guards came and ordered them to be still or be flogged. Again silence fell over the cell.

"What's your name, laddie?"

Ramsey blinked in the darkness. His eyes had adjusted to the dim light now. "Ramsey Monroe," he offered.

"Monroe, is it? We're mostly MacDonalds. The prisons are full of MacDonalds. Those of us not dead are here waiting to die."

Ramsey looked around. True enough, they were all emaciated-looking. There was no question about it, it wouldn't take long to die here. Those who got ill probably did not recover.

He put his hands on his aching head. Why the hell had he fought in the first place? He didn't really give a damn about the prince. Still, he was sure all the MacPherson boys and their father were dead, and if he got out, if he survived, he would be able to take over Cluny. He was still Glynis's rightful husband. He pursed his lips and thought about her. If he got out, he would find her and teach her a lesson. Things would be different this time. Her father wasn't around for her to run to. She was alone and she would need a protector. But more important, he would have Cluny, one of the richest estates in the Highlands.

But how to get out? He was tired of all this. Tired of being held in damp, miserable cells, tired of being treated like a criminal. Surely there was a way he could ingratiate himself to his captors, surely there was a way he could find to make them let him out.

Everyone said there was a network in London, a group of wealthy, influential people who were secretly Jacobites and who helped those escaping. If someone could find out who these people were, wouldn't the British find the information useful? An idea began to form in his mind, an idea that might well get him out of this hellhole.

Even though it was November, there were numerous strollers along the Seine. It was a mild day and many wanted to take advantage of the good weather before the cold of December set in.

James walked along the river, his hands in his pockets, his head down, as he was deep in thought. Paris, he knew, was a beautiful city. Like London, Paris was divided by a great river. But the Thames was crowded and the city's worse slums lined the waterfront. Paris was different. Parks lined the Seine, and it had a tranquil, rural appearance, an atmosphere that could almost make him believe he was in the country. Not that Paris lacked slums. Hardly. It was simply that they did not blight the riverbanks.

Yes, he thought sadly, if he must be an exile, Paris was one of the better cities in which to spend his days—more so if one spoke French, as he did. The added advantages were that he had lived there as a student at the Scots college and knew the city. As part of the prince's entourage, he was welcome at court and was able to meet many influential men.

At that moment, James looked up. Walking toward him was a vision of loveliness. As wonderful as was this fall day, its glory faded before the woman who approached him. No, she wasn't really walking, it seemed to him as if she were floating.

She was dressed in a stylish, low-cut russet gown and wore over it a black velvet cloak. Her curly brown hair was loose and fell in ringlets over her shoulders. It blew ever so slightly in the afternoon breeze. Her face was perfectly heart-shaped and her lips full and inviting. Her skin had a tawny hue and her eyes were a golden color. It wasn't simply that she was beautiful, it was the uniqueness of her beauty that made him unable to turn away from her. To his surprise, she returned his gaze, and then stopped directly in front of him.

"Monsieur, did I not see you at the reception? At Versailles? Were you not one of the brave Jacobites presented to the king?"

James bowed, took her gloved hand, and kissed it.

"Mademoiselle, I am indeed one of those who was at court. But I must be going blind that you escaped me unnoticed. Had I been presented to you, we would be dancing yet."

She laughed a little and smiled. It was not a coquettish smile, but, rather, a genuine smile, a very nice smile. "You need not flatter me so much. I was late arriving, and was always near the back of the room."

"Then I should have searched the room. Forgive my boldness, since we did not meet under ordinary circumstances, might I introduce myself now?"

Again the dazzling smile. She nodded.

"James MacPherson of Cluny." Again he bent and kissed her hand.

"I am Aimée Doucet. I live at court."

"I live at court" meant that she was either a lady-in-waiting to the queen, or that she was one of the ravishing women Madame de Pompadour kept at court for the pleasure of influential men. James decided it was more likely the latter than the former.

"Are you free to stroll with me?" he asked, bowing slightly again, and wishing all this formality would be over. With the French, it was always a slow and painful journey to familiarity, and after that, an often unexpectedly short trip to intimacy.

"It would be a pleasure," she returned. "I suspect we will not have many more days such as this. Soon Paris will be unbearably drizzly and rainy. But then the king will no doubt move the court to the south of France. It is so much more healthful."

"How long have you lived at court, Mademoiselle Doucet?"

"Two years, but please, you may call me Aimée."

"And are you from Paris?"

Aimée shook her head. "I was born on Saint Domingue and sent to France by my father when I was sixteen. And, yes, to satisfy your curiosity, my grandmother was a slave from Africa. A Frenchman took her for his mistress and their child, my mother, married a Frenchman. I am what they call a quadroon."

"I can only observe that your ancestry has produced a most stunning beauty."

She smiled again. It was an enchanting smile, and, James decided, an inviting smile.

"May I visit you at court?"

"But of course. I should like that very much."

They walked on for a while, and he picked a flower and gave it to her. In order to make conversation, he mentioned Laurie. "There's a Scots girl at court now. Her name is Laurie Lewis."

"Ah, yes. I've met her. She is a very attractive redhead."

"Yes, that's the one. She was once engaged to my brother."

Aimée seemed to digest the information. "Perhaps I should not say this, but she is a strange girl. An odd man visits her often. She seems totally smitten with him, but she does not go with him or leave court. It is most unusual."

James could think the man was none but Angus Ross. Aimée seemed unusually observant, and he reminded himself that the women of the court were almost all informants. But what of Laurie? Was she an informant to Madame de Pompadour, or to someone else?

"You're thinking about this Laurie, aren't you?"

"Yes."

Aimée smiled again. "Let me find out more."

He wasn't sure he should trust her, but somehow it didn't seem to matter in this case. It was not as if he had confided in her. Besides, he wanted to see her again— and he thought as he watched her expression and again felt drawn to her full lips, that perhaps this was a woman he could lose himself in. Perhaps she was the one for whom he had been waiting.

December first brought yet more rain to London. Ramsey cursed the rain as he stood in the prison yard. They had the opportunity to exercise too infrequently as it was, and heaven knew the fresh air, wet or otherwise, was welcome. But he resented the fact that it was raining at just the time he was granted exercise time. It was the third time this week it had occurred, and he felt more and more resentful.

He looked furtively at his fellow prisoners. They were a rough lot. As soon as he began thinking about talking to his captors, he realized how very careful he would have to be. If anyone got wind of it, his fellow inmates would kill him.

There would be no time except out in the yard. But if the guards didn't listen to him, what excuse would he give the others for having spoken with them? And if he feigned illness, they might not take him away to the infirmary. They might just leave him in his cell to languish, and surely he would be robbed of what little he had left by the MacDonalds. They didn't seem to like him anyway.

Finally, Ramsey screwed up his courage and ambled toward one of the guards, a big, impassive brute of a man.

"Tell the prefect I must see him," he whispered. "No, don't say anything. No one must know."

The guard looked meanly at him. "Get away from me, you filth!" With that he kicked Ramsey in the stomach and Ramsey doubled up, rolling to the ground with a grunt. Had the brute understood? Had he kicked him to cover his request, or had he just kicked him?

Ramsey didn't have a clue, but he scrambled to his feet

and made for the far corner of the yard. Water dripped from the roof onto his face.

"What was all that about?" one of the MacDonalds demanded.

"I asked the bastard to let me go to the infirmary. I'm sick."

"Like a fox," MacDonald replied. "You'll not get out of here that easy."

Ramsey let out his breath and watched as the MacDonald ambled off. He was suspicious, but not too suspicious.

Ramsey sat slumped in the corner of his cell. It had been two days since his bold attempt to talk with the prefect of Newgate Prison, but as yet no one had responded and he had begun to believe that the guard had not understood his urgent plea.

Somehow, some way, he had to get out of there. He felt as if he were going mad in the dank misery of this cell. How long did they intend keeping them here? Were they truly going to send them off to some godforsaken colony, where they would live out their wretched lives as indentured servants?

The door to the cell opened and Ramsey watched as two guards entered, torches in hand. One leaned over him and kicked him roughly. It was the same guard to whom he had spoken in the yard.

"You! Get up! I need you for a work detail!"

Ramsey staggered to his feet, wondering why the guard felt it necessary to keep kicking him. But he buried his anger and followed them out of the cell.

The two guards walked on either side of him down the long stone corridor. Here and there water trickled onto the floor from the rocks that lined the prison walls. More often, small rodents scattered as they approached.

It seemed miles through the corridors and finally up several flights of stairs. The air improved markedly and soon they left behind the central part of the prison. At last they came to a large wooden door, and one of the guards opened it and pushed him inside.

At the far end of the elongated room there was a window, and in front of it, a desk. Behind the desk a small man sat. He had a tight, narrow face and wore a slightly yellowed wig.

"What is your name?" the man asked without waiting.

"Ramsey Monroe."

The man wrote it down and pointed Ramsey to a straight-backed chair. At the same time, he waved the guards out of the room.

"You wanted to see me. What about?"

"I think I can help you—well, I think I can help the cause of King George."

The man scowled. "The forces of King George? You're a Jacobite. You're in prison for supporting your ruddy 'Bonnie Prince Charlie.' "

"Why don't we say that I've had a change of heart," Ramsey said, leaning over.

"Just why should I believe you know anything of value?"

Ramsey shrugged. "I didn't say I knew anything of value. But I have the ability to find out things that may indeed interest you."

"Such as—?"

"I know there is an organization here in London that gives aid to Jacobites."

"I see," the man said. "And exactly what is it you want?"

"I want to get out of prison. I want to go back to Scotland."

The man grunted. "I shall have to consult with others. Your suggestion, or should I call it an offer, is rather interesting."

Ramsey suddenly stiffened. "You can't send me back to that cell. The others will be suspicious."

"Well, their suspicions would be well grounded, wouldn't they?"

A chill passed down Ramsey's spine, but he held his tongue.

The man nodded. "I'll have you put somewhere safe." He called for the guards, and once again Ramsey found himself walking through Newgate Prison. This time the walk was not so long. He wasn't put into a cell, but, rather, into a room. It was a long, narrow room with a bunk and a washbasin. Ramsey took immediate advantage of it, cleaning himself up as best he could. There was no doubt in his mind that they would accept his offer. He smiled happily. He knew where to find money and he knew where to go when he returned to Scotland.

"I was hoping it would snow on Christmas," Glynis lamented as she looked out the window and into the front yard.

"We're fortunate to be alive and together," Carrick said. They were nine in all as they sat around in the gaily decorated drawing room in Mrs. Pinkney's spacious house: Carrick, Robert, and she, who lived with Mrs. Pinkney; Benjamin and Frannie MacIsaac, who lived with a family named Hart; Cameron MacKay, Bruce Randonald, John Fraser, and Nora MacNeil, who lived with the Harveys.

Mrs. Pinkney brought in yet another plate of food and Carrick saw to pouring more Scotch. "Few may we be, but we'll have a proper Christmas *Ceilidh* anyway!"

A *Ceilidh* it might be, Glynis thought, but it would not be like the ones at home, if for no other reason than that they had to be careful not to be too raucous and arouse the suspicion of the neighbors. It was well known that Mrs.

Pinkney, a widow, rented out rooms, but if the house were vibrating with the sound of fiddle music and the stomping of step dancing, those who lived nearby might well question what was going on.

Her mind wandered over past *Ceilidh*s. They were often practical as well as fun. It was common to include "milling frolics." A large piece of newly wove fabric would be spread out on the floor and everyone gathered around it and pounded it to the tune of the fiddle so that it might be softened.

There would be much drink, singing, and step dancing. After a while they would gather in a circle—not just adults but children as well. Children were always included in all the celebrations. They would hold hands and go around the circle, each one telling a tale until the children were fast asleep and everyone was tired and ready to go to bed.

Tonight there would only be music, food, and tales. A subdued *Ceilidh* to celebrate Christmas.

"I suppose now that they've banned the kilt and the speaking of the Gaelic in Scotland, they'll ban the *Ceilidh* as well," Carrick said bitterly.

It was true that people were both saddened and outraged at the banning of the kilt. To the British it was the very symbol of the Highlands and Jacobites. But to the Scots it was far more than a badge of identification. The rich had kilts that were sewn and somewhat stylized. But a true kilt was a great length of cloth that made the Highlander self-sufficient, as it often served as both bed and tent as well as dress. In order to put on a proper kilt, a man would be naked and he would lay the great length of wool on the ground with a leather belt lying across it under the middle. He would then fold it into pleats end to end and lay on top of it. He would pull one end over his shoulder and down his front and fasten the belt to secure everything.

He was well covered and able to run through the thick heather with his legs free.

"What are we?" John Fraser asked. "We're what we wear and what we speak and what we sing. They've taken it all away."

Robert turned to her and squeezed her hand. "A tale, Glynis. Give us a tale to make us feel at home and free. Unless they cut out our tongues, they can't take away our tales."

Glynis leaned back in the rocking chair and took a sip of Scotch. Memories of *Ceilidhs* past still swirled in her head, and though she shared their sadness, her memories gave her hope.

"Robert's right," she said softly. "No one can take our tales, and as long as we remember, we can speak our language and weave our kilts even if we must speak and wear them secretly. The harder they try to kill what we are, the stronger will become our memories." She smiled. "I'll tell a tale of Ewen MacLachlan. Who has not heard of our great Scots Hercules, the master of the caber toss, the strongest man in all Scots history, Ewen MacLachlan?"

"Who indeed?" they all replied in unison.

"He was building a bridge across the great River Clyde, when his wife, Annie MacLachlan, came to tell him the giant, MacCall, had challenged him and would, that night, come to their home atop the mountain overlooking the Clyde.

" 'Dear me, no.' Old Ewen, strong through he was, shook in his boots and begged his wife to help him. 'You're as clever a lass as can be found in the Highlands. MacCall will eat me alive. I'm strong, but I'm no match for a giant.'

" 'I'll think on it,' old Annie replied. And so she went to her cupboard and drew out her nine woolen threads of different colors. She braided them into three braids and she wore one over her heart, one on her wrist, and one on her right arm. She knew she could not fail at anything she undertook as long as she wore her strands of nine colors.

"And so she thought and thought. And at last she went to all her neighbors and borrowed one and twenty iron griddles. She came home and kneaded them into the middle of her bread cakes and baked them in her oven. While they were cooking, she dressed her husband as a small boy and made him crawl into the cradle. She covered him with sheepskins and told him to follow her lead.

" 'I have great faith in you,' Ewen told his wife.

"When the giant came, his very footsteps caused the house to shake, but old Annie remained calm and cool.

" 'Are you hungry, MacCall? I've bread cakes and tins of fresh butter.'

" 'I am indeed,' MacCall the giant answered. He sat down and in a moment screamed out, 'My teeth are broken! My teeth are broken.'

"Annie feigned surprise. 'Gracious me. Ewen eats four loaves a day! Never once have his teeth broken.'

"Ashamed, the giant took another loaf, and he cried out again. 'More teeth! I've lost more teeth!'

" 'I don't understand,' Annie said, shaking her head. 'But now I must tend to the baby.'

"The giant followed her, and when she uncovered Ewen dressed as he was, as a baby, the giant let out a terrible cry. 'If this be his baby and that be the bread he eats, I want no part of Ewen MacLachlan.' Terrified, the giant MacCall ran down the mountainside and all the way to England!"

They all laughed and clapped and Carrick took the fiddle and began to play. "Just a few tunes," he said.

Robert put his arm around Glynis, and she rested her head on his shoulder. It was Christmas and soon it would be New Year's. Perhaps the New Year would bring change; perhaps it would even bring hope.

Chapter Twelve

December 1746

The last day of December was brisk, but not so cold that a walk in the garden was impossible.

"Walking here is like a stroll back in time," James said as he stopped briefly to look at one of the statues.

Aimée's luxurious hair was hidden beneath the hood of her velvet cloak, just as her figure, which rivaled that of the statue of Aphrodite before which he stood, was a mystery beneath the folds of an all-encompassing wrap.

"You must be frozen," she said in a voice filled with concern. "Don't you own a warm cloak? Did you leave it in Scotland?"

James smiled down at her as he turned and they resumed walking. "Ah, my little French lassie, don't worry. I'm not in the least bit cold. We're a hardy people who in winter let the wind swirl around our bare legs."

"I've yet to see you in your kilt," she mused.

He loved the smile on her face. She was a master of subtle flirtation and of innuendo. He had to remind himself over and over that she belonged to the royal household, that she was a woman of experience. Perhaps, he thought, that was why he wanted her. He admitted to being tired of inexperienced young women who giggled the time away and could speak of nothing save their latest gown. Aimée was highly intelligent as well as sophisticated. She could talk of music, art, or politics with ease. Of these, he suspected she knew most about politics and was no doubt a master of palace intrigue. Yes, he would have to be careful with her, but caution did not rule out a liaison. At this moment they were dancing—not a stylized dance like the minuet, but the compelling dance of slow seduction.

"My kilt? I must model it for you."

Aimée laughed gently. "I'm sure you look quite handsome in it. Now, tell me the truth, don't you have a cloak?"

"I have one, but I feel no need of it till the snow falls. The climate here is really much warmer than in Scotland."

"I don't mind confessing that I am quite chilly."

"Should we go back to the palace?"

"No. Even in a place so large there is no privacy. The walls have ears, the palace is alive with eavesdroppers. Follow me. At the far end of the garden is a small cottage. It has a fireplace and is well furnished. We can go there and I will fix us some tea."

"That is an irresistible invitation."

He took her arm and they walked on, weaving down the intersecting paths as Aimée headed for this rendezvous, which he assumed she had quite carefully planned so that they might be quite alone.

The cottage was as she had described it. Small with a large fireplace and furnished with lounges and comfortable chairs. It did not escape him that behind a drape there was a large bed, nor was he surprised to find the fire burning merrily in the hearth.

Aimée discarded her cloak to reveal a golden gown that like other gowns he had seen her in, fell off her shoulders and dipped daringly low.

He sat down and watched Aimée as she went about the business of making him the promised cup of tea. "You're a mysterious woman," he ventured.

"Not so mysterious. I know we will end up making love, and so do you. I simply felt it better to bring you here, away from the prying eyes and wagging tongues of the palace."

James was taken aback by her candor. He had suspected they would have a longer dance of seduction, that she would tease him and that today would not be the day. Her bluntness, her apparent desire for him, surprised him completely. "Lady, you surprise me," he said as she brought the teacups to the small table and sat down primly.

"As long as you are surprised and not shocked. But some things must come first, James MacPherson. It is vital that we talk," she said earnestly.

Again she surprised him. He had not expected an immediate request for a conversation.

"Please don't be puzzled," she said, guessing his thoughts. "If you were another man, I might try my wiles on you and then ask you questions. But I think you are smarter than that. Besides, our aims are not in opposition to one another. I believe we are on the same side."

He looked into her eyes and saw that she did not flinch. Still, he reminded himself that Laurie could look as widely into a man's eyes and lie her head off. Still, he was sure this woman was being truthful, and, he admitted, he would have to be doubly careful because he wanted to believe her so much.

"Go on," he urged.

"I am Madame de Pompadour's confidante. I shall not insult your intelligence by telling you what that means. Madame holds the interest of our king close to her heart, and sometimes things become—well, shall I say, most complicated."

"I am sure they are not so complicated that Madame cannot handle them. Madame de Pompadour is renowned for her skill at, shall I say, diplomacy."

"I will explain the problem. But first let me say that there is much intrigue at court and much intrigue even among your own people. I am not speaking of the simplicity of opposing sides in an argument, but of sides within sides, puzzles within puzzles."

James nodded.

"It is this way. Our king and Madame de Pompadour wish to support your young Prince Charles. But his presence in France is awkward. There are influential men who resent the money spent on him and on his entourage. There are also those who say we cannot have peace with England as long as he is here. Some want us to cease our support of him, others want to send him back to Italy. Still others want both. Most upsetting, there are a few who believe his death would solve many problems. We could not help him if he were dead—but if we simply withdrew our support it would hurt our king's position with the pope. You will understand that Madame is appalled at the thought of an assassination, especially on French soil. She will do anything to prevent this."

James smiled. "These views do not surprise me, nor does Madame's concern."

"Does it surprise you to know that your prince was allowed to escape Scotland?"

James opened his mouth slightly. "Yes," he said without hesitation.

"It is obvious if you think about it. There was a price

on his head while he was in Scotland. He was hunted. But what do you do when you capture a prince? If you behead him or hang him, you risk an uprising—at least if you are the king of England and you are already not very popular. If assassinated in England, it could be equal trouble. Ah, but if he escapes, he becomes someone else's problem."

"I don't quite understand," James admitted. "I quite see the logic of what you say about capturing him—but how is he a problem now?"

"The British king still wants Prince Charles dead. He wants him assassinated here, in France. That way it cannot reflect on him."

"But he is protected here."

Aimée smiled. "Not from his own, James. There are spies among you, spies who work for the British. They will kill your prince, and my king will be blamed. As I told you, there are also forces here who would see him dead. If those forces in France unite with those sent from Britain to kill him—it will be difficult to prevent his murder."

"Laurie—" James repeated her name in a low voice. Glynis had seen Laurie with her cousin Angus Ross, and Glynis was suspicious at the time. Laurie had known everything and everything had been betrayed by someone. Not that Laurie was the only spy. But now she was in Paris and she had lied to him about Colin being dead and about having been in France. Laurie was there for a reason, that much seemed clear.

"Laurie," Aimée said, repeating the name. "You believe she is the one?"

James nodded. "One of them—but to be sure, we must set a trap."

Aimée smiled. "Yes. You see, I told you we could work together."

James drained his teacup and stood. He walked behind her chair and ran his hands through the mass of thick curls, then down over her bare shoulders. She closed her eyes and leaned back and whispered, "Yes—now is the time."

James let his hands roam over her breasts, which pressed against the material of her dress. Yes, now was the time—in fact, a little pleasure was long past due. The details of their new arrangement to trap Laurie and the other spies could wait a little.

Glynis put on her cape. Outside, it was once again raining, and although her walk back to Mrs. Pinkney's house was short, she dreaded the cold wind. January, she decided, was much more inclement than December had been.

Wealthy Jacobite families in England had reached out to the refugees, helping when they could and finding work for those who were qualified. Robert had begun tutoring and Glynis became daytime governess to three small children in one of the families where Robert tutored.

Mrs. Pinkney could be persuaded to take no more than a nominal amount for room and board, so employment meant they were able to survive without selling any more of Glynis's jewelry. It also helped the time to pass. It was quite impossible to make the voyage to the colonies before late spring.

If it had not been raining, Glynis thought, she would have enjoyed her walk along the tree-lined streets of Mayfair. But the short, gray days of winter made her pensive and a trifle depressed. Scotland was no less gray, and in the north the days of winter were even shorter. The mitigating factor was the snow, she decided. When it did snow in London, which was rarely, it was thin and watery and seemed to turn to dirty slush instantly. But in Scotland, when it snowed, it was white and clean. It hid the soot of Inverness, and in the country it gave the land a cloak of virgin white marked only by the paw prints of small animals, sheep, and the little dogs that herded them with barks and gentle snaps to the leg.

She let herself into the house and found she was grateful that no one was around. She went directly to their room and sat in the darkness, not even bothering to light a lamp. The fire burned slowly in the fireplace, and she sank into one of two large chairs, her eyes fixed on the only light, that emanating from the low flames and hot, burning embers.

She tried to think about the future, about her and Robert going to the colonies and building a new life together. She tried, but her dreams of the future could not entirely wipe out her sentimental remembrance of things past.

Perhaps, she reasoned, her mood was owing to a Christmas that had been pleasant but left her longing for Christmases past. There was no midnight mass followed by a gay party and Christmas morning breakfast. There had been only a clandestine mass—dangerous for the celebrants. There was no winter hunting, no rides on the sledge through the pristine snow, no gathering by the fire to tell stories.

Tears began to run down her face, inexplicable tears. Perhaps her mood was due to other things—no, she did not want to think about that just yet. The complications of their life were already manifold.

She turned her head slightly when Robert came in.

"Glynis?" he whispered.

He was so considerate. Perhaps he thought her asleep. "I'm here, in front of the fire."

"Sitting in the dark?"

"Yes, just thinking."

Robert came to her and bent down. He kissed her cheek gently and with his hand, he brushed her cheek. "You've been crying," he said gently.

"I know how fortunate we are, I just don't know what's wrong with me."

He sat down on the floor in front of her and took her hand in his. "A lot has happened. Friends and relatives killed and missing. Glynis, your sadness is natural."

"I love you so much—it isn't you—I just can't seem to get control of myself. Robert, I don't want to go to the colonies. I want to go home. I'm homesick." She heard her own voice break into a sob.

He was on his knees and he wrapped his arms around her. It was like a cloak of security, and she leaned her head on his shoulder. "I miss Cluny, I miss Scotland."

She felt him nod his agreement. "We can't book passage till April, Glynis. We have time to think about this."

"We have to do the right thing," she said with determination. "I'm being a baby." She sat up. "I know everything has changed and I know that things are not as I remember them. But I love Scotland—so much of me—of us—is there."

"You're no baby, Glynis. You're brave and strong. That you love Scotland as I do is nothing to be ashamed of—it is our future and we must give our decision some real thought. We must find out what is happening—if in fact a future there is possible."

"Yes, I know."

"Now, I've brought you some good news for a change."

"Tell me."

"I've just found out that James is alive and well. He's with the prince in Paris, and apparently living quite well at court."

"Thank heavens!" Glynis leaned back in the chair. "Oh, Robert! He's still alive! He's really alive!"

Robert kissed her again. "That did seem to cheer you up."

"It will never be the same without Stewart, but James is

alive and I'm certain my father is in hiding. Now, if only I knew about Colin—but somehow I'm sure he's alive too. Robert, we could start over. We could save the land of our forefathers. We could rebuild."

Robert kissed her again. He loved her all the more for wanting to go home, for wanting to rebuild. She knew as well as he what a daunting task that would be. Still, she wanted it, and he knew that deep in his heart he wanted it too.

Ramsey now sat in a cozy room located in a mansion off Gough Square. It was the first time he had been taken out of Newgate Prison, and although he wasn't yet free, he had begun for the first time to feel free.

He had met with various officials in the prison. But each time he had been returned to his small room. The room was certainly a cut above the cell he had previously occupied, but still he was angered that they would or could not seem to accept the fact that he was in a position to help them in return for certain favors. But today it had been different. He'd been given new clothes and driven to this house. Once there, he had been escorted inside and taken to this room, where he had been told to wait.

He looked up when the heavy ornately carved door opened. The man who entered wore a fine blue suit, a ruffled shirt, and a white wig. His face was moon-shaped and his eyes were a watery, faded blue.

"Ramsey Monroe, is it?"

"Yes."

"I will be known to you only as Frederick. We will be meeting from time to time, though not here."

"Does that mean my offer to, uh, help has been accepted?"

"You may say that. I would like to remind you that

should you betray us, you will be hanged without a second thought."

"I won't betray you."

The man made a funny sound from deep inside his throat. His face twisted slightly and he sneered. "A man who will betray one side will betray another. Don't get the idea I have any respect for you—none of us does. If you keep your bargain and give us useful information, you'll be given your freedom, you'll be returned to Scotland, and you can claim your wife's land. If your venture leads to nothing, you'll be sent back to prison, and if you tell anyone of your agreement with us, you'll be hanged. Do I make myself clear?"

"Yes." Ramsey stared at him. He hated all of them. He hated the English and the Jacobites. Yet he knew he could find those in London who were helping the Jacobites— those Jacobites who were active and disloyal to their king. That was what the British wanted, and for that they offered him his freedom and the opportunity to claim Cluny for his own. In return, he had only to make his pledge of allegiance to George II and he would be given Cluny and all the MacPherson estates because of his marriage to Glynis and the fact the others were dead. He smiled to himself. The icing on the cake would be finding Glynis herself. He still fantasized about teaching her a lesson.

"I shall meet with you in ten days time," the man called Frederick said. "You will come to a pub called the Elephant and Castle. It's near the Thames, across London Bridge on the south side. You will come at exactly ten P.M. and ask for Frederick."

"Yes, sir," Ramsey said, forcing a smile.

Frederick stood up. "You may leave by the back door now. On the table by that door you will find some money. Go find lodging, get yourself some clothes, and get to work."

Without even turning, Frederick left, closing the door behind him and leaving Ramsey alone.

March brought chilly rain to London as well as high winds. Glynis stared out the window into the garden. The grass was green and she was certain in a few weeks the flowers would begin to bloom. The crocus were up, but not yet out. And one day soon—perhaps in May—they would leave England forever, if indeed they decided to go.

Robert's tutoring had expanded into full days, so that his time passed much more quickly than hers. Even Carrick had found work in construction. It was most lonely for her on Saturdays, when Robert was working and she was not.

Finally, Glynis stood and put down her embroidery. She determined to go out for a walk no matter how rainy it was. She put on her hooded cloak, left a note for Robert, and went out into the gray afternoon.

It soon proved to be less miserable out than it looked, and Glynis noted that in the west, blue sky was beginning to show through the gray clouds. She walked along the lane that bordered the Royal Hunting Reserve, watching as the birds picked at worms in the grass.

Glynis reached the corner and turned left toward Tyburn, the fearful place where so many were executed. There stood what was known as the "Tyburn tree." It was a permanent triangular gallows. She walked this way not because of the gallows, but in spite of them. The side of the road on which she walked was part of the hunting reserve. It was wooded and quite lovely.

Glynis was nearly at the crossroads when she saw him, and she stopped in sheer terror and ducked behind a large tree near the iron fence that marked off the reserve.

Could it be? Her heart pounded and she felt on the verge of hysteria—the man she had seen walking along looked for all the world like Ramsey. She had to be mistaken.

She peeked out; he had crossed the street and disappeared. She leaned against the tree trunk. Her heart was still beating hard and she couldn't think what to do. Should she tell Robert? No! He would be horrified, he might even want to find Ramsey and call him out. Such a thing would end their chances of escaping to the colonies or of returning to Scotland. Robert felt strongly about the fact that she was still married. It was only that they had both believed Ramsey dead—but now, dear heaven, if he were still alive, what did it mean?

Glynis warred with herself. She couldn't move, her mind was a jumble. She bit her lip and decided she absolutely could not tell Robert, especially now. There was nothing she could do except return home and pretend the whole incident had not happened. Perhaps it was not Ramsey, perhaps she felt guilty and only imagined she had seen him.

But no matter how hard she tried, she could not erase the image from her memory.

"Glynis, where have you been?" Robert took her hands and pulled her inside. The foyer was empty and they were alone in the house except for the servants.

As she walked home, it had begun to rain furiously and she was soaked to the bone.

"My heavens, you'll get ill walking out in the rain like that."

Glynis fought to compose herself. "I just had to get out—restlessness, you know."

He smiled at her. "I do know. But you look as if you've seen a ghost. You haven't, have you?"

His eyes danced with merriment, and she knew he was

teasing her. Still, she had seen a ghost, a ghost who could destroy her whole life.

"Come," Robert said, leading her to their room.

He took off her wet cloak and hung it up. He unlaced her dress and hung it carefully over a chair close to the fire. She hardly moved, and now he stood and looked at her. She was wearing only her filmy undergarments and they were also wet.

His eyes devoured her, and she felt warm under his gaze in spite of everything. He could make her forget; he could make her forget what she had seen.

He turned away and quickly set a fire in the hearth, and when it was burning merrily, he turned to her and slowly finished removing her clothing.

For a long while he stared at her, and he felt his mouth go dry with desire. It was always the same for him when he looked at her. She was the most incredible of women. Her skin was so white and her hair so dark. Her eyes were green, their pupils ringed with gold. Her eyes compelled him, they were the mirror of her soul, they spoke of her intelligence and loyalty, of all the things he truly loved about her.

Her neck was swanlike and her breasts were perfect. As he gazed at her, he thought they seemed a trifle plumper and even more desirable than they had been, were that possible. Her nipples were erect, like pink stones in mounds of soft, white sensitive flesh. Her waist was small and her hips rounded and seductive. Her legs were long, and when he looked at them all he could think of was how she wrapped them around him when they made love. Far from ebbing, his passion for her had grown with each passing day and with every encounter, regardless of how frequent.

He drew her into his arms and kissed her even as he began to undress. She reached out to him, eagerly helping.

She undid his shirt and finally his belt and breeches. He shed them quickly and pulled her to floor in front of the now-roaring fire.

He lay her down on the Russian-bear skin that was in front of the fireplace. Her skin smelled of rain and her hair of spring. She was rare and sensual and his breath came short now as he kissed her and began to caress her, arousing her to a fever pitch, to a desire that bound them together in a search for mutual satisfaction.

"How I love to watch you!" he said, toying with her till she cried out and her glorious hips moved to reach his taunting hand. She turned her head this way and that, lost in his tormenting caresses.

After a moment, when her panting had ceased, it was her turn and she slithered down his body. He felt her lips around him and he moved to her tender yet knowing caresses, but he did not allow himself pleasure—she could have it more than once, but he had to wait. Not that he minded the waiting. It was better, so much better.

"Stop now, my little minx." He drew her up to him and rolled over so that he straddled her. She grasped him around the shoulders and lifted herself to him, wrapping her long legs around his waist. Unable to hold back longer, he felt his pleasure and hers as she quivered beneath him.

For a long while they lay next to each other in the darkness of the early evening before the flickering fire. It was as it always was, and yet tonight he sensed more. She seemed to be clinging to him, as if for the first time since he had known her she were afraid.

Ramsey had been sitting in the pub for hours. But he did not drink heavily. Rather, he sipped his brew slowly, listening to as many conversations as he could. He listened for Irish and Scots brogues. He knew this was the right ort of neighborhood. It was a poor area, an area where many Catholics lived. Not that there were not wealthy Catholics in England, there were many. It would be the wealthy Catholics who would be housing and hiding escapees, but the poor would know who they were and how to get in touch with them. He did not know exactly where to look, but he had decided that a pub in this neighborhood would make a good beginning. And though he met Frederick every few weeks, he was able to report enough so that his new masters knew he was trying.

Finally, he drained his mug of beer and ordered another. He was staring glumly into it when he felt a hand on the back of his shoulder. He turned around to see a large, burly man whose expression was all but obscured by facial hair.

"You're alone. A man ought not drink alone."

The stranger sat down, and Ramsey nodded.

"And you're a slow drinker too," the stranger observed. "I've been watching you."

Ramsey shifted uneasily. Was he so conspicuous? He had thought he was being rather subtle. "Is it a crime to drink slowly?" he asked, trying to sound nonplussed.

The stranger shook his head. "It's simply been my experience that a man who drinks slowly is less interested in drink than in information. I see you listening."

Ramsey felt uncomfortable and shifted in his chair. "I don't know what you're talking about."

"It's all right, friend. I hear your brogue. If you need help, you must go to Mayfair and watch the houses near the Royal Hunting Reserve. You'll eventually find the right house."

Ramsey shrugged and drank a little more.

The stranger stood up and pushed his chair back. "It pays to be careful. I understand."

Again Ramsey nodded. He followed the man with his

eyes and wondered if he should follow. In the end, he decided not to follow. He thought about Mayfair. He had been in that area already. At that time he had just walked the streets adjacent to the Royal Hunting Reserve. But now, he thought, he must go back there and be more observant. Had the stranger guessed what he wanted? Well, watching houses in Mayfair could do no harm.

James took Aimée's cloak and hung it on a rack by the door. The apartment in which he lived was modest, as he felt it was his responsibility to conserve funds. In fact, his family's accounts in France, to which he had access, were quite ample. But there was no need to drain them by living lavishly. Money would be needed to rebuild.

"What, no manservant?" Aimée asked, smiling.

"I gave him the night off," James said, ushering her out of the foyer and into his main room. He had found this apartment on Boulevard St. Germain and was well satisfied with it. It was the entire top floor of a fine house, and from the balcony one could see the spires of Nôtre-Dame on the Île de la Cité in the middle of the Seine. "In any case, although I trust him, it is perhaps better that we are alone."

"I'm certain you are right. Well, James MacPherson, this is the first time I have been to your den of iniquity."

"It has not seen many iniquities from this tenant. You are the first woman to grace these rooms since I came here last October."

"You are so handsome, I find that hard to believe, although I do believe it. This place looks like you. Very quiet, very male. It is quite untouched by a woman's hand."

He looked around, not that he hadn't seen his apartment before, but because her comment made him want to see it through her eyes. It was filled with books and papers. The furnishings he had chosen more for comfort than for looks. It was better than most of the exiles had, and yet it wasn't at all ornate. It lacked decoration and gave the impression that it was more of a place to eat, sleep, and study than it was a home. He laughed. "Now that you mention it, I do believe I have recreated my student apartment."

"I see you have read all the papers."

"Yes, and I admit I am less than proud of my young prince."

"Madame de Pompadour says he has made a bad mistake."

It had now been revealed that Prince Charles, angered by inactivity, had secretly gone to Spain late in January. He had gone on his own initiative to try to convince the Spanish king, Ferdinand VI, to come to his aid, as the French had not. He had asked for large sums of money, arms, and one of Ferdinand's sisters as his bride to seal the bargain. But the Spanish wanted no more trouble with England than they already had. They were polite, but they made it clear that Charles should return to France at once. Rumor had it that his father was furious with him and thus, in a temperamental mood, he moved in with his banker and refused to see his father's messengers.

"Madame de Pompadour is right. How does this affect our mutual interest?"

Aimée shrugged. "It does not, really. The central problem still exists. But it does make him harder to protect, harder to watch, when he runs off doing as he pleases and makes his own father angry."

James nodded his agreement. It was not just his father either. Young Henry, the prince's brother, was in Paris as well. He was a learned young man, far more intelligent than the prince, far less interested in obtaining power. He had made it clear he wanted no part of the intrigues that went on. He believed firmly that the old Jacobites were dying off and that European powers had no interest in supporting the Stuart cause. Furthermore, their father seemed to be losing interest. He seemed to know he was now too old to rule and that his son, having failed to cause a full rebellion, would never rule. That which had not been clear before seemed clear now, and it was obvious to James as he and Aimée discussed it. But still the young prince had to be protected; he had to be safely gotten back to Italy. That, naturally, would have been easy enough had he agreed to go, but he would not agree.

"Have you learned anything?" James asked as he showed Aimée to a table on the balcony and proceeded to open a bottle of wine. She looked utterly ravishing in her russet gown. Her hair was piled high and curls cascaded from the pinnacle down onto her long, lovely neck. Her ever so slightly slanted eyes glimmered in the candlelight.

"Your Laurie Lewis visits an Angus Ross with great regularity. They are most definitely lovers, though strange ones, I must admit. On several occasions she has made love to other men, and he has conspired to watch." She smiled and added, "I've heard that some men find such perversions exciting."

James did not feel any surprise with her information. "Is there more?"

She smiled seductively and sipped her wine. "Of course, there is always more. But you will have to find more for yourself."

Her eyes twinkled with merriment. She was teasing him, and he well knew it. "Is this to be a hunt?"

"Of course. I carry what you seek on my person, but you must find it."

It was an invitation. He stood up and went behind her chair, placing his hands on her shoulders. He moved his hands down and across her breasts, stopping when he reached her deep cleavage. Then without another word he plunged his fingers into her dress and withdrew a letter. "I believe I have found it," he said, smiling.

She puckered her full lips. "I made it far too easy for you."

"I shall take a long time thanking you when we have finished our wine."

He unfolded the note and held it up to the light. "Ah, me," he said after a minute. "The plot thickens."

The note was from someone who signed himself only as "Frederick." It was also from London. It gave instructions to Ross to continue to survey the prince and be ready to act when it was decided to act. Clearly the British did not want the assassination to be too soon. They wanted the French to be truly fed up with Charles when it happened. James knew full well that if there were many more incidents like Charles's recent trip to Spain, it would not be long before the time would indeed be right.

"How did you come by this?"

Aimée laughed again. It was like music on the night air. "Let us just say that Monsieur Ross does have a manservant and that he is in the employ of Madame."

"Madame is very smart."

"Madame is very influential."

James bent over again and kissed her shoulder. He could not be with her long before he wanted her. She was incredible to look at and truly incredible in bed.

She finished her wine and stood up, turning in his arms.

He kissed her lips and could still taste the wine on them. "I should like to kiss wine from your breasts," he whispered into her ear.

"Then do so," she murmured back. "Will you be as slow as before, my Scots lover?"

She reached down and touched him intimately. "You

are so—so—" she said breathlessly. "Strong, yes, stronger than any of my previous lovers."

He felt inflamed by her hand on him and by her words. He swept her up into his arms. He picked up the wine bottle too. In moments he would be lapping wine off her soft breasts while she squirmed beneath him. Then, as she had done before, she would wrap herself around him like a snake, and he would feel wondrously entrapped by her sinuous body. She excited him in a way other women had failed to excite him. Now, as he deposited her on the bed, he looked forward to hours of lovemaking that would repeat themselves in the morning, when he could have her again.

The long table in Mrs. Pinkney's dining room was set with a white damask cloth, sparkling silver, and fine crystal. In the center a vase held freshly cut flowers. March had brought forth flowers to the gardens of England and so, even if it were cloudy, there was a riot of color around all the fine houses of Mayfair and in all the parks and squares.

Glynis felt divided as she had never before. A part of her wanted nothing more than to return to Scotland with Robert. She knew the population had been decimated, the land raped, even burned. But she wanted to go home, she wanted to rebuild. Still, the memory of seeing Ramsey haunted her. If they went home, he would eventually find her. She was still legally his wife. Robert would fight him— Robert might well be killed. She was terrified of the thought of Robert being killed, terrified of Ramsey. And now she had other matters with which to be concerned— the choice was becoming no choice. They would have to go to the colonies and try to start over. At least, she told herself, Ramsey would not find them there, or if he did, there would be little he could do.

In spite of her distractions, Glynis cleaned her plate.

"You're silent, but you've a good appetite," Robert joked.

"I'm sorry. I guess I'm not a good conversationalist."

"Well, no wonder, with so much on your mind," Mrs. Pinkney said.

Carrick, who always wolfed down his food, now gulped his wine. "Well, there's no use fretting. We just can't get any passage to America till at least July. They're using all the free space to deport half of Scotland to serve as indentured servants."

Robert shook his head. He wasn't sure if the delay was a good thing or a bad one. He and Glynis talked often, and though she wanted to go home, she now seemed to waver and speak of the advantages of settling in a new land. It was as if she were trying to talk herself into it, and so, he thought with some relief, the decision had at least been temporarily put off. But that did not seem to please her either.

Glynis was on edge, but he could seem to do nothing to make her relax. He just assumed it was the accumulation of all that had happened. Her mind and thoughts were jumbled.

"Where do they send most of them?" Glynis asked.

"South or to the Caribbean. They can't send them to Boston, because apparently the colonists there are too independent-minded. The authorities don't feel that Irish and Scots revolutionaries are what's needed."

Robert smiled at Carrick's comment. "True, wherever we go, we cause trouble."

"You haven't caused me any," Mrs. Pinkney said. "I shall be most sorry when you're gone. The house will seem so empty."

"At the rate we're going, we will be here for some time." Robert smiled. "It's good to know we're welcome."

"July," Glynis said as if it were a million years away. And to herself she thought, July—it would be too late.

"Are you all right?" Robert asked, turning to her with concern.

"I'm fine." She smiled reassuringly at him.

"We'll just take every day as it comes," Robert said. "At least there is no urgency."

Glynis shivered. There was urgency. He just did not know it.

Chapter Thirteen

March 1747

Ramsey hovered behind the hedge and watched as Robert Forbes left Mrs. Pinkney's house. Robert Forbes! Not just any Scots Jacobite exile, but a man he truly hated! A man on whom he intended taking revenge. Ramsey felt his heart beat wildly. It was perfect, so perfect he could hardly contain himself. Ah, the sweet circumstances that had brought him to this moment, this almost miraculous encounter! He sucked in his breath and copied down the address of the house. Undoubtedly it was owned by a Jacobite and full of escaped exiles.

Ramsey was about to move on, when out of the corner of his eye he saw the door again open. The woman who stepped outside was unmistakable. It was Glynis! He pressed his lips together and swore. They were together! Robert and Glynis were together!

For a long while he stood stock-still. He watched as she

crossed the road, turned down a side street, and walked in the opposite direction from that taken by Robert Forbes.

This, he thought, complicated his situation immensely. Only moments before he had thought that he would tell Frederick about this house when next they met. Frederick was growing impatient for information, and Ramsey had been delighted at seeing Robert Forbes. He could take his revenge on Robert and placate Frederick all at once. But Glynis's presence in the house would necessitate a change of plans. She would not return to Scotland with him willingly. He would have to find a way to make her accompany him and still have Robert Forbes and whoever else was in the house arrested. He sunk his hands into his pockets and began to walk. He began to think about Glynis. She would do anything for Robert Forbes. The thought made him angry, but at the same time he realized that her desire to protect Robert could lead to a solution to his problem. A plan began to take form in his mind. It was a plan that would suit all aspects of his desire for revenge and at the same time placate Frederick.

James MacPherson tossed on his side. He was by any standards a sound sleeper, but one who moved about his bed a great deal and always awoke in the morning to find the covers on the floor. That morning was no exception. First it was the chill of the early morning that caused him to awaken partially, but the pounding on his front door quickly brought him to full wakefulness.

He wrapped himself in his robe and went to the door, unbolting it. To his surprise, Aimée stood on the threshold, her cloak pulled tightly about her.

"Come in," he said. "This must be urgent."

Aimée nodded and slipped inside the door.

James undid her cloak, and as he did so, he bent to kiss her. "An unexpected pleasure."

The gown she wore that morning—the last day of March—was unlike most of her gowns. It was quite plain, and yet he thought that she was so exquisite and her looks so exotic, even the plainest gown looked well on her.

"Some of my news will be pleasurable," she said. "The rest will necessitate some action."

"Come, let us have some tea and you tell me what has brought you here so early."

She touched his cheek gently. "Something that could not wait till evening, *mon amour.* Are you alone?"

"Yes. I dismissed my servant. I decided not to risk having someone know too much."

Aimée laughed. "That's because I told you about Angus Ross's servant."

"Perhaps," he said as he put the kettle on the fire and set out the teapot.

"How strange to have a man making tea."

"If you stayed here with me, I would make you tea every morning."

She smiled but she did not respond with wishes or promises.

"We have learned—ah, James, I must trust you. What I am about to tell you must not be told even to your prince. Perhaps, I should say, especially to your prince."

He sat down opposite her. "Then it shall remain our secret."

"I assure you the prince will be told by his father when the time is right. When all is in order."

James nodded. "Tell me this mysterious news."

"We have learned that the father of Prince Charles, James II, will in a few months time renounce all claims to the British throne. Further, his youngest son, Henry, will become a cardinal."

James looked at her for a long while in stunned silence. Not that the decision to do either of these things was odd. The pretender to the throne of England, the Stuart king, the leader of the Jacobites, had realized what many had known a year before at Culloden. So few could not win against so many. Moreover, now the Scots had been starved, exiled to the colonies, and imprisoned. Nearly all the leaders whom Charles had brought with him from Scotland to France were busy trying to get commissions in the French army. The remainder were old, far too old to lead a new rebellion. Henry, Charles's brother, had no talent for court intrigues. He was an aesthetic, a withdrawn and deeply religious young man. Hence the decisions made perfect sense, but no one who knew Charles would think they would make sense to him.

"The prince will be devastated. I doubt he will renounce his claim, although I believe he should . . . for his own safety and because he will never be king."

"You are quite right," Aimée agreed. "And even if he does not renounce his claim, he will soon be in less danger given this decision by his brother and father. Of course he will remain in danger until this information is public knowledge."

"And when will that be?"

"May," she answered. "After the information is made public, I think Louis will make arrangements for Prince Charles to leave France."

That was hardly a surprise either, James thought. Charles's presence was a great drain on the treasury, an impediment to peace with England, and a great trouble to Louis personally.

"In the meantime, we have reason to believe the prince is in grave danger. James, we have learned of a plot in the making."

"And this is your bad news?"

"Yes. If he survives, if this plot is foiled, he will, in all likelihood, be all right until the announcements regarding Henry and James are made. Once the renunciation of the throne has been made, well, as I said, he will be too unimportant to be assassinated."

"Tell me what you know, Aimée."

He stood up, took the kettle off the fire, and filled the teapot. Then he sat back down.

"We know it involves Laurie Lewis and her cousin Angus Ross. They are working for the British and have contacts with those in France who would see your young prince dead. He is to attend the opera. We believe it will happen there."

James nodded. It was understood that he would have to stop this assassination, because the French would make no public moves. King Louis wanted to have his cake and eat it too. He wanted to support and protect Prince Charles without actually supporting and protecting Prince Charles.

Aimée poured the tea into their cups and she immediately took a long sip of hers.

"What are you thinking?" she asked.

"I am thinking that I will have to initiate a small plot. I am also thinking that I would like to invite you to join me in bed. I have been awakened far too early."

Aimée blushed. "And are you going to sleep if I come to bed with you?"

He reached out for her, caressing her intimately. "I will sleep only after I have ravished you."

Every morning at nine, Glynis came to the Forster house to care for the three youngest children: Claudia who was just four years of age; Barlow, six; and Chilton, eight. In the afternoon, Barlow and Chilton were sent to Robert, who conducted private classes for some ten children in a classroom provided by a group of families who did not wish their children to be educated in schools run by the Church of England.

For her part, Glynis read to all three children, supervised their play, coached them in French, and fed them their lunch. Since Barlow and Chilton were relatively self-sufficient, they often played or studied on their own, leaving Glynis alone with little Claudia, whose age demanded more attention.

The large nursery was on the second floor and its windows faced the back garden. It was a splendidly large room, airy and filled with light.

It was midafternoon, and Glynis sat on the floor with Claudia. Between them was a large pile of building blocks.

"It fell down," Claudia said in a small voice.

Glynis smiled at her young charge. "It fell down because the base was not large enough. Look, if you put four blocks on the bottom, you can build it higher."

Claudia looked quizzically at the blocks and then, following Glynis's advice, she began to build a new tower, this one with a four-block base.

"Good," Glynis said as she heard the knock on the door. It was, she assumed, the butler with their afternoon tray of milk and cookies. "He's a bit early," she said under her breath.

It was indeed the butler, but he was not bearing a tray of milk and cookies. Rather, he held out an envelope to her. "This was delivered a few minutes ago, Miss Glynis. I was instructed to bring it to you."

Perplexed, Glynis took the proffered envelope. There was no name on the outside. The butler turned and left. Glynis glanced at Claudia, who was busily constructing her tower. Glynis opened the envelope and took out the neatly written note. She had read no more than one line, when her hand began to shake uncontrollably.

Dear Glynis,

How glad I am to know that my wife is alive and well. How shocked I am to discover she is living with another man.

You will understand that I do not approve of such a situation and indeed intend to bring it to an end. Not that you would leave your lover willingly. Knowing this, I have devised a little scheme to make it easier for you.

Robert Forbes is among the "wanted," and I suppose you are as well. But you can count on me for protection. Yes, it is true. Here in London I have made friends in high places. Naturally, my new "friends" will want to know about you and Robert as well as about others in the house and those who own the house, those you work for, and even their children. What a lovely little girl the Forster child is, what a pity it would be for her to grow up in Newgate Prison with her parents and everyone else involved in the sheltering of fugitives. I am sure you will want to learn how to keep this from happening, dear Glynis. You will meet me at five-thirty today at the gallows. Don't be late, my darling, I have missed you so much.

Lovingly,
Ramsey

Glynis had to hold the letter firmly with both hands in order to read it. He was in London! She *had* seen him! He knew where she was and what she did! He knew about Robert—it was as if someone had sat on her chest. She felt she couldn't breathe and her hand would not stop shaking. She couldn't think of what to do, of how to respond. But then it came to her. She had no choice, she had to see him and find out what he wanted. She had to protect the people who had helped them, and she had to protect Robert and the exiles. Glynis wrapped herself in her own arms and began to rock back and forth as she tried to clear her head and overcome her fear. Never before had she known this kind of fear. She hadn't been this afraid in battle. She hadn't been this afraid in the cell when she was almost raped. But now she had something to protect—she had others to think about as well as herself. She could not let Robert be hanged, nor could she put the others in danger. Whatever Ramsey wanted, she realized how strong was his leverage. She had nothing with which to bargain.

"Oh, it fell down again," Claudia said, clapping her hands together.

Glynis looked at the little blond girl. She didn't look as perplexed as she might be. "I guess I built it too high," she finally said.

Glynis forced herself to smile as she allowed the child to drag her back to reality and out of the realm of her imagination. An imagination now filled with thoughts of horrible realities.

"Can we go down to the garden?" Claudia suddenly asked.

The sun was shining outside; the spring flowers were in bloom. "Yes, of course," Glynis quickly replied. Perhaps Claudia would amuse herself for a while in her playhouse. Perhaps she would wander in the garden or play alone with her dolls. Glynis wasn't at all sure how she would cope with the rest of the afternoon, she only hoped that she could. Ramsey's veiled threats and promised protection filled her thoughts. She couldn't concentrate and she realized with something less than resignation that this would likely be the longest afternoon of her life. She might not be able to rest after she heard his proposal, but she cer-

ainly could not even think with it hanging over her head
ke a benevolent death threat.

The late afternoon was even more lovely than the day
ad been. As if on cue, April brought a vibrant blue sky
vith great puffy white clouds on the distant horizon. The
un was warm, and everywhere flowers were in bloom. It
hould have been a day for happiness and rejoicing, but
or Glynis it was a terrible day, a day filled with apprehen-
ion and a strong feeling of helplessness. She made her
vay to Tyburn in a trance, and now she stood slightly to
ne side of the Tyburn tree, trembling in the sunlight as
f it were mid-February. Having her meet him there, in the
place of execution, was like an unspoken threat. It was a
place of dying, and she felt as if she were dying inside.

Never had she felt so cold. It was as if her body were
lead and her mind had run amok. She could not turn
ff her imagination, and when she told herself that her
houghts were anxiety-fed fantasies, a voice inside firmly
eminded her that the situation was real, the dangers were
manifold, and that the outcome could only be disastrous.

"How pale you are, dear Glynis, have you not been out
n the sun enough?"

Ramsey Monroe rounded the gallows and came up
ehind her. Glynis jumped and turned toward him, her
mouth slightly open.

"Ah, you are a treasure when you are frightened."

"I'm not frightened of you," she managed to say. And
hat part was true. In and of himself, Ramsey was not
rightening. She was terrified of what he could do to others,
o people she had come to love as her own family, and,
most of all, to Robert.

"Don't lie to me, Glynis. I can see the fear in your lovely

green eyes. You're a trapped cat, Glynis. And cats fear being trapped."

His words took her back to their wedding night. The night he had tried to force himself on her; the night she had scratched and bitten and finally held him off with a pistol. She had quoted the family motto then, and now he threw it back at her. She fought answering him in kind; she fought to maintain her dignity just as she fought to hide her dread. "What is it you want?"

"Can't you guess, my dear wife? I want you. I want you to come home with me to Scotland. I can arrange everything. If you come, I can arrange it so that your lover, dear Robert Forbes, is deported rather than hanged in Kennington Common. Let me make this very clear, Glynis, the house is watched, so there is no running away. He will be arrested—it is really only a matter of whether he is sentenced to exile or to death. Here, do look at my list."

He held out his list, and Glynis took it. Robert's name headed the list, then Carrick's. After that came Mrs. Pinkney and the Forsters, followed by the names of four other families, twelve fugitives, and a priest who saw to their spiritual needs.

"And you will see to it that none of them is hanged if I come with you?" she asked.

"That is the arrangement. Glynis, I'm sure you know I have always wanted you back. We'll go home and start over, we'll rebuild Cluny. It will be our estate."

She shivered. He didn't know her brothers were still alive and she had no intention of telling him.

"How can I trust you to keep your promise?"

"I can only give you my word."

"That would be the word of a traitor," she said without blinking.

"I could argue that those who instigated the rebellion

are traitors. I personally have seen the light and given my allegiance to King George."

"You are a traitor to your own people. Why do you want me, Ramsey? If I come, you will never possess me, I will never love you or sleep with you. I will always hate you."

"I will have the land and your family's wealth. And you will be deprived of what you most desire. That alone will give me pleasure."

Glynis looked at him hard. It would only be temporary. Her brothers would eventually come back. James, who was in Paris, would already have secured and moved the family wealth for safekeeping. Ramsey was a fool. But for the moment he did hold Robert's fate and the fate of the others in his hands. Going with him seemed the only way to save them. If Robert were alive, no matter where he was, there was a chance for them.

"Give me your word," she demanded.

"I give you my word. They will all be safe if you return immediately with me to Scotland."

Glynis nodded.

Ramsey smiled broadly. "Meet me here tomorrow afternoon just as you have today. Bring nothing with you that will cause suspicion. We'll leave London immediately."

Ramsey stepped closer to her and then roughly yanked her into his arms. He forced a kiss on her lips, and she struggled to get free of him. But he refused to let her go and so she bit his lip, tasting his blood in her own mouth.

"Bitch!" he cried out, pushing her away and wiping his mouth with his handkerchief.

"That was not part of our bargain," Glynis said, her eyes narrowed.

"Tomorrow afternoon," Ramsey muttered. "Don't be late."

* * *

The stale smell of beer filled the noisy pub. In a far corner, a group of five men played darts. But most sat around small tables or stood by the bar, drinking ale and talking loudly.

Ramsey sat at a small table in the corner with Frederick.

"You haven't touched your ale," Frederick said, lifting his brow and staring into Ramsey's eyes.

"I have information."

"And about time. Frankly, I was about to have you returned to Newgate."

"I have complete information," Ramsey added. "But first an addendum to our bargain."

Frederick laughed. "You've got freedom, a full pardon, and some money. What possible addendum do you think I would agree to?"

"It's not a big thing I ask. And I assure you my information is well worth having."

"Well, what the hell do you want?" Frederick asked, taking a big gulp of his ale.

"I want your word that none of the people on this list will be arrested until I have left for Scotland with my wife. It's quite simple. A matter of personal safety, really."

Frederick frowned. "Your wife?"

"Yes, she is among the exiles in London. I want to take her home."

Home? It was hard to know what Ramsey was talking about, Frederick thought to himself. His information regarding the state of Scotland was that it was far from a desirable place to be. Food was short, the Highland economy—such as it had been in the first place—was in shambles. The population was starving and many of the grand castles belonging to the so-called aristocracy had been burned to the ground. Frederick screwed up his face.

"I suppose there is no harm in allowing you to take your wife and leave before the arrests."

"And as her male relatives are all dead, I will control the land?"

"Yes, we discussed that before."

Ramsey nodded with satisfaction. He reached into his pocket and withdrew a long, carefully written list. "Here," he said. "But nothing happens till the day after tomorrow. We leave tomorrow night."

Frederick scanned the list. His narrow lips formed a smirk of satisfaction. Among those on the list was one clan chieftain. This late in the day, a chieftain was a big catch. The others had all been commanders at Culloden. He said nothing to Ramsey, but he well knew that charges against Mrs. Pinkney would never stand. She would be let go immediately. Her influence reached far too high into the seat of power—her lover was a member of the royal family.

The day turned out to be far nicer than the early morning would have indicated. The sky was clear, and along the Seine a brisk wind blew the new blossoms that filled the flower beds. Paris was coming alive with spring.

James walked by the river and then sat on a bench near one of the many bridges that spanned the rambling waters that dissected the city and so defined its character.

After a prolonged few hours of lovemaking, and a delightful breakfast together on the terrace of his apartment, Aimée had returned to court. He had dressed, read a little, and sometime after two set forth on his walk. All his life, walking or riding in the woods had helped him think. Today he had much to think about.

First, he considered the whole. The trouble with clandestine activity was that it gave him cause to trust no one, alas not even the beautiful woman with whom he was having a delightful dalliance. Or, he thought more soberly, especially such a woman, a woman trained in the art of subterfuge. Carefully, he thought of all Aimée had told him. It made perfect sense. He tried to think of why she might not be telling the truth, of all the reasons Madame de Pompadour might instruct her to lie. After a long examination of the various possibilities, he decided that she was telling the truth, though a small part of his mind reserved total judgment as he reminded himself how very much he wanted her to be telling the truth.

Next he contemplated Laurie and her cousin, the British agents and their possible alliance with Frenchmen who wanted the prince dead. Again the sides were logically drawn.

He turned his thoughts to the prince himself. To his habits, to his desires, and to his personality and character. He was a man with many fine attributes, most of which James admired. But there were several characteristics that could not be overlooked. The first was the prince's deep belief that he had survived so far because the Almighty protected him. James did not disregard his own religion, but he knew full well that those who surrounded the prince had saved him many times. Granted, they may have been there because of the Almighty, but that made the prince no different from any other man. He was vulnerable and he refused to recognize his own vulnerability. As result of his belief in divine protection, the second negative characteristic came into play. The prince was more than a trifle foolhardy, and he tended to play at subterfuge. He wrote notes using code words, he often went around in disguise, he assumed false identities, and he felt one hundred percent protected by these acts.

The main drawback of this last characteristic was obvious. It made it difficult to protect the prince, especially in public places, where he thought he wandered unrecognized, when, in fact, everyone knew who he was.

If he went to the prince and told him there was a plot to assassinate him at the opera, the prince would simply ask, "How will anyone know me?" He might also go to Louis for protection, thus alerting the plotters to the fact that their identity had been discovered, or he might try to switch disguises and allude even his own bodyguards.

The problem was twofold. First, the prince had to be protected without his knowledge or the knowledge of the French civil service, and, second, the plotters had to be captured and exposed. How to do this? James now focused on the central problem. And just in case Aimée was not telling him everything, he decided to keep the plan a total secret known only to himself.

Glynis could not think when she had ever felt more miserable. It was a perfect spring day, a day when all of nature was being reborn. "But I am dying," she said to herself as she leaned by the side of the great stone arch.

"My dear, I was afraid you would have second thoughts. But I see you are here, thus ensuring the continued health of your lover."

Ramsey was again at her side. He always seemed to materialize out of nowhere. She carried only a small satchel made of tapestry and was dressed plainly in a day dress and a warm cloak. But in her satchel she carried her pistol. As soon as it was safe, she would move it and carry it at her side, beneath her cloak. Silently, she vowed she would never be without it. Ramsey had blackmailed her into leaving Robert. But if he ever touched her, she vowed she would kill him.

"I'm glad you're loyal to your lover. Not that you were ever loyal to me."

Glynis looked him steadily. "You lied to me. You told me Robert was wed. I'd have never married you otherwise."

He took her satchel and led her to a carriage that was parked down the lane.

"So, you admit you loved him from the start, that you married me only to make him notice you."

"I told you our marriage was a mistake. I offered you your freedom. I admit to having made a terrible error, I was childish and hurt that Robert was engaged to Margaret. I didn't mean to hurt you."

He looked into her eyes, and in his she could see only anger and hatred.

"You married me to get even with Robert Forbes and I married you for your money, Glynis. Well, now we shall both keep our bargain. Robert Forbes will always want you, at least until the day he dies, and I will have your family's money."

Glynis shuddered. Didn't he realize that Robert would find her? "You have kept your word, haven't you?"

"Of course, my dear. I wouldn't betray you."

Glynis leaned back against the leather seat of the coach and closed her eyes. She was too distraught even for tears. "Where are we going?"

"To Portsmouth to take a vessel to Inverness."

Glynis pressed her full lips together. She felt emotionally drained and physically ill. She could not, in her wildest dreams, imagine how she was going to survive an ocean voyage.

Robert lit the lamps and looked around the room in disbelief. Glynis was always waiting for him when he came home. But she was not there, and the room bore no evidence that she had been there. Panic started to creep over him as he remembered the last time she had not been waiting—that day she had been taken by soldiers.

He began to feel more apprehensive, but he told himself over and over that she was probably out walking. Yet he felt an intuitive disquiet that grew into a deep-seated anxiety.

He left the room and encountered Mrs. Pinkney in the downstairs hall. "Is Glynis resting?" she asked.

Robert frowned. "She's not upstairs. Have you seen her?"

Mrs. Pinkney smiled warmly. "No, but no doubt she is out walking. It's a lovely evening and no doubt in her condition she needs fresh air and exercise. We haven't discussed your proposed voyage to the colonies, you know. I mean, in her condition I fear it will have to be postponed."

Robert felt stunned, and for a moment he could not move. "Condition?" he said, leaning toward Mrs. Pinkney. "Of what condition do you speak?"

Mrs. Pinkney bit her lip and stepped back. "Oh, dear! I have spoken out of turn! I'm so embarrassed. I just assumed—that—well, you two had talked—"

"About what?" Robert pressed. "For heaven's sake, woman, Glynis isn't here."

"I'm sure she's just walking. This really is for the two of you to discuss."

"No! I want to know now what you mean."

"Well, her condition. She looks, well, she seems to be pregnant. I've known so many young women, I can usually tell when they're pregnant. Am I wrong? I was so sure."

"Pregnant?" Robert said the word aloud, and it sounded even stranger when it came from his lips. But of course! He had noticed she'd put on a little weight, that she ate more and that sometimes in the morning she was quite ill. He had noticed her changing moods, too, but he had just assumed it was all frustration over their situation, over their decision whether to return to Scotland or go to the colonies. Now it came crashing down on him. Glynis was pregnant! He felt rather stupid that he was surprised. They slept together enough, the shocking part was that it hadn't happened sooner.

"Please, don't tell her I said anything."

Robert nodded dumbly. "I really must find her," he muttered. He left Mrs. Pinkney stuttering and apologizing in the hall. He flew out the front door. If she were walking, she had probably gone to walk along the lane that bordered the Royal Hunting Reserve.

He walked along the lane, then began to scour the nearby streets. He could find her nowhere. He encountered others and asked them. He walked back to the lane, but still could not find Glynis. A deeper panic began to seize him, and he found himself running home, back to Mrs. Pinkney's. Glynis would surely be there, she had to be there. A child! They were going to have a child. He felt excited and apprehensive all at once. Most of all, he wanted to hold her, to tell her it would be all right, to tell her he was there to protect her and their unborn child.

Robert flung open the front door. He ran up the stairs two at a time and opened the door to their room. He looked around with a sinking feeling. Glynis was not there. He turned and left the room, heading downstairs to the dining room. Everyone was gathered around the table, eating supper. Glynis was not there either.

"You haven't found her yet," Mrs. Pinkney said with concern.

"No," Robert answered. He felt utterly helpless. Where should he look for her?

"Maybe one of the children became ill. She could easily still be at the Forsters," Carrick suggested.

"Of course," Robert replied. "I'll go right over there."

He turned on his heel and walked briskly toward the

Forster residence a few blocks away. How foolish I am! he thought to himself. Of course, that was where she would be. It was only natural that if one of the children were ill, she would remain after hours.

He turned the corner and there, parked outside the Forster house, were two dark carriages. Something was surely wrong. He increased his pace and leapt up the steps to the front door, knocking on it loudly.

It was opened by a tall, thin man whom Robert did not recognize. He stepped in, and only then did he realize he had stepped into the middle of some sort of problem. Behind the door, two policemen stood at the ready. Just inside the reception room, the Forsters and their children hovered in a group. Mrs. Forster was pale-faced, her husband was agitated.

"What's going on?" Robert asked.

"Judging from your description, I assume you are Robert Forbes?" the man who had opened the door said without emotion.

It was pointless to deny his identity. "Yes, I am Robert Forbes."

"In the name of the king, I place you under arrest," the man replied.

Robert felt a sinking sensation. He addressed the Forsters. "Where is Glynis? Do you know where she is?" His voice was almost pleading. Had she been arrested too?

Both of the Forsters shook their heads and Robert turned to the man who was obviously an inspector of police. "Has my wife been arrested?"

"Your wife?" The inspector raised his brow. "You may call her your wife, but it is our understanding that she is the wife of one Ramsey Monroe. No, she has not been arrested, she is on her way home with her husband."

Robert felt the blood drain from his face. Glynis was with Ramsey? A vague picture of what was happening began to take shape in his mind. Ramsey had somehow forced Glynis to go with him and arranged to have the others arrested. But he did not ask about Mrs. Pinkney or the others at her house. Perhaps they did not know about everyone. Primarily, his thoughts were with Glynis. She was pregnant with their child and she was with Ramsey. He could not even think about the implications—it was true that she was Ramsey's wife. After all was said and done, they were married, and in the absence of her father, Ramsey could force Glynis to stay with him. It was the law. Robert pressed his lips together. Ramsey was a traitor, a miserable bastard, and he would abuse Glynis. There was nothing to do but fight to get free. Then he would find Ramsey and he would duel him. He and Glynis belonged together. They were truly wed in a spiritual way she had never been wed to Ramsey.

Robert said no more for fear of telling the police something they may not have known. They were all herded into the waiting carriages and in moments were headed through the streets of London for Newgate Prison.

The evening was warm and those attending the opera were glittering in their refinery. Many who attended the opera came to see and be seen. But to his credit, Prince Charles, who had been reared in Italy, was a true lover of the art.

As was usual when he went out, the prince adorned a disguise. Tonight his tightly curled, white powdered wig was gone. In its place he wore a black wig and dark garments. Somehow, when James looked at him, he felt as if he were looking at a privateer turned dandy. Not only was the disguise a bit silly, it also did not serve its purpose. The prince was quite recognizable. Even so, James thought. The disguise would prove useful in the long run.

"I'm so glad you decided to come," the prince said, turning to James. "I would have never guessed that you even liked the opera."

"I have not been to one in a very long time," James said as they stepped out of the ornate carriage and into the well-dressed milling crowd.

James looked around. He saw several gendarmes, burly Paris police. Not members of the court bodyguard or military, but simply Paris police. He breathed a sigh of relief. They could absolutely be counted on, if for no other reason than they would not know what was happening.

"Opera is a relatively new art in France, you know." The prince smiled. He did adore lecturing on any subject with which he was familiar.

"Yes, it was imported from Italy a mere hundred years ago. But, you know, Italian opera is all about voice, French opera is all about drama."

"I've heard that," James said, his eyes darting around the crowd. Amid them the assassin lurked. Everything depended on his timing, on his knowing exactly when to act.

"For ever so long the most popular of French operas were written by Lully—no doubt because of his collaborators. One of his librettos was written by Molière, and Philippe Quinault, who was very talented as well, was another."

"I've read Molière," James said abstractedly.

"Tonight we'll see *Hippolyte et Aricie*. Rameau's music is an absolute delight. It has a kind of imposing grandeur—"

The prince's hands danced in the air, and in his peripheral vision, James saw the flash as the pistol was drawn.

"Pickpocket! And dressed as a gentleman!" James shouted. With considerable force James pushed the stunned prince into the arms of the two Paris police, who seized him immediately, shielding him.

"That one too!" James shouted. He pointed to the assassin, who was trapped in the crowd. But James did not wait for the police, he grabbed the man himself. "See! He has a pistol!"

The crowd oohed and aahed and stepped back.

In his captor's arms, the prince struggled in vain. He looked at James in disbelief and in turn James said, "I know you, O'Sullivan!" For some time O'Sullivan had been the name used by the prince when they were on the run in Scotland. On hearing it, the prince settled down immediately.

"This man must be his accomplice," James said, still holding the man who had the pistol.

One of the policemen blew his whistle, and in moments a police wagon galloped up.

The crowd was murmuring and muttering, but the bell for the curtain sounded. Seemingly assured that this was nothing but the case of a tawdry pickpocket and his armed accomplice, the opera lovers began to disappear into the depths of the opera house.

The prince and disarmed assassin were taken away, and James looked at one of the policemen. "I will come along to press charges and have a word with the prefect."

"It is not necessary, sir. You can certainly stay and enjoy the opera."

"No, I must speak with the prefect," James said. "I shall just ride along with you."

Both the prince and the assassin were securely tied with their hands behind their backs. Charles looked quite placid, aware by now that he was a player in some drama he had yet to learn about. Oddly, he actually seemed to be enjoying himself. The assassin, by contrast, looked completely distressed.

In moments the carriage was clattering across the cobblestones on the way to the police station.

* * *

The two prisoners were taken into the police station and James followed. They were made to stay in the hall while James was shown into the office of the prefect of police.

"James MacPherson," he said, standing straight before the prefect. "Palace business. I am part of the personal guard of Prince Charles, who lives under the protection of your king, Louis."

The prefect clicked his heels officiously. "I am at your service."

"I was certain I could count on that," James said. And it was true, he had counted on it. Common policemen, and indeed the public at large, had no knowledge of the assorted intrigues of the French court, of British efforts to kill the prince, of the squabbles and fights within the prince's entourage. All they knew was that Prince Charles was under the protection of their king. And Charles was immensely popular in France.

"The gentleman in the black wig is the prince," James confided.

"Mon Dieu!" the prefect said as his face paled.

"It is quite all right. The second man is a would-be assassin. I shouted 'pickpocket' to avoid a major incident. Let us say that it would be most embarrassing for anyone to even know of this assassination attempt."

"Indeed, most embarrassing. What may I do to assist you?"

"Please provide an escort for the prince to his home— he lives with the Duc de Bouillon, and I should like to question and take charge of the assassin."

"By all means. It is something that should be handled by the palace."

James smiled. He turned away and returned to the outer office, where the two arrested men stood. He walked to the prince and whispered in his ear, "Everything is all right, your highness. You will be taken home. I must stay here and interrogate this man who would have assassinated you."

"Assassinated me?" Prince Charles paled, or at least he seemed paler than usual. "I do not understand all this."

James smiled. "Trust me. I will explain it later. Just go home and bolt your door. I want you to speak to no one until next you speak to me."

The prefect, who had been standing in the doorway, gave the gendarmes orders and the prince was immediately released and escorted from the station. James turned to the assassin. "We shall have a long talk," he said in a low, ominous voice.

Long before, James had learned that the threat was worse than the act—the promise of torture was more effective than the torture itself. He could see the fear in the eyes of the assassin. He would most certainly talk, and with any luck, Laurie Lewis and Angus Ross would be caught.

Chapter Fourteen

April 1747

It was completely dark except for a tiny crack of light under the door, and another high on the wall where the stones were crumbling with age. Robert shook his head, but no matter, it still pounded. He couldn't recall how many times he had been hit, only that there had been five of them and that finally three of them had held him while the others kicked and punched him, swearing as they did so.

Instinctively, he clung to the shadows as his cell door was opened and four guards entered, their bludgeons in hand.

"Get on yer feet!" one of them shouted. The door ajar now, Robert could see the light beyond the shadowy, dank darkness of his cell. He struggled to his feet lest they hit him again.

They didn't tell him where they were taking him as they

pushed him out the door and into the corridor. He blinked in the bright light. Perhaps they were taking him to be beaten again—no, why bother? They could have done that in the cell. Perhaps they would hang him? Yes, that was a real possibility. He didn't fear dying, but he was afraid for Glynis, for their unborn child. He had spent the entire miserable night unable to think of anything else. The memory of her sustained him and helped him heal. He hadn't felt the pain so severely when he'd been able to concentrate on his memory of her.

He staggered down the hall with the guards on either side of him. His clothes were now stained and in tatters. His eye was swollen, and blood was caked on his face where his nose had bled. But all and all, he was able to walk and he felt better than he should have after so long a beating.

They went outside and crossed a large courtyard, then they entered another wing of the prison and went up a flight of stairs. They stopped in front of a door and he was pushed roughly inside. Behind a desk there sat a moon-faced man dressed in gentlemen's clothes rather than the garb of those who worked in the prison.

He waved the guards away and motioned Robert to a straight-backed wooden chair.

He steepled his fat fingers and looked into Robert's face with watery blue eyes. "And you are Robert Forbes."

"Am I so famous?"

"No. I just wanted to see you."

Robert nodded. "Where are the others?"

"The others—by that I presume you mean those arrested with you?"

"Yes."

"I'm not obligated to tell you anything, but I will. And do allow me to apologize for the reception you seem to have had at Newgate Prison. It's—shall I say, customary, to beat new prisoners."

Robert didn't say anything. He just shrugged. He supposed the same might have happened to an English prisoner in a Scots jail—were there such a thing.

"Oh, good. A liberal. I love liberals," the moon-faced man said sarcastically. "Now, let me see, the others—well, Mrs. Pinkney is quite comfortable in her home. That is because she is well connected, a charming woman of uncertain morals who has given her affections to a personage of some power. She is quite distraught, but she will be just fine. The Forsters are under arrest, but will be let go shortly. They are rich. The rest are all here, awaiting trial like yourself."

"Glynis? Where is Glynis?"

"Ah, Mrs. Ramsey Monroe. She is the reason I asked to see you. I have done business with a jackal, I do not like Mr. Monroe. I'm almost sorry to say that your Glynis Mac-Pherson is with him, and no doubt on her way to Scotland. That was part of our arrangement."

"She would not have gone with him willingly," Robert said, staring into the man's rheumy eyes.

"I should think not. Who would? No, she went because he promised you would not be hanged, even though I am afraid that was not his to promise and he did in fact make no such request. He was quite proud of having convinced her of his 'influence.' It is why I call him a jackal. He lied to her and he had you arrested just hours after he left England with her."

Robert was not surprised that Glynis would sacrifice herself for him and for the others. He had suspected as much from the first moment he had heard she was with Ramsey. Still, he felt a terrible loss and he felt fear as well. Ramsey was a bastard. He probably had not yet discovered she was pregnant. "For whatever reason, I thank you for telling me."

"It is my own way of getting even with a jackal. And how can knowing the truth help you?"

Robert could not answer. Was the man so dense? Knowing raised his spirits as well as his resolve. Glynis loved him, he loved her. She loved him enough to sacrifice for him. Now he had to find a way to get free. He had to find her and release her from Ramsey's grasp.

"One other thing," the man with the moon face said. "Monroe is claiming the MacPherson land. He is, after all, her husband."

Ramsey had married her for her money and position—though Robert was sure little was left of either. He did not mention that her brothers were alive, or that her father might be in hiding. Certainly Glynis would not tell Ramsey either. The less Ramsey knew, the better, and the same went for the British authorities.

"How long before I go to trial?"

"Who knows? Weeks, months? Maybe you'll eventually be released. Arrests have slowed a bit, rumors are flying."

Robert again just nodded.

"Guards!" the man called out. Almost immediately the door opened and his guards were again on either side of him.

"Take him down to the cells where the others are. Don't beat him anymore. He's had his initiation to Newgate."

They grumbled and led him away. Robert felt a surge of hope. He would be with the others—there was strength in numbers.

Glynis stood on deck and thanked God it was spring. The sun was warm even as they headed north, and that was some small comfort among a basket full of miseries.

It wasn't stormy, but the North Sea was never calm, and the great swells caused the vessel to pitch and roll. Again

Glynis felt the vomit in her throat. Motion illness consumed her in a way it never had before.

"Ill again," Ramsey said unsympathetically. He had come out of the steerage and stood on the deck behind her. "One can hardly imagine a more beautiful day, Glynis. I can't imagine whatever is the matter with you."

He stared hard at her. Her face was paler than it had ever been and her hair seemed darker as a result. Sick or not, she was stunningly beautiful, and he fantasied about possessing her. It would happen one day—he would catch her off guard and overpower her. But at this moment, however tempting she was, he had decided not to touch her. He wanted to be alone with her. He wanted no scene to which there were witnesses. He frowned slightly. In spite of her illness, she seemed to be a bit plumper and her breasts, always full, seemed larger.

"Are you putting on weight?" he asked.

Glynis leaned over the rail and vomited into the sky-blue sea. She turned on him angrily. "I'm pregnant, you fool!"

Ramsey stared back at her in disbelief, then his expression gradually changed to hatred. "Whore," he spat out. "Is it Robert's bastard?"

"Who else's would it be?" He asked only to hurt her, to make her say it. He was such a despicable creature. "Of course it is," she returned, screaming back at him.

"A little bastard child. Well, you need not think I will give it my name."

Glynis narrowed her eyes. "I didn't ask you to."

"True, you didn't. I trust you know the law is quite clear in these matters."

Glynis felt confused as well as ill. The truth was, she had no idea what he was talking about, though she was certain he would tell her.

"I will take over your estates, and when all the details

are seen to, I will decide what to do with you and your bastard. Though my inclination is to give it up."

Glynis felt herself go as stiff as a board. Take the child away? Did he have that power? Without her father or her brothers, what were her rights? Did she have any? Especially as Ramsey seemed to have the support of the British and she was a Jacobite. She took a deep breath rather than answer him. If she got angry or hysterical, it would give him pleasure. If she even looked distressed, it would give him pleasure. She silently vowed to give him no pleasure— no sexual pleasure, no emotional pleasure—not even the pleasure of seeing her suffer. There was nothing to do but put up with him until the child was born. Then she would consider her options. But she knew one thing for certain, she would never give her child up. Never. Silently, she prayed for strength.

One could not ask for a more romantic locale, nor a more beautiful woman. The suite to which James was taken was in the central section of the palace at Versailles. It was a large suite with a balcony that looked out on the magnificent gardens from which the scent of a thousand blooming flowers floated on the clear night air.

The inner walls, paneling, doors, and even the chimney pieces were decorated with gilded stucco, while the ceiling of this, one of the six grand apartments, had a huge mythological painting. The whole place was sumptuous and ornate, and yet seductive because of the assault on all of one's senses.

"This is not my apartment," Aimée was quick to tell him. "Madame de Pompadour has seen to it that we may use it tonight."

James raised his brow and looked around. On the balcony a small table was set for two. Champagne chilled in a silver bucket, and covered silver dishes held a variety of exquisite cuisine created by Jean-Jacques, Madame's own chef.

The center room was filled with luxurious divans, and on a table nearby, brandy and glasses had been laid out for future use. Beyond the main room was a bedroom with a huge canopied four-poster. Adjacent to the bedroom was an exceptionally large bath steaming with hot, perfumed water. If he were to choose one word to describe his surroundings, it would be sensual, and it was the same word he would have used to describe Aimée, who was dressed in a diaphanous white gown of layered chiffon, cut low and trimmed with gold embroidered flowers. Her hair tumbled loose over her shoulders, and her beautiful golden catlike eyes caressed him from beneath thick, dark lashes. Her mouth was wonderful to behold. It was full and promising.

"Do you like it?" she asked in her seductive, husky voice.

"Not as much as I like my hostess."

"There, you see, you always say the right thing, my lover."

"And to what do I owe the use of these surroundings?"

"Madame and the king are very pleased with the most discreet way in which matters were handled. It appeared to one and all that instead of British assassins working in concert with disgruntled Frenchmen of power, the entire matter was nothing more than a tawdry experience with petty crooks. I congratulate you on the grand illusion."

James smiled. "There is still the matter of Laurie and Ross."

"The hired assassin gave evidence against them. They are both in the Bastille and will remain there for some time to come. At least until the prince is safely on his way to Italy."

James nodded. Charles would not be happy to leave

France, but it was most certainly for the best. It was over. Peace had to come, and with it a gradual rebuilding— even in Scotland. Once the peace was made, things would gradually begin to change. British rule in Scotland would be harsh, but not as harsh as it was now.

"Let us not talk of politics tonight," Aimée said softly. She came to him, seemingly floating across the room till she was at his side. "What is your pleasure, a bath before dinner?"

He smiled; it seemed a splendid idea. He lifted her into his arms and carried her into the bath. She stood in front of him and began to undress him slowly, touching him softly as she did so.

She was a woman of experience and training. She made no false moves and she knew where to touch him—and when to stop. He felt his skin hot as he in turn undressed her, letting her veils of clothing drop to the floor slowly. He ran his fingers over her skin and held her rounded buttocks tightly, moving against her till he felt he would burst.

She laughed and danced away from him, lifting her shapely leg and climbing into the hot water. He followed instantly, submerging himself in the water and sitting behind her so that their legs were stretched out before them and her buttocks were up against him.

He touched her swelling breasts. Her nipples were large and dark. He rubbed them slowly with his fingers, drawing them out till they were taut. She leaned back, her head on his shoulder, and moaned as he touched her most sensitive spot. She groaned and wiggled against him. He continued, and she glowed warm, her breath coming in short gasps, her moans growing louder. He was like a sword, but he vowed to wait. Watching her was sheer pleasure. Suddenly she went stiff and let out a loud groan as her pleasure spread over her and she shook in his arms.

He leaned over and gently bit her ear. "Much more to come, my love."

He emerged from the water dripping, and she stood up. But she did not take a towel to dry herself. Instead, she stood against him and slithered down his body till she was in front of him. He closed his eyes as he felt her close around him. He smiled as she worked her magic. The night was young, he would be ready again after dinner, and yet again by midnight. She was the mistress of arousal and satisfaction. And yet, it would end. Sadly, he felt it would end that night.

The doors to the cell were opened and Robert was pushed inside with considerable force. It wasn't totally dark in this large dungeon, nor was he alone. He closed his eyes for a moment and then opened them. It had been bright outside, and it took a moment for his eyes to adjust to this dimmer light.

"Are you Scots?" someone shouted.

"Aye," Robert replied. "Robert Forbes."

"Robert!" The voice was familiar and Robert felt arms helping him to his feet. His eyes were fully adjusted to the dim light as he looked into Colin's face.

"In the name of heaven," he breathed. "Colin MacPherson. Is that you?"

"None other, my friend. None other."

They embraced and Robert realized they were both crying unashamedly glad to have found each other.

"Where's Glynis? I thought she was with you."

"She was, up until my arrest. She's with Ramsey. As I understand it, she agreed to go with him if I wasn't hanged. He lied to her—I will be tried like everyone else."

"I'm here too," Carrick said as he came forward.

"My old friend and my new friend," Robert said, looking

around. Colin looked gaunt, dirty, and disheveled, as were the rest of them. Robert supposed after his beating that he scarcely looked any better. "Colin, how did you get here?"

"My death sentence was commuted and I was sentenced to exile. I came here to await a ship to the colonies. I came via an unpleasant sea voyage."

"We have to get out of here," Robert said with determination. "I have to get Glynis back. That bastard Ramsey has taken her back to Scotland." He did not say that Glynis was pregnant. He had no desire to explain to everyone in the cell about him and Glynis. She was still married to Ramsey—they wouldn't understand.

Colin inhaled slowly and let out his breath. He understood all that was unspoken. Robert most certainly intended killing Ramsey. And, like Robert, he knew that as long as Ramsey was with Glynis, she was in danger. She could fend him off for a time, but eventually he would take her by surprise. "He'll hurt her," Colin said in a near whisper. "Even Glynis cannot bargain with the devil."

"There's no breaking out of here," a voice from the corner said. They both turned and saw that the voice belonged to Father O'Brien, an Irish priest who had long tended the spiritual needs of the Jacobite exiles in London. There were many priests in Newgate, so many, they had become something of an embarrassment to the government.

"Is it so secure?" Robert asked.

"It is," the priest responded. "But there is no need for undue concern. The pressure has been great on King George. There will likely be no more hangings. I'd say we were all headed for the pleasures of indentured servitude on some Caribbean isle."

"I'd as soon hang as work all day for some bastard and

then die young of one of those tropical fevers,'' Carrick
intoned glumly.

Robert began pacing the cell. "How often are we fed?"

"Twice a day, once in the morning and once at night."

"At the same time?" Robert asked.

"More or less," Carrick replied.

"Do they let us out for exercise?"

"Every few days, but we're heavily guarded by soldiers."

Robert nodded. He walked to the barred window and
stared out into the courtyard. A group of prisoners was
being marched around as he watched. Then, through the
gates, a wagon was admitted. It was driven right across the
courtyard, circumventing the prisoners. It stopped on the
far side, and some of the guards gave up their posts to
help unload it of what appeared to be foodstuffs. He silently
noted the procedure. If one were on the outside, it was
certainly possible to break in.

"Did I ever mention how obvious you are, Robert?"

Colin was leaning over his shoulder and Robert half
laughed.

"I can all but see your mind work," Colin added.

"I hope, if the time ever comes, that you're as quick."

"I'd probably be too nervous."

Robert turned around slowly and finally sat down with
Colin. There wasn't a man in there he wouldn't want to
see escape, but in truth, no successful escape could involve
more than two. But this was not the time for planning. It
was too soon and he had yet to get the full lay of the land.

The May sun was warm and the rolling hills sprouted
wildflowers among the rocks. Sheep were grazed lazily
where the sparse grass grew.

Silently, Glynis thanked heaven that the nausea that had
plagued her mornings was now gone. In fact, in every

physical sense she felt healthy and strong. Unconsciously, she touched her swelling stomach. It was the child growing inside her that made her strong. It was Robert's child, it was part of their future, part of Scotland's future.

There was so much to do! So much had changed! Everyone had worked hard before the rebellion and its terrible aftermath, and they rewarded themselves for their own work. It seemed that every night the pipes had played and young dancers twirled around. There had been a carefree gaiety that filled the valleys and echoed off the barren mountains. Now it was all gone, and in its place was sorrow for what had been taken away.

Strangers were not welcomed, and there was no hospitality, no trust left. That was what they had taken away, Glynis thought bitterly. They had taken away the trust of the people by turning neighbor against neighbor and son against father. Now, when strangers approached, everyone hid. Strangers were feared, food was short, crops had been destroyed. But it wasn't only the material things that had been destroyed. The spirit of the people had been sucked away with the banning of the kilt, the pipes, and even the use of their own language, Gaelic.

Glynis glanced at Ramsey, who drove the wagon, and she vowed that somehow she would escape him with her child. But she knew full well she had to stay until the child was born. No matter what his threats, no matter how miserable she was, she could not risk leaving until she was strong enough. Her only comfort was her knowledge that Robert was alive, that her bargain with the devil saved his life.

"We'll be near Cluny tomorrow," Ramsey said without looking at her.

"Cluny," she said softly. What had they done to her home? A feeling of nostalgia gripped her, and in her mind's eye she saw the foolish young girl she had been.

Again she chastised herself for ever marrying Ramsey, for creating the situation that now threatened to destroy their future, their child's future.

"I shall be master of Cluny," Ramsey said cockily. "I like the title. And you, Glynis, my dear, will be mistress of Cluny whether you like it or not. You will act the part of my wife, you will devote yourself to me. Of course all that will have to wait until the birth of your bastard child."

He turned and smiled meanly at her.

"You will never have me," she said evenly. If he touched her, she had decided she would have to kill him. The thought of his hands on her made her skin crawl.

"I don't want you. You're little more than a whore. I'll take a mistress to satisfy my needs."

Glynis did not answer him. He probably would do just that.

They reached the top of a rise and Ramsey stopped the wagon to rest the horses. There were a few more hills, then the valley and the glens of Cluny. And the lake. Glynis thought of the cool, clear water. She wanted desperately to plunge into those waters, to bathe, to wash away all thoughts of Ramsey Monroe.

James walked along the Seine with Aimée at his side. The sun was setting, and the easy-flowing waters of the river seemed to shimmer with bands of glimmering gold. Flowers were in bloom everywhere, and graceful trees dipped into the water as if sipping it. He felt a certain sadness. She had not said so, but he was sure Aimée intended ending their affair that day. He had thought it would end after their most wonderful night together in the suite belonging to Madame de Pompadour, but it had not. Their business was over, and Aimée had other duties. In a few moments he felt she would explain those duties and ask him to understand. He wanted to make it easier for her because although he loved her, he understood. Love—it had taken him some time to realize he loved her and almost as long to realize the impossibility of the situation.

"You seem distracted," he said.

"I am. Something quite dangerous has happened."

James had been unprepared for such a revelation. "What?"

"Ross has escaped from custody. The girl is still in prison, but Ross somehow escaped."

"The prince—"

"Is in no danger, my darling. It is you. The man has apparently gone quite mad. Since the night he was taken, he has done nothing but rave about you."

She stopped walking and stepped in front of him in order to look into his eyes. "I know how fearless you are, but you must take all caution. The mad are exceptionally dangerous, and I am told he is truly quite mad."

"I'm not afraid of him, but I will be cautious."

"You must promise me. I could not bear to lose you."

He looked into her eyes and saw what he had not seen before. It was a softness, a vulnerability.

"I thought you would end our affair when our business had been completed. I thought that was why you wanted to see me today."

She looked away shyly and shook her head.

"Aimée, does that mean you love me?" It was as if the question had simply fallen out of his mouth.

She looked up at him again and her lips formed the word, yes. Then, leaning against him, she said, "Do you need to ask?"

"I warn you, I am a jealous man," he told her as he wrapped his arms around her.

She suddenly began to cry. Not hysterically, but softly,

nd she leaned against him. "I was afraid you could not
accept me—my past."

Dear heaven, is that what she had thought he meant!
'Aimée, I have no trouble with your past—it is your future
hat concerns me. My darling Aimée. I love you too."

She pressed against him. "I will leave court. I will follow
you anywhere."

He wrapped her in his arms and hugged her ferociously.
She was kind and beautiful and intelligent. "Come home
with me now," he whispered.

"I shall be your loving mistress forever."

"You shall be my loving wife forever."

Aimée lifted her arms and encircled his neck. She kissed
him—tenderly at first and then with increasing passion.

"Come," he said. "Come home with me."

The wagon jolted down the path that led to Cluny castle.
The previous day's sun had been devoured by the rolling
fog that drifted across the land, carried by cooler winds
from the North Sea. How it affected the scenery—how it
affected her! Gone was the vibrant green of the trees, the
brilliant wildflowers, the feeling that one could reach out
and touch each rock. Now the flowers hid from the sudden
cold, and the trees in the glen were draped with moss that
hung like spiderwebs from their crooked limbs. On the
lichen-covered land, mushrooms grew rootless, their poi-
sonous bright red heads the only color in the ghostly fog.

It was so eerie that Glynis shivered in spite of her cape,
in spite of the fact that it was May and this fog was just a
temporary delay of spring. She closed her eyes against it,
against the ghosts of Culloden Moor, against the sight of
the fallen soldiers, against the knowledge that her brother
Stewart was among the fallen and was now among the
ghosts of this enchanted land.

Glynis opened her eyes when she heard Ramsey swear loudly. She wished with all her heart she had left them closed. Before her was Cluny—a great, empty stone skeleton marked by the fire that had raged through it, had eaten its fine furnishings, had ravaged its artwork, had left it a mere scar on the land, like some ancient ruin.

The emotion that rose inside her was so strong, she could not speak.

"I've inherited nothing!" Ramsey ranted. "It's been burned and looted and I've been left with nothing!"

Glynis ignored him as she could not ignore what stood in front of her. The place of her childhood memories was destroyed. It was as if it had never been.

She was in a daze as she climbed out of the wagon without his assistance. Ramsey had so wanted the wealth of Cluny—now he had nothing but the shell of what had been. Still, she knew there was wealth here, it was a wealth he could not see or understand. It belonged to him on paper, but it would never really belong to him.

She ran into the castle and stood for a silent moment in the entry hall. The stones could not be burned, but they were covered with charcoal, and a fine black dust covered everything. All the wood—the house inside the castle—was gone. She walked down the long corridor and stared into empty, burned-out rooms. She climbed the stone stairs and found piles upon piles of rubble.

She stood in the doorway of her father's study and looked in. Ashes replaced books, debris had taken the place of a lifetime of recollections.

Glynis looked and tried to understand, and slowly it came to her that the rubble was not random. It had been swept into piles and left in corners. A little chill passed through her. She turned to the pile in the corner and bent over, moving bits of wood and charred pieces of cloth. Then she spied a scorched wooden frame and she picked up, turning it slowly in her hands. It was the frame that had once held the miniature portrait of her mother. But the painting had not been burned, its tiny canvas cut from the frame.

A frown covered Glynis's face and then another chill passed over her. Someone had been there. They had carefully swept the rubble and gone through it. Someone had been there—but who?

"Glynis!"

Ramsey called out and instinctively she hid the frame, shoving it back into the pile.

"I'm in here."

Ramsey came in and looked around. His face was set in a deep, angry scowl. "I was tricked," he muttered.

Glynis ignored him. Cluny had to be restored. She didn't give a damn about Ramsey and his claim to own it. She cared only that it was her home, her family's home, and somehow she would find a way to make it the home of her unborn child. She turned on him in a fury. "Tricked? Go to hell, you traitor!"

The late afternoon sun poured in through the window of the spacious music room. Margaret Campbell, her blond hair loosely tied back with a ribbon, held her violin while her cousin Tilly accompanied her on the harpsichord.

It was an easy piece and Margaret knew it by heart. Her eyes strayed around the room, and it occurred to her that it was the first time she had been in this room when the sun was bright. At night the music room was a magical place. But now she noted that the rug was faded and worn and the paint on the walls was cracking ever so slightly.

In the opposite corner of the room, her father lay on a chaise longue, *The Daily Advertiser* in front of his face. It was his custom to come to the music room at two every afternoon and read his newspaper while she and Tilly played. He said he found it relaxing, and Margaret was sure he was right. More often than not, she found him sound asleep behind the paper, his mouth open while his snores added a certain cadence to whatever piece was being played.

But her father was not asleep today; in fact, he seemed unusually engrossed in the news, more engrossed than he had been since they left Edinburgh for London.

The piece came to an end and Margaret let her violin drop to her side. The silence caused her father to peek out from behind the paper. "Done already?"

Margaret laid her violin down and walked across the room. "You seem very interested in what you're reading," she observed.

"It seems that some of the Jacobites who escaped have been rounded up right here in London."

The very mention of the Jacobites caused her to feel uneasy. And her father's pleasure at news of the arrests was yet another reminder or how unlike her bellicose family she was. The Rising had been a nightmare, and now Scotland was a nightmare. She wished it would all go away, that everyone would forget it happened, that the persecutions would stop and everything would return to normal.

But she reminded herself of the reason they were in London. Her father was to be presented at court and given an award by the king for his part in the Battle of Culloden.

How she wished that were over too! How she hated it all! Her clan had chosen to support King George, but they had suffered hideous losses and the other clans had suffered even more. It was too terrible to think about. She could not condemn her father or any of her relatives, but in her heart she could not blame those who had taken part in the Rising either. To her, fighting did not seem a thing for which one should get an award. But then, she knew she was inconsistent too. She was still proud of her father; he was the master of the family.

"Does the arrest of the Jacobites trouble you?" her father asked.

She hardly knew how to answer. She shrugged. "I wish the persecutions to be over."

"They serve little purpose," her father agreed.

She was surprised by his mild tone. She had thought he would be angry.

"Who was arrested?" Margaret asked.

"There's a list here." Her father ran his finger down the page. "Oh, my," he said after a moment.

Margaret saw the flash of recognition in her father's eyes, and she all but took the paper away from him. "Who?" she persisted.

"Robert Forbes. The young man who used to court you."

"Please tell me they won't hang him."

Her father set the paper down and looked up into her eyes. "Do you still love him?"

Tilly, who had been at the harpsichord, sensed the coming of a personal conversation and hastily left the room.

Margaret ran her hands nervously over her blue taffeta dress. "No, but it pains me to think of him in jail."

Her father nodded. His daughter was a beautiful woman. She wasn't crying, and she had been able to look into his eyes. He knew she was telling the truth, and it was a good thing too. She was to marry a man he had picked himself, a loyalist and a hero. Still, he remembered Robert Forbes with some fondness. He was an honorable man, and he supposed he had done what he saw fit.

"Papa—" Margaret looked imploringly at him.

"You don't have to ask me. I'll speak with the powers that be tomorrow. Perhaps I can arrange to have him released."

"Papa, I really don't love Robert, but I would like to see

him, to speak to him myself." Even as she said it, she was not sure it was true. She had suppressed all thoughts of Robert for a long while, but deep inside she had a residue of feeling for him—for the way she had felt when he kissed her, for the way he held her when they danced.

"How do I know he doesn't still love you?"

Margaret smiled. "Dear Father, I don't think he ever really did love me. I suspected it long ago, and I'm sure of it now."

"I can't imagine him not loving you."

"That is because you're my father." She kissed him on the cheek. "Please do go tomorrow."

Her father nodded. "And I will see if I can arrange to have you see him."

"Thank you," she said.

James poured two glasses of wine and sat down at the table opposite Aimée. She looked content, but he knew it took little to arouse the fire within her. They had lived together for a few weeks now, yet their passion for each other had not eased off.

"How long will we stay in France?" Aimée asked.

"Not long. I will try to help recapture Ross. And then, if you're still willing, I'll have to make arrangements for you to accompany me to Scotland."

"I'm quite willing, more than willing." She reached across the table and covered his hand with hers.

"Aimée, Scotland is not Paris. I don't know how to prepare you for Highland life, especially now."

"I did not always live at court."

"I'm afraid you will miss the splendor and elegance, the creature comforts."

"Such things can grow boring. I think I would miss nothing as much as you."

A sudden noise was followed by the even larger noise—
Aimée slumped across the table and all James saw for a
single instant was the expression of surprise on her beautiful face, then the frozen beauty of sudden death. His movement was automatic as he dove under the table. A shot
from the assassin's second pistol reverberated through the
small room, and he saw the feet of a man as he stepped
to one side of the entrance to the room. James rolled, his
movements erratic. The assassin had time to reload. A third
shot missed and James was behind the wall. He clutched
his own pistol and thanked heaven he had not taken it
off.

"Come out and show yourself!" he shouted. "You're a
coward!" No one had to tell James who it was.

"You may live and I may die. Or perhaps it will be the
other way around," Ross said from the other side of the
wall. "But no matter, you will have no happiness. She's
dead. Such a touching moment!"

James swore loudly, and he felt a tremor of deep anger
sweep through him, a hatred he felt not even in the heat
of battle. The expression on Aimée's face was frozen before
his eyes—one minute the living, breathing expression of
love, the next she was taken by the angel of death, the
victim of a madman, a spy, a traitor.

Should he burst through the door and confront the
monster who had, in one split second, deprived him of
the only woman he had ever truly loved? Or should he
stand there, against the wall, waiting for Ross to take that
step?

He gripped his pistol and listened. They were surely
back to back, a wall separating them. The balcony door
was open on Ross's side of the wall. But it was three floors
to the street below.

Ross could not escape that way. If he ran for the door,
James knew he would hear him.

A noise came from the opposite direction. Aimée, who had slumped sideways, fell onto the floor, tumbling from the straight-backed chair in which she had been sitting when Ross's bullet had struck.

The noise was enough. It spooked Ross, who bolted for the front door, turned swiftly, and took one step through the entrance. He fired at Ross's back just as Ross was about to fling the door open.

Ross crumpled and fell in front of the door, his hand already on the latch.

James let his pistol drop to his side as he carefully approached the body. He kicked Ross over with the tip of his boot and stared into the face of the would-be assassin. "Burn in hell," he muttered as he looked at Ross's twisted expression.

He walked slowly back to the dining room where Aimée lay crumpled on the floor.

Tears suddenly filled his eyes. In death she had saved his life when she had fallen from the chair, causing Ross to try to run.

He bent down and sat on the floor, cradling her in his arms and rocking her back and forth. "I love you," he said aloud. His words hung in the still air. He felt alone, more alone than he had ever felt in his entire life.

"You're leaving," the guard said as he escorted Robert to the gate of Newgate Prison.

"Leaving?" Robert was stunned. He had not yet been tried, he was given no clothes, he was simply taken from the cell he shared with the others and marched across the courtyard to the main gate. "I don't understand."

"Few get out of here, and thems that do don't ask stupid questions," the guard muttered as he shoved Robert through the gate and out onto the road.

"Robert!" The voice that called to him was clear and sweet, but it wasn't Glynis's voice. He felt a stabbing pain, a desire for her even as he saw Margaret Campbell standing by a carriage. She wore a plain blue frock and a large bonnet to shield her face from the sun.

"Margaret," he said, looking at her. She was fresh and clean and seemed somehow unreal in this setting.

"Please, get in the carriage, Robert."

"You'll never get the smell out."

"I don't care. It's not really my carriage anyway. I've brought you some clean clothes and some money. I've even rented you a room for two weeks."

"I hardly know what to say. Do I owe my freedom to you?"

"To my father. Please, let's be off. This neighborhood is fearful."

"Could we stop at a public bath on the way to this room?"

She smiled. "Of course."

He climbed into the carriage after her and listened as she gave the driver directions. "I can hardly believe your father is responsible for my unexpected release."

"He saw your name in the paper. He said he always liked you. You've a full pardon."

Robert laughed. "How ironic, and how very British. A full pardon? I've not been convicted of anything."

"Please, just accept it for what it's worth."

He looked at her steadily. "Dear heaven, I know what it's worth."

"My father has considerable influence now."

"That seems quite obvious. Tell him I thank him."

"I will. I'm getting married next week," she said, touching his arm.

"I'm glad for you, Margaret. I hope you love him."

"It's a made marriage, you know that. But I can learn to love him. He's a good man."

Listening to her brought another stab of pain. She accepted it all so readily—not like Glynis. Glynis would never accept Ramsey. He and Glynis truly loved each other, and he knew now they always had. Youth and stupidity had kept them apart, but they'd always been fated for each other. He couldn't tell Margaret how he felt, but even as he sat in this carriage with her he knew that he would move heaven and earth to get Glynis back.

"You and Glynis found each other, didn't you?" Margaret said suddenly.

Robert nodded. "I was a fool not to know it sooner."

Margaret smiled. "I knew it."

"I'm sorry."

"Don't be. I'm not, not really. It's all worked out, Robert. You'll find her and be together with her again. I know you will."

The carriage came to a halt in front of the baths. "I'll come back in a few minutes."

Margaret shook her head. "Your room is not far from here. I've written the address down. The clothes and the money are in this satchel. We should say good-bye now, Robert."

She kissed her two fingers and touched his cheek gently. "Go and find Glynis," she whispered. "Go and be happy."

Chapter Fifteen

June 1747

For more than a week the fog engulfed Cluny. It hung low to the ground, and over the lake it floated like the ghosts of the past.

Ramsey ignored the upper floors of the castle, but he cleaned two small rooms on the main floor and insisted they would live there till more repairs could be made.

Glynis slept on a bedroll in one corner, he took the other. She lay awake at night till she heard him snoring. She could only be grateful that he left her alone. Not that he didn't threaten her daily. Each day it was the same. "I don't want you now. You're fat and full of child. But after the child is born, then I will make you my wife, Glynis. My real wife."

She did not bother to reply. If he forced himself on her, she had vowed she would kill him. If he left her alone, she would take the baby and run away—where she was not sure, how she would survive she was not certain, but she had no intention of allowing him to take her child from her.

Glynis rubbed her eyes. In the late afternoon she was always tired, and she assumed it was merely a symptom of her condition.

But there was no time to rest. Even if they did so for far different reasons, Glynis wanted to rebuild Cluny. In any case, the stores of food that had once existed were now gone. Survival depended on hard work. Every day since they had arrived, Glynis worked in the garden that had once been the cook's domain. She found onions growing beneath the earth, and she dug them up and then reworked the earth. She planted cabbages in the hope that they would grow. If so, she could keep them by leaving them in the ground for the snows of winter to cover and preserve. Then she would peel off the frozen outside leaves and utilize the rest of the cabbage in a soup.

Glynis stood up and wiped her hands on her apron. It was nearly four o'clock, and as usual she felt tired. But she did not go to her bedroll. Instead, she climbed the back staircase to the second floor, where she again sought her father's study. Each day she went there and sat on the floor in the silence, her eyes glued on the pile of debris in the corner. She had brought some pillows to sit on. There, in that room, she felt closer to her father, her family, and all of her past memories. It was not a room Ramsey came to—it was uncontaminated by visits from him.

Glynis opened the door and stepped into the partially lit room. She stopped short as she heard a creaking sound like footsteps on dry wood.

Puzzled, Glynis looked about her. "Hello?" she said not too loudly. But no one answered and the room remained in shadowy silence. Her eyes adjusted to the light and she made a small noise of surprise. The debris had disappeared! The room was swept clean.

Glynis lifted her hand to her mouth. What did this mean? Who had been in there?

She turned suddenly and closed the door. Then she ran downstairs to find Ramsey. He was talking to a young woman who stood on the threshold of the front entrance.

Ramsey turned around. "Ah, Glynis. This is Guenna. She'll be working here."

Guenna was a small but well-built girl of no more than seventeen. She had clear skin, brown hair, and large doe-like eyes. Her breasts were full and overflowing her simple dress. Ramsey was leering at her, his intentions quite clear.

"This is my wife," he told the girl. No one could have missed the sarcasm in his voice. Glynis wondered if Guenna knew what she was getting into. Glynis gave Ramsey no satisfaction and simply murmured, "Hello."

"I should like it if you would sleep upstairs from now on," Ramsey said coldly.

Glynis nodded. "Did you clean out my father's study for me?"

"Of course not, if you want it clean, do it yourself."

He hadn't really understood her. He had thought her question was a request. But his answer was quite clear. He hadn't been the one who had removed the debris.

"I'll take my things upstairs now," Glynis said softly.

Ramsey did not bother to reply. He took Guenna's arm and guided her away, his eyes glued on her breasts. Ramsey would soon sleep with Guenna, if in fact he had not already.

While James waited in the small room in the offices used by the prison officials, he paced restlessly. Ross was dead, and if he could have, James knew he would have killed him ten times over for shooting Aimée.

But Aimée was gone and so was Ross. Laurie, whatever she was, or had been, was not a murderer. The thought of Laurie suffering in prison bothered him, even though he knew she was far from innocent.

The door opened and a large prison matron with greasy hair pushed Laurie inside. James pursed his lips, trying to hide his surprise. Her appearance was shocking. Her long, red hair was a tangled mass, and her white skin was caked with dirt. Her dress was badly torn, and there were scratch marks on her face and shoulders. She grasped the edge of the table around which he had been pacing and held on to it tightly. Her brown eyes were huge and haunted looking.

"Laurie." He said her name sharply, and she turned to him as if she honestly had not seen him before, as if the sound of her own name had brought her back into the world.

"James MacPherson." She stumbled over the words. "Please help me!" Tears welled in her eyes and ran down her face, creating rivers in the dirt that covered her face. She fell in front of him, grasping his ankles.

"You were part of a plot to assassinate the prince."

"I didn't do anything. I just listened and told Ross . . ."

"You betrayed us—you passed information to the British before the battle. You betrayed my brother."

She blinked up at him. "I went to the duke, I had Colin's sentence commuted. I tried to see him before he was sent to London, but he wouldn't talk to me."

James frowned at her. Colin's sentence had been commuted and he had heard he was in prison in London. She was probably telling the truth. She had a conscience of sorts; clearly she had been unable to live with the idea of Colin being hanged.

"Colin was not the only one you betrayed."

"He was the only one I could help!" She was sobbing

and she tried to wipe her face with her skirt. She looked like a scared cinder girl as she crouched in front of him, begging and imploring.

Laurie was truly pitiful. "Why did you do it?" he asked.

"Ross. I love him so. I would do anything for him, anything."

James paused. He had to tell her. And even though she was who she was, he had no desire to cause her the kind of pain he himself felt.

"What is it? Something has happened to him. Tell me!" Her voice was filled with sheer panic.

"He's dead," James said without embellishment.

She whimpered and hugged herself even as her sobs overcame her.

"He killed Aimée; he killed the woman I loved."

She looked up at him as if trying to understand his words. "I don't understand. He was in prison."

James shook his head. "He broke free. He tried to kill me, but he shot Aimée instead."

Her sobs continued unabated. "I'm so sorry," she whimpered.

"It won't bring her back."

Laurie sniffed. "They'll hang me. I'm so frightened. I don't want to die," she whispered. "I can't stand it here though. If I'm to stay here, I'd just as soon die."

"You look terrible. What's happened to you?"

"The women down there are animals. They fight over food, they tore my dress, they—"

He waved his hand in a motion that bade her to stop. It was quite obvious that her ordeal among hardened criminals had a profound effect on her.

"Did you love Ross before you met Colin?"

She nodded, then added, "Colin was always good to me."

"You chose the wrong man to love."

"I know—he wasn't even always nice to me."

James did not comment. He well knew there were women who let men treat them badly, who even liked it and were excited by it. Laurie was clearly one of those women. Ross had enslaved her with desire. She was nothing more than his puppet; she was a child.

"I'll get you out of here," he promised. "But you in turn must promise to stay in France."

"What will I do? How will I support myself?"

"As a nanny. I'll find a position for you. It's not the worst life."

Laurie nodded. "Thank you."

James turned to leave, and as he did so, she grasped his knees. "Please don't be long, please get me out as soon as possible."

"Today," he said, taking her hand and pulling her to her feet. It was, he decided, the right thing to do. He believed she had tried to help Colin. He felt he had to do the same for her in spite of everything.

Glynis's clear green eyes compelled him to her side. She was before the fire, her hair tied primly back, her shawl covering her shoulders.

Robert traced her full, moist lips with his finger and then bent and kissed her on the mouth, which opened to him even as his hands toyed with her earlobes. His face dropped and he kissed her long neck, her ears, then her lips once more.

He reached back and pulled the ribbon from her hair, loosening it over her shoulders as he pushed her shawl away. Dark hair on white shoulders, lips puckered, inviting eyes. Glynis was innocence and passion, she was fire in his arms.

He kissed her swelling breasts—first one and then the

other. He pushed away the fabric of her dress to reveal her perfection. He nursed on one breast and toyed with the other. She moaned and twisted in his arms and they were lying down, both naked, both enflamed.

"Glynis, Glynis!" Her name was on his lips and he opened his eyes to find himself alone in the small room Margaret had rented for him. He was wet with perspiration and his mouth was dry. He was ready for lovemaking and yet alone, still clinging to the reality of his dream, which was fading all too rapidly.

He turned over on his back and stared at the ceiling in the early morning light. "I have to get out of London," he said aloud. "I have to find her as soon as possible." But first, he knew full well, he had to get Colin. They would leave together. They would go home to find Glynis.

For a brief moment he thought of Margaret. He owed her a great deal. He thought of the note on the dresser. She had asked to meet him tomorrow in St. James's Park. He was going to the rendezvous, but he wondered what she wanted. When they had last spoken, he had gotten the idea it was for the only time. He felt puzzled. Still, he knew he would go to meet with her.

Robert cast Margaret from his thoughts and again tossed on his stomach. He closed his eyes to seek sleep, to recapture his dream, to hold Glynis even if it was only in his sleep.

"Be safe," he whispered to her image. "Please, be safe."

"Now you look rather more like the Robert Forbes I remember," Margaret said as she opened her cape slightly. It was warmer than it usually was this time of year, but in fact the June weather was highly unpredictable.

The pathways of St. James's Park meandered under gracious trees and around flower beds. They neared the lake in the middle of the park, and Margaret sat on a bench. Robert sat beside her.

"The most exotic waterfowl frequent this lake," Margaret said. "See, look, there are some pelicans."

Robert looked at the ungainly birds. "And more ducks than one could hope to see in a lifetime."

"I suppose you wonder why I asked you to meet me," she said, turning to him.

"I'm quite sure it was not to discuss waterfowl, however exotic and impressive."

She bit her lip. "I rather hoped when I sent you the message it would be undeliverable—that you would be gone."

"Did you want me gone?"

To his surprise, she nodded. Then she looked up into his face. "Robert, disturbing news has just reached me— well, no, I shouldn't say 'reached me.' It is information I admit I solicited."

"What information might that be?"

"I've learned that Colin MacPherson was in jail with you."

"Is that unusual? There are hundreds of Scots in Newgate. Not a few have been hanged in Kennington Common."

"The hangings have stopped."

"I'm suitably grateful and so is my neck," he said a bit sarcastically.

"I don't blame you for being bitter."

He looked down. "I'm sorry, Margaret. I certainly have no cause to blame you or to be caustic with you."

"I know you don't mean to be bitter, I know how deeply you felt, how you must feel now."

He just nodded and looked into her face. She was empathetic as well as kind.

"Robert, you must leave London. You must go home.

You have a pardon, you can return to Scotland and find Glynis."

"I intend doing just that."

"I know you well. I know you want to get Colin out of jail too. Robert, I beg you, don't do anything foolish. Don't do anything that will cause them to take your pardon away and send you back to prison."

"That's what this is about."

"When I found out Colin was with you, I knew what you were thinking."

"You're too perceptive."

"Please give this up. Colin is in no danger. He's only to be deported."

"The ships used for deportation are hellholes, Margaret. More than half the deportees die before they reach the colonies. I can't leave him there. I hate leaving any of them there."

"I can't help you get him out. I would if I could. Robert, it's too dangerous, much too dangerous for you to try to—to facilitate a prison break."

"You seem quite convinced that I will not succeed."

"I hardly see how you could."

"And will you turn me in—will you alert the authorities because you believe I will try to get Colin out?"

"No. But if you're caught, I won't be able to help you." Robert turned and took her hands in his. "You've done more than anyone else could or would do under the circumstances, Margaret."

"I've done nothing but give you a chance—I just don't want you to lose it."

"I understand." He stood up and held out his hand to her. "When will you be married? The man is very fortunate to be marrying you."

"In a week's time. We'll go to the seaside, and then eventually back to Edinburgh."

Robert took in the information. "Well then, since you have been in London longer than I, why don't you tell me about this charming park."

"You have given me no comfort at all. I was hoping you would promise to leave and not to try to get Colin out of jail."

Robert looked into her cornflower-blue eyes. "I try never to make promises I may not be able to keep."

She shook her head. "Very well. You are far too stubborn a man for me to reason with. Come along, I'll show you the park."

He walked with her for a while. "This park would not be here were it not for Henry the VIII."

Robert laughed spontaneously at the irony of her comment. "Margaret, neither would we. It was Henry who brought Protestantism to England, and his daughter who beheaded our Mary Queen of Scots!"

Margaret looked back at him. "I hadn't thought of that," she said in a near whisper.

July's sun bore down on her garden. It was too short a growing season, Glynis lamented. Still, the turnips had miraculously grown on their own through the months of neglect before her return.

She finished thinning the carrots, hoping that there would be a large crop of small ones, and that not too many would be misshapen and entangled. The vegetable that had grown the best were the potatoes. No one had dug up the previous crop, and so they had branched out, multiplying tenfold. Together, these three things would be good in soup. With luck, she would be able to shoot a deer, and if not, she could only hope there was sufficient small game to support them through the coming winter. She shook her head to dispel thoughts of winter. It was midsummer,

and she knew she was only thinking ahead because someone had to, and Ramsey didn't seem at all concerned.

She glanced toward the house. Ramsey was no doubt
occupied with Guenna. Glynis felt a wave of sympathy for
the girl, who was not among the brightest of women but
who seemed to have a good heart and who, it could not
be denied, worked hard.

If only one could say the same for Ramsey. At first he had
been angry to discover his "domain" had been reduced to
a burned-out castle and acres of land occupied by hungry
peasants.

Only a few of the sheep survived the British slaughter,
and it would take time for the herds to be rebuilt. The
chickens had all been killed long ago, but much to Glynis's
joy, the cow had survived. Still, everything was in disrepair.
Those who had worked in the castle and on the surrounding land had left and gone back to eke out a living
farther away.

Ramsey could have worked, as she and Guenna did, but
he did not, Glynis thought angrily. He could have repaired
the barn, built some crude furniture, even helped in the
garden. But he chose to do none of these things. Instead,
he spent his days drinking and his nights with Guenna.
He declared himself the lord of the manor, and as if he
had taken leave of his senses and not noticed that the
manor was in utter disrepair and decay, he sat most of the
day in one of the few chairs remaining, and issued orders
neither of them followed.

But he stayed away from her—because he knew she
always had her pistol at the ready, she thought with satisfaction. But in her heart she knew that was not the only
reason. He was waiting. When she had the child, he would
come for her. He threatened her on a regular basis, and
yet she could not bring herself to kill him then. She wasn't
even sure she could kill him if he tried to attack her. She

could fight him, but she knew more now than she had known a few years earlier. She knew now that the taking of another life was a powerful experience and that even in self-defense, as had been the case on the battlefield, it was an act that diminished the killer. Then, too, she knew that the baby within her had given her a new reverence for life.

Glynis was deep in thought when Guenna's scream shattered the quiet of the afternoon. She jumped to her feet, her fingers closing around the pistol in her apron pocket as she ran toward the back entrance of the castle.

Guenna burst out the door as if chased by the devil himself. Her brown hair blew in the wind and her eyes were large with fear. "It's haunted!" she shrieked, virtually throwing herself into Glynis's arms.

"Haunted? What are you talking about?" Glynis asked, trying not to sound too harsh. Guenna was shaking, and the color had completely drained from her face.

"It's haunted! The castle is haunted! I've heard it before, but I've never seen it."

Glynis frowned at her. "Heard what, seen what?"

"The ghost, the ghost! I hear it all the time, but today I saw it!"

"Where did you see it?"

"Upstairs—I went to sweep out the room where you sleep."

Glynis wrapped Guenna in a hug. "Come, you show me."

Guenna cringed and wouldn't move. She was rooted to the spot where she stood.

They had an odd relationship, Glynis thought. Ramsey had expected her to be jealous—though she did not know just why he had assumed this. He seemed stunned that they liked each other, that they worked together and even sometimes talked pleasantly to pass the time of day.

Guenna just took for granted that he had taken her for his mistress while his wife was pregnant. Glynis had not bothered to correct her impression because, for the time being, it did not matter what she thought, and she was grateful for Guenna's help, grateful that Guenna satisfied Ramsey's needs so that he left her alone. They had come to naturally divide the work. Guenna tended the cow, cleaned the rooms they used, and carried water. For her part, Glynis did the gardening, cooked, and sewed.

"I'm sure you imagined it. Come along, I'll go with you."

Guenna shook her head vigorously. "I saw it! I saw it! I really did."

"Tell me what you saw exactly."

"It was tall and thin, very thin. A man, I think. It had long, long, white hair and eyes—oh, the eyes were horrible!"

"And you saw this in the room where I sleep?"

"Yes, you must not sleep there anymore. I'm sure it's dangerous. It walked right through the wall."

"Well, if it was a ghost, I suppose it could do that," Glynis said, still trying to suppress a smile. No wonder the English called the Highlanders "Irish." They shared a similar lore—a thousand stories of little people, fairies, and ghosts.

"I know you don't believe me."

"Please, come with me. Show me, perhaps we can find something."

Guenna bit her lip, then she nodded and reluctantly allowed Glynis to lead her by the arm up to the room that had once been her father's study.

Glynis walked into the room while Guenna clung to the doorway.

"There! There! Look!"

Guenna pointed to the stone floor. Again her eyes were filled with terror.

Glynis looked down. Across the floor, on the smooth stone, there were partial footprints—gray-white footprints. She stared at them in disbelief. They ended right at the wall.

"I hear it at night. I hear it dragging its chains on the stones! It's a ghost, believe me. It lives in the walls and it's very angry."

"I've lived here all my life," Glynis said. "I've never heard or seen any ghosts, nor did anyone else."

"Then it must be among the recently departed," she whispered as once again she crossed herself. Again her naturally large eyes seemed even larger, and Glynis could see that her fear was quite real.

"Have you ever seen it downstairs?"

"No, but I've heard it—as I said, at night."

Again Glynis bent over, and this time she wiped the mysterious footprint with her finger. Then she lifted her finger and tasted it. It tasted for all the world like flour.

"That's its essence," Guenna said. "You have to be very careful of it. It might enchant you."

Glynis did not say that it was not essence of ghost, but, rather, flour. She could not, in any case, have convinced Guenna of that fact.

"Shall I go tell the laird?"

The laird? Was that what Ramsey made her call him? He was completely mad!

"I wouldn't," Glynis said calmly. "He might be angry and we wouldn't want to make him angry."

"Oh, no. I don't want that."

"Guenna, don't worry. If it is a ghost, it has no reason to dislike you."

Guenna nodded, but her expression showed she was still ill at ease.

"Just don't come up here anymore," Glynis reiterated.

"But you sleep here. What will you do?"

"I suppose if I see it, I shall try to engage it in conversation."

"You're so brave."

"I'm not, really," Glynis said. She almost smiled as it occurred to her that a ghost might be better company than Ramsey, or even poor Guenna.

"You're good to me. Not everyone would be under the circumstances of my being here and all."

"I'm glad you're here. It's all right. I'm afraid the truth is, I don't much care what Ramsey does or does not do."

Guenna nodded again, and Glynis could see the relief in her eyes. She was still afraid of the ghost, but she was not afraid of her. "Let's go have some tea," Glynis suggested. By this time, she well knew that Ramsey would be asleep. He always slept after lunch, and usually for several hours till he woke up and began again to drink.

"We'll talk," Glynis said, guiding Guenna away from the flour footprints and thinking that when she was alone, she would have to investigate this matter further.

"Get out of here, you filth! Don't be skulking around, ya hear?" The rotund man that shooed him away was short of leg and loud of voice, Robert thought with amusement. But who could help yelling, he *was* skulking. As for being called filth, well, that was part of his disguise. He was dressed in rags and sat on a flat wagon without sides, which he propelled with one leg, stretching the other out on the wagon so it would appear he was an invalid. It was an appropriate ruse. Everyone noticed him, yet no one really saw him. If asked, they would all simply say there was no one there, just an invalid.

Laboriously, Robert scooted his way down the uneven,

cobbled road. Behind him, the great iron gates of Newgate stood, dwarfing the heavily armed guards who watched them.

Each day for a week Robert had come to the gates. He had stationed his wagon as close as he dared, and there he begged for money from all those who passed. Those who entered the prison were primarily policemen, solicitors, or judges. But there were others, and it was the others that Robert watched with the most intense interest.

The delivery wagon he had noted the very first day he had been thrust into the cell with Colin appeared three times a week. It came more or less at the same time each day, and was admitted without question. Its goods were unloaded through its back doors and consisted mostly of food for the administrators and prison guards.

It interested Robert now, as it had when he first saw it. He deemed it to be the best way in—and possibly out, of the prison. First, its design was perfect. The driver's bench was up front, the cargo was taken out the back. The wagon had high wooden sides and a top. It was rather like a small house on wheels, and a man could easily hide behind the boxes that filled the back.

The prisoners were walked in the prison yard at the same time every day. The trick, Robert thought, was to have the wagon arrive a bit off schedule, at the same time as the prisoners were in the yard exercising. Thus, the first problem was for him to have control of the wagon for several hours. The second problem was to create a distraction once inside the prison yard, enough of a distraction that Colin and Carrick could seize the opportunity and hop into the back of the wagon and hide.

Today he had watched again just to make certain he understood the routine that was followed. Twice the drivers had been different; this clearly meant that the prison guards were not expecting any one driver.

Tomorrow, he thought as he took refuge behind an old stone building, he would have to follow the wagon and see where it came from. He dusted himself off, and now, pulling his cart, rejoined the pedestrians on the street. He hoped he could finish off his reconnaissance and act in the next few days. The danger of Colin being moved or sent back to a ship in order to sail to the colonies was ever present.

Ramsey looked at Guenna lustfully as he sipped his Scotch by the light of the fire. He put the glass down and motioned her to come to him.

"Don't be reluctant," he slurred. "You should know what an honor it is to sleep with the laird, to be my chosen mistress."

Guenna said nothing. His breath smelled of whisky and she turned her head slightly to one side.

"Turn around and give us a kiss!" He seized her chin and turned her face to his, pressing his lips on hers even as he pushed down the shoulders of her dress.

Guenna squirmed in his arms and he kissed the top of her breasts.

"Damn, you country girls have too many laces in your bodice," he muttered as he fumbled with her corset. She had such lovely plump breasts. He adored it when her nipples were just barely covered and he knew he had but to dip down into her dress to feel them. But tonight he decided he wanted her breasts entirely free.

"You're not wearing undergarments, are you?"

"You told me not to," Guenna answered. He was so unpredictable.

"That's right. I like to have you ready, so to speak."

He pulled down her dress. "Oh, I like that! Leave yourself that way!"

Her corset was loosened and her breasts hung over the top of it, but it was still laced tightly farther down and it pulled her waist in and made her buttocks seem even more rounded and more inviting.

"Like two delicious melons," he muttered as he reached out and caressed her backside. Then he slapped her playfully and she jumped slightly. "Bad little girl, you need a spanking."

But he did not spank her again. Instead, he pushed her down to the bed and flung himself across her. Taking a nipple in his mouth, he sucked hard on it till she tried to push him away.

"Be good!" he ordered, and fearfully, Guenna stopped struggling.

He pulled on her other nipple and went back to sucking it. Then, quite suddenly he let go of her. "What's that sound?"

He was straddling her, but now he sat upright.

"It's the ghost rattling his chains," Guenna said, her voice quivering.

Ramsey continued to listen, but the sound stopped. "Ghosts," he mumbled. "Ghosts."

He looked back at her and savagely began kissing her again while she thrashed about. Then, with all his strength, he turned her over and slapped her behind. She raised it obligingly, and he entered her from the rear even as he seized her breasts and held them tightly.

"One day I'll do this to Glynis," he muttered. "One day soon."

James MacPherson once again walked down the Hall of Mirrors at Versailles feeling small and dwarfed by its splendor.

Behind the great mirrors were the royal apartments, one

of which he had spent the night in with Aimée. As he passed the door he felt a stabbing pain of loss. It was, he acknowledged, a feeling with which he was becoming all too familiar.

He stood before the door that led into the private royal apartment of the king and wondered why he was there. A summons from the king was not that common, nor indeed was it to be ignored.

Even Prince Charles had to await a royal summons, and they were rare indeed.

James took a deep breath and entered the room when the door was opened. A silent servant bowed deeply, then backed out of the ornate room into which he was ushered.

The room, large and spacious, was filled with priceless art objects. Each piece of furniture was a masterpiece and distinct from any other in existence. The tables were all inlaid, the furniture covered with exquisite tapestry or unique needlepoint. He looked around at the elegance and felt as if his breath had been sucked away.

"You like my little hideaway?"

James fell into a deep bow as the king came in from another room of the royal apartment. He was dressed in a gold robe and wearing his tightly curled white wig.

"It is stunning," he replied.

"Being surrounded by beautiful things has a calming effect on the soul," the king said with a royal flutter of his bejeweled fingers. Versailles—Fontainebleau—Chambord—Francis the First built them all, but it is I who have properly furnished them. But, of course, I did not summon you simply to show off my art."

"I am honored to be received by his majesty."

"I am honored to have you. Even among your countrymen it is difficult to find a truly trustworthy man. I am told by Madame that you are most trustworthy, a man of great honor."

"She praises me too highly."

"I think not. She hardly ever praises too highly, though she can truly heap damnation on those whom she abhors."

"In that case, I am glad to be in her good books."

"You are, believe me. I want first to express my sorrow for your loss."

"She was a beautiful and intelligent woman, it is not my loss alone."

"Yes, you are quite right. To change the subject, I suppose you wonder why I have asked you to come, since I have already told you it was not to view my treasures."

"It is unusual, your majesty. A royal summons is not an everyday occurrence."

"I have a job for you. There is gold, quite a lot of gold, which is to be transported to Scotland. It is to pay back the chieftains who fought so bravely. A portion of it is for your own family, and I have set aside a special reward for you."

"You are most generous."

"I should like you to transport this gold and to be in charge of its distribution."

"It is an honor to be so trusted by your highness."

"You will sail when a ship is readied. You will have to leave Paris immediately. Do you have any difficulty with that schedule."

"Not at all, your highness. I am eager to get home."

"Excellent, excellent. You will find the money has already been loaded, except, of course, for the personal reward I mentioned."

The king walked across the room and opened an armoire. He returned and handed James a small but heavy bag.

"Thank you," James said with another deep bow.

"Be on your way, then. Safe journey."

James left the king's apartment and found a guard waiting to escort him first home, then to Dunkirk. Only in the privacy of his bedroom, while packing, did he open the bag. It contained many louis d'or coins and a handful of priceless gems. He closed his eyes for a moment and imagined Cluny. He knew full well that all of Scotland had been looted and burned. It would be a miracle if Cluny had escaped. The money and jewels he held would rebuild. He smiled to himself. This made going home much easier, even though he would make the journey alone, without his beloved Aimée.

Chapter Sixteen

Late July 1747

Robert, dressed as a gentleman of means, was wearing a fine suit, well-shined boots, and a proper powdered white wig. He drove a carriage that gave the impression of affluence. To all intents and purpose, he appeared to be a gentleman out for a morning ride or on his way to his business in that part of London known as the City.

The day was cloudy, and again it threatened to rain. It should have been fine weather, but storms that had plagued the Mediterranean for weeks continued to deposit rain on London and its environs.

Robert guided his carriage down Holborn Viaduct past the church of St. Sepulchre. It was one of the oldest churches in London, and each time a prisoner was sent from Newgate to Tyburn to be executed, its bells pealed out and those who knew the prisoner, or the faithful if he had no friends, brought a small bunch of flowers and left it at the door of the ancient church. In the past few months, owing to the many executions of Scots, the church entrance had seldom been without flowers.

Viaduct turned into Newgate, and the prison came into sight. But Robert drove past its iron gates and depressing stone walls. He turned up St. Martins le Grand and from there he pulled into a mews not far from Goldsmith's Hall.

Robert looked about warily and concluded that he had selected his position well. Each morning since he had been observing it, the wagon bearing supplies for the prison traveled down St. Martins le Grand, passing by this small mews. He brought the carriage to a halt by the side of the road and waited. The mews was not busy, and that pleased him all the more. He tethered the horses, and leaving the carriage just off the main road, in the mews, went back onto St. Martins le Grand.

He waited, praying he was on time, praying that all would go according to schedule. At last he saw the delivery wagon clattering down the street. Robert hurried to the middle of the road and flagged it down. It came to a halt, and the perplexed driver looked down on him.

"Come with me, young man, I require your assistance!" Robert ordered.

The wagon driver scowled and muttered, "I got business, I got deliveries," he answered.

"I'll make it worth your while. Just come along, I'm sure you know better than to argue with a gentleman!"

"But I got to go to the prison," the driver protested.

"I am a close friend of Lord Haggerty's, as well as of the prison warden. I shall explain your delay. Come along."

The driver shrugged and climbed down.

"This way," Robert motioned. He led the driver into the mews and stopped at the first door. It had clearly once been a shop, but now it was closed. Robert had rented it for one week, no questions asked.

"What's going on?" the driver protested. He turned back to look into Robert's face, but it was too late. Robert's fist met his jaw, and with one more blow the driver staggered to the dusty floor of the shop just inside the door. Robert quickly dragged him inside, closed the door, and pulled down the shade. There had been no one in the mews. He breathed a sigh of relief.

Quickly, he bound and gagged the man, then dragged him behind the unused counter.

Robert took a bundle from a chair by the door. He had put it there the day before. He unwrapped it, took out the clothing on top of the pile, and quickly changed from his gentleman's suit into the clothes he had left in the shop. When he was dressed, he hurried outside to the delivery wagon, which the driver had left just in front of the mews on St. Martins le Grand. Robert climbed up into the driver's seat and, whistling, drove off toward Newgate Prison. He checked his watch. He was right on time.

When the guard at the gate saw the approaching wagon, he called out, and the great gates of Newgate swung open. Robert drove inside. The prisoners were walking around. Colin and Carrick stood to one side. Robert smiled. He and Colin had talked about somehow using this delivery wagon as a way to escape. He hoped now that Colin remembered their conversation.

He brought the wagon to a halt and got out to open the back.

As two of the guards came around the back and began to unload the supplies, Robert eased his way around the wagon and, using it for cover from both the prisoners and the guards, quickly lit his fire caps from the embers of the pipe that was clenched between his teeth and rolled them across the ground. He hurriedly stepped back into the open. Robert saw Colin staring at him, and in that one split second of eye contact Colin seemed to know what had to be done.

As the guards, arms full, moved away from the wagon, the sharp sound of the firecrackers filled the courtyard, reverberating off the stone walls and causing the horses to whinny and rear up.

The guards ran for cover, and in the confusion Colin and Carrick sprinted for the wagon. They scrambled inside and hid as far back as possible. The guards were rounding up the prisoners now, and Robert soothed the horses and swore loudly.

A guard looked at him suspiciously.

"Who fired them shots?" Robert cried out. "I thought I was dead, that's what I thought!"

"Take your wagon and get out of here, we have to search all the prisoners now!"

The guard seemed angry. It was clear he hated trouble on his watch. Robert climbed into the driver's seat once again and headed out the prison gates. The guards had all been on the other side of the wagon with the majority of the prisoners, but if other prisoners had seen Carrick and Colin, they did not call out. If anyone had realized he had sent the firecrackers rolling across the yard, they did not alert the guards.

Robert drove slowly down the street till he turned the corner and he could no longer be seen from the prison. They would round up all the prisoners now. They would search them and count them. That would be when they'd discover that two were missing.

Robert spurred the horses on. He returned the way he had come and drew up near the mews. He opened the back of the wagon and Carrick and Colin hurried out. Robert slapped the lead horse and sent him on his way.

With luck, the wagon would continue on driverless, and no doubt back from whence it had come.

"This way," Robert motioned them. He let them into the empty shop and pointed behind the counter, to the bound and gagged driver. He mouthed directions. "Don't talk. He must not hear your voices or see you. There are clothes in those bundles."

They quickly changed, as did he. The driver, conscious but behind the counter, could not see them.

"Bring your prison clothes," Robert mouthed.

Hurriedly, and all three dressed as gentlemen, they left the shop in the mews and climbed into the carriage Robert had left parked on the street. In moments they trotted off.

"What will happen to the poor bastard whose wagon you took?" Colin asked.

"I put a note to the warden in one of the boxes that was unloaded. They should find him shortly."

"They'll be looking all over London for us," Colin said, shaking his head.

"Maybe not," Robert answered, a slight smirk covering his face. "I mentioned to the warden that it might be wise to keep this quiet. After all, it's not a good idea for people to know how simple it is to break out of Newgate. Besides, it would reflect badly on the poor fellow—not running a tight ship and all that."

The three of them laughed. "Are we going home?" Colin asked Robert.

Robert nodded. "We're going home to find Glynis."

"It's a long road," Colin said as he thought of the journey.

"And a dangerous one," Carrick added.

"We'll start tonight," Robert assured them. But already his mind was wandering. Glynis filled his every thought. The vision of her with Ramsey would spur him on. Still, there was no quick way to travel so far. It would take more than a month to get to Cluny. They could not travel by sea, and even by the quickest land route it was over six hundred miles.

Each day it grew warmer, but as welcome as the heat of the sun was after winter's dampness, it meant that water had to be brought to irrigate the garden. Glynis and Guenna carried buckets from the well and carefully drizzled the water over the rapidly growing vegetables.

It was near high noon and Glynis watched as Guenna used her final bucket of water. "We've both worked hard," Glynis said, wiping her brow. She felt bad that Guenna now had to do most of the lifting because she was seven months pregnant. "I think we deserve a dip in the lake."

They both knew that Ramsey was, by this time, drinking. He cared little about how either of them spent their days as long as his meals were brought on time and Guenna was available when he desired her.

"Do we dare?" Guenna asked.

Glynis smiled; Guenna liked to swim in the lake as much as she, although Guenna was reluctant when the water was cold. But now the lake had warmed up, and it was extremely pleasant.

"I think we dare. I'd race you to the lake, but in my present state I'm sure you would win."

"It's much too warm to run," Guenna replied as she stood up and brushed out her skirt.

Together, they began walking toward the lake. When they reached it, they stepped into a secluded clearing and shed their clothes, then they both hurried into the water to wash their hair, their bodies, and to swim and frolic. Rare were the days when it was possible to enjoy oneself so much.

"I've never known a person with child to go swimming," Guenna said.

Glynis laughed. "I'm sure it won't hurt."

Guenna washed her hair and herself. When she was finished, she began swimming parallel to the shore. She waved to Glynis, who was floating on the calm water, enjoying the sun.

Farther down the lake, Guenna pulled herself out of the lake and lay on a warm, flat rock. It was a wonderful feeling, the heat from the rock on one side of her body and the heat of the sun on the other.

She closed her eyes, and all the hard work of the morning overtook her at once. She felt herself drifting off to sleep.

The sound that caused her to open her eyes was a rustling in the brush. As it grew louder, she sat up and listened. Was it an animal?

She felt her heart pounding, and when the brush suddenly parted, her hands flew to cover her nakedness.

But she dropped them quickly to cross herself as she saw the apparition—its long white hair blowing in the breeze, its hollow eyes staring at her, its yellowed, paperlike skin glistening. The apparition held its arms out toward her, and Guenna screamed and slid off her rock. Splashing into the water, she swam away without even looking back. She screamed again, and it was Glynis for whom she screamed.

Down the beach, Glynis stopped floating and treaded water. The first scream was muffled, but the second she heard clear as a bell. She swam to Guenna, who was swimming toward her as if being chased by a monster.

They met halfway and swam to shallow water. "What is it?" Glynis said as she stood up.

"The ghost! I saw it by the shore. It came and stared at me! I know you think I'm just a foolish girl, but it is a ghost, the same one I saw in the castle."

Guenna was as pale as a ghost herself. He eyes were huge and, as before, her fright was obviously genuine.

"Let's get dressed and look for your ghost," Glynis suggested.

"It's horrible," Guenna shuddered. "It seemed to be beckoning me—it was horrible."

They went to the clearing and both dressed hurriedly.

"At least it didn't take our clothes," Glynis said.

"What would a ghost do with clothes? Please don't joke. When you've seen it, you'll understand."

Glynis said no more. She tied back her wet hair and pulled on her boots. Guenna had dressed rapidly, as if clothes made her feel more secure in the presence of an aberration.

"Let's go," Glynis said, leading the way down the path toward the place where Guenna had gone ashore to sun herself.

"I don't want to find it," Guenna moaned. "I don't ever want to see or hear it again."

"Well, I certainly want to find it," Glynis said with determination. "If I'm to live in a haunted castle, I certainly want to know who it is that's haunting me."

They walked on, and Guenna pulled on Glynis's skirt, and when Glynis turned around, Guenna had lifted her finger to her lips. Glynis stood stock-still.

Glynis heard a rustling and what sounded like footsteps on the dry lichen. She motioned Guenna to follow, and she herself plunged into the brush, parting it and moving forward with Guenna in her wake holding on to her skirt.

Suddenly they stepped from thick brush into a clearing, and it was then that Glynis caught a glimpse of something. She stopped short at the sight of the creature with long, white hair.

"Stop!" she shouted.

"You saw it! That's it! Let's run," Guenna begged.

But Glynis did not feel like running away. Instead, she pursued the creature out of the clearing and once again into the brush. But no matter where she looked, or how hard she listened, the noise of its footsteps was gone, and there were no tracks and no more noise. It was as if it had disappeared into thin air.

"It's gone," Guenna whispered. "See, it's disappeared into the air. Only a ghost could do that."

"I'm quite certain your ghost is mortal," Glynis said, trying to gain her own composure. But she hoped Guenna would not ask too many questions. She herself could not explain how it could have disappeared into thin air or walk through a wall. Still, she felt certain it was not an apparition.

"At least you believe I saw something," Guenna said with a bit of relief in her voice. "I was beginning to think I was going mad."

"You're not going mad."

"I've never heard of a ghost that comes out in daylight. Could it be something else? Should I carry a cross?"

Guenna was typical of many Highland women. She had heard tales of ghosts and such since childhood. She firmly believed in the supernatural and doubtless she felt guilty about her relationship with Ramsey. Perhaps she even thought the ghost had been sent to punish her. Superstition mixed easily with religion on both sides of the Irish Sea. Still, she had seen something. She just wasn't sure what. She certainly could not explain where it had gone, although she was sure it had gone somewhere.

"I don't think you need to carry a cross," Glynis said. "I'll find out what or who our ghost is, eventually."

And you'll be on your way to Scotland in ten days time. Was that what the over confident King Louis had told him? Or had he just said he would leave for Dunkirk in ten days time? James looked out the window at the sheets of wind and rain—a warm summer wind and an equally warm rain, but nonetheless, the weather had been terrible and he had been delayed for weeks as one storm after another battered the coast of France, making it impossible for him to sail.

It all brought back Robert's descriptions of the long wait the prince and his followers had before they could sail for Scotland. But that had been spring and now they were in the full blush of summer, and yet the weather was once again prohibitive.

James left the sight of the wind and rain as he walked away from the window and left the room above the tavern where he was staying.

He went down the winding wooden staircase and into the main room of the tavern. He supposed it was a tavern, at least in England that was what it would have been called, although this place did not look at all like an English tavern. Its walls were made of stone, it was slightly below street level, and it had a musty though not entirely unpleasant smell.

Behind a wooden bar were stacks of dusty wine bottles and beneath a cloth, wheels of a dozen or more kinds of cheese, many of which had rather distinct odors of their own. In a large bucket there were loaves and loaves of hard French bread.

There were seven people in this candlelit half cellar. They sat three at one table and four at another and drank wine while they ate bread and cheese. They talked to one another in rapid French, and by their gesticulating, he could only assume the subject was politics. Had he cared to, he could have sat close enough to eavesdrop, but he did not, so he chose a table in the farthest corner of the room. In a moment the proprietor, a round-faced bald man wearing an oilskin apron, came and asked him what he wanted. He ordered a bottle of burgundy, a loaf of bread, and some Brie.

Dunkirk was the most northerly town in all France, and from its port men had been sailing for centuries. France, James contemplated, was a strange country. The people of its coastal regions were adventurous and willing to go to strange lands to colonize. But the rest of the population could not be moved. To populate their colonies the French had to empty their prisons. But then, many Englishmen were deported to the colonies as well. Still, there were more, even many Scots and Irish, who ventured forth freely, eager to start a new life in a new land.

The proprietor brought him his wine, bread, and cheese and James, who had been lost in thought, looked up to see a hesitant young woman descending the stairs.

He was not the only one who looked up. The sight of an unescorted woman in such a place was something of a surprise.

She was dressed well and extremely modestly. Her bonnet cast a shadow over her face, but she had a good figure. She took a table not far from his. There were few, in any case, from which to choose.

When the proprietor came over, she ordered some bread and cheese in a hesitant French. He immediately recognized that she was, in fact, Scots.

James got up and left his table. Walking to hers, he bowed from the waist. "Please, allow me to introduce myself, madam," he said in Gaelic. "I am James MacPherson of Cluny, on my way home to Scotland and awaiting the sailing of *Le Bellona*. It is most unusual for a single young woman to be alone in such a place, may I invite you to join me?"

She looked up at him from beneath her bonnet with clear green eyes like those of his sister. But her hair was not dark like Glynis's hair; rather, it was a unique strawberry blond. In fact, her hair was virtually a mark of identification. In all of Scotland, those with strawberry-blond hair raced their ancestry to Clan Diarmid or one of its many septs.

"Thank you. That's very kind," she answered shyly. "I am Sorcha Diarmid."

James bowed again slightly and escorted her to his table several feet away. He pulled out the chair for her.

"Normally I would not speak with a strange man," she said quickly.

James smiled warmly. "Perhaps our circumstances allow us to break the normal rules of formality."

She nodded. "I broke them because you are one of my countrymen and because I, too, am to sail on *Le Bellona*."

"It is unusual to see a woman traveling alone."

"I have no choice," she replied. "And I came down here only because I am hungry."

The proprietor brought her food, and James, without asking, poured her a glass of wine. "Now that you are no longer unescorted, please have some wine."

"Thank you."

She sipped a little, but immediately tore off some bread, spread it with cheese, and began to eat. She did indeed seem hungry.

"May I ask how it is that you are alone?"

"My father and I have been living in Paris with the other exiles. My father died three weeks ago, so I have decided to return to Scotland to try to find my relatives. I have no one in France, and rumor has it the prince will soon return with his entourage and most of the other exiles to Italy. I don't even speak Italian."

She might not have spoken Italian, and her French was hesitant, but otherwise she seemed well educated and well spoken. She was, he noted, also very pretty.

"That's a bold and very brave decision," he said sincerely. "It's a dangerous trip for a man, but for a woman traveling alone, the dangers are multiplied tenfold."

"I have only begun to realize that. But what was I to do? It was just as dangerous for me to remain in France. I'm afraid I had no desire to become the mistress of some well-off Frenchman. No, I want to go home. I miss Scotland."

James nodded and looked into her eyes. "I must be honest with you. I am probably wanted in Scotland. I have been traveling with the prince for many months now and was with him when he escaped Culloden Moor. I have also just recently lost the woman I loved and am still in mourning for her. But if you are willing, you are welcome to travel with me. I shall do my best to protect you from the hazards of traveling alone, and if you were willing to pose as my wife, we might be considerably less suspicious than otherwise."

She looked at him steadily. If she was shocked by his proposal, she did not appear so. Rather, she seemed to be thinking of the advantages, which he knew could be many.

"What would you expect of me in private?" she asked.

"Absolutely nothing, save perhaps conversation and companionship that two people traveling together might in any case expect."

"I would not have to sleep with you?" she asked forthrightly. And then added, "I would not, in any case, but I want to set things straight before I except your offer—which certainly has merits."

James smiled. "Were I you, I would also want to know the rules. Let me assure you I will be a perfect gentleman. I regard this as a practical arrangement for both of us."

She smiled. "Then I accept your offer, James MacPherson of Cluny."

James sipped more wine. She was not only attractive but cheerful. He liked that and he felt his spirits rise. He was tired of being alone. At least they could play cards and talk. The sea voyage, if they ever sailed, was three to four weeks, and from there it was a long ride to Cluny.

"Are you staying in this inn?"

"I saw you last night, though you did not see me. I believe I am in the room across the hall."

"Do you perchance play chess?"

"I do, yes."

He grinned. "I'll see if I can borrow the board and pieces from the innkeeper. Could we play this evening?"

"I would like that," she replied.

"I look forward to it myself."

"Work, work, work," Ramsey said aloud as he sat in his chair and watched Guenna piling firewood near the hearth.

"It's summer now, but when the nights get cold you'll be glad it's here," she said, not looking at him. His laziness was intolerable, she thought. But, of course, it was not her place to comment. The only thing he had the slightest energy for was lovemaking, and the more he drank, the less frequent that became too. Although she was not complaining. In truth, she found him quite disgusting, and she did not now, nor had she ever enjoyed being with him. It was a matter of survival, a matter of having food to eat and a roof over her head.

Ramsey took a long swig of his whisky and then belched loudly. "How's your ghost, you stupid girl?"

Guenna turned and looked at him. He was always belittling her, telling her she was stupid and the like. "You're good for only one thing," he said again and again. But his wife was not like that. Glynis was kind and thoughtful. She worked as hard as if she were a servant, and when they talked, Glynis always treated her as an equal. In fact, Glynis had begun to teach her to read.

"I haven't seen the ghost lately," she answered without looking at him. Long before, she had discovered that prolonged eye contact caused him to become physical with her, as if he thought that when she looked at him, she desired him. Nothing could have been further from the truth.

"Maybe Glynis scared it away," he said drunkenly.

"I still hear it at night," Guenna said. "So does Mistress Glynis."

"I don't hear anything."

Guenna bit her tongue to keep from saying "You're usually so drunk, you wouldn't hear St. Peter calling."

Suddenly Ramsey pulled himself out of his chair and walked unsteadily toward the staircase. "I'm going to look for your ghost, girl. Perhaps I'll offer it some drink."

Guenna crossed herself. "It's not good to laugh at such," she whispered. "The dead can be powerful."

"Only if they're not buried. The stench can be powerful," Ramsey slurred.

As he went up the stairs, he seemed to sober slightly and Guenna watched him, wondering if he would, in fact, see the ghost. In her heart she hoped the spirit would remain unseen, but she thought, if anyone was going to encounter it, she hoped it would be Ramsey.

Ramsey rambled along the second floor corridor, carefully avoiding charred timbers. He poked his head into each of the empty rooms. When he came to Glynis's room he looked in there as well. But it was empty, and she was, as usual, in the garden or down by the lake. There was absolutely nothing in the room save her neatly made bed roll, her cloak, and her change of clothes. A brush and comb were set in front of a bit of broken mirror she had found amid the rubble.

He muttered under his breath and closed the door. He

looked at the staircase that led to the third floor and began to climb it. It was darker in the third floor corridor because the only window was at the far end and all the doors to the various rooms were closed. But he knew there was nothing in any of them, because when they had first come they had explored the entire burned-out shell of the castle.

"Ghost! Are you there, ghost?" he called out drunkenly. "Here, ghosty, here, ghosty . . . come to Ramsey."

Suddenly the light from the far window was blocked by a tall, gaunt apparition, its arms spread wide, its long, white hair flowing in the wind, its face obscured by cloth pulled around it. It let out a baleful wail, and Ramsey, his whole body shaking, shrieked and stumbled back down the staircase, cursing and shaking.

"It is a ghost! It is a ghost!" he screamed as he finally reached the first floor. Glynis had come inside on hearing the commotion, and Guenna stood pale-faced, looking at Ramsey, who immediately vomited even as he clutched the rail.

"It is a ghost!" he cried out.

Glynis stared at him without sympathy. "I don't hold with ghosts, but if a ghost it is, it is no doubt the ghost of my ancestor risen from the dead to let you know you do not own Cluny, Ramsey Monroe, and that you do not belong here." Her green eyes had narrowed.

"Get out of my sight, you pregnant bitch!" he shouted hysterically. "Leave me alone!"

Glynis still looked hard at him. She touched her stomach and glanced at Guenna. When the time came, it would be Guenna she had to count on. She knew full well that Ramsey would not even go to fetch the doctor for her. He was insane, but she did not underestimate him. He was dangerous too.

* * *

The August sun was hot when Colin, Carrick, and Robert reached Ayr. It was in Ayr that they decided to break up and travel separately so as not to be so obvious.

Robert decided to travel up the east coast of Scotland and up the great glen to Inverness and then west to Cluny. This route avoided most of the higher mountains, and was by far the fastest of the land routes.

It's a little out of my way, Robert thought as he approached the home of William MacInnes, the fisherman who had many months ago taken Carrick, Glynis, and him away from Ayr and farther south. He intended buying Sampson back. It would mean a lot to Glynis, as she had raised him from a foal.

If he closed his eyes, he could see her now astride Sampson. Her magnificent hair would be blowing in the wind and she would be sitting sure in the saddle. Suddenly, he saw her on the field of battle and remembered how stunned he was when she appeared and took the reins of his horse, leading him away, saving him from certain death.

The truth was, he could think of nothing but Glynis and the fact that she was pregnant with their child. The thought of her with Ramsey tormented him. And it tormented him more now than before since he knew she must be growing close to her time. He had counted it out over and over. There was no way around it, the child must be due in late August or early September. He could not know for sure, but he remembered when first her moods began to change. That, he now assumed, must have been in the first or second month of her pregnancy. What a fool he had been not to see it! But then, Mrs. Pinkney had assured him that men did not usually notice these things and that the only reason she knew was because she was a woman and, indeed, the mother of several children.

He recalled a conversation he had with Colin and Carrick before they separated.

"I can see you're thinking about your coming fatherhood," Carrick had said, winking.

"I think of nothing else," Robert admitted.

"What will you name it?" Colin asked.

Robert laughed. "If Glynis agrees, Debra if it is a girl and Stewart if it's a boy."

Colin smiled. "Debra was my mother's name."

"Yes, I know," Robert said thoughtfully, then he looked at Colin. "I pray it is not born till I reach her."

Colin nodded. He, too, was worried about Glynis. But he tried not to speak of it because his concern only caused Robert to suffer more.

"She's a strong woman," Carrick said by way of comforting them both.

Robert discarded his thoughts and looked into the distance. In a crude corral Sampson stood by the fence, looking out at them. He suddenly whinnied.

"It's almost as if he remembers me," Robert said to himself. He tried to imagine how Sampson would react to seeing Glynis again.

"The sea has been kind to us," James said as he leaned over the rail and watched the rolling swells.

"Perhaps because all the really bad weather delayed us for so long—I won't complain, I was so afraid I'd be ill."

Sorcha was wearing the same dark blue day dress as when he had met her nearly a month earlier. He now considered their meeting sheer providence. They had sailed the next week after repairs were made to the vessel, and from the day they left the weather had been excellent.

"I think you have the makings of a seaman," he said, stealing a sideways glance at her. Sorcha did not have the exotic appeal of Aimée, but she was, nonetheless, a beautiful woman of great intelligence and good humor. She did not deserve to be compared to anyone else, because she was quite unique.

At chess, she beat him as often as he beat her. At cards, it was the same. And she certainly had no difficulty holding her own in any conversation. Her laugh and sweet smile filled him with good humor.

"How much longer do you think we'll be at sea?" she asked.

"Another week," James answered. "Will you go directly home when we are set ashore?"

She turned and faced him. "I have no home left. I can go only to where it was."

James felt a sudden pang at the thought of not seeing her again, and indeed of not being with her day after day. In such circumstances people grew close quickly, and it was with surprise that he suddenly realized he had some feeling for her. Was he simply filling a void caused by Aimée's death? He wasn't sure, but of one thing he was certain. The two women were nothing alike save the fact that they were both beautiful and both bright.

"I shall miss you," she said, looking into his face. "I've enjoyed your company and we've become good friends."

It was impulse alone that caused him to put his hands on her slim shoulders and draw her into his arms. He bent and kissed her, and the passion of the kiss also surprised him, as did the warmth of her body, the movement of her lips, the honesty in her eyes.

He drew back and they looked at each other. "I'm sorry—we had a pact. I didn't mean to violate it."

She didn't move. She neither came closer nor pulled away. She only looked up at him, then softly she said, "Don't be. I wanted you to kiss me."

A chill ran through him. He drew her into his arms

gain, this time closer, and he held her tightly and then
issed her, this time for longer and with more passion.
Ier lips moved beneath his, and he was certain she felt
s he did. Had this angel been sent to help heal him?

"Come home with me," he said urgently. "Come home
ith me till we are both sure this is right. If it is, we shall
e married."

"Do you think it is right?"

"Yes, but perhaps we both need time."

"I think it is right too—James, we are fortunate to have
ound each other."

He ran his hands over her and was again surprised at
ne excitement she caused him to feel. He wanted to make
ove to her, to feel her beneath him, to hear her laughter—
es, he needed that. He needed laughter and hope and a
uture. Suddenly it seemed to him as if he would, in fact,
ave just that.

Chapter Seventeen

September 1747

Glynis sat up and stretched. It was hard to get up fro[m] the bedroll now, hard to struggle to her feet because he[r] time was close and she was heavy with child.

"So awkward," she murmured to herself. "I'm just s[o] absurd looking."

She struggled into her clothes, such as they were. Sh[e] had let out the two dresses she had brought with her ti[l] it was no longer possible to let them out further. Desperat[e] she had asked Guenna to help her. Guenna was able t[o] find some material—well-worn material to be sure—b[ut] together they had managed to stitch together two loos[e] fitting garments, which Glynis wore gratefully.

Glynis went to the small, low table she had constructe[d] using a slab of wood and four rocks. She lifted her satch[el] to retrieve her pistol and in sheer panic threw the ba[g] aside. "My pistol," she whispered. It was gone!

Glynis felt her heart beating rapidly. Did Ramsey have it? She shook slightly. He would probably kill the child and her eventually. He hated her and hated her unborn child even more. If she were dead, no one would challenge his right to Cluny—or so he believed, because he had no idea her brothers were still alive.

She touched her stomach and felt ill. Without her pistol, how would she protect her child?

She tried to think what to do. Should she behave as if she had not discovered it was gone? Ramsey was not the type to hide any advantage for long. If he had taken the pistol, which seemed most likely, he would let her know it soon enough. If he had not taken it, he would not know she didn't have it.

She thought about Guenna, but dismissed the idea. Guenna did not like Ramsey any more than she did, but she had no intention of killing him. She was biding her time. They both were.

Finally, Glynis decided to brave Ramsey. She went downstairs, where Guenna already had a fire in the hearth and water boiling for morning tea. "Good morning," she said cheerfully.

"Good morning, Guenna. Where's Ramsey?"

"Sleeping it off. He wanted me last night every way but standing on my head, he did."

Glynis smiled. Guenna was an earthy girl, a typical crofter's daughter. She was a hard worker and good-natured, and so loyal. Glynis had long ago vowed to keep her after Ramsey was gone—if ever he was gone. But her statement was puzzling.

"Were you together all night, then?" she asked. She almost never asked Guenna about Ramsey.

Guenna turned and nodded. "Yes, unfortunately. If he carried half the water I do, or worked even a third as hard, he wouldn't be of a mind to be lifting his kilt half so often as he does.''

Glynis could not help laughing. Guenna was funny.

Guenna laughed too.

"You're sure he didn't get up and leave you during the night?"

"Quite sure."

If Ramsey had not taken her pistol, who, then? She didn't want to upset Guenna by telling her it was missing. Guenna too, thought of it as protection, and Guenna looked to her to take care of anyone who might try to molest them including her ghost. Certainly Ramsey, drunk and lecherous as he was, could not be counted on.

Guenna made the tea and brought her a cup. "It'll warm your insides. It's quite chilly this morning. Fall is coming."

It certainly was not as warm as it had been, but it did not seem fall-like either. "Thank you, Guenna," she said, taking the tea. She drained her cup quickly.

"Some bread? An egg?" Guenna offered.

Glynis shook her head. Had she put the pistol on the table? Maybe her brain was getting addled. Maybe she had left it with her other pile of things. "I'll be back," she said abstractedly.

Guenna nodded and watched as she climbed the stairs. Glynis was vaguely aware of thinking that Guenna probably thought her odd indeed.

Glynis looked around the room as she stood in the doorway. She had piled her sheepskins in one corner of her father's former study. It was a barren room now that the bookcases and floors had been burned. But the fireplace and mantel remained, and she was able to keep a small fire going during the night to take the chill off. There was nothing in her room save the mantel, her makeshift table, and her bedroll. She looked again under and around everything. It was gone. The pistol was gone.

Glynis suddenly tensed as she listened. She heard a sound in the walls, a kind of dragging sound. Her heart began beating faster—what could it be? It was hardly the sound of mice or rats, as she had told Guenna it must be. This was a far heavier sound than the skittering and scattering sound that rodents might make.

She continued to listen, willing the sound to come again. When it did, it was more like a step and then the sound of dragging. It sounded like an invalid walking across a sand-covered floor.

Again her mind darted back to the footprints that had been there the first time Guenna had seen her so-called ghost. She remembered the taste of the grayish-white powder. It was surely flour. But who had walked through flour and left footsteps on the floor that led right up to the base of the wall—footsteps that simply vanished into thin air?

Was there a ghost? No, she did not believe in ghosts.

Glynis walked to the wall, to exactly where the mysterious footsteps had come to an end. To exactly where the sound seemed to originate.

Sunlight poured into the room from outside. Glynis was staring at the wall and feeling it with her hands, when suddenly it gave way and moved to one side with an ever so slight noise. Glynis gasped. The wall gave way to an opening of some three feet. She ran back to her bedroll next to which she kept a small lantern. From the low flame she lit a candle and then, making sure the door to her room was closed, she returned to the opening in the wall. She slipped into the opening and slid it closed behind her. She held the candle up.

There was a rough flat surface and then a narrow winding stone staircase. Below the reach of the candle's light, it was pitch black. "A passageway," she whispered to herself.

Glynis followed the steep steps downward, holding the candle in one hand and feeling the wall with the other. It was slow going, but she moved onward, her curiosity easily overcoming her fear. Whatever was down there must be friendly. It could have molested her a hundred times as she slept in the room above. She was quite certain of one thing. It was no ghost.

How was it she had spent so many months sleeping in this room and not known of the passageway? When had it been built? A thousand questions filled her mind.

At long last, the steps came to an end and Glynis stepped into a large room. She held up her candle and gasped. The room was comfortably furnished with a few pieces that had been in various rooms before the fire. There was a hearth, and in it a fire flickered. It must connect with one of the chimneys, she thought. When they joined, the smoke mixed and no one knew of this secret room, a quite comfortable room deep under the main floor.

Glynis raised her candle. There was a picture over the fireplace. It was the painting of her mother! She stared at it for a moment, transfixed with the similarity between them.

She moved around, and then saw the other entrance. It was on the far side of the room, to one side of the bed. There was a large bag of flour too—it was like one of the bags that Cook used to keep in the kitchen. It was half gone, and flour was spilled all around it.

Suddenly, the apparition appeared in the other entrance, framed by the darkness behind it, illuminated only by the dim candlelight.

Glynis suppressed her scream and miraculously did not drop her candle. The apparition was no ghost, but, rather a man. He was tall and gaunt with hollow cheeks and sunken sockets. He was dressed in a nightshirt that hung loosely on his body. His hair was snow white and fell well below his shoulders, scraggly and unkempt. His facial hair was also white and his beard was exceptionally long.

Glynis walked closer and he didn't move.

Then suddenly he took a step toward her and lifted his skeletal hand. His dry lips moved and she could see there was a questioning expression in his face. "Debra," he hoarsely whispered. "Debra, is that you at last?"

Glynis shivered so violently, she almost dropped the candle, "Father?" she murmured. "Oh, Father."

Glynis staggered forward and the gaunt old man whom she scarcely recognized pulled her into his arms.

"Debra, I thought you'd never come. But it's much too dangerous for you here."

Glynis looked up into his eyes. "Father, I'm not Debra. I'm Glynis, your daughter."

"Daughter?" He repeated the word as if it were in a foreign language. He said her name. "Glynis." Then he asked, "Where's Debra?"

"Father, Debra died a long time ago. Try to remember."

Tears suddenly began to flow down his hollow cheeks. "No, no! You're Debra!"

What had happened to him? He was so frail, and he seemed so old. And yet it had been only a few years—but she knew there had been a price on his head. She knew he had been living from hand to mouth for a long time, and, in fact, until a few minutes before, she had not been certain he was alive. Still, she had not expected to find him this way—he was ill and clearly disoriented. The strain of day-to-day life, all the losses—his mind had surely snapped.

"Why are you living down here? What is this place?"

"Secret hiding place. Safe from the soldiers. I have to stay here."

She nodded. The last thing she wanted was for Ramsey to discover her father. He would be furious, because as long as her father was alive, his claim to the estate through their marriage was invalid. Her father was weak. Ramse might even kill him if he knew he were still alive.

"Our castle is full of strangers," her father said. "I trie to scare them away, but they won't go. I tried and tried but only one of them is afraid of me."

"You mustn't do that. They must not know you're here."

"But you know."

"I'm your daughter, Glynis. Glynis . . . besides, I won' tell them."

"Glynis," he said again, but she was sure he still though she was her mother.

"What are you living on?" she asked.

"I don't have much food. But I have what I could sav from the fire."

Glynis nodded. "I'll bring you food. Father, for the tim being you must stay here."

"I'm worried about you, my darling Debra. Will you b safe?"

"Yes, you must not worry, Father. No one will bothe me."

He nodded. "When will you come back?"

"Soon," she whispered. "As soon as I can."

"Do you have to go now?"

Glynis shook her head. "I can stay for a while. I'll rea to you. Get into bed and I'll read to you."

"I have only a few books," he told her, pointing ol toward a shelf of dog-eared volumes.

Glynis covered him after he climbed into the bed. H was like a child, hardly the strong-willed father she ha known.

She ran through a mental list of doctors who lived i the vicinity, but she knew they were all gone. She coul not even find one to come and deliver her child, no le: care for her father.

She selected a book and began to read to him. In moments he had closed his eyes and was snoring peacefully. Glynis stayed for a while, then returned to her room, sliding the secret door closed after her. She decided it was likely that it was built after the revolution, when the Stuart king had been sent from England and William and Mary had been placed on the throne. There had been two previous Risings of the Scots—neither had been as decisively defeated as this most recent one. Yes, most likely that was when the passageway and the secret room had been constructed.

She lay for hours thinking about her father. He had been running from the British like an animal, living off the land. Clearly the months of loneliness and deprivation had affected his mind. She wondered if he would ever return to normal, or if these terrible changes in him were permanent.

James MacPherson and Sorcha Diarmid landed at Loch nan Uamh at dawn on September 4. It was a frosty, misty morning, and the ground beneath their boots crackled slightly. It felt good to be on land after so many days at sea, better to be in Scotland, and better yet to be headed home. James turned to Sorcha and grinned, then he picked her up and twirled her around. "We're home!" he shouted, and they joined hands and quickly danced an impromptu dance to the accompaniment of the sailors clapping hands.

But inside, James had warned himself over and over about what he would find. It would not be the same, it would all need to be rebuilt.

"I haven't seen Cluny personally," Andrew MacDonald had told him before he left Paris. "But I heard all the chieftains' castles were burned."

At the same time, James knew things were a trifle better. The wanton violence had ceased, and though scarcities plagued the land, people were beginning to rebuild their lives. The clans were still strong; a man's identity was more important than his material possessions. Still, there were new laws and apparently they were strict indeed. The wearing of the kilt was banned, as was the tartan. Did they really think a man needed his plaid to know his clan?

"You'll see the changes everywhere," he was warned. "You'll see the results of the law. Highland women dye or soak their husbands' kilts in vats of mud and the men are obligated to sew their kilts together to make breeches. Scotland has both changed and remained the same."

"We'll go into town and buy a horse and wagon," James told Sorcha. "It's a long ride home to Cluny, and I think we'll need a wagon in any case."

"Can you afford it?" Sorcha asked with concern.

James thought of the treasure he carried, and he almost laughed. "More than one horse and wagon if necessary."

"And with two would we get there twice as fast?"

"Come, my witty woman. We'll have to stay the night in the village."

Even the village had changed, James thought as they walked down its streets. The Act of Union had brought the Lowlands under English law when the Stuarts had first been replaced by William and Mary. But the Highlands had remained under the control of the clan chieftains until their defeat on Culloden Moor. As a result, Catholicism remained the sole religion of the Highlands.

Now there were two Protestant churches in the village, and the man from whom they bought their horse and wagon muttered, "They're everywhere converting and helping the poor. And their schools will come next."

Neither Sorcha nor he answered the man, but when they were alone in the tiny room he rented for them, Sorcha sat down on the bed and shook her head. "It's not bad, you know. If they build schools the way they have in the Lowlands, not just the wealthy will be educated."

"You're right," James agreed. "But education for all will be fought because all change is fought. But it's a good thing. Maybe all that has happened will turn out for the best."

Sorcha pulled off her boots and began to undo her dress. James watched her for a moment, then, as he always did, he turned away, affording her the privacy he had promised her when they began their voyage.

"Turn around," she said softly. "Please turn around, James."

He did so slowly and was surprised to see she had taken off her dress and stood, not in her heavy nightdress, but in a more seductive white nightgown trimmed in light green ribbons.

Her gorgeous strawberry-blond hair cascaded over her shoulders, and for the first time he realized what a very good figure she had. On all previous occasions he had seen her ready for bed, if he saw her at all. She wore a heavy flannel nightdress, and most of the time she was under the covers.

But tonight she stood before him revealed, a half smile on her lovely oval-shaped face.

He stared at her with admiration. Her breasts were not large, but they were wonderfully shaped, almost tilted upward. Her waist was tiny and her hips rounded.

He felt his mouth dry. "You tempt me."

She held out her arms. "I intended to not only tempt you, but satisfy you."

"Are you sure?"

She stepped into his waiting arms and lifted her face t
his. "I'm sure," she whispered. "Come, my love, make m
a woman."

It had not occurred to him that he was to be her first, bu
why was he surprised? She was modest and well-mannerec
clearly she had been sheltered.

He bent and kissed her deeply. Her lips were sweet an
he could feel her warm body against him. He covered he
breasts with his hands and felt them through the thi
material of her nightdress.

"You smell of flowers."

She moved seductively in his arms, and again he kisse
her, this time on the neck, and then on the ear.

He lifted her in his arms and took her to the bed. H
lay her down and discarded his own clothes quickly, emba
rassed by his own state of excitement.

He lay down next to her. "I must be gentle with you,"
he whispered. "Gentle and slow."

He undid the ribbons of her gown and pushed the mate
rial aside. He looked with fascination at her upturne
nipple, all rosy and soft. He touched it lightly with hi
tongue, and immediately her tiny nipple hardened. H
touched the other with his fingers and aroused it as wel
"You're lovely," he said, feeling awestruck as she moane
slightly and returned his kisses with wanton passion.

He stroked her thighs and kissed her till she twisted i
his arms and he felt her body warm and glowing. The
he touched her intimately, aware that he must hold hi
own pleasure till she was fully ready, till she opened hersel
to him and he could enter her without causing her pair

She moaned again and again, turning in his arms as h
rubbed her gently, causing her to feel an incredible ter
sion. Then he slid down her, and while he toyed with he
nipples between thumb and forefinger, he kissed her i
that most intimate of places.

Sorcha moaned again and again. She could not help herself. He created a sensation she had never dreamed existed. "Oh, James," she gasped, and then she seized him and held him tightly as her whole body shook with pleasure. She was panting and shaking as he looked down on her and kissed her damp lips. "Now we'll make love," he said with a smile.

Glynis staggered down the steep stairs with a basket of food. "Father—" she called out softly.

Her father appeared out of the shadows. No wonder Guenna had thought him a ghost. He was so tall and so thin and he moved silently.

"I thought I had dreamed you were here last night, Debra. Is it really you?"

She didn't know how to answer him except to persist in calling him Father and hoping that he would come to understand that she was his daughter and not his long-dead wife. "It's Glynis, your daughter," she said again.

"Glynis—" Again he repeated her name, but it was as if he were familiar with it without truly understanding who she was. Still, he accepted her. He knew she was someone who was close to him.

"I've brought some food," she said, uncovering a large pot of soup.

He leaned into it and inhaled deeply. "Smells good, Debra."

"You must eat some. Let me help you."

She helped him and noticed that his right hand shook when he held the spoon. She took it from him and fed him slowly, then she wiped his mouth off.

When he finished eating, he reached out and touched her hair. "Debra, you are round with child. When are you expecting?"

"Soon," Glynis said, taking her father's hand. "I'm Glynis, Father. This will be your grandchild." She took his hand and pressed it to her.

A smile crept across his face. "It moves," he said, and for the first time his eyes glimmered slightly.

"Oh, Father." Tears began to run down her face, and she held him to her. If only he knew her for who she was! She wanted him to know she was pregnant—she wanted him to know there was a future.

"I must sleep now," he muttered. Glynis nodded and helped him to his bed. He was so very ill.

She sat by his bed and watched as he passed into a deep sleep. What was she to do now? She had intended running away with her child as soon as it was born so that Ramsey could not take it from her. But how could she leave her father here? She shook her head in frustration. What was she going to do? She turned again—maybe she should tell Guenna about her father. Tomorrow, for the first time since they had come back to Cluny, Ramsey had announced he was going into Inverness. Doubtless, she thought, he had run out of Scotch.

Glynis turned restlessly in her sleep, then for some inexplicable reason she came fully awake. The half-moon shone through the window, making the room incredibly bright. Outside, the night was clear and the stars shone brightly.

Suddenly, Glynis felt a pain. Not a sharp pain, but a prolonged pain. She drew in her breath—she waited, and again the pain came, this time sharper. In a moment she felt a dampness, and she reached down to find a jellylike liquid. Her heart raced. "Guenna! Guenna!" she called out.

She tried to sit up, but just as she pulled herself up,
nother pain came and she fell backward again.
Guenna!" She was starting to panic.

At the door of her room she saw a circle of light, the
oor opened, and Guenna stood holding the lantern.

"Guenna! I think my water's broken! I—" Her words
aught in her throat.

Guenna set down the candle and came running to her
ide. She pulled back the covers and saw the liquid that
overed the bed. "That's what it is," she said. "Your
ime has come. I'll have to go and get some things, Glynis.
Iold on, count between your pains so I'll know how long
t is."

Glynis nodded as Guenna disappeared. Ramsey was still
way, and somehow that made her glad. He was probably
lrunk in the Inverness tavern, drunk and womanizing. In
ler heart she wished he would never come back.

Another pain racked her body, and she counted as
Juenna had directed.

Another and another and another. They seemed to be
hree minutes apart. Where was Guenna? She held fast as
mother pain came, and she panted as Guenna had told
ler she must.

It seemed like an eternity before Guenna reappeared.
he immediately put a kettle on the fire and lit five lanterns.
Ifter that she laid out some clean oilcloth beneath Glynis,
truggling to arrange it properly. Over it she put a softer
loth. All the while, Glynis felt the pains coming, ebbing,
eceding, like the waves on the shore. She was aware of
erspiration on her brow.

"Spread your legs apart," Guenna directed. She had
iled pillows beneath Glynis's head so she was sitting up.
"Bend your knees and spread as wide as you can."

Glynis winced. The position was far from comfortable

and the pains were terrible. The next one that came wa
so strong, she screamed.

"It's all right to scream as loud as you like," Guenn
said. "You won't be long. You're built for birthing, you'r
lucky."

Glynis did not feel at all lucky, as the next pain wa
hideous.

"Pant, pant like a dog."

Glynis closed her eyes and panted, but she stopped t
shriek as the severest of all the pains surged throug
her.

"I can feel its head," Guenna said. "When I tell you t
push, you must push. Then you must pant."

Glynis's body dripped perspiration. When the next pai
came, she pushed and then she panted. "I can't stand i
I can't stand anymore!"

"You can. Push!"

Glynis gritted her teeth and pushed, and as she did s
she screamed again.

"It's coming! It's coming! Again, again!"

Glynis pushed hard and felt a sudden release.

"Oh, it's a wee girl!" Guenna cried out joyfully.

"Oh!" Glynis shuddered. It was another pain but no
as severe.

"Just the afterbirth," Guenna said. She was holding th
cleaned baby and Glynis heard it shriek loudly.

With her eyes blurry, she saw Guenna cut the umbilica
cord and then wrap the baby tightly in swaddling clothes
Smiling, Guenna handed her the baby. "Your daughter,"
she said as she wiped Glynis's forehead.

Glynis looked at the little girl. "She's beautiful, than
you."

"I'll get you cleaned up, and then you should get som
rest."

Glynis nodded. She felt incredibly tired, more tired than he had ever been.

Guenna removed the soiled clothes and tidied up. She helped Glynis wash and put on a clean nightdress. Then he left her to return to bed.

No sooner had Guenna left than the wall slipped open and her father appeared.

Glynis held her finger to her lips, and he did not speak. At least he had understood when she told him not to show himself to anyone else.

He kissed her on the cheek and smiled. "She's a beautiful child, Debra."

She did not correct him. She kissed him tenderly on the cheek instead. "She's your grandchild," she said.

He looked into her eyes. His expression was troubled, as if he were struggling to understand. He bent and kissed the child. After that he stood up straight, turned, and left.

Glynis stared as he disappeared into the passageway. Again she asked herself how she could protect her child from Ramsey and somehow save her father. But she was too tired to even think of it tonight. She was too tired to think of anything.

Nearly a week passed and Glynis was feeling quite herself, though she still had not told Guenna about her father and she still did not know what to do. Ramsey would surely want to get rid of the child, and if he found her father, he would kill him.

She was sitting in the study on a chair Guenna had brought from downstairs. Little Debra slept soundly on the bedroll.

"You're worried, aren't you?" Guenna said.

"I don't know what I'll do when Ramsey comes back."

"Maybe he won't come back," Guenna said. "I'd say good riddance to bad rubbish."

"He'll come back," Glynis said dejectedly, and almost as if her dreaded moment were ordained, she turned toward the window. It was the unmistakable sound of hoof-beats. She was halfway to the window when she remembered that Ramsey had taken the wagon.

She looked out the window and felt her whole body fill with joy. The horse whose hooves she had heard was Sampson, and the rider was Robert!

"Robert! Robert!" she called from the window, and then ran past Guenna, flying down the stairs and outside.

"Robert!"

He lifted her off the ground and spun her around, kissing her as soon as he set her down. "Mrs. Pinkney said you were pregnant," he said breathlessly.

"And so I was till last week," she said, hugging him. "I can't believe it's you! I can't believe it's over!"

He bent down again and kissed her more deeply, more passionately. "I've missed you," he breathed in her ear.

"And I you. I've thought of you every second."

"Is the child all right?"

Glynis nodded. "You have a daughter."

He smiled and kissed her again. "I hope she's as beautiful as her mother."

Glynis took his hand. "Come with me." She led him inside and up the stairs.

"Where's Ramsey?"

"He's gone to Inverness. He's been gone over a week now."

"Well, we'll have a surprise for him when he comes home," Robert said, grinning.

Glynis led him to the study, where Guenna was just closing the shutters to keep out the sun. "The baby's asleep," she whispered.

Glynis took Guenna's hand. "This is my Robert," she said. "Guenna was my midwife. She's taken care of me."

"And she keeps the ghosts away from me."

Robert gave Guenna a hug. "My thanks."

Guenna blushed and, picking up her skirts, hurried out of the room.

Robert went to the bedroll and looked down at his daughter. Tears filled his eyes. "She is beautiful," he said softly.

He stood up again and kissed Glynis. Her lips moved under his, and though he knew she was not yet ready to make love so soon after giving birth, he kissed her and hugged her.

They sat down together and Robert held her close. There was no need for words even though there was much to say. She had to tell him about her father.

Glynis was feeling warm and comfortable in Robert's arms, and he was near sleep, having traveled so far so fast. She moved in his arms and then sat up, startled as the door was kicked open.

Ramsey, wild-eyed and pointing a rifle, stared at them.

Robert sat up suddenly, and Glynis's hand flew to her mouth in horror and surprise.

"How touching," Ramsey spit out. "A bastard child in the bed and the two lovers ready to make another."

Self-consciously, Glynis pulled up her dress. She had been feeding the baby.

Ramsey moved closer till he was standing at the foot of the bedroll, his rifle pointed at Glynis. "One of you will die," he said drunkenly.

"And the other will kill you," Robert said, staring him down.

Robert moved slightly, and Ramsey took a step closer. "Don't go for your pistol or I'll kill her. No one will take Cluny away from me. I'm the laird!"

"You're a drunk," Robert said evenly. "And Colin is on his way here and James is alive."

Ramsey narrowed his eyes. "Say your prayers, Glynis!"

Glynis saw the glint of the pistol, and the shot rang out. Ramsey fell over the foot of the bed, blood gushing from his back. Standing in the now-open passageway, Duncan MacPherson held Glynis's pistol.

"Father," Glynis breathed.

Robert stared at the old man, who held the smoking pistol. "Thank you, sir," he said.

"You're my son," Duncan MacPherson muttered.

"My father is ill," Glynis explained. "There's a secret room downstairs. He's been hiding there for a long, long while. I believe he has apoplexy."

"Your father's a strong man. He'll get better."

Glynis nodded. "From now on, everything will get better.

August 1749

The night was warm and insects sang a discordant melody as the waters of the lake lapped ashore on the rocks. Glynis stood close to Robert, looking into the rippling waters as the full moon was reflected upward.

"It's the moon underwater," Glynis murmured. "It's my twenty-third birthday and I can't think of anything to wish for. James is happily married, Colin is engaged, and we have a most delightful daughter. Even Guenna has found a husband." She could not say that her father had fully recovered, but he had a remarkable relationship with little Debra, and each day he spent with his granddaughter, he seemed to improve. Dr. Cameron, recently returned to Inverness, explained that that her father had suffered a stroke.

"The moon underwater has been good to me, good to us," Glynis said in a half whisper.

He reached out and touched her shoulders. "Make a silly wish, then."

Glynis laughed and the music of her laugh filled the trees. She turned with a mischievous look and suddenly began to take off her clothes.

He watched her with fascination. She was as beautiful as the day he had first possessed her. Her white skin glowed in the moonlight, her dark hair fell down to her full breasts. She turned, then, and jumped off the rock into the water.

He watched her, quickly stripped, and followed her into the cold water of the lake. He swam hard till they were even with each other.

"Catch me if you can," she called out, and she swam even faster, headed for the great flat rock at the end of the lake.

He touched her just before they reached the rock. "I've caught you, and what is my reward?"

She stood up in the shallow water, and droplets of the lake fell from her body. Her nipples were taut and hard and cold from the lake, her hair was in a thousand wet ringlets. She was as he always remembered her that first night. He pulled her into his arms and kissed her passionately. "Come to me, my wife."

His eager hands caressed her, taunting her even as he devoured her with kisses from head to toe. He lifted her to the flat rock.

"It's still warm from the sun," she said as he kissed her nipples yet again and then slipped down to where he could caress her more intimately.

"Oh, my darling," she whispered. "This is what I wished for. The moon underwater always hears me."

He felt her shudder as he continued this most intimate of all caresses, and he guessed she wanted him to continue.

Her hips undulated, and then he heard and felt her as she reached her pleasure. He waited only a moment before he again kissed her neck and her breasts. In a few minutes she would be warm and again desirous. She was everything to him, and they were everything to each other.

ABOUT THE AUTHOR

Joyce Carlow lives in Ontario, Canada. She has published five romances with Zebra: *Timeswept, A Timeless Treasure, Timeswept Passion, So Speaks the Heart,* and *Defiant Captive.* Her newest Zebra historical romance, *Highland Fire,* will be published in June, 1999. Joyce loves hearing from readers, and you may write to her c/o Zebra Books. Please include a self-addressed stamped envelope if you wish a response.

BOOK YOUR PLACE ON OUR WEBSITE AND MAKE THE READING CONNECTION!

We've created a customized website just for our very special readers, where you can get the inside scoop on everything that's going on with Zebra, Pinnacle and Kensington books.

When you come online, you'll have the exciting opportunity to:

- View covers of upcoming books
- Read sample chapters
- Learn about our future publishing schedule (listed by publication month *and author*)
- Find out when your favorite authors will be visiting a city near you
- Search for and order backlist books from our online catalog
- Check out author bios and background information
- Send e-mail to your favorite authors
- Meet the Kensington staff online
- Join us in weekly chats with authors, readers and other guests
- Get writing guidelines
- AND MUCH MORE!

**Visit our website at
http://www.zebrabooks.com**

ROMANCE FROM HANNAH HOWELL

MY VALIANT KNIGHT   (0-8217-5595-1, $5.50/$7.00)

In 13th-century Scotland, a knight had to prove his loyalty to the King. Sir Gabel de Amalville sets out to crush the rebellious Mac-Nairn clan. To do so, he plans to seize Ainslee of Kengarvey, the daughter of Duggan MacNairn. It is not long before he realizes that she is more warrior than maid . . . and that he is passionately drawn to her sensual beauty.

ONLY FOR YOU   (0-8217-5943-4, $5.99/$7.50)

The Scottish beauty, Saxan Honey Todd, gallops across the English countryside after Botolf, Earl of Regenford, whom she believes killed her twin brother. But when an enemy stalks him, they both flee and Botolf takes her to his castle feigning as his bride. They fight side by side to face the danger surrounding them and to establish a true love.

UNCONQUERED   (0-8217-5417-3, $5.99/$7.50)

Eada of Pevensey gains possession of a mysterious box that leaves her with the gift of second sight. Now she can "see" the Norman invader coming to annex her lands. The reluctant soldier for William the Conqueror, Drogo de Toulon, is to seize the Pevensey lands, but is met with resistance by a woman who sets him afire. As war rages across England they find a bond that joins them body and soul.

WILD ROSES   (0-8217-5677-X, $5.99/$7.50)

Ella Carson is sought by her vile uncle to return to Philadelphia so that he may swindle her inheritance. Harrigan Mahoney is the hired help determined to drag her from Wyoming. To dissuade him from leading them to her grudging relatives, Ella's last resort is to seduce him. When her scheme affects her own emotions, wild passion erupts between the two.

A TASTE OF FIRE   (0-8217-5804-7, $5.99/$7.50)

A deathbed vow sends Antonie Ramirez to Texas searching for cattle rancher Royal Bancroft, to repay him for saving her family's life. Immediately, Royal saw that she had a wild, free spirit. He would have to let her ride with him and fight at his side for his land . . . as well as accept her as his flaming beloved.

Available wherever paperbacks are sold, or order direct from the Publisher. Send cover price plus 50¢ per copy for mailing and handling to Kensington Publishing Corp., Consumer Orders, or call (toll free) 888-345-BOOK, to place your order using Mastercard or Visa. Residents of New York and Tennessee must include sales tax. DO NOT SEND CASH.